JUMPERS

Also by Christopher G. Moore

Novels in the Vincent Calvino crime fiction series

Spirit House o *Asia Hand* o *Zero Hour in Phnom Penh*
Comfort Zone o *The Big Weird* o *Cold Hit*
Minor Wife o *Pattaya 24/7* o *The Risk of Infidelity Index*
Paying Back Jack o *The Corruptionist* o *9 Gold Bullets*
Missing in Rangoon o *The Marriage Tree* o *Crackdown*

Other novels

A Killing Smile o *A Bewitching Smile* o *A Haunting Smile*
His Lordship's Arsenal o *Tokyo Joe* o *Red Sky Falling*
God of Darkness o *Chairs* o *Waiting for the Lady*
Gambling on Magic o *The Wisdom of Beer*

Non-fiction

Heart Talk o *The Vincent Calvino Reader's Guide*
The Cultural Detective o *Faking It in Bangkok*
Fear and Loathing in Bangkok o *The Age of Dis-Consent*

Anthologies

Bangkok Noir o *Phnom Penh Noir*
The Orwell Brigade

JUMPERS

A VINCENT CALVINO NOVEL

CHRISTOPHER G. MOORE

Heaven Lake Press

Distributed in Thailand by:
Asia Document Bureau Ltd.
P.O. Box 1029
Nana Post Office
Bangkok 10112 Thailand
Fax: (662) 260-4578
Web site: http://www.heavenlakepress.com
email: editorial@heavenlakepress.com

First published in Thailand
by Heaven Lake Press, an imprint
of Asia Document Bureau Ltd.
Printed in Thailand

Heaven Lake Press paperback edition 2016

Jacket design: K. Jiamsomboon
Author's portrait : Peter Klashorst © 2015

ISBN 978-616-7503-34-9

For Mike Herrin and Francis Reynolds

"The life of man is of no greater importance to
the universe than that of an oyster."
— David Hume, *On Suicide*

"The thought of suicide is a great consolation:
by means of it one gets through many a dark night."
— Friedrich Nietzsche

"But in the end one needs more courage to live than
to kill himself."
— Albert Camus

Part I

ONE

CALVINO LIKED CONFIDENT, outspoken women, so he'd asked Fon to dinner. She worked in the film business. She hired out her services as a local fixer and location scout for Hollywood productions, television commercials, reality shows, and European TV dramas. Based on her work experiences, her opinion of white people—farang, as they were known here—was low. Farang who chose to live in Thailand were even lower in her estimation. Fon could have been a Wikipedia illustration on the subject of "Familiarity breeds contempt." She was also proof of another platitude: that no man is a hero to his valet—or in her case, to his local fixer.

"If you hit your stride in Thailand, it means you were likely in the slow lane at home," she'd once said to Calvino. "Your slow lane is our fast lane. Insane, right?"

The start of the rainy season had come with a blanket of dark clouds rolling in like waves. They embraced and subdued the Sukhumvit Road skyline beyond Lake Ratchada as Calvino stood looking out from his eleventh floor balcony. Then a crooked fissure of bright light cut through, followed by a sharp clap of thunder, filling the air with the sweet smell of rain. Closing the balcony door behind him, he strode purposefully across the sitting room to the kitchen as the rain slanted down to the street below. Keith Jarrett's elegant jazz piano accompanied the sound of the downpour, which within minutes would have all the cars in the street plowing through the foul run-off.

Soon his date was due to arrive. He'd met Fon on the set of a low-budget film. Calvino had had a cameo part as a Soi Cowboy bar owner who loved to cook. She'd challenged him after the take about his knowledge of cooking in general and Thai food in particular. He'd gamely offered to cook her a Thai dinner. Wednesday was her day off from the film production company that currently employed her as a translator and fixer. With the sudden rain and flash flood, it was a given that she'd be running late, stuck in traffic somewhere.

The prevailing wisdom was that Thailand was riddled with guns, mafia, military uniforms, and irony. Fon's name proved the last point; it translated as Rain. The country's recent political storms had left a trail of mafia and soldiers wading hip-deep through the debris as a flood of change carried the unconnected out to sea.

Calvino dialed Fon's number and got the recorded message in Thai that her phone wasn't in service. The workings of the phone service in Thailand remained a deep mystery to him. Sometimes it worked, but at other times—especially when it rained—the system clotted up like fatty blood, giving the phones a digital heart attack. He'd try again later. He had a Thai meal to prepare and a skeptical woman to entertain. She'd promised to bring a copy of the rough cut of *Monsoon Angel*. He'd sweated too much on the set, and his makeup had left snail trails that made him look like a character from a horror film. New makeup had been applied and the scene reshot three more times until the director sighed, shook his head, and went outside to smoke a cigarette.

To Calvino the greatest mysteries weren't in movies; they were people in plain sight, carrying inside their heads their secret lives. Calvino wondered what Fon's secret life was. Like most people she was guarded; she protected herself. But part of the seduction of a new relationship was the unearthing of those secrets, watching them unfold. Coiled inside any person was a serpent on guard duty, and going too fast invited an aggressive and quick reaction. He planned to proceed with caution as he climbed down her mental ladder into the interior for a look around in the dim light.

He tried to phone her again, with no luck. In the kitchen he'd set out the ingredients to make the ever-popular Thai salad called som tam: a pile of shredded green papaya, toasted peanuts, two cloves of peeled garlic, three red chili peppers, a small pile of shrimp, palm sugar, six cherry tomatoes, and two cut limes. He toyed with adding a third chili pepper. The difference between two and three chili peppers, he knew from personal experience, was the difference between a .22 cal and .45 cal round.

Earlier that day, at a roadside stand on Sukhumvit Road, he had observed a couple of street food vendors making som tam as a kind of informal cooking class. The unstable metal tables and plastic chairs were filled with a lunchtime office worker crowd huddled over their plates, fork in one hand, smartphone in the other, talking, chewing, and posting selfies. One woman, while a thumb massaged her cellphone screen, dropped a forkful of som tam on the pavement. A cat as fat as a pig grabbed it and ran for cover under the shade of a motorcycle, hunching down. He'd never seen a cat eating som tam with three chili peppers—an exotic scene, he thought—and he was struck once again by the unpredictable, messy, and opportunistic nature of the world. He remembered that cats, like people, survive by adapting their tastes and calculating risks. Scavengers who trailed behind the predators maintained a large contingent on the streets of Bangkok, marking the human species territory in the urban animal kingdom.

Watching the cat, he temporarily forgot his mission. He turned back as the cook threw peanuts into the mush. As someone who had eaten Thai food for years, it surprised him how little he knew about the process of making it. He'd assumed that he knew what som tam was. As a longtime resident of Bangkok, Calvino had fallen into the old-hand attitude that he understood how things worked there, that his understanding wasn't some tour guide fantasy but a multi-layered kind of knowledge. Like a card counter in Atlantic City, he believed he'd mastered the system. That was a mistake.

In reality there are many recipes for som tam. Each one has the same name, even though the ingredients vary. To call som tam a papaya salad would be like calling tom yam gung shrimp soup. Ingredients are everything, Calvino thought. It doesn't matter what you're putting together: a salad, a chair, a woman, a friend, or a theory. Ingredients must be defined, tested, evaluated.

Calvino pounded the thin strips of papaya. The sound of the pestle against the mortar made his mouth water. He pinched a bit of the fruit between his thumb and forefinger and put it in his mouth. Sour taste exploded as if he'd blown up an invisible bridge at the point where his tongue disappeared down his gullet. Looking down at the mixture, it occurred to him that the wooden pestle in his hand could have passed for a medieval dildo. Upcountry, in every village, street vendors and housewives pounded the mortar with the pestle, and the sounds of this ancient food preparation ritual, like the sounds of love-making, sent out waves of deep sensations and cravings to everyone within earshot. In modern cities, with food and sex prepackaged and reheated in a microwave oven or online, humanity had lost part of its sound inventory and narrowed its understanding of the world.

Calvino carefully worked the pestle with a natural cadence and rhythm he had seen and heard hundreds of times upcountry and on the back sois in Bangkok. It was a register of tones that echoed across space, alerting an audience to the concert in progress, making the eyes brighten, the wet mouth drool, and the anticipation build. The musicality of the preparation was part of the som tam pleasure. The som tam concert had no fixed time. Morning, afternoon, or night, someone would take up the beat, and soon an orchestra would join in, up and down the soi. Calvino checked the time. It was 5:33 p.m.

He added two thin, crinkled red chili peppers. He pushed aside the third pepper. There was a difference between food and a substance used by riot control police to subdue protestors. The pestle smashed them open and seedy guts mixed with the papaya. The steamy smells birthed a new Calvino's Laws: Eating a death defying three-chili som tam without breaking into a sweat was proof that a man's body can cope with pain, and a man who doesn't feel pain or sweat is to be feared.

He threw in the third chili.

Next he added garlic and then a twist of lime, all the time pounding and splashing in fish sauce. Rising to walk over to the fridge, he retrieved the tomatoes and hog plums. He washed the fruit in the sink and carried it to where he'd been working. Picking up the pestle, he continued pulverizing the ingredients. Then he poured in a dash from a bottle of Johnnie Walker Black. Every chef had a secret ingredient, an add-on, a Keith Jarrett flourish, and a splash of whiskey was his.

He leaned over, smacked his lips, and breathed in the heady vapors. His cellphone rang. He licked his thumb and reached over to answer the call on the fourth ring. He was certain it was Fon phoning to say she was running late.

He was wrong. On the other end was an American named Paul Steed.

Paul Steed was an old client whom he hadn't heard from in more than a year. Like a lot of foreigners in Calvino's life, Steed had come to Calvino's door for the most profoundly banal reason—he'd wanted to find someone who was missing. And he had in mind that Calvino had a reputation for finding people who didn't want to be found. Apparently he also believed Calvino had an ability to make a "Thai problem" disappear. For someone like Paul, those were two invaluable assets. Calvino was like a resident beekeeper called by drunks after they stumbled over a hive. A swarm of bees was one step behind as they speed-dialed Bangkok's expat private investigator.

Paul offered, "I hope that I've interrupted a moment of passion."

Calvino remembered that Paul was still testing a beta sense of humor that never quite seemed to progress from the adolescent stage.

"It's okay. I'm still at the pounding stage."

"You sound disappointed," said Paul.

"That's because I am. What can I do for you?"

Paul paused for a moment as music blaring in the background at his end filled the silence. Calvino turned down the Keith Jarrett.

"What's that you're listening to?" asked Calvino.

This was the sort of question you'd ask an adolescent.

"Man, come on! You don't know the Clash song 'Should I Stay or Should I Go'? I thought everyone knew the Clash."

"Okay, you found someone who doesn't. So you phoned on a rainy night to educate me about music?"

That tipped Paul into another moment of silence filled by the lyrics of the song.

"I have a bit of an emergency."

"Paul, there is rule—I call it a Calvino's Law—and it goes like this: There is no 'bit' attached to the word 'emergency.' Can you turn down the music? I'm having trouble hearing you."

A moment later Paul, or someone else at his end, lowered the volume.

"I'm at Raphael's studio. His girlfriend is here. Raphael is dead. I don't know what to do. Or who to phone. Fuck, maybe I should just get out with the girl and let someone else deal with it."

"Raphael? The painter?"

Calvino knew Raphael Pascal. What were the chances of there being two Raphaels in Bangkok who knew Paul? Still, the shock of hearing news of the man's death automatically prompted the question.

"It's the same guy I hired you to find last year, remember?"

"I might have missed the Clash, but my memory hasn't gone missing."

Calvino stared at the som tam, smelling the diesel-strength fumes. He said nothing more, leaving Paul Steed to wonder at the other end if he was still listening.

In fact, over the last year, Calvino had learned various things about Raphael. Some of the information was trivial. For instance, Raphael had been named after a famous High Renaissance Italian painter named Raffaello Sanzio da Urbino. With a name like that, you either live under its shadow or you find a way to break out and make your own place under the sun. In Raphael's case, he'd been double handicapped with the family name Pascal, the surname of a French genius. The product of a French mother and an Italian father, Raphael had been born in the Quebec commune where they met. Being a child of parents who lived in a commune outside Montreal had given him a number of strange ideas about life, art, philosophy, living, and death.

Calvino had bought one of Raphael's paintings, a nightscape of Bangkok's Chinatown as the sky filled with Chinese New Year's fireworks. In Raphael's painting a slim, long-haired Asian woman ran naked and barefoot at night along a street illuminated by the fireworks bursting overhead. Raphael's wildly post-modern interpretation of Galileo Chini's 1913 painting of Chinese New Year in Bangkok struck Calvino as original; he'd made Chini's painting his own. Chini, a distant relative of Calvino's, was an artist of whom only a handful of collectors and historians had any knowledge. He hadn't lived in the age of social media and Raphael did. A lot of people followed Raphael Pascal on Facebook, and his account had been blocked multiple times for his paintings of nudes. But no one had the details of Raphael: where he lived, what he looked like. His background was a mystery. In his favor was youth—Raphael was twenty-six years old. He went out of his way to create the aura of a painter without a face, without a past, and without a future. It was his thing.

Calvino had gone to Raphael's studio a number of times. The first time was simply to find him, to convert him from a missing person to a found person. Then he returned a couple of times to sit for a portrait. The portrait Raphael had done now hung on Calvino's office wall.

"You know, the young guy from Montreal?" said Paul Steed, breaking the silence. "You bought one of his paintings, right? It's just gone up in value."

"Yeah. Raphael. Reddish beard. Thin. Blue eyes."

Calvino saw no reason to establish his personal connection to the painter. Paul wanted something from him. He had a feeling that this wasn't the time to pass along this additional information.

"That's him."

"Phone the police," said Calvino.

"He's dead."

"That's all the more reason to phone them, Paul. That's their job. They need to investigate."

"Their job is finding money. Raphael left a bunch of cash in his studio. I call the cops, and what happens to the money?"

Calvino caught the wet glimmer of lime juice and small pearls of the fruit that glistened along the side of the pestle. Som tam needed the right amount of lime, he thought. Too much spoiled the taste; not enough, and something important was missing. Lime juice, like money, had an unmistakable flavor.

"What happened to him?"

Calvino heard a woman in the background, sobbing, blowing her nose, jabbering incoherently in Thai. The cycle repeated itself as a series of breath-clutching storms, each of which flushed out a new round of tears. For the residents of Thailand, the monsoon of tears lacked a defined season. The forecasters gave no warning, and the military rulers blamed the corrupt politicians as disloyal sowers of tear clouds that failed to heal a parched, burnt-out land.

"Killed himself. His girlfriend who found the body called me. And now I'm calling you."

Calvino knew that the death of a farang was like one of those chain letters where, if you break the chain and fail to pass it on, something bad thing will happen to you.

"I'm sorry the kid's dead. Call the police and the duty officer at the Canadian embassy. Let them handle it. They know what to do. If there's money, photograph it with your phone and send me a copy if you want. Tell the cops you have pictures of the cash. No need to say anything else. They'll understand."

"His girlfriend, Tuk, found a note beside his body. Handwritten. Dated today."

"Give the note to the police. It's evidence."

"Calvino, I just arrived. I don't have all the facts. I don't know what's evidence and what's not. How things can get twisted. You know what I'm saying? Can you come?"

"How did he kill himself?"

The list ran through Calvino's head: jumper, overdose, razor blade, gunshot …

"An overdose. He'd talked about killing himself."

Calvino sensed that Paul was determined to have him come to Raphael's studio.

"I'm sorry he's dead, but there's nothing I can do."

"Something you should know: he wrote your name in the suicide note. He named you executor. Basically he left all his paintings to you. I thought you should read what it says before the police arrive."

"Why didn't you say so before?" asked Calvino, pinching some som tam from the bowl and pushing it into his mouth.

After ending the call with Paul Steed, he got the call he'd been waiting for.

"Fon, something's come up," he said. "An emergency."

"You're standing me up?"

She sounded pissed off.

"Someone I know has committed suicide and I've been called to the scene."

He could hear the taxicab radio in the background giving an update on Bangkok traffic.

"Sorry, Khun Vinny. And about the rough cut … More bad news."

He waited for her to continue.

"Was I terrible?"

"Your Soi Cowboy bar scene was cut."

The som tum was three-chili hot. The lime cut some of the pain, but he wanted to feel the burn go deep. He had a feeling it was going to be a long, three-chili night.

TWO

IT WAS STILL the evening rush hour as Calvino queued for the MRT train to Huai Khwang station. When the train came it was standing room only. Packed close around him, straphangers commuted back to their rooms, lost in the digital worlds of their smartphone screens. He looked at their faces. None of them looked back. They were on another kind of journey. Calvino wondered if he was the only one on the way to investigate a young dead man, or the only farang in the carriage who smelled of som tam.

At Huai Khwang station Calvino queued again, this time for a motorcycle taxi. It had stopped raining, but flooding on the streets had slowed down the traffic to a crawl. Overlooking Ratchadapisek Road, the district's main, multi-lane drag, were Las Vegas-style exteriors for soapy massage joints, with neon names like Cleopatra, Utopia, Amsterdam, and Victoria's Secret. Raphael's studio was nestled in a building on a narrow, nondescript sub-soi. It was a neighborhood with concrete buildings and small, cheap rooms. He saw a couple of young women in tight jeans and low-cut tops walking in Nike track shoes, trying not to get their shoes sodden. They smiled as Calvino's motorcycle taxi passed.

"You like girls?" asked his driver, looking back. "You want a young girl? What kind of girl you want?"

Yeah, I like girls, Calvino thought. What I don't like are girls who are subcontracted by motorcycle taxi drivers. I find somehow it destroys the possibility of romance.

The driver lost interest in driving as he continued with his questions. The sexual transaction business had offered a far more lucrative possibility. He hit a patch of water, sending the dank run-off up Calvino's legs. This was the time to start being afraid. Death by distraction was another way to commit suicide, Calvino thought, as he signaled for the motorcycle driver to pull to the curb.

"You want a boy?"

"I'm meeting an ex-wife. She has a gun. She was very angry on the phone. Three chili peppers hot, but beautiful. You want to come along? You talk to her for me?"

The driver pulled to the curb.

"You get off here. I go home now."

It wasn't a request; it was an order. Calvino climbed off the back of the motorcycle. The driver hadn't waited for money.

Calvino watched him do a U-turn and head back to the taxi queue at the MRT station. In a way, he was sorry the driver hadn't stuck around after the invitation.

The evening had got off to a bad start. A broken date, his film debut dead on a editing room floor, som tam half-prepared and abandoned, the suicide of an acquaintance, not to mention the ruined possibility of sex. With his trouser legs tucked inside his calf-high rubber boots, he looked like a farm laborer leaving a small wake behind as he sloshed down the flooded street to Raphael's building. Broken pavement, open manholes, and snakes were all real possibilities in the murky water. Walking barefoot down a flooded street in Bangkok wasn't good karma, and wearing shoes and socks would be a waste of good money. Only rubber boots, a sturdy umbrella, and a sense of humor could get anyone down one of the old sub-sois like the one to

Raphael's apartment building. The flooded pavement was lined with ugly, squat concrete structures with too much dark glass and too little cement, roosting grounds for the staff—employees also known as sex workers, prostitutes, or whores—who slipped into working names like Pat, Apple, Orange, Pepsi, Kiss, and Pie. He passed a couple of women sharing an umbrella, giggling at the farang with his pants stuffed into his boots. He used to be a man of style, he thought. In the Bangkok rain, no one had any style in the gravy colored flood.

The downpour had come during the dead time between the end of the sex-work day shift and the beginning of the night shift. Raphael lived in a neighborhood with a high ratio of such workers. On the sub-soi, removed from their customers who knew them as Fork or Mind or Lake, they would curl up inside their cheap rooms, listening to the rain outside, alongside three roommates who gathered like a litter to sleep through the daylight hours. Up front a daytime shift of workers warmed their place inside a series of glass bowls, swimming like a school of fish in twenty-four-hour evening gowns. But these fish were fishers themselves, waiting to catch a customer's eye and sink their hook in deep.

Calvino shifted his boots on the pavement, looking for a relatively shallow patch. Finding one, he stared up at Raphael's building, a box of five floors with no lift. It reminded him of a building type he knew from Brooklyn, where they were called walk-ups. The height of the building likely explained why Raphael had elected not to join the ranks of the jumpers, the expats who jumped off high-rise condo balconies. Ten floors minimum were highly recommended to get the job done—though no one who actually jumped from a tenth floor was among the experts who made the recommendation.

Calvino pushed the button on the wall for Raphael's third-floor painting studio, which doubled as flophouse.

The entrance door buzzer chirped and Calvino opened the outside glass door. He walked through the narrow lobby and up to the third floor. The door to one unit was open, and he saw two pairs of shoes on the outside. They were dry as a bone. The shoe owners had been inside for some time, he thought, as he pulled off his boots. And it looked like the cops still hadn't been called. He walked in.

"Where is he?"

Paul Steed nodded at the bedroom. On the sofa, knees together, a young Thai woman with a box of tissues sat with her face in her hands.

"That's Tuk," said Paul. "She's pretty busted up."

She came across as racked with grief and in no shape to talk. Appearances were one thing, but it was unclear which wheels and cogs still moving inside her head were operating the tear gears.

"Look at this note first. You'll see why I phoned you. Read it."

Calvino ignored him and stepped inside the bedroom. He saw Raphael's body on the bed. A large dog with long golden fur slept in the corner. He watched to see the dog's ribcage expanding and contracting, as it slowly inhaled and exhaled. It was a big breed—a golden retriever. Apparently it had the sort of temperament that allowed it to sleep through hurricanes, volcanic eruptions, and suicides. He waited for Paul and the girl to join him. They stayed away. Finally Calvino walked back to the sitting room.

"Let me read his note," Calvino said.

Paul, and then the crying woman, watched as Calvino read the handwriting on a sheet of A4 paper.

"I find it beside his bed," said Tuk.

Those were her first words since his arrival.

"And the cash?"

"Where he leave it, next to his bed," she said.

"I remember his dog," said Calvino. "Charlie."

Calvino saw the way Tuk looked to Paul for reassurance and comfort. Whatever connection the two of them had, it was designed to pump out a basement of tears.

"Why you talk about a dog? Raphael is dead," she said.

"The dog is something else to deal with," said Calvino.

"Honey, he's right. Even the will says Vincent is to take care of his dog."

Honey, he called her, thought Calvino. Wasn't Tuk supposed to be Raphael's girlfriend? Either the "honey" was evidence of a quick rebound by her, or she'd been jumping the mattress trampoline with Paul before Raphael's death. In Bangkok the meaning of "girlfriend" was as porous as that of "democracy" or "freedom." It was easier to wring the tears out of a working girl than to shake loose all the men hiding in the places where tears were made.

As suicide notes went, Raphael's wasn't a long manifesto but something orderly, sweet, and short:

My Last Will and Testament

I wish that all of my property be disposed of as follows:

I leave Tuk the $2,000 that I put under my mattress because where I am going there is no rainy day.

I have left $500 in cash for Joy at Cleopatra's, which she can keep herself or share with her friends, Monday and Guess.

I want my body cremated at Wat That Thong on Ekkamai Road. I leave $300 dollars to the monks for their trouble. No ceremony, no prayers, just the burning of the body, ashes spread in the Chao Phraya River.

I leave to my maid, Oi, 5,000 baht for the trouble of cleaning up my mess.

I leave to my landlady, P'Pensiri, 18,000 baht for two months' rent, in case she has trouble renting the room again.

I leave to the police, for their trouble, 25,000 baht.

I leave to Vincent Calvino, who once told me that one day every boxer realizes he can no longer throw or take a punch, and he can choose to become either a trainer or a drunk, 15,000 baht to look after Charlie. And I leave him all of my art, my paintings. Why? Because Calvino's great-grandfather was a famous painter who lived in Bangkok. He can do whatever he wishes with the paintings, including burning them and scattering their ashes with my own in the Chao Phraya.

If there is anything else of value, I donate it to Gavin and my fellow volunteers at the Bangkok Suicide Hotline for their good work.

For everyone: This isn't your fault. There was nothing you could have said or done to stop me. What I've done by ending my life is the only rational act a person can take once he understands that things are not what they seem, that we've been lied to and our reality has been fabricated, and that once you tear that facade down, there is nothing behind it. To keep living, if you know what I know, is to live as a coward. Moral courage means one thing— once you have a glimpse of what we are and what we are not, you have no other choice but to stop the lie. You must stop living.

Raphael Pascal

Calvino looked up from the note at Paul, who had joined Tuk on the sofa. She looked scared, anxious, ready to jump out of her skin. The confident nightlife face she no doubt usually wore had collapsed. A revolving fan swept the main room. A soft hum came from an air-conditioner in the bedroom. The music he'd heard over the phone had been turned off.

Calvino made a note of the surroundings. The sitting room was sparsely furnished with an old, paint-splattered sofa and one chair. Paintings, dozens and dozens of them in various stages of completion, were scattered over the floor. In every direction were images of women—nudes, half-nudes, frightened, innocent, diseased, disturbed—alone, in pairs, and threes. Some images were pure pornography, others parodies of Andy Warhol, others reminiscent of Lucian Freud with their emotional complexity, and still others of Francis Bacon, as if an egg had hatched a monster. Calvino carefully stepped around and between the paintings strewn across the floor. He had inherited from Raphael Pascal a body of work with a riot of conflicting brush strokes, styles, motifs, and compositions. He remembered the day Raphael had appeared in his office wearing a T-shirt with the image of Caravaggio on the front, and the scene before him was as if Caravaggio had returned to this world, had a psychedelic experience, and checked back out.

On an old wooden table were chipped mugs with dozens of brushes, some with tiny heads to detail the iris of an eye, others large and blunt for backgrounds. In front were his mixing bowls—an omelet with swirls of yellow, orange, red, and blue spilling out over the edges and onto the table. Then there were the long 20 ml tubes of paint: titanium white, ivory black, cadmium red, alizarin crimson, ultramarine blue, cadmium yellow light, and cadmium yellow. Calvino glanced at the condition of the paints and concluded that Raphael must have been painting right up to the end.

Some of the tubes had been squeezed flat, others were fresh and full, and all were scattered in apparent disorder on the table. The odors of paint, linseed oil, and turpentine competed with the smell of death to fill the room. Some of the canvases had been stretched inside simple black wooden frames, many of them stacked and several more hanging on the walls. Framed and unframed together, he guessed there were over a hundred paintings.

One painting that caught Calvino's eye hung above the sofa. He examined it more closely. Pictured there were figures on a reclining position on a sofa—the same sofa before him now, with every blotch of paint reproduced exactly. The immediate impact on the viewer was disorientation. Calvino knew that Raphael had titled this painting Degrees of Freedom I. He had seen it before when he had sat for Raphael. It was a self-portrait of the artist in Muay Thai trunks, painting a young mem-farang, her eyes blank, with the handle of a butcher's knife sticking out of her chest.

Calvino had also seen the other paintings in the six-part series. His own portrait had been labeled by the artist as number six.

"I can't make any sense of it," said Paul, looking vaguely toward the painting. "I have no fucking idea what to do. I don't need this."

He was getting worked up, and a bit of spittle formed along the sides of his mouth.

"Stop feeling sorry for yourself," said Calvino. "No one needs this. You brought me here because you want me to hold your hand, is that it?"

"Like I said on the phone, I wanted you to see the condition of this place before the cops come. Sorry if I came across the wrong way."

Calvino shook his head.

"You'd better tell me what happened, before the police arrive."

He told himself he should have stayed at the condo. Now it was too late to go back. He had no answers because he wasn't even certain of the questions. He suspected that over the year he'd got to know Raphael that the artist had been playing some kind of game, and freedom was the prize. If being dead meant being free, then Raphael had on one level succeeded.

Calvino stood at the bedroom door looking at the body of the man who had painted the dozens of canvases scattered on the wooden floor, hanging on the walls, and leaning eight or nine deep against the wall. The art world and the police world would have to find a way to make sense of each other inside this apartment.

"Were you doing drugs with him?"

"That's not what happened, I swear," Paul protested. "Tuk phoned me. I phoned you."

"Be prepared for the police to give you a drug test. Her too," he added, gesturing at Tuk, who sat with her box of tissues, saying little.

"Let them test me. I'm clean. She is too."

Calvino watched them exchange looks.

"Let's move on," said Calvino. "You hired me last year to find Raphael. The police will want to question me about your relationship with him. I'll have to tell them you hired me."

"Christ, it *is* getting complicated," said Paul.

"Death usually is. Let's have a look at the body before the police arrive."

"You already see it," said Tuk from the chair.

"I want us to see it together so I can ask some questions. The police are going to ask the same ones."

Paul glanced toward the bedroom.

"Count me out. The dog doesn't like me. She growled at me last time I went inside."

"In that case, me and your honey will go inside," said Calvino.

Paul flinched at hearing Calvino use his term of endearment.

"She's pretty broken up."

Calvino stopped himself in the bedroom doorway.

"What's the connection between Tuk and you?"

"I know her from around," said Paul.

"You'll have to do better than that with the police," said Calvino.

He found that to truly understand geometry, the place to start was with a triangle. He figured the love triangle must be one of the oldest bits of human relationship geometry discovered by mankind.

"And she was also Raphael's girlfriend," said Calvino.

Paul shrugged.

"For what it's worth, I didn't know until she called me and gave me this address. She didn't have anyone else to turn to."

"Is that what she told you?" asked Calvino. "Or is that your opinion?"

Paul's jaw went slack like a man who'd been double-crossed once by a woman and was still surprised when it happened again. Calvino guessed this attitude had worked to keep Paul happily blind—he didn't want to know. He liked the part of the triangle he occupied.

"And was that the reason you phoned me?" he continued. "You couldn't think of anyone else?"

"Vinny, you saw his suicide note. You knew him. He liked you. Who else should I have called?"

In Calvino's world there was always a reason a woman gave for calling you and not somebody else. There was always one for being late or not showing up. One that on the surface made a lot of sense, one that you wanted to believe was the true one. He thought of Fon and wondered if his cancelled date could be salvaged, or if like his role in the movie, this opportunity had been left on the cutting room floor.

Calvino would have expected that a massage girl who was also a girlfriend might have camped out near the body to mark her territory. Tuk followed him inside the bedroom. She stood beside the bed, looking at Raphael and then back at Calvino, waiting for him to say something.

"What time did you find him?"

She stared at the lifeless body.

"*Torn bai*. In the afternoon," she said, the Thai vagueness of time kicking in.

"What time in the afternoon? One o'clock, three o'clock, four o'clock ...?"

The questions rattled her, and she gave him a puzzled look. "*Jam mai dai.*"

Calvino pointed at the bottle of Mekhong on the floor and two glasses.

"Was he still alive when you arrived?"

She nodded.

"Now it's getting complicated," Calvino said, turning to Paul, who stood in the doorway. "She was with him when he died."

"Maybe she shouldn't tell the police that," said Paul. "What difference does it make, if he killed himself?"

"The police might think it makes a big difference," said Calvino. Turning back to the girl, he asked, "Did you see him take the drugs?"

"I see. What can I do? I say, no, don't do like that. But he not listen to me."

"What massage parlor did you say that you worked for?" he asked her.

She looked offended.

"I used to work at Five Star," she said.

It was a large, fancy massage parlor that catered to Chinese customers.

"Now I work as hostess at Lady's in Trouble. You know it?"

"It's a mostly Chinese nightclub," said Paul. "It draws a few farang but not many."

"You two know each other from the club?" asked Calvino.

"Correct," said Paul.

"Customers rich, mainly Chinese," said Tuk.

The talk of money worked to clean her pipes. She gave Calvino the feeling that she could track the scent of money like a bloodhound.

Tuk looked to be in her early twenties and was dressed in shorts and a tank top. Her eyes ashen, burnt-out holes from crying, she tried to read Calvino's expression. She looked like a schoolgirl on a sad occasion, except for one important detail—no schoolgirl had enough experience to talk about her customers like items on a spreadsheet. Calvino gave away nothing, as he hadn't made up his mind about her or her relationships with Raphael or Paul.

Wadded-up tissues had been scattered beside the bed till it looked like the floor of a soapy massage room. The golden retriever stirred, crept forward, and sniffed at Calvino's damp pant cuffs. Charlie's large head slowly rose from between her paws. Her tail banged against the floor as she recognized Calvino as a soft touch for a snack.

"The dog likes you," said Paul. "They say a dog is a good judge of character."

"Feed a dog and his view of your character is always in your favor," said Calvino.

He scratched the dog's head. Calvino and Charlie studied each other for a moment, before he turned his attention back to Raphael Pascal, curled up on his right side as if sleeping, dreaming, the rumpled sheets covering part of his left leg below the knee.

Raphael lay naked from the waist up. He'd dressed for his final voyage to the next world in a pair of blue and black gym trunks, the sort of baggy nylon trunks worn by boxers at Muay Thai fights. Raphael's hands showed that deliberate planning had gone into his costume of death. He'd wrapped them like the hands of a boxer. But there was no fight in him now. He'd gone down for the count.

"What do we do?" asked Paul, standing in the doorway.

He still stood with one foot in the bedroom door, the other in the sitting room.

"I'll phone a friend," said Calvino.

Calvino phoned General Pratt, now retired, who at that moment turned out to be practicing on the tenor saxophone. Pratt's wife, Manee, had answered the phone and asked him to call back after had Pratt finished. She said how excited she was to see Calvino in a movie. He didn't have the heart to tell her the news that his scene had been cut. There was a pause and he heard Pratt playing in the background. He told Manee it couldn't wait.

When Pratt came on the phone, he sounded irritated by the interruption.

"Vincent, I was about to phone you. How is your som tam experiment working out?" said Pratt. "Weren't you on a hot date tonight with a movie star?"

"She isn't a movie star. She's a fixer for movie people. The point is, our movie together got cancelled."

Pratt laughed, "I get it. She stood you up for the leading man."

"That would have been better than the real reason."

"Which is?"

"I'm in Huai Kwang looking at a dead body, Pratt. Looks like he committed suicide. I know the deceased. His girlfriend is here. So is another foreigner."

"Is he dead, too?"

Calvino glanced over at Paul. "Not as far as I can tell. Paul is his name. But Raphael, the artist, I told you about him. He's dead." He saw Paul cringe has Calvino spoke his name. Some people could stand the sight of blood; others could stand hearing their name given to the police. Calvino figured Paul had a whole lot of things that made him nervous. Paul's face twisted, reminding Calvino of something William Burroughs once had written, "A functioning police state needs no police." Informers and fear did the dirty work, and that took care of most things.

"Who is Paul?"

"Paul Steed's an old missing person client, and I thought you might have a name of someone at Huai Khwang Police station to call."

He did.

Calvino looked over at Tuk. Exhausted from crying, she knelt beside the mattress with her head on the bed beside Raphael's. The crumpled sheets, pressed between her long, polished nails, were damp from tears. Her little dance of grief had a practiced feeling about it. But then, he thought, she worked as a paid performer, and mastering emotional display was a big part of her skill set.

"Raphael ..."

She stuttered, then stopped before finishing her thought. Like an old-fashioned flash bulb taking a picture of something floating through her head.

Finally she said, "He love the dog. I think he love her more than me."

That set off a fresh round of bawling, dry heaves, coughing and blubbering as if her payday depended on it. All her impressive array of sound effects filtered through to Pratt's end.

"Is that the girlfriend crying in the background?"

Calvino looked at Tuk, who now had an arm draped over the body. She was a mess curled up in the fetal postion. Dead bodies were known to cause that effect.

"That's her. I need a hand, and not with my som tam. You remember, last year I had a missing person, a young painter from Canada?"

"What about him?"

"It looks like he killed himself."

"When?"

"The air conditioner is on full blast. It's hard to say how long he's been dead. From the girl, it was in the afternoon."

Calvino paused.

"Yeah, I'm at his place. Raphael Pascal is his name. This girlfriend discovered the body."

"Get the time, Vincent. And ask her why the delay in calling the police or emergency services."

Calvino turned back to Tuk.

"Tuk, why didn't you call the police hours ago?"

"I am scared." Her voice did that little shutter number. "Police no good."

"I heard her," said Pratt.

"She's vague on the time," Calvino said.

"It's not the meek who inherit the earth. It's the vague," said Pratt.

"*Hamlet?*" asked Calvino, thinking Pratt had pulled another Shakespeare out of his policeman's hat.

"Ask her what kind of drug he took," said Pratt.

Tuk looked confused when Calvino asked her.

"*Mai loo.*"

"She doesn't know," said Calvino.

Tuk was the kind of woman who managed to be many things to men, but her knowledge of chemistry wouldn't have been a strong point.

"They'll find it in the autopsy."

Calvino sat on the edge of the bed, looking at the bottle of Mekhong and the two unwashed glasses.

"What was your deal with Raphael?" asked Calvino. He sounded cold and unfeeling because her hysterics finally got to him; he was tired of her act and wanted to get down to business. If nothing else, she looked like the kind of girl who understood business.

"He was kind to me," said Tuk.

The world she lived in was one in which rich Chinese came and went, and though they left mountains of cash behind, they failed to give even small change of kindness. He saw Paul Steed swallow hard and take a deep breath as Calvino told him to prepare himself for the police.

Calvino locked eyes with her for a moment. "You can't take kindness to the bank."

"You don't believe me? You don't understand me?"

"Affirmative to the first question; negative to the second."

He caught a glint in her eye that signaled the show of respect two sharks give as they glide past each other.

THREE

NIGHTFALL. OUTSIDE THE third-floor window, neon signs flashed from the massage parlors and nightclubs lining Ratchadapisek Road, and the night-shift workers were on their way to their fishbowls and evening gowns. Pratt stood in the bedroom with three uniformed cops. Their walkie-talkies squawked with static, intermingled with a dispatcher's voice an octave too high. They were distracted by Raphael's artwork, a full gallery of paintings—many of them of nude models. This wasn't a crime scene that police training had prepared them for.

Calvino watched as they walked around the nudes—grotesque figures with disfigured breasts and stomachs, and large bushy mounds between their legs. No matter where they looked, the floor or walls, there was another assault on their senses, what monks and teachers had told them was sinful and wrong, and what secretly they watched alone on websites. They repressed their feelings behind a series of smiles, frowns, snickers, sighs, and some sounds that flashed like the neon outside. Pratt and the medical officer entered the bedroom to examine the body. One uniformed cop stood outside the studio, and another outside the building, telling curious neighbors to move along. But the neighbors did what the curious do. They stood their ground. An old man asked who was being hauled off to jail. It was a natural question for the occupants of a building in the area.

The senior officer sat on a chair questioning Tuk, who was perched on the sofa next to Paul, nervously kneading his hands. Stopping briefly to blow her nose, Tuk told the interrogators how she had used her own key to get into the apartment. No, they didn't live together. But they spent a lot of time together. Yes, they were lovers. No, that wasn't her in the painting on the wall, or the ones on the floor, but yes, he had painted her once and had given her the painting to keep. Tuk started crying again.

When the group had reassembled in the sitting room, Pratt read Raphael Pascal's will and suicide note and translated it into Thai for the benefit of the officer, the medical examiner, and the junior cops. After he finished, Tuk produced in her right hand a bundle of hundred dollar bills, saying she'd found the money in an envelope under the mattress. The envelope had Calvino's name and address on the upper left-hand side.

Pratt spotted the name on the envelope but said nothing.

"It's money I gave Raphael for a painting," Calvino said.

"Can I keep it?" she asked, looking at the cops.

Pratt exchanged a glance with Calvino. It was Pratt's call in one way, and in another, as a retired cop, he was now out of the loop, no longer an active player in the ever-shifting power structure of the Bangkok based police force. With all the cash on hand, this was a moment of truth and the moment Calvino had wanted Pratt to be around to witness.

"Looks like from his will, it's your money," Pratt replied.

The other cops showed no emotion. Pratt wasn't a working cop but a retired general. His reputation for honesty was legendary, and he wasn't someone they were about to cross.

"Thank you, sir," she managed to say, over a trembling lower lip.

Calvino wanted to applaud her performance.

A medical officer came out of the bedroom with a bottle of white powder in a zipper bag in one hand and a half-full bottle of Mekhong whiskey in the other. He'd found the bottle with the two glasses in plain sight. The combination of drugs and liquor was a familiar story, providing an effective one-two punch that would put any fighter down for the count. Raphael had left behind all the ingredients for the perfect suicide recipe, not unlike som tam with a five-chili-pepper ending, swallowed in one big gulp with head thrown back.

There wasn't much else for Tuk to tell him.

"He left twenty-five thousand baht for the police," said Paul, "for your trouble."

The cops exchanged glances, with no one making the first move toward that small pile of notes.

"Vincent," he continued, "tell them it's all right to take the money. It's what Raphael wanted."

As a large number of uniforms walked in and out of the apartment, Calvino watched as they stepped around and between the paintings scattered around the room at odd angles. Hanging over the sofa, *Degrees of Freedom I*, with its female subject wearing only a butcher knife, caused them to lose track of their own questions and miss half the girl's answers as well. One of the cops laughed as he looked at it, a reaction that signified not amusement but either confusion or embarrassment.

Volunteers from the Por Tek Tung Foundation—the locals sometimes called them "body snatchers"—appeared at the entrance to the apartment with a gurney. Charlie barked as they entered the bedroom. She was taking a stand, fur raised on the back of her neck as she growled at the volunteers. No one would be taking away Raphael as far as she was concerned. Calvino found her leash and collar in the top of a closet. Pulling it down, he slipped it over Charlie's head and led her out of the bedroom. The volunteers from the foundation heaved Raphael's body into a body bag and placed it on the gurney.

Tuk and Paul watched as the loaded gurney rolled in front of them and out the door, leaving tire tracks over half a dozen paintings. Pratt followed them outside.

Calvino pulled the dog into the kitchen, opened the fridge and found some Greek yogurt. He took it out and fed the dog from the container. After Charlie emptied the container, he gave her a couple of slices of bread from the fridge and watched as she wolfed them down too. When Pratt returned, he found Calvino petting the dog.

"You're lucky they didn't take that envelope with your name on it," said Pratt.

"It wasn't a crime scene," said Calvino.

"That's not the answer I want to hear, Vincent."

"I gave it to him months ago. I have no idea why he kept it under his mattress," said Calvino. "What else do you want me to say?"

Pratt said nothing and returned to the sitting room, where the medical examiner was packing up. Pratt had taken a photo of the suicide note with his cellphone camera. He studied it and conferred with the medical examiner. He'd found no fresh bruises, cuts, or other signs of violence. There were older marks, though, the kind of purple marks that might be left on a body that had entered a Muay Thai ring.

"No problem. Suicide," said the examiner.

The remaining police officers nodded as he repeated himself: "Suicide."

It was the magic word that warded off the evil of a murder investigation and months of paperwork.

"Keep the place and contents locked for the next few days. Once we have the autopsy report back, you can clean it out."

"What about the dog?" asked Calvino.

"Take care of her. After all, she's our only material witness," said Pratt with a smile.

Late the following morning in Calvino's office, having heard the news of Raphael's death, Ratana was dressed in funeral black, her eyes puffy and dark-ringed. Hearing Calvino conversing in the next room, she just sat at her desk, staring at the blank computer screen and ripping tissue after tissue from a box on her desk to dab her eyes. She took a deep breath before rising and walking toward Calvino, feeling wounded as she exhaled. She carried a notepad on which she'd scribbled down information about the funeral arrangements. She glanced at the wall where she'd hung Raphael's sketch of her. When a man draws a woman, she thought, it can be more intimate than sex. When he dies, the loss can be more painful than that of a lover. She'd connected with Raphael when he'd visited the office. The bond between them would have been hard for her to describe—one of knowing, seeing, and feeling. The kid had an ability to get under a woman's skin. Ratana was no exception.

She spotted Charlie, with her head on her paws, in a corner of Calvino's office next to his briefcase and the umbrella stand. Calvino sat on his office sofa, his back to the door, leaning forward, scratching Charlie's neck and talking in his cellphone. He hadn't noticed the flecks of white paper around Charlie's mouth.

She waited until he ended his call.

"How much money did Raphael leave for his funeral?"

Calvino turned around.

"Three hundred dollars."

"I've not checked the exchange rate, but it will be a lot more than three hundred dollars."

"How much more?"

She glanced at her notes.

"The sala for three nights, five monks, food, and the cremation come to about fifty thousand baht. Just so you know."

Calvino slowly shook his head and looked up at his own portrait painted by Raphael, hanging on his office wall.

"That'd be around fifteen hundred dollars to cover a full send-off. But he was an artist," said Calvino, "and three hundred dollars was a lot of money for him. He wanted a quick, no-fuss, no-mess cremation. Three hundred covers your basic burning charge."

"I feel so sad," said Ratana with a dreamy glazed over look of someone locked into an old memory. "He was so special. I think we should honor him and pay whatever it costs. I will pay the difference," she said.

"The executor covers the funeral expenses," said Calvino.

"What about his family?"

"His father is dead. He's not been in contact with his mother for years. As far as I can see, he had no close relatives," said Calvino.

It wasn't just Ratana who was lobbying for a three-day funeral; it was also Pratt's idea. Pratt wanted to check out Raphael's friends. Maybe one of them might explain why a young man like Raphael had wanted to kill himself.

"Let's plan on the three days and the monks," said Calvino. "I'll take care of the difference."

"Pratt said he could get the Thai price."

The authorities hated farang suicides. They made for bad press and gave potential tourists a queasy feeling as they scrolled through web pages of sandy beaches and smiling locals. The drug angle might catch the curiosity of some brass in the department who had troubles with their own kids and drugs. Only this wasn't in the same league. Being reckless with drugs wasn't the same as using them to check out permanently. Some said it was an imaginary line. Inside

Pratt's world, most of time he saw the bodies of those who crossed to the wrong side. Lost, depressed and lonely people stumbled over the line, and sometimes they sprinted over it. From Pratt's point of view: Drugs were drugs, and drugs were a problem. His attitude to drugs was part of the reason Pratt had been informally asked to assist in the investigation. There was an off chance at the funeral that the cops might find information about who had supplied Raphael with the controlled drug that had killed him.

"Will you sell his paintings? Who will buy them?" she asked, her face a mask of grief, the back of her hand flicking away a tear rolling down her cheek. "I would never sell the painting he did of me."

"A decision about his stuff comes later. You phoned the Canadian embassy, right?" Calvino asked, changing the subject before Ratana completely dissolved into an emotional storm. "What'd they say?"

She shrugged, followed by her standard expression that read, "You know they mean well."

"They have someone working on notifying kin," she said. "But they have nothing for us. Mr. Google is my friend. He helped me find Raphael's mother's last address in Paris. But she left it a couple of years ago, and there was no forwarding address. The father died years ago. Suicide."

Like infidelity, hooliganism, and alcoholism, suicide had a folder in a person's DNA file. "Suicides tends to run in families," said Calvino. "Anything else?"

"The embassy said they'd send someone to the funeral."

She looked at her boss and then at the painting Raphael had painted of him. The artist had captured something of Calvino's cagey, ironic, questioning manner, and also the slightly uncomfortable look as wrinkles appeared around his eyes when he pretended not to be disturbed.

"You sent the embassy a scan of Raphael's suicide note?" asked Calvino.

"I did. But they aren't commenting on that. They don't want to be seen as approving or disapproving it."

"If Raphael's mother suddenly appears with a complaint about the arrangements, the embassy can give her my number."

"They already have your number. But no one has any idea how to contact her in France—if she's still in France, that is. The embassy can't even confirm she's alive. They also have the office number. They definitely know who you are."

She disappeared from his office, closing the door behind her.

He heard her in the next room. She inhaled as if she was doing her yoga exercises. Her mood that morning was cold, remote. Calvino wasn't surprised; it was Ratana's way of dealing with emotional overload. The dead young artist, his golden retriever, now a fixture in Calvino's office, a studio full of abandoned art, and the phone calls for a funeral: so many things had accumulated until she had no space left to move in. Raphael Pascal's paintings now invaded her every thought. Calvino had given her JPEGs of each one with its title, and she'd begun typing out an inventory. Each time she looked at one of them on her screen, she started to cry. Calvino opened his door and saw her standing in front of the sketch Raphael had done of her. She sighed and returned to her seat. He closed the door and went back to his desk.

A moment later, hands on her hips, she stormed back into Calvino's office.

"That dog ate a roll of toilet paper. She stole it from my desk," said Ratana, pointing at Charlie. "She chewed through a roll of toilet paper and threw up under my chair."

Calvino's hand came away with soggy bits of toilet paper from the edge of Charlie's mouth.

"She usually specializes in eating homework," he said. "May be we can get her a website and sell the service."

Ratana didn't see the humor in the situation. "Do you plan to keep Charlie at the office, Khun Vinny?"

"Only for a couple of days, until I can find a new owner."

She saw his eyes soften in the way they mellowed when he made a plea for her to understand and to give him time.

"McPhail likes dogs," she said.

"He's at the top of my list."

FOUR

RAPHAEL PASCAL'S BODY remained behind a steel door inside the Police Hospital morgue. The authorities waited for Calvino to complete the arrangements at the wat before transferring the body to the sala. Pratt had seen the preliminary autopsy report confirming that Pascal had ingested high levels of a drug called pentobarbital, a short-acting barbiturate sometimes used in low-rent countries to execute condemned prisoners. It had also been used on humans in small doses to control convulsions, and by vets as anesthesia to operate on animals. As a suicide drug, a hundred milliliters of the oral solution mixed well with Mekhong liquor, according to some. Bottoms up, lights out.

It would be difficult to trace the source of the drug found in Raphael's studio. But one senior cop who wasn't in the pocket of the Chinese influences inside the department had information from a couple of informants that the drug was being smuggled into the country from China. The street value of a lethal dose was around five hundred dollars. The senior policeman, General Sirichai, an old friend of Pratt's, was unhappy that the local Chinese mafia was growing in size and influence. Sirichai, gathering intel before Raphael's death related to the suicides of three Thai nationals, had learned that a Chinese connection was responsible for trafficking the pentobarbital into Thailand. He asked Pratt to find out if Raphael had any Chinese underworld connections.

"I am retired," Pratt had told him.

"It's because you're on the outside that you can help."

Nattapong, who was senior in command to Sirichai, had a reputation for going easy on those plugged into the Chinese operated section of the underworld network. It was only a matter of time until the difference in opinion within the department would turn into a South China Sea–type territorial conflict. Pratt's intervention was a gamble. He might help delay or even avoid a showdown. He was no longer in the department and therefore had the appearance of standing clear of the factions. The premise was that no one would expect Pratt's involvement, or if they did, they would respect his motives as not being tied to the promotion game. On the down side, Pratt carried the baggage of a clean cop, and among the company of bent coppers there was unspoken agreement that the non-corrupt had to be isolated and carefully watched.

It was raining again when Pratt left police headquarters. Motorcycles sheltered under walkways and bridges. The traffic moved slowly on Silom Road. It was the kind of day meant for driving to a wat to arrange for a funeral—gloomy and confining like a coffin with the lid nailed shut.

Pratt braked as a bus in front of him changed lanes without signaling. Maybe Raphael Pascal hadn't seen it coming either, he thought. The close call made his heart pump.

Nobody but a suicide ever thought the last time had really arrived and they wouldn't be back for another. People always believed there was a next last time; they could never imagine the absence of next—except when a person chose the timing of their death. Raphael Pascal appeared to have known it was his last time. He was done with "next." There would be no next last time. He'd finished. He'd left his brushes and paints behind and crossed the line into nothingness voluntarily.

Paul Steed struck Pratt as the kind of farang who suffered from a prolonged adolescent immaturity. How many times had he heard single farang men say, "Thai women are fantastic, beautiful, gorgeous, sweet, irresistible." The surface was the place where such farang lived, danced, drank, and dreamed—until one night one of those fantastic, beautiful, gorgeous, sweet, and irresistible women pulled him deep in a tunnel from which he'd never escape. That had been Pratt's first impression of Paul Steed. It wasn't a particularly good one. He'd given Steed the benefit of doubt because he'd been Calvino's client. At the same time, he was exactly the kind of foreigner Calvino should have turned away.

Pratt made it a rule not to interfere in Calvino's business, even when saying something would save both of them a great deal of trouble. He told himself the problem with farang like Paul Steed was they were easy to underestimate when one forgot that they often had a cornered dog's capacity to fight and survive. Steed may have acted like a fool, but in a pinch he might not be one.

Pratt considered Steed's options and tried to think them through. To give Steed credit, it was true that when he had showed up at the scene, he'd understood that if he had called the cops immediately, the first thing they would have done would have been to arrest him. Pratt could see it from the cops' point of view, too. What was this foreigner doing inside Pascal's apartment? Was he gay? No, he wasn't. He went to the rescue of a Thai woman named Tuk, crying her eyes out in the bedroom next to the body of a man she admitted was her boyfriend. She worked in a nightclub frequented by rich Chinese who didn't work at regular jobs and traveled on red PRC passports.

The dead boyfriend was dressed in Muay Thai gear, his hands wrapped, ready for the gloves. Steed explained that, no, it wasn't a love triangle that ended in murder. No, it wasn't like the daytime Thai soap operas. Yes, the studio was in an area with a dodgy reputation, the girlfriend dodgy too, and Steed's reason for being present hard to swallow. In such a neighborhood, most people and their activities were dodgy. Pascal looked like he'd been in some kind of boxing match. When the medical examiner had looked Steed over, he'd checked his knuckles for evidence of scrapes, cuts, or bruises. None were found. Never mind. He might have used gloves like O.J. Simpson and tossed them before calling the police.

Yes, Paul Steed had seen the options at this crossroads of his life, and he knew that everything that he did next would determine where he'd be spending time for the next dozen years.

The possibility must have crossed his mind that Tuk had used him, as she used all men—it was her trade—luring him to the scene with misdirection and timing that had to work perfectly. She had to get him as his adrenaline was still surging and before he figured out he was just another brush to paint a different kind of death scene. Steed had stumbled into Tuk's world, and in that world women in ball gowns didn't just dance the dance with a customer. She had more in mind: pulling him down to where he'd need a lot of money to push himself back up.

The senior officer at the scene had pulled Pratt to the side and asked for his opinion. What were they to make of the death? They had walked in and what had they found? Among other things, they found a middle-aged farang private investigator who, on the one hand, was a personal friend of a retired police general and, on the other hand, had worked for a client who appeared to have connections to this sleazy world of Chinese nightclubs and massage parlors. Neither of those associations was a normal, run-of-the-mill matter, unless the farang was a gangster. Pratt had watched as the officer looked Calvino and Steed over, trying to make sense of the two men's presence. He'd counseled Calvino in the past to try to see things, if only for a moment, through the eyes of the police.

The investigating cop had sized Paul Steed up as a man who had got himself mixed up with the wrong people and found himself on the wrong side of the line. His assessment of Steed was close to Pratt's own. True enough, Tuk told them she worked in a nightclub, a polite way of saying she was a high-class hooker. But she planned to go straight, she claimed, and was about to quit when this happened. He saw the cops rolling their eyeballs.

Moneymaking machines lacked the software to unplug themselves; they worked on the floor of a specialized money exchange system that economists overlooked. Tuk hadn't needed a Harvard MBA to understand the rules of the finance game in the Bangkok night world, rules that in any case weren't written in any textbook.

If she'd simply called the cops, the money Raphael had left, including her own two grand, nicely piled in neat stacks, might have suffered shrinkage. Had the thought crossed her mind to run off with the cash—to just say, fuck it, he's dead, and if I don't take it, the cops will? She must have felt something for the guy, Pratt told himself. Finding him dead like that meant something in her karma was testing her. Maybe she saw it as a chance to make merit, and stealing a dead man's money was the other side of the merit coin.

No doubt she had worried the cops would be suspicious and try to stitch her up as having had something to do with his death, and this explained her slowness to involve the police. However, the medical examiner hadn't found a mark on his body that wasn't consistent with a Muay Thai boxer. Pratt had a feeling she'd simply panicked.

He glimpsed what must have gone through her head. She'd thought, "Who do I know who can give me some protection?" She ran through her contact list of names, and Steed popped out as her best bet. She'd read him, thought

Pratt, as the kind of farang she could control. She told herself that with Steed at her side, she'd feel safer. He'd feel sorry for her, and she could always offer him a couple of thousand baht for his trouble. When the time came, if she did consider handing him money, she must have laughed, realizing that it had only been an idea, and a stupid one. But she still thought the cops might not try pulling a fast one with a farang in the room. She got bonus points when Vincent Calvino was pulled onto the playing field. Investigating officers distracted by the two farang would go easier on her as they concentrated on the foreign men. Calvino and Steed also would trigger the alpha male reflex and focus suspicion on the outsider males.

There had been a time gap between when Calvino arrived on the scene and the estimated time of death in the autopsy report. Somewhere in the range of seven to ten hours of unexplained time had elapsed and was unaccounted for. Maybe Steed had sought a different outcome, one that had them taking the money plus emptying Raphael's ATM account—the kind of quick money scheme thought up by an emotional adolescent with an addiction-to-women problem. Why did farang crave to wear a hero's halo with a woman from a bar, a nightclub, or massage parlor? Pratt would never understand that level of stupidity.

Steed had knowingly put himself at the scene of a wrongful death because he had answered her distress call. He had liked this idea of being the knight coming to the rescue until his mature side whispered a couple of disturbing questions to which he had no answer. It occurred to him then that he ran the risk of having his farang ass in leg irons in an overcrowded Thai prison, eating rats and rice and killing cockroaches while those around him shivered with fevers in the tropical heat. It was this vision that kept even the stupidest farang in line most of the time. Thailand was a nice place, judging by outside appearances, but scratch the surface and things quickly turned dangerous and ugly. If you wanted your version of reality, you arranged witnesses and evidence in one way, and if you wanted another story, you had to know which people and evidence had to be massaged. Whatever the story, it had to be good for the money, it had to be possible in the law of physics and it had to avoid jail time.

Pratt also sought to understand Steed's motives for dragging Calvino into the situation. In his career he'd come across many desperate people, including farang, who'd do anything to anyone if it meant they could slip under the net. The key was finding the small flaws in the explanations they sold to themselves and the police.

Steed, in his own mind, had only accelerated the inevitable call to the police by tipping off Calvino first. It might have seemed to him that he was doing Calvino a big favor. Why not let him get his feet wet from the start—dive right into the death scene and the will just happen to have provided a perfect cover; it showed Calvino was a person of interest. Steed had visualized the setup. The cops, in uniform and carrying guns, would march through the door, and what would they find? Two middle-aged farang and a young Thai woman, all broken up over the dead boyfriend in the bedroom.

The cops at the scene, including Pratt, would figure that all three knew the deceased. The woman would be in a state of shock. They would find the body of her boyfriend with her weeping at his side, and two farang in a sitting room littered with pornographic paintings over every surface except the ceiling, and no one would know exactly what happened. The police would ask themselves if this guy had really killed himself, or had he had some assistance? They would investigate the people present and examine the setting for clues. Was it murder made to look like suicide? Of course they would ask themselves that question. But it wasn't easy to answer in many cases. The best criminal minds were Oscar-winning set designers and casting directors. That reminded Pratt that once Calvino had a walkon role in a local film but it had been edited out. He hoped that history wasn't an omen.

It was still raining as Pratt drove into the parking lot of Wat That Thong in Ekkamai. Opening his umbrella as he climbed out of the car, he reached into the back seat for a package with incense sticks, candles, and fresh orchids that he'd bought at the market. He locked the car and walked to the main entrance. The gold sheen on the bell-shaped chedi loomed before him as a dull and somber force. At any one time there might be a dozen or more funerals with coffins and mourners scattered among the salas. The traffic sounds from Sukhumvit Road and the rain faded as he walked into the temple grounds.

Pratt was early for his appointment. The timing was deliberate. He had arrived early to perform a merit ceremony in memory of his parents.

FIVE

UNDER AN UMBRELLA Calvino emerged from the Ekkamai BTS station wearing a black shirt, black tie, and black trousers. He crossed through the large parking lot in front of Wat That Thong. The lot was packed with cars, SUVs, vans, and motorcycles. He spotted Pratt's car with its police sticker on the windshield. The sun had set, and the light rain had tamed the heat. Crowds of mourners filtered through the main entrance, some stopping to read a blackboard with the names of the deceased and the numbers of corresponding salas written in chalk. Inside, paved paths wound through the grounds to the ordination hall, to the cloisters with the monks' living quarters in the back of the compound, and to the salas, each including a brightly lit hall with windows facing the pavilion.

Everyone had come to pay their last respects. At each of the sala entrances, mourners removed their shoes, knelt in front of the coffin, lit incense sticks, put them in an urn, waied the coffin, and said a prayer before finding a seat, while the monks, already seated, began their chanting. Behind it all was an ancient desire to experience the rituals of grief and loss. Calvino had visited this wat many times before. Its ceremonies followed a timeless routine. Nothing had changed in centuries as a dozen salas located in the wat had monks performing the same rituals as the hum of voices merged into one. As Calvino took in the sound of chanting mantras and the smell of incense in the wet air, he was reminded that he had entered the theatre of death.

It's just the way people are, thought Calvino.

Like a pilgrim, he joined the flow of foot traffic along the walkways inside the wat, passing through waves of incense and chanting that drifted into the open night air from the salas. The rain had stopped. The umbrellas had been folded and put away. The sun was gone, but the air through which the mourners moved was still hot and stifling. Seven o'clock was funeral rush hour at the wat. Today Raphael's was one of two funerals for foreigners among more than a dozen simultaneous services, each begun with doors open as the dead awaited the living—like a dozen orchestras, each with its own set of fans and supporters, crowding around its departed maestro's temporary stage and shrine. The mourners mingled in clusters in the walkway outside their assigned sala and ignored mourners from adjacent salas who gathered a few feet away. The crowd consisted mostly of Thais, with a few foreigners who bulged out like raisins on a loaf of bread. You couldn't miss them. Calvino was another raisin looking for a loaf.

Removing his shoes and leaving them outside, Calvino entered sala hall number 6. The number had appeared next to Raphael Pascal's name on the blackboard outside. After three days his name, written in white chalk, would be wiped clean to make way for the next name. In front of Raphael's coffin was a photograph. At twenty-six years old he looked like a kid. It occurred to Calvino that through middle-aged eyes most people in their mid-twenties appeared more childlike than adult. The photo caught Raphael's faraway look, as if he was focused on something behind the photographer, as if he were in a different space. He wore a T-shirt with an image of Caravaggio. Raphael stared out from the framed photograph as if looking at the audience. Dozens of floral arrangements were placed in rows behind the photo. Each one bore the name of a person, family, or company in large script on a banner across the wreath. Calvino saw his own wreath of red roses in the front row. Ratana had ordered it from a floral shop near the office. His name, misspelled as "Wincent Calvino," was splashed in large black letters across the banner. Confusing a W with a V wasn't uncommon in Thailand. He smiled at the mistake, thinking that funerals, like books and movies, need editors. The monks edited the rough edges of grief until it could be embraced.

After Calvino finished his ritual of respect, he took a seat next to Pratt.

"You're late," his friend said.

"I had to feed and walk the dog."

Pratt nodded.

"Ratana told me about the toilet paper–eating retriever."

He smiled at the thought of Calvino dealing with the dog.

"Charlie's got a future working in the Thai education system."

Pratt let the small talk drop as he glanced into the sala, which was filling up fast.

"It's standing room only," said Calvino, glancing back at the rows of folding chairs filled with people.

"For someone who was a missing person just last year, he seems to have made a lot of friends."

"Deduct the plainclothes police working the crowd," said Calvino.

"They are doing their job," said Pratt.

Calvino didn't want to push Pratt about what they were after. Not yet. It was easier to change the subject.

He leaned in closer to Pratt, whispering, "If I die before you, don't play Bach at my funeral."

Pratt smiled and nodded.

"I'll keep the music a surprise."

"And see they spell my name with a V," he said.

"I'll check the chalkboard."

Calvino counted the number of working girls who showed up to pay their last respects. Bar owner funerals produced a busload of twenty-something women crying for the loss of their big boss. Losing a steady customer in any business affected the bottom line, but losing a boss collapsed the balance sheet. Ordinary expat funerals—if there was such a thing—rarely attracted scores of strange, unattached women. In truth expats often remembered such women better by their numbers than their names. Raphael Pascal's funeral attendees were closer to a bar owner's crowd. On this opening night the ceremony had drawn an impressive number of soapy massage and nightclub female staff.

Raphael must have invested a lot of money for such a turnout, Calvino thought as he checked out the back rows. A dense colony of young, smartly dressed women in black had poured their slender bodies into over-tight slacks or stylish skirts that revealed their goods. Calvino counted seventeen young women—a bar owner funeral score—who dressed like bats at a cave fashion show. But judge them not, he thought. They'd made an effort and shelled our hard-earned money to attend Raphael's funeral. They deserved respect. Once or twice Calvino thought he might have recognized a body type or face he remembered from one of Raphael's paintings, but he couldn't be sure.

Seated ahead of the contingent of women were a dozen male expats with mem-farang scattered among them. He caught a couple of the men half-turning in their seats, looking over the women in the seats behind as if a fishbowl had materialized inside the sala. One of them whispered, "Seventeen beauties!" Smiles were exchanged. Not even death stopped the working girl's quantum-like world of creating a business opportunity from nothingness.

Piped cantatas by Johann Sebastian Bach played from speakers hung from the ceiling. Calvino guessed the

49

selection had been Pratt's suggestion. Ratana had consulted Pratt on the arrangements. All day long the two of them had talked on the phone about the details. There had to be music. What music was appropriate for a dead farang painter of pornographic images? In Pratt's mind, Bach's cantatas fit the bill. Who could resist the catchy vocals of "My time has come" and "His time has come," repeated over and over as if in disbelief that the time had actually arrived? Bach was a gloomy bastard, thought Calvino. It was the kind of music that made suicide an acceptable option. But what did it really matter? The music, like the flowers and the food, were for the living.

Pratt and Calvino sat in the front row, reserved for family. On the opposite side of the aisle, Paul and Tuk sat close together on a bench. In the row behind the family pews sat a half-dozen undercover cops, each with close-cropped hair, erect posture, identical white shirts, and black ties. Every few minutes one of them, who looked like the officer in charge, excused himself, exited the sala to take photos of the mourners outside, and returned to take more photos of those inside. No one was fooled about the identity of the photographer. Raphael had committed suicide, and it was reported in the papers and appeared as an item in the expat social media feeds like Thai Visa.

Still Calvino marveled at how the sala was jammed with mainly young people—the lost generation, as Pratt called them. Calvino had his own theory: suicides, like car crashes, attract gawking strangers.

Once the Bach stopped, the monks seated on an elevated platform chanted Buddhist mantras.

After the monks finished chanting, the ceremony ended. There was no sermon. No one stood up and said anything about the deceased. The end of the monks' duties signaled the arrival of the food. Attendants handed out Styrofoam bowls of tom yung gung, thick with fresh prawns. Pratt had negotiated a good price but had underestimated the number of mourners by a factor of three. They started at the front and worked their way to the back. Under his watchful eye, the undercover cops declined the offer.

People relaxed once the monks left the sala. Calvino got up and walked over to the pew with Paul Steed and Tuk and sat next to her.

"Tuk, have you recognized any of the people?" asked Calvino, glancing at the mourners behind their bench. "Point out anyone who came to Raphael's studio."

"Is this really the time, Calvino?" said Paul.

Calvino's eyes narrowed. He let out a short New York sigh, which in the old days had been a precursor to an act of violence.

"As Bach said, 'His time has come.' He left some people money. I want to see they get what he left them. Understood?"

Paul stared at Raphael's coffin, thinking about how to reply.

"It's okay, I guess."

Just then, it was as if Calvino had a moment of clarity about his ex-client. Paul Steed was thirty-five years old, an age when a man had either realized his potential in life or fallen behind younger, up-and-coming colleagues. It was the time a man saw his future as part of a crowd waiting on a platform for a train. That train wasn't late because it would never arrive. Either a man accepted his place on the platform or he became desperate to make one last chance to break out.

Paul's reply was as close to an approval as he was likely to get. Calvino grabbed the opening and crawled through.

"Three names. Which one is Joy? Do you see Oi, his maid? Or P'Pensiri, his landlady?"

Tuk looked to Paul for approval or permission. After a brief search through the faces in the room, she pointed out the three women. The maid and landlady knew each other and were finishing their soup. Joy sat with the soapy massage contingent.

Calvino had the money in white envelopes with the names in both English and Thai on the front. Ratana's neat handwriting was easy to read in both languages. He invited Joy to join him outside the sala. Outside the entrance she followed him through the pools of light reflecting off the wet surface between pavilions. Joy's nose and eye work had been first-rate, Calvino thought. Joy's height was slightly above average; he guessed it to be about 170 cm. Her black skirt was tight and short—the style favored by a certain segment of female university students, and copied by a segment of upscale hookers catering to men's schoolgirl fantasies.

"Raphael left you some money."

She took a cigarette out of a small black handbag and lit it.

"He was a very kind man," she said, smiling as she exhaled smoke out of her nose.

Whenever a hooker called a man very kind, Calvino knew, what she really meant was he was a sucker who overpaid for services. Thai schools had successfully prevented them from learning anything remotely useful so they were on their own, and like all semi-feral people learned that to survive in nature without any special skills you need a patron or two or three.

"Did you model for him?"

Joy nodded as she flicked the ash.

"I did."

"Did he pay you to model?"

She nodded.

"You modeled in the nude?"

"That is his style."

"Any idea why he asked you to model?"

She thought for a moment.

"He knows Joy think about suicide. Like a lot of trans, I not accepted or fit in. I want to shock him. Get a reaction or something. Joy not know he so serious. Now it is different. I understand him. A trans looks for little expressions. Joy understand him very much."

Joy watched Calvino's face, carefully waiting for a reaction. She was a transgender with the ambience of a beautiful natural-born woman. She'd unlocked a door that, once gone through, allowed no turning back.

"He say he was freak. He say being born in the wrong world was more difficult than being born in the wrong body. I say, 'I don't know about other worlds, but this one is pretty shitty.' "

Calvino sorted through the envelopes, finding the one with her name on it.

"There's five hundred dollars inside."

Her eyes filled with tears. She dropped the cigarette. It hissed as it hit a puddle of rainwater. Joy found a tissue in her handbag and dabbed at her eyes so as not to ruin her makeup.

"Last time I sit for him, I tell him I have money problem. I owe money to a Chinese loan man for my last operation. If I can't pay what this asshole want, he say he hire someone to throw acid on my face. I have no one who help me. I tell Raphael that."

"When was the last time you saw him?"

"Last week."

"Did you ever do drugs with him?"

"Never. He not like that."

"What about his girlfriend, Tuk? Did you see her with drugs?"

"I only see her ask him for money. If she use his money for drugs, I don't know. Tuk don't like me. Jealous too much. We not talk. Say hello, goodbye, that kind of thing."

"And you don't much like Tuk," said Calvino.

Joy slowly smiled.

"Not really."

"When you were at Raphael's apartment, did you ever see the farang Tuk is with now?"

She shook her head.

"I not see him before. I think maybe he her farang customer."

He watched her turn the envelope with the cash over and over again in her large hands. She was thinking about the money.

"Pay the loan shark, Joy. Move on. And give me your phone number. If I have any more questions, I'll phone you."

Calvino put Joy's phone number in his cellphone and, returning to the sala, sat next to Oi, who tilted her head to the side, wondering what he wanted. She was a simple, slightly overweight woman who'd slammed at high speed into her late thirties, retaining the faint afterglow of youth like a dead star. Wearing no makeup and a one-size-fits-all dress from a street market, Oi curled her toes in her sandals as if seeking to steady herself.

"Raphael remembered you in his will, Oi."

She looked at the envelope with her name on it. From the expression on her face, Calvino could see that something had frightened her.

"It's okay. Take it. He wanted you to have it."

"Thank you, sir," she said.

"Where are you from?"

"Burma."

"Did you model for Raphael?"

She smiled.

"Me? No, I am not beautiful enough. I am old, I told him."

"But he wanted to paint you."

"He said I am beautiful," she said, blushing as she looked down. "No one ever called Oi beautiful."

Calvino remembered her portrait. It was a nude. Raphael had used his imagination to restore her body to its original, pre-motherhood condition.

If Joy had been born into the wrong body, Oi had been born into a woman's body but with the different curse of being plain—until she finally met someone who could see the soft, gentle beauty underneath.

"Do you have any kids in Burma?"

She held up two fingers.

Relaxing a bit, she confided, "A boy and a girl. They stayed in my village with my mother. When he painted me, he asked me what I wanted in life. I said I didn't want anything. He insisted, so I told him the truth. I wanted my boy to stay in school. But I didn't have money for a school uniform, books, and fees. It costs two months' salary. He asked me why I wanted him to go to school. I said so he can have good jobs and not be like his mother. If he can have high education and understand the world, he won't have to wait for other people to tell him what to think. He can have a real life. That's what I told him."

"When you cleaned his place, did you ever find any drugs?"

She shook her head.

"He didn't do drugs. I'm sure."

He waited for her to add something else, something that seemed to be on the tip of her tongue.

"But you found something more dangerous," he said.

"I don't want trouble."

"No one has to know, Oi."

"I left it. I didn't take it," she said.

She sounded frightened.

"Left what?"

"A little notebook with names and money numbers next to them."

"The names of models?"

"Police, government people."

"How do you know that?"

"Titles next to the names."

Calvino remembered a Calvino's Law from the past: The first person to question at a possible crime scene is the maid. She'll know where her boss keeps stuff hidden.

"Are you sure you don't have the notebook?"

She looked shocked at the thought of possessing something so toxic.

"I look at it and put it back. One of the models knocked at the door, wanting to use the toilet."

"Where did you put it back?"

"I was cleaning the water heater box and the cover fell off. I found the notebook inside wrapped in bubble and stuffed in a plastic bag from Foodland."

"Is the bag still inside the water heater?"

She shrugged.

"I never touched it again. I was too afraid to look. It's bad luck for me."

Thanking Oi, Calvino rose to find a third woman to present with money and questions: Raphael's landlady.

By the time Calvino sat down with P'Pensiri, the last of the undercover cops had left the sala. He spotted Pratt at the front talking to Paul and Tuk, no doubt digging deeper into the substrata of their connection with Raphael's short life. At some layer was someone who had sold Raphael the drug he'd used to kill himself. Calvino could see Paul and Tuk shaking their heads, perhaps in answer to that very question. The other thing the two detectives didn't have was a motive. A little notebook recording bribe payments hidden in a bathroom water heater screamed motive, yes, but a piece of evidence with no chronology attached could be a deadend. Raphael had rented the studio for less than two years. It felt like a place with a history of bad vibes that might go back further than that.

P'Pensiri looked less like the grandmother and more like a big sister the 'P' prefix to her name suggested. Raphael's legacies had gone through three generations. The last stop was P'Pensiri, whose elegance in old age came from a past long gone. She wore a little too much lipstick, and her fingernail polish was chipped on the right ring finger. Otherwise she was the perfect image of a granny.

"The dear boy said I reminded him of his great aunt, who had studied piano in Paris after World War II. She lived a full, racy life. Played in jazz bars. Slept with Ernest Hemingway and Scott Fitzgerald. No one, he said, expected her to drown herself in the Seine. It's not what people expect if you've had a good life. Of course, if you are depressed, ill, without family or friends, killing yourself isn't a surprise. He smiled when he said that his family had a history of surprising people."

Calvino interrupted: "P'Pensiri, do you have a record of the tenants before Raphael?"

"Mr. Calvino, I have records for everything."

"Why did the last tenant leave?"

She scrunched up her face, jaw firm, going into the grinder-like mode of thinking.

"A musician from England named Harrison. He told me he played in a band that worked a circuit of local nightclubs."

"Why did he leave?"

"You know, I never did find out. He disappeared. No note or phone call. Left most of his belongings."

The studio did indeed have a history.

As P'Pensiri finished her answer, a hand pressed on Calvino's shoulder. He looked up.

"I hear that you're looking for me," said a farang. "Raphael was my client. Here's my card. Phone me and we can find a time and place to talk."

Calvino recognized Gavin de Bruin's face from Raphael's painting of him. The portrait had captured the man—mid-thirties, clean-shaven, thick around the middle, blue eyes, fare complexion. A charismatic presence. Everything about him was in the middle of the bell curve except that he appeared to benefit from some kind of personal power source of unknown origin. He seemed to be friendly with P'Pensiri, who chatted with the others in his group. Calvino asked Gavin about his entourage, and he laughed.

"I'm not a celebrity. My colleagues work as volunteers at the Bangkok Suicide Hotline. Raphael was a volunteer there too."

Calvino watched as Gavin led his little group into the night. He returned to sit next to Pratt.

"Who was the farang?"

He handed Pratt the business card Gavin de Bruin had given him. "Bangkok Suicide Hotline, Psychologist and Counselor" appeared in small print under his name.

"An NGO," said Pratt, handing the card back.

"He was Raphael's shrink. The one who gave him the dog."

"And who were the others with him?"

"Volunteers who work the phones for the hotline. Raphael volunteered time there helping out on the phones."

"Did they say where they were going?"

"I heard one of them mention the Bamboo Bar restaurant on Soi 3, Sukhumvit Road."

"Maybe one of them might have information about the drug. Why not join them?"

It was Pratt's way of saying, "I need a favor." By rights, he could have said, "You brought me into this. Now you're going to help me get to the bottom of the drug deal."

It was a real problem for detectives in Bangkok that any one crime was likely to be linked to another, and that one might be linked to another and so on, and as the investigation expanded, the trail was likely to lead to a destination no investigator wanted to arrive at: the untouchables.

"I don't know, Pratt. Their job is to talk people out of killing themselves, not to give out the phone numbers of drug dealers," said Calvino. "Besides, I wasn't invited."

"A suicide hotline picks up all kinds of information," said Pratt.

Taps were periodically put on the phone lines of such organizations. Pratt knew of several cases that had been cleared by evidence gleaned from listening to conversations with hotline callers.

"You don't need an invitation, Vincent. You show up to make plans to give him back the dog."

Pratt was right. The dog was a good excuse. Calvino would miss her, though.

"I'll return Charlie to him. It's his dog, after all."

"The dog didn't take Raphael's mind off killing himself."

"What did you get from Paul Steed?" asked Calvino.

Paul and Tuk had left while Calvino and Pratt were talking, passing by the two without acknowledgement. The sala had cleared of almost everyone except some young women in the back who huddled together, talking quietly.

"I didn't expect a kiss," said Calvino, "but at least they could have said goodbye."

"I asked Paul about why he hired you last year to find Raphael."

Given the turnout at Raphael's funeral, it was difficult to believe he had ever truly been a missing person.

"What did he say?" Calvino asked.

"The same story he told me at Raphael's studio."

Steed had told Pratt he'd hired Calvino to find Raphael Pascal a year before. His story was that waiting for a late evening flight to Bangkok, he'd been drinking in a bar in downtown New York and got into a conversation with Eric Tremblay, a guy from Montreal, and they talked about women, French food, and baseball. Tremblay lit up after Paul told him that he lived in Bangkok. Tremblay and Raphael had been friends, and Tremblay wanted to hear from him. Could Paul help? Steed had told Calvino the guy he met was an old family friend who'd lost touch with Raphael and wanted to re-establish contact. In other words, Paul had stayed on story.

"Why didn't you just sent a message through his Facebook page," Pratt had asked Paul, "and save yourself some money?"

Calvino had asked Paul the same question the day he came to the office to hire him for a missing person case. He had Raphael's page on his computer screen and turned the screen around to show the potential client. Paul laughed and told him the story of meeting Tremblay.

The friend, according to Paul, had tried Facebook but heard nothing back. They'd had a disagreement in the past and Raphael may have held a grudge. The guy in the bar had regrets and not healing the past with Raphael was one of them.

"I said I'd see if I could find him," Calvino said, "or find someone who could find him."

"And you believed his story?"

"I had no reason to question it. I saw it as just another missing person case."

Calvino started to leave, unfolding his umbrella as a light rain started.

"Vincent!" Pratt called after him.

Calvino turned, the umbrella above his head.

"When you see Gavin de Bruin again, ask him when was the last time Raphael worked on the hotline. Maybe he could give you the names of the people Raphael talked to.

I know all of this is confidential and can't be disclosed, but we have to be realistic. Others have taken this drug and died in Thailand. I'd like to put a stop to that."

"I'll ask him."

Calvino could feel the gears of the universe, impersonal and random, starting to move as he walked out the wat entrance in the rain. The clouds the color of grief, grey and low, pressed against the earth. Calvino watched a rising sea of umbrellas pouring out of the salas. Another night of mourning behind them, rain above their head, walking ahead into the place of the living. He stopped to slap a mosquito dead on his exposed arm, leaving a small splatter of his blood. Headlights from a car illuminated the death scene on his arm. He reminded himself that Bhuddists were prohibited from to killing even a mosquito. To kill one on the grounds of wat fell into the category of a bad omen. The mosquito might be a rebirthed spirit flying to a new life from one of the salas. He brushed the mosquito off his arm and kept on walking.

SIX

CALVINO RODE ON the Skytrain and got off at Nana station. He walked between the vendor stalls on Sukhumvit selling Viagra, T-shirts, wallets, watches, wooden frogs, dildos, and porn. Reaching the lights at the Nana–Soi 3 intersection, he crossed to the Soi 3 side and entered the Bamboo Bar restaurant. The interior was like a non-airconditioned railroad apartment. The tables in front were where spooks, with lines of sweat beadings on their faces, were taken for their final examination in profiling Middle Eastern men. All around, bearded men with eyes sunk deep in gray faces showed their yellow teeth as they dipped ragged pieces of naan into plates of hummus or leaned back to take hits from a hookah pipe.

At the far end of the room, Calvino pushed through double glass doors and felt the air-conditioning hit his face. The room was a cool enclave. Modern technology provided a refuge for those tired of desert heat and the pungent smell of smoke coming from the hookah users. He spotted Gavin de Bruin and his crew seated at a long table, talking amongst themselves as they devoured the Middle Eastern fare by hand, using forks to snag pickles and strips of beef. A waitress came with two more baskets of Indian bread.

"Mr. Calvino, please join us," Gavin said. "We were just talking about you."

Calvino pulled a chair out and squeezed it next to Gavin, who showed no surprise that the private investigator had showed up. Calvino got a better look at the volunteers who had sat in the back of the sala, near where the Ratchadapisek Road night-shift workers had roosted. A handful of the younger diners looked around Raphael's age, but for the first time Calvino saw that Gavin wasn't the oldest member of the group. One from England and one from Australia were old enough to be retirees, and two more farang who had unknotted their black ties looked to be in in their fifties. Two well-dressed mem-farang, both in their early thirties, seated together, leaned toward each other to say something as Calvino sat down.

"Talking about me? Sorry I missed the conversation," said Calvino.

"And about Charlie, of course, and why Raphael asked you to look after her," said Gavin.

One of the younger men said, "I wondered if you knew about Charlie's history."

"Every woman has a history," said Calvino. "You think you know it until you hear someone else's version. So why don't you tell me about Charlie's history?"

He turned to order a beer from the waitress.

"Raphael was her second owner," said one of the women.

That surprised Calvino, and looking confused, he turned to Gavin.

"I thought you gave Charlie to him?"

"Before she went to live with Raphael," said the woman, "Charlie lived with another person."

Obviously she had forgotten the person's name.

"Roger Stanton," said another volunteer.

"Yes, it was Roger," said the woman. "I remember his face. Just couldn't recall his name."

"She has a checkered history," said Calvino.

"A tragic one, unfortunately. Charlie's previous owner also passed on."

"Killed himself," said Calvino. "That's what you're saying."

"We no longer call Charlie our rescue dog," said one of the women volunteers.

"And do you think Raphael left her to me because I was suicidal or because he wanted to break the chain of dead owners?"

"That's what we were discussing," said Gavin.

The table of people who'd attended the funeral fell quiet as a morgue. It was as if they had frozen in time and place. He wouldn't say that any one of them looked ready to stand on the ledge of a high-rise balcony, deciding whether to jump or go back to bingeing on *Game of Thrones*. Calvino had expected the muted atmosphere of a wake. Instead he found nothing to suggest they shared a sense of deep depression or despair. Maybe they'd become immune to those feelings, having dealt repeatedly with people killing themselves. The volunteers had their rituals to express regret when losing a caller. Now they'd lost one of their own and coped in much the same way, through the ritual of sharing food, memories, and pain, and talking about their feelings.

One of the volunteers at the other end of the table cleared her voice and said, "Raphael will be missed. He had a rare talent and even more rare intelligence. Perhaps people like him aren't meant for this world."

"I've never met anyone who was," said Calvino.

One of his Calvino's Laws sprang to mind: Fitness was earned by surviving danger, and living another day knowing the risk never diminished and one day you would be unlucky. "Is this my lucky day?" That was the one question no one had little control over to determine.

Calvino watched a couple of skinny hookers in high heels enter the air-conditioned room on the arms of two farang who could have passed as TSA anal-cavity-search agents.

"He volunteered for the late-night shift," said Gavin. "It's fair to say that Raphael stopped half a dozen potential jumpers. Six people who would otherwise be dead are walking around because of him."

"He never told me," said Calvino.

"He wouldn't. He had a natural empathy. People related to him. He'd already saved those lives when someone he counseled made the balcony jump. He resigned from the hotline after the sixth death on his watch. He said it was an omen and I should try and understand."

"Maybe that explains why he left the residue of his estate to your hotline. But as far as I can tell, other than his paintings he didn't have very much of anything of material value. A computer, his clothes, a little cash, and that's about it."

Calvino saw a moment of anguish wash over Gavin de Bruin's face. It was one of those genuine emotions it was difficult to hide.

"It's the thought that counts, wouldn't you agree, Mr. Calvino?"

The whole table listened. Calvino thought it was a good time to tell them about the will.

"I wanted to tell you … As his executor, I'll make an inventory and let you know what the hotline can expect. Don't get your hopes up too high, though."

Gavin shrugged as if he wasn't all that interested. Calvino's advice didn't even register with the other volunteers. They seemed to live in an alternative reality where money wasn't important.

"About his suicide," Gavin said, "I feel, looking back, that it was inevitable. Did you know him well?"

"No, I can't say I did," said Calvino. It had taken him a lifetime to understand he hadn't ever fully knew anyone well—tear down one wall, and another appears, was the lesson of Bangkok life.

"He told me you bought one of his paintings. And that you modeled for his freedom series."

"Don't look surprised," said Calvino. "I guess I knew him as well as anyone. He had an unknowable quality that emerged from pockets of silence, gaps in his story, from wanting something that had no name. With Raphael it was best not to have expectations. He told me that he had finished his series. Did he have a buyer for it?"

"I recall that he did," said Gavin. "Some rich Chinese guy in Hong Kong, but he didn't get into the details. He hated business. His art was his life, and he was particularly proud of the finished series. Every week he'd phone and ask when I was coming to see all six of them. I kept putting him off. The delay frustrated him, but I had my reasons. I felt as long as I kept him waiting, he would get on, think about painting, live his life, and see that his talent shouldn't be destroyed. I naively believed I was buying time. But Raphael saw through the fear game."

That was the real takeaway—not a takeaway as in pizza or Chinese food. People who wanted something bad enough were forced to come out in the open. Gavin de Bruin had wanted Raphael to live. Raphael wanted to close the books by receiving Gavin's approval of the paintings. That had been their little game. From the circumstances, it looked like Raphael finally lost interest in Gavin's approval and made his move.

Calvino drifted from the conversation, his head filled with Hong Kong and speculation about what kind of deal had been made for the paintings. It was another complication. A photo album of smiles is handed to you, and your job is to match the smiles without knowing whom they belonged to. For all you know they belong to falling angels, thought Calvino. The falling angels had been pushed out by Pratt's face asking him for a favor.

Calvino raised his bottle.

"Here's to the memory of Raphael Pascal," he said. "By the way, does anyone know where he got the pentobarbital?"

No one around the table responded by raising a glass. They shut Calvino out, stared at him as if he'd committed a grievous social error.

"Did I say something wrong?"

He looked around the table. No one met his eyes. The volunteers shared a communal synchronicity, and Calvino had ruptured it. It was as if everyone had rechecked their winning lottery ticket number and saw that in fact they were losers. They'd stopped eating, reaching for food, or tipping back their beer.

Gavin cleared his throat. But rather than making a speech, he made it sweet and simple.

"Mr. Calvino and I are going for a walk," he said, as he pushed back his chair.

He pulled out a couple of thousand-baht notes from his wallet and handed them to a waitress.

Outside the restaurant men with Middle Eastern faces, flanked by a row of open grills, sweated as they turned long skewers with thick slabs of lamb and chicken. They watched over the hot coals, cigarettes in the sides of their mouths, the smoke rising out into the hot Bangkok night. A heavy traffic of people around them flowed like a retreat out of Aleppo. Nothing about the people, the food, or the hookahs seemed connected to what anyone thought was Thailand. Calvino and Gavin de Bruin walked away from the entrance and stopped at the curb, looking for a taxi. Nothing on the road moved. The traffic light at Sukhumvit was red. The cops in the police box on the corner were taking their sweet time to manually switch it to green.

Gavin watched the traffic backing up on Soi 3. He started to say something but couldn't find the words.

Finally he said to Calvino, "Some police at the wat were asking around about that drug. The volunteers feel they were ambushed. They'd gone to pay their last respects to a friend but instead ran into a police interrogation. Checkpoint harassment by the police had turned into a franchise, making everywhere a potential checkpoint, including a funeral. The drug link was enough for the police to question us like criminals. What will the police ask us next? Will they search our apartments, go through our computers, looking for whatever they can find? Calvino, you know that in these times, the police have absolute power. They can do whatever the hell they like. No one feels comfortable in their presence."

He let Gavin vent, releasing his feelings of helplessness and ill ease that came with living in a dictatorship.

"What did you tell them?"

Gavin inhaled the smoke that drifted out of the restaurant.

"I said I didn't know anything about how Raphael got access to *that* drug."

"Aren't shrinks in the emotional comfort business?"

"You're confusing me with a Bangkok bar owner."

That made Calvino smile.

"Yeah? I might have made a mistake. It wouldn't be the first time."

He stepped out onto the soi and looked down at Sukhumvit. The red light still hadn't changed.

Glancing back at Gavin, he said, "Raphael was a regular member of your organization, but he also went to you for therapy. Am I right?"

"We are a tight group who maintain an equilibrium by sticking together when times turn sour. Working a hotline isn't suited to an idealist. They burn out. In the real world the time comes when there's nothing you can say or do that will make a difference. You lose someone you tried to rescue. I teach the volunteers to accept that. When I first met Raphael, all he wanted to talk about was art, noir crime fiction, and noir films. He came to our meetings three or four times. I encouraged him to keep attending. I thought it would take him into a world that was dark but where he could help others. People who need emotional support are often the best to give support to others."

Calvino had seen Raphael's modest library—noir crime fiction, horror, philosophy, and books about painters and poets. But all Raphael had wanted to talk about was the dark books, the ones focused on violence and death. He collected Leonardo Sciascia's books, and from the look of it, Raphael had a full set of the Italian's novels. That made him a fan, and Calvino knew that you can learn a lot about a person's attitudes, tastes, values, and insecurities from the authors he collects.

Gavin had seen the library as well on those afternoons when he had gone for a modeling session.

"Sciascia was the author who dismissed reality and truth as two dead ends," said Gavin. "I told Raphael to be careful about reading books written by bitter men who failed to change the world. Most middle-class authors have never witnessed a murder or had to kill someone. It's no different from a priest giving a couple advice about wedding night sex. Wouldn't you agree, Mr. Calvino?"

"I've had my wedding nights. But that doesn't make me an expert."

"But you've seen death up close."

Calvino shot him a look as the traffic began to inch forward. He gestured for a taxi to stop.

"What's your point?" asked Calvino.

"A man's library and art collection are evidence of his worldview."

"John Waters said, 'If you go home with someone and they don't have books, don't fuck them.' "

Gavin took this as a test, and replied, "If you followed that rule in Thailand, you'd remain celibate."

Calvino grinned.

"Raphael had books."

And not all of them were on the bookshelf, he added silently. Since the dawn of books real readers had always had a secret place for forbidden books. The notebook was one such book, and it had been hidden in the bathroom water heater.

Calvino stepped down from the curb and rapped his knuckles on the window. The driver powered the window down. Calvino gave him his office address and opened the back door.

"Time for Charlie's walk," he said, holding the door open for Gavin. "And I've got something I want to give you."

SEVEN

CHARLIE HAD PICKED up their scent even before Calvino unlocked his office door. Calvino worked the key as Charlie jumped against the door, barking. Across the sub-soi a couple of neon lights flickered on.

"Charlie, quiet!" said Gavin through the door.

The barking stopped.

Calvino opened the door and the golden retriever sat in the doorway, tail wagging, beating against the floor with a thump, thump. Gavin gave a hand command and Charlie approached him and sat at his feet. He patted her on the head.

"I'll go along with you," said Gavin.

Calvino walked into his office and emerged with the leash. Gavin knelt on one knee, gave Charlie a hug and put her head through the chain collar. The obedience of the dog was the best evidence that the person giving the orders had earned the position of alpha. Calvino led the way down the stairs to the sub-soi.

"I don't understand why Raphael gave Charlie to me," said Calvino. "Why not return him to you?"

"He knew Charlie's history."

An old woman watched the two men with umbrellas walking a large dog below her second-story window.

"Charlie had a caretaker before Raphael. He unfortunately committed suicide," said Gavin. "I'd like to think he would have done it sooner and with less reflection had Charlie not been in his life. Raphael finished a painting of the two of us—master and dog, the unequal power, the absence of control. In the painting Charlie and I are looking at something we can both see but the observer can't. I thought why that angle? No exotic nudes or disfigured perspectives or distorted features; he painted me as a 'true' photographic image."

"You might have been the only 'real' person in his life," said Calvino.

"He never believed that 'real' or 'true' existed in his heart, or in nature, or in reality. He told me that it came to him one night as he thought about the painting he was doing of Charlie and me. The dog's perspective measured the world, my perspective measured a different world, but fundamentally they were the same, a distorted, limited, and incomplete truth. He said the problem is that almost everyone is convinced they possess the absolute truth. In this case dog and man were locked in two versions of the same fantasy."

They walked awhile before Calvino broke the silence.

"Why Raphael left me the dog is a mystery," said Calvino. "What am I going to do with her? She's huge."

The rain had let up, and Calvino folded his umbrella.

Gavin laughed.

"He left you Charlie for a reason. It was Raphael's message to me that my belief in Charlie as a mental health solution was useless. In his mind it was time for Charlie to retire to a permanent home, one that wasn't some ridiculous transitory, romantic plan to convert a suicidal person to a normal life. He told me once, 'No dog can save you from the endless psychotropic drugs, the hospital committals, the counseling, the monitoring, until gradually there's no difference between you and any other species of animal.' "

By the time Gavin had finished speaking, they'd returned to Calvino's office. Charlie, rather than going to her corner, lay down on the floor next to Gavin, who sat on the couch.

"Here's what I wanted to give you," said Calvino, balancing the painting of Gavin and Charlie on his desk.

Gavin smiled and studied the painting with fresh eyes.

"How about a drink?" Calvino offered.

Pulling his bottle of Johnnie Walker Black from his desk drawer, he set out two glasses and poured two generous double shots into each.

Gavin took one of the glasses.

"How did you meet Raphael?" asked Calvino.

"We first met one morning at a Muay Thai gym in Chatuchak."

That answer hadn't been on Calvino's short list. He'd figured Raphael had gone to him for counseling.

"When he died," Calvino said, "Raphael was wearing Muay Thai trunks, and his hands were wrapped as for a fight. Seriously, you first met him …"

"In the ring. It was in the center of an open-air gym. There weren't a lot of foreigners at the gym that day. That may be one reason the two of us were paired off. A former champion ran the gym. One of the training exercises was to practice clinching. Raphael didn't say much as the coach shouted instructions in Thai. I translated for him.

"The clinch is a key part of Muay Thai. The boxers embrace in the ring, looking for a window to use a knee, an elbow, or a leg sweep against the opponent. It's a death-like struggle. I hit Raphael with a knee, catching him in the chest. He went down hard. He was groggy when he got to his feet. I could see he was hurting, but I also saw that he wanted to continue.

"He motioned me with his gloves that he wanted more. We clinched again, and I did the same move a minute later, drove a knee into his chest. He gasped and fell to his knees, trying to catch his breath. I squatted next to him and asked him if he was all right. Raphael said he never felt better."

Calvino drank his whiskey and sat back in his chair, rethinking how he saw Gavin de Bruin and Raphael Pascal. People truly are mysteries, he thought.

"Raphael didn't seem like the boxer type to me."

Gavin smiled.

"People get into boxing for different reasons. Some to beat up other people, others to learn self-defense ... and still others take it up for the punishment it inflicts on them. Some people invite pain. Raphael was one of them. He and I trained together for a few months. One day I got him to tell me a bit about himself. He told me how he'd worked at a private mental hospital in Montreal, and how his parents had been hippies who met in a commune. I asked him why he opened himself up for a knee or elbow during a clinch, as if he was inviting his opponent to hurt him. The basics of boxing are offense and defense. His defense was intentionally sloppy. He had no answer for me.

"Then, one day after another workout, he told me that he was a painter, and that boxing was his way to stay connected with pain. He believed humanity's natural condition was shaped by our experience of pain and suffering, that modern times have separated the well-off from pain, sealed them in a pain-free place. And that was why art had become shit, why life was boring, why people gave up and killed themselves. They had stopped feeling an essential ingredient of life, stopped accepting pain as a necessary part of living. He said any state of being without pain was artificial. Pain avoidance was a refusal to prepare for death. It created the illusion that there was something worth living for, some grand purpose once pain had been defeated. He said there could never be a defeat of pain. To believe otherwise was to believe a lie, but people preferred their illusions even if it cost them the truth. He thought that rather than fearing pain as we've been taught, we should embrace it.

"You know how the clinch works in Muay Thai?"

Calvino answered, "The two boxers move close enough to wrap their arms around the other guy's neck. Then it's all knees and elbows trading blows to the body."

"For Raphael, the clinch was a chance to look into someone's face and use it like a mirror. Reflected in an opponent's eyes was the image of his own pain. He said Muay Thai pain collapsed his perception of himself and his surroundings, crumpled it up, and dumped him deep into the animal pit from which there was no escape. The two boxers trade pain until one boxer surrenders or is knocked out. Win or lose, you get beat up. Your body carries around that beating for days afterwards. It's waiting for you when you turn over in bed, or when you pull off your shirt, or when you try to wash yourself in the shower. Even when it seems to have faded away, the body memory of the punishment floods your brain and seeks renewal. Then you're back at the gym, fueling up your body to run on pain again. You might think, well, Raphael was what we call in English a masochist. But you'd have missed the point."

"Which is?"

"Raphael tested himself against pain, and he painted best when he was hurt. He translated the suffering of pain into his art. He thrived on real, in-your-guts, physical pain. The usual pain from everyday emotional heartache wasn't enough. He said painting is physical work, like what a mechanic does on a car. You work with your hands. Look at a painter's hands, he said, and you'll see they're fieldwork-hardened like a rice farmer's. So he always left an opening for the other boxer, one that didn't look too obvious. His opponent was almost invited to see the opening. He'd get kneed hard and keep going back for more. Raphael was a young man in search of teachers—boxing was one. Others were Charlie, his father, and you."

"Me, his teacher? That's seriously deranged, mental," said Calvino, tapping his head with his forefinger.

Gavin sipped and then, putting down his glass, held the whiskey against his tongue and swallowed slowly.

"How others see us isn't always the way we see ourselves. It was his way of looking at the world. He felt that whenever you see reality a little too clearly, those inside the fog will disagree. You argue with them; they don't listen. They call you a depressive. You know what they do with depressed people. The doctors pump you up with enough medication to shut you up. We argued about the meaning of sanity, and I told him that riddle would never be solved. It came out that I'd trained as psychologist. That made him defensive, but when he told me about his own experience working in a mental hospital, it created a bond.

"Later we talked about my boxing history. I'd boxed in my hometown of Utrecht. It's a nice little university town in the Netherlands. My father encouraged me. So from age thirteen to nineteen—my teen years—I boxed. I put away the gloves once I went off to university. Raphael thought that abandonment of what I loved was a stain. It was as if I'd sucker-punched him. He asked to be paired with a different sparring partner. He avoided eye contact with me. I recall that we didn't talk for a couple of weeks.

"Then I took him out for a drink and told him that I didn't judge him. I wasn't his counselor. Yeah, I counseled expats with emotional and psychological issues, but when I went to the gym, I was in that space I remembered from my teens. 'Muay Thai is a time machine for me,' I told Raphael. 'For me it's a pain machine,' he replied. He explained how he was oversensitive around counselors as he'd had a bad chain of experiences where they'd let him down. In Raphael's mind, his ideas about pain, life, and the decision to end his life were perfectly sane and rational. Entering the world was an irrational act; he'd had no choice about that decision. But leaving this world, that was within his control, and to him it was an act of supreme sanity.He argued that it was the insane who worshipped a reality painted in false colors, forms, shapes, and images. If that's what they wanted, fine. He would not go along with their conspiracy."

Gavin had a strange way of talking about the dead. Calvino put his insights down as nuggets collected by a skilled counselor and psychologist. Their job was to hear out the patient and solve the mystery behind the mask. After a case in Rangoon had crashed into his life, Calvino had been a patient himself. He remembered the mental marching up and down the field as the shrink watched him trying to find the goal post. But this was something else. Gavin had delivered punishing blows to Raphael's body and head. Any time you hit another person, that act of violence goes deep inside the mind of the person on the receiving end. No one ever forgets what it was like to be beat up—what it was like to offer yourself to be beaten up. Calvino saw Raphael's paintings in a new light. They had talked for hours about artists and painting. He hardly remembered what he'd said to Raphael that made him think that he was a teacher.

Gavin reached down and stroked Charlie's head. The dog slept on her side, eyes closed, getting petted in her sleep. Calvino refilled Gavin's glass and his own, laying the painting down on his desk. He sat in his office chair, elbows on the chair arms, watching Gavin with the sleeping dog.

"Did he say why he painted the 6 Degrees of Freedom series?" Calvino asked. "What it meant to him? It isn't obvious. I Googled the phrase and what do you think turned up? Pages and endless pages of links about what the degrees of freedom meant in mathematics, chemistry, engineering, and robotics. I found tons of technical jargon and equations. I got a headache trying to understand the complicated equations. I gave up searching. I thought I was looking in the wrong place, that I was missing something. None of what I found had a remote connection to what he painted. You might be able to help me out."

"Raphael once said that a perfectly planned death could be ruined by one wrong word from a therapist," Gavin replied, "or destroyed by an intelligent, well-meaning theorist. I know I've given you the impression Raphael came to the gym just to experience the pain. Because he thought that pain was a better, more accurate teacher about life than pleasure. But he also studied Muay Thai boxers in a different way. I noticed him one day sitting alone and watching from the side. I asked him what he was doing. He said he was counting each boxer's movement. It was mechanical. Boxers displayed the limits of six degrees of freedom, he said. Every Muay Thai move could be classified as up and down, left and right, forward and backward, the roll, the yaw, or the pitch. No different from a boat or an aircraft. But in the clinch each degree of freedom was reduced. The clinch altered the body's movement—it was connected with the other boxer. Two machines seeking an opening to land a knee, elbow, or head butt. But the clinch can do something unexpected as well.

"When both boxers' lock their bodies together, they lose their individual mobility. Two bodies tangled up don't make one body; it's a condition intended to be broken by violence. But until the blow landed, there is a brief moment when the boxers experience zero degrees of freedom. Raphael wanted to understand what that condition of being meant. To be unfree, all six possibilities closed down for a moment, gave him a glimpse into a deeper reality. This was the ultimate lesson of Muay Thai—the pain, but also the clinch itself."

Gavin drank his whiskey. Charlie slept on her side near his feet. Calvino had just let him talk; no targeted line of questioning had set off Gavin to freely share his theories and recollections. With Gavin, talking was a professional hazard, and no stakeouts, snooping around corners, or tailing were required of the investigator. It hadn't taken much to send that talk car rolling downhill. But as someone in the private investigation business had once told Calvino, clients who confess their innocence in persuasive detail were, in some cases, giving reliable evidence of their guilt.

Calvino broke the silence.

"I had a friend who once said, 'As long as it pays good, it makes no difference to me.' He also said, 'It's the creed for most working girls.' "

Gavin said, "Pretty much. What's a prostitute's real job? She's paid not for sex but for an illusion that it matters. She makes a man forget the futility of rolling the same stone up the mountain every day."

Calvino stretched in his chair. It was after midnight.

"Raphael's views must have won him a lot of friends and party invitations."

"I'm afraid I've talked too much. As he appointed you as his executor, I thought you might want to know more about him. There was a side to Raphael you may not have seen …"

Gavin rose to his feet. Charlie lifted her head, eyes open, watching Gavin.

"The bottle's not finished. Have another drink," said Calvino. "Sit down if you have more to say."

Gavin considered the invitation. He shook his head.

"It's best to call it a night."

He'd broken off as if he was about to say something more and changed his mind.

"If you think of anything else, phone or email me," said Calvino. "Will you go to the wat tomorrow night?"

Gavin gave a slight nod.

"Sure, I'll be there. If you really want insight into how his mind worked, Raphael set down his views on a web page. I'll give you the URL. Unless you already have it."

Calvino shook head.

"No. But I'd like to have a look. Thanks."

"I created the page and encouraged him to write about his feelings, his parents, and his daily life. He didn't mention it to you? I find that strange. Most of what I told you tonight came from Raphael's own words."

Calvino handed him a pen and paper and Gavin wrote out the address.

"After you've looked at it, if you have any questions, we can talk again tomorrow. Will the police be there?"

Calvino nodded.

"You can count on it," said Calvino. "About Charlie ..."

Calvino looked over at the dog.

"Take her with you. Living in an office is no life for a dog," he said. "Or are you in a condo with a no-pets rule?"

"I have a small house. Charlie's not a problem."

The dog lifted her head upon hearing her name. Gavin touched Charlie's neck and she was on her feet.

"She's lost two caregivers in a year," said Gavin. "It's time she has someone who won't be leaving her behind. I think that's one reason Raphael left her with you. He sized you up as the last person who'd kill himself."

"Is that on his website?"

"No, it's only a personal observation."

"What are you saying exactly?"

"Don't take it personally. Most people are fragile. They are afraid and cling to their narrow corner of life. It's what they know, and that's good enough."

Calvino walked Gavin to the door, and Charlie trailed behind as if sensing it was time to go home.

"It seems Charlie has made her choice."

Gavin bent down to put on her leash.

"Raphael was clever about people," said Gavin, "especially for someone so young. He said that he wrote what he called his case for suicide for me, so I'd understand what he believed was rational and logical. Imagine, an artist worrying about rationality? He left you his artwork. I suspect he had something in mind. Charlie was to be our link. He knew that I'd come around for her sooner or later. He suspected that you'd have many questions, and as I was the one he'd confided in, he must have planned that we'd have no choice but to work together."

"The big mistake is going too deep into a working girl's life."

Calvino was thinking about the notebook Raphael's maid had found.

"It's the only way to know someone," said Gavin.

That perspective was to be expected from a mental health professional, Calvino thought. For them knowing the interior of a mind is the goal. But most interiors are basic. To dig into the depths is to find a grave-sized hole.

"I'd say there are people whose depths you don't want to know."

Calvino walked Gavin down the stairs to the sub-soi. The sign on the massage parlor, No Hands Clapping, remained on. A couple of the massage girls loitered in front, watching the two men and the dog walk out of the soi. They waited for a taxi at the mouth of Soi 33. The third taxi driver agreed to Charlie getting into the back. As the taxi pulled away from the curb, Charlie pressed her nose against the inside glass, looking in Calvino's direction. He'd begun to like the idea of taking care of a dog again. At the same time, he had to admit that Charlie had likely made the right choice. Even a dog sensed that some owners shouldered bigger rocks to push up the mountain.

Part II

ONE

THE NEXT DAY Calvino, eyes wide open, taking short deep breaths, sat in his office reading through the numbers and names, nicknames, rank, and unit. It was the proverbial smoking gun. Billowing smoke and thunder as if someone had handed him the keys to hell and he'd unlocked the door. He had gone back first thing to Raphael's studio with a screwdriver. He'd removed the water heater panel and found the plastic Foodland bag with the little notebook inside. He'd been leafing through it all morning. Would someone have killed to get hold of that book? That was a question with only one plain answer. Had someone killed Raphael for the notebook and made it look like a suicide? That answer wasn't as simple.

He hadn't told Pratt about the notebook. He hadn't told Ratana, either. The notebook remained a secret between him and Oi, Raphael's maid. He was reasonably certain she wasn't talking about it. It lay open on his desk, and he was feeling like a scrap metal collector who'd stumbled across a cache of cobalt-60. How to contain the radiation?

The last entry in the notebook was dated March, three months earlier. That ruled out a prior tenant stashing it; Raphael or someone else had hidden it during his time at the studio. No bar, club, or massage parlor name appeared anywhere on or in the notebook. The writer had exercised caution. Discretion was the byword in the bribery game—

lights out, door closed, CCTV cameras switched off, no witnesses ... the usual checklist to ensure a private space in which to deny any payment was ever made.

The system would have worked like a charm until the notebook recording names, dates, and amounts disappeared.

Chasing down the chain of title would be a challenge. The notebook might have come out of the back office of any one of hundreds of nighttime establishments. It smelled of extortion, blackmail, and double-cross—in other words it smelled like fresh blood spilled on the floor.

Calvino examined it like a puzzle that, if solved, would rip the mask off the anonymous notebook owner. When the criminal became the victim, the only rule that could be counted on was someone would die. Calvino sat back in his office chair, wondering exactly who had stolen it and how it had ended up inside Raphael's water heater. But for its accidental discovery by Oi, a Burmese maid who had taught herself to read and write Thai, it had been a good hiding place.

Paul and Tuk had been in the studio for hours and had had every opportunity to remove it. Either they were unaware of it or they figured it was so toxic that it was better to leave it. As with most evidence, the conclusion depended on how an investigator read the intentions of the person of interest. In the end, Calvino scratched his head and turned back to his computer screen. He repeated to himself—Raphael killed himself. He wasn't murdered for a notebook or any other motive. That was what he believed to be true. He'd been at the scene, seen the body, read the autopsy report. He'd questioned a dozen people, and every avenue pointed to the same conclusion: suicide. But the notebook opened a new road leading to a destination where evil's door swung open. Some vital component was missing in the equation. He couldn't interview Raphael. But he could investigate Raphael's own words for a clue. People couldn't help revealing themselves in all kinds of small ways. They left footprints to be followed.

Raphael had the models write their stories on their portraits; paint and words together formed the finished piece of art. He finished his coffee as he prepared to dive head first into the sea of Raphael's own words. The artist seemed to have planned his suicide as a work of art, but other forces had been present and suggested his death also fit the plans of others.

This wasn't Calvino's first case of suicide that carried a whiff of murder. Once, in Pattaya, Calvino had been sitting on the balcony of his sea-view hotel room, reading Graham Greene's *The Quiet American*, when something unthinkable happened. He looked up in time to meet the terrified eyes of a young Thai woman, a silent scream on her lips, in free fall from the room above him. He'd experienced blindingly intense feelings as his mind struggled to think anything but "What can I do now?" Remembering that moment rekindled the feeling of being a witness to the cold chill of a death in progress.

There had been other death scenes he'd attended. McPhail had once asked him, "What's it like to see so many dead people? You must get used to it."

It had been a sobering moment.

"It's part of the job. You deal with it."

"You have a cast iron stomach," said McPhail. "I don't want to know. I don't want to see those things. I don't want to hear about them."

McPhail spoke for most people. Avoiding someone else's death is second only to avoiding one's own, Calvino figured.

Calvino's initiation into suicide and murder had arrived with his first case in Bangkok. An English stockbroker was found with a bullet in his head. The police concluded he had shot himself. In fact, it wasn't suicide—Ben Hoadly had been murdered. And there was Alan Osborne's son, Rob, whose murder in Rangoon had been set up to look like a suicide. Rob had been young and idealistic, like Raphael. Youthful idealism seemed to come with a high casualty rate.

Raphael had in many ways been a man-child. The stuff they found in his body was no ordinary drug; it was one of those last-exit drugs that suicidal people exchange information about on the Internet. The nature of the drug, like the handwritten will that doubled as a suicide note— in its own way a work of art—acted as another powerful piece of evidence that he had intended to kill himself. In addition, there was no clear evidence of a murder motive. But Calvino knew he'd entered an age when evidence and facts no longer carried the same force and conviction as in the age of idealism.

And anyway, motive wasn't enough. There was no physical evidence of murder to brush under the investigative carpet. The police had driven in with a backhoe when what they needed was a pair of fine tweezers.

In Calvino's other cases, there had always been some detail that didn't fit the suicide story. Raphael, in contrast, had been planning his demise for a long time. He had created a sort of online diary dedicated to self-murder. Calvino opened the page and began to scroll down, reading as he went. The second night of Raphael's funeral lay ahead as Calvino began applying his tweezers to a mountain of information in search of some detail contradicting the verdict of suicide.

TWO

WE ALL HAVE two stories: one we tell others about ourselves, and the story that we tell to ourselves. This is my own story ... I am not the first foreigner to come to the Land of Smiles as a test of whether life is worth living. I knew even then that if the answer turned out to be no, then Thailand would be the place to put away childish things and get on with advancing the end of life. That said, I have long felt the "end of life" phrase to be tiresome and distorting. No one can say where "life" begins and where "life" ends. Even someone half-educated like me understands that the gap between the two is not a trivial matter.

I am in my second year of living in Bangkok. I am of the generation that has no future. I believe things will get much worse for us. That's the way it is. But acceptance of that reality does not stop me from wishing to end my life before the world does the same. I have worked the suicide hotline. I know the lies people tell themselves. I know it is easy to talk about suicide to get attention. Talk is talk, right? Most people who call the hotline want someone to listen. "Hey, look, it's me here! Pay attention!" And artists are like hotline callers. What artist doesn't want attention?

There it is ... I want attention for my art, but none for the decision to end my life.

It is an artistic decision.

I am not interested in being rescued. I paint ... I will die. These are two things I have in my control. All else is flux, a blur, a dream you wake up from sooner or later.

Why don't I just get on with it? I offer two reasons. Think of them as bullshit excuses if you like. The first one is that I am decoding the book of life from Tuk's cellphone. She works in a nightclub frequented by rich Chinese. Just hold on, hold on to that thought for a moment: beautiful woman … bad men … dangerous business. What about the second reason? Hold on, be patient. One reason at a time.

I have hacked into her cellphone. I know things. Things I should not know.

Most afternoons I read Tuk's text messages. You would be surprised what people with a lot to lose will text to a working girl. I read her messages while she sleeps in the next room, exhausted from the physical demands of her line of work. Each day brings a fresh series of mixed media messages—a story composed of words, smiley faces, photographs, voice messages, animations, talking emoji and videos. Looking at the content, I can see that she never loses her focus or forgets who is at the other end. She displays the emotional range of a raccoon communicating with a fish in a small pond.

Within her cellphone are many exchanges, copied and pasted. Romantic spam. There is a list of names for Chinese customers, another list for Japanese and a third list for farang and others. I am on the farang list: Ace, Alfie, Bjorn, Buck, Cesar, Denny, Eddy, Felix, Ivan, Jerry, Karl, Kurt, Mat, Niko, Pat, Paul, Randy, Raphael, Robin, Shane, Steve, Wally, Yusuf and Zack. (The boldface is mine, not hers.) She is a businesswoman with a mission to increase her profits each quarter.

The book of her life has many chapters, with many emoji. Tuk and her Thai friends exchange them constantly. They live beyond the grasp of language. A series of emoji shared electronically might express their deepest feelings, for which they have no words. Her clients underestimate her, and Tuk works that ignorance, keeping it in her favour. Why do I encourage her to return here every day? Her ambition anchors her to life … mine leads me to sail away from life's shore. I want to understand the pull of life through her eyes. To give things a second chance, a think-through.

Narcissism keeps alive the strange belief that our lives are unique. But all those emotions and feelings are as common as dirt. They are nothing special ... you are nothing special ... I am nothing special. I don't lie to myself.

I am just another foreigner who lost his job, boarded a plane to Thailand and believed a fresh start would make everything right. A few months into the new place, I asked myself: Is life worth living? I heard that question repeated time after time by callers to the suicide hotline. They thought I must have the answer to it. What a joke! Did they really want my honest opinion? No one ever wants honesty or truth, because they're afraid of it.

I would not tell my callers that, of course. I would tell them, "It depends on what you want." I would listen for that hint of ambition that drives Tuk and millions of other people. The caller would tell me to forget about ambition ... He had run out of cash and his Thai girlfriend no longer sent him happy faces. He felt his luck had run out. He was in a free fall. He would whisper about joining the jumpers' club.

Sometimes I wanted to scream, "Fucking jump!" Because what difference does it make in the long run? Either you jump or old age and disease push you off the ledge. (Gavin: Don't worry ... I never actually said that to any caller.) But I am not that shabby guy in the back row of an AA meeting, secretly passing a flask down the line. I am that shabby guy who drinks at home and goes out to meetings to listen to other empty shadows talk about finding God.

I am finishing a series of paintings ... and that's my second reason for staying alive for now. A rich guy in Hong Kong says he will buy the series. Lang, my money guy, found him. I planned six paintings. I call the series "6 Degrees of Freedom." It will be my contribution to the memory of my father, the Freedom Place commune and its members.

The series is also a personal reminder that no matter how many hundreds of paintings I finish, I can never escape from those six degrees of freedom. That is what the commune believed. The degrees of freedom mark our boundary, and when you hit a boundary and can go no further, you feel many things—horror, sadness, desperation … It's not that you don't fall off the edge of the world. You discover no one cares.

My studio is a miniature of the commune of my childhood. People are free to come and go as they like. They can leave things, take things, share things, drink, eat, strip nude, love and hate. I paint them. I give them freedom. Once they have tasted the sweetness of freedom, they return. That means I should be about the happiest guy in the world, right? If only life worked out in a simple way like that, but it doesn't.

I have known guys drunk off their faces who do stupid shit and end up dead. Like the guy who was fucking his girlfriend on the balcony with enough kinetic energy that both of them went over the top of the railing. Splat, they went … twelve floors down, slamming onto the roof of a red Honda Jazz illegally parked in a clearly signed handicap-only parking place. It was actually the dead girl's car. The press played up the irony. As if death needs an invitation to the irony mystery ball.

Welcome to my personal irony ball. I am Raphael Pascal, your host. I am an artist. I am also a practitioner of the art of Muay Thai boxing. The art lies in knowing when to throw a punch and where you want it to land … and also what you hope it will do once it connects.

Painting is the same, except you don't land a physical punch with your body. My body does something else. My weapon is the brush or knife, and I use these tools to inflict myself on the canvas. Using my left hand to mix the precise colour, my right hand to pick up the brush, I lean in close until I clinch with it. I want to restore the person to mint condition. And by "mint condition" I don't mean the sort of happy fiction used to sell toothpaste.

When I was very small, I spent hours in my father's garage, watching him restore old cars. I watched him work with those worn out, used up, rusted, dented and battered car bodies. He taught me the art of reimagining what is true. He also taught me how to box.

It feels good to restore things to their true nature. To know you can take the pain of getting hit.

Over time I learned to make my moves as a painter—quick and decisive, a curve, a line, a shadow ... and the painting takes form. In my studio I jab with my brushes, and in the ring with my knees, elbows and head. I am in search of a pattern I can see and feel and taste. Pain helps me to focus my mind. As my father used to say, pain is your friend. Don't treat it like an enemy.

Painting and boxing are arts of technique—intuitive, inspired and merciless—surprising you and aiming to knock your lights out. Techniques take time to learn, and then more time to unlearn and overcome. The skills and knowledge to kill yourself need thought, design ... and not an empty cliché that says, "I'm tired of living." It is not the pain that is the problem. It is the meaningless of suffering.

If you click <u>here</u>, you can see a draft of my current suicide note, and the history of updates I have made to it over the past year. I have archived the changes as I have painted, studied Tuk's cellphone, boxed, fucked and debated. Did a money dance with Tuk's Chinese connection, Lang, who gets into fits of schoolgirl giggles. It is a front. But who doesn't have more fronts than money to finance them?

At last count I have 72 versions of my suicide note. I like that number. I have a thing about numbers. 72 is a number with heavy baggage. Some say that Muslim martyrs are promised 72 virgins waiting for them in paradise.

Here's a short history of my suicide note writing ...

Reading on, Calvino noted that Raphael had written a new suicide note every Saturday for nearly two years. Close to a hundred notes. It had become a habit to make a suicide note, photograph it, print it, and then hide it behind one of his framed paintings, a different one every time. He also made a collage of the notes, with photographs of the paintings lacquered onto a wooden surface. Each note expressed his state of mind at that moment: he gave the time of day, the day of the week, month, and year. Each was written as if he was going to die that day, as if he'd stopped living at that time and place. After a while, as Gavin had observed, it became a game that Raphael played with himself—a recursive loop of suicide notes feeding back on the author, who continued to live one more life, one more day. It was a mental exercise. Each day that he decided to stop living, a model would arrive, and he would decide this wasn't the day to die.

... If that doesn't make me Hamlet, what does? Writing in the third person about myself gives me a feeling of what it is like when you are dead. Our lives exist inside the first person "I" or "me." We die in the first person ... but what is written next can only be written in one way—in the third person.

The Bach fugues were written by and for those who were unshakeable in their belief of God. Their particular sound echoed from their channel to emotional certainty. That channel is shutting down. Some people kill themselves because they see no point in sticking around once those beliefs have evaporated. They have done enough shopping and find nothing else to buy. The world has divided itself into believers and non-believers, and the former are making a last, desperate effort to reclaim the mental space that Bach once carved out as theirs.

In my last session with Gavin, I told him about my work at the hospital in Montreal. He asked what I remembered most. I told him I realized that a hospice is a place for the dying to be cared for until they die, but a mental hospital is a place where a patient who wishes to die is forced to live.

Gavin, my Muay Thai buddy and counselor, you rock!

You understand and talk Muay Thai. It is my paintings you don't get. Just like you don't get my wish to jump onto the raft out of his life. You've given me a chance with the hotline. I appreciate that confidence. I don't think I have betrayed you with any caller. I did my best each time to defend the old black-and-white world that pushed them into a grey funk. I lied to them. Sweet-talked them. Coaxed them. Pleaded like the best of the volunteers. They desperately wanted me to give them my consent to live. I gave it.

My boxing and painting careers have taught me the art of dancing on my toes and going more than one round. To be ready. To be prepared.

What I left out of my discussion with Gavin was this ... When the time comes, I won't be the victim of a whim, an impulse. To even call me a victim is to buy into the "life is precious and to be treasured" point of view. Once a puppet looks up and sees the strings by which he is dangling, he cannot go back.

"Muay bplum" is the Thai term for wrestling from the clinch in the Muay Thai ring. Bplum has another meaning—it also means "rape" in Thai. In both cases the clinch is about physical force and the lack of consent. There is another possibility rattling around that no one talks about—being forced to remain in life without one's consent. Either you maintain a relationship with life ... or you break the clinch, cut the strings on the puppet and drop out of the performance.

I don't need anyone's consent to stay alive ... or not.

In Bangkok lies and liars come pre-assembled, pre-packaged, even pre-plugged in. All brands are available. My motto is ... Believe nothing you are told. Never kneel to authority. Don't consent to lies in return for comfort. And never glance up unless you are prepared to deal with the strings.

THREE

MANY OF THE same faces turned up for the second night of Raphael's funeral. The previous evening it had rained, but this time the hue of sky was robin egg blue. The sun had turned Bangkok into an oven. Inside the sala the mourners sat in sweat-soaked clothing, shivering in the air-conditioning. Seemingly half-suffocated, they looked like they'd spent too long in a sauna.

An old friend of Calvino's who was English, Alan Osborne, used the phrase "like a bad penny" for the recurrence of someone or something counterfeit. In any pocket of change, sooner or later a bad penny showed up. When you discovered it, you would quietly pass it along to the next sucker, only to find a day or two later that someone had passed it back to you. Calvino had a feeling that Oi, Raphael's maid, had passed him a bad penny on the first night by telling him about the bribery notebook. Sometimes passing the bad penny along isn't an option. Calvino couldn't spend it. He couldn't even tell anyone about it. With this bad penny he'd have to just keep it in his pocket and wait for the owner to show up. He sensed the owner would be waiting for him on the second night. Whoever it was would be sweating not from the present heat but from the fear of being dropped in a boiling pot.

"None of the volunteers had anything useful to pass on about the drug," he told Pratt.

Pratt clenched his jaw, sighed, and stared at Raphael's coffin.

"That's unfortunate," he finally said.

"The volunteers are civilians. They know the world from looking at it through a particular window. It's no surprise asking them drew a total blank."

"In the last year, pentobarbital has turned up in several other suicide cases. Thai suicides that don't make the *Bangkok Post*."

Pratt knew how to throw a punch. This one came as a knockout. Only the greenest farang could assume he understood the tensions and conflicts inside the real lives of Thais from reading the *Bangkok Post*.

Pentobarbital was Pratt's bad penny. Illegally obtained drugs like this one were a relay race, a passing down the line, hand to hand, until the ultimate user popped it into his mouth and swallowed it down with Mekhong whiskey. The chain might be long or short. Pratt was right that foreigners, while consumers of all things Thai, barely had an idea how things really worked or were distributed in a system that was beyond their experience.

That left open the question of who had passed the pentobarbital to Raphael. Whoever it was, that person, an accomplice in the death, might be among the people at the funeral. Looking over the crowd in the sala, Calvino wondered who among them might have assisted Raphael. Had he or she helped others to kill themselves using the drug? Calvino listened to the drone of the monks' chanting, thinking not only about the drug supplier but also the owner of the bribery notebook. Pratt and Calvino sat side by side, jingling their bad pennies in silence.

In Thailand there was always another reason layered below the first one, like Russian nesting dolls. Pratt's volunteering for the funeral arrangements had a second reason: he owed a favor to an old friend, a couple of years his junior, who had one year until retirement from the police department, and Pratt worried he might not survive that long. There had been considerable turnover among the department brass since the coup. Through witch-hunts, self-imposed exiles, and public humiliations, the mood had changed inside the department. Ever-changing suspicions meant it was hard to know who could be trusted, and the senior brass tied to a short military leash.

Internal fights over territory created enemies and raised suspicions. Cops Pratt had known for years had stopped talking to him, partly because he was noted for his honesty. What had once been a virtue had become a liability. He thought about all those years before he'd been part of the department; the police force he'd joined had been different. Or had he, as a young officer freshly returned from America, wanted to see something that had never been there?

Pratt's friend in the department, whom he was trying to help, had been assigned responsibility to head a foreign suicide/murder task force and report with a recommendation in sixty days. It was an impractical assignment with an impossible deadline—another dark, gloomy cloud casting shadows over the friend's future. Looking back, he could see now that it was inevitable that the junta would call for swift, bold action in every arena.

Raphael Pascal's death had been widely reported in the local Thai press. It was a good story to sell newspapers— "Young Canadian, controversial painter of prostitutes, kills himself with pentobarbital." His death contained all of the elements the media loved to run with. After a Thai journalist snapped a headshot of Charlie inside Raphael's studio, they played up the survival of the suicide's loyal golden retriever as well. Within hours, a couple of anonymous posters on Facebook and Twitter had floated a number of cover-up conspiracy theories that suggested murder. Nothing the Thai police spokesman said had stopped the speculation.

The rumors had tarnished the country's reputation and were discouraging tourism. Legal action was threatened against anyone in the social media posting such rumors. Politics had taken over the department; politics was in the driver's seat, and there was only room for one driver.

Pratt had been advised to keep a low profile while making quiet inquiries in the hope he might flush out the dealer. Policing was managing the pressure cooker so it didn't blow up in the face of the powerful. Like a Thai funeral, department politics had many ancient beliefs, practices, and rituals. Pratt knew what worked most of the time and the boundaries beyond which no one was prepared to venture. Such knowledge should bring wisdom, he thought to himself. Only the knowledge was always incomplete, and one of the things wisdom instructed was never to trust someone like Pratt who no longer had skin in the game.

During the chanting, Pratt thought how Calvino had avoided mentioning any of the suicide cases he'd worked, or even the suicides that he'd witnessed. He could tell that Calvino was holding back on him. Pratt could write it off as funeral sala sadness, but it didn't stop him from wondering if Calvino had shut down part of his mind, pushed it away, or anchored it deep beneath the surface of his conscious mind. Mourning the loss of someone could have that effect. But what if the pressure on Calvino got out of control? Then what? But Pratt had no idea what was going on inside Calvino's head. Half the time he didn't even know his own thoughts.

Watching a man on his way to a funeral was to see him for the first time, Pratt thought. Shakespeare talked about death, of course. Pratt struggled to remember the line from *Measure for Measure*.

The monks put down their fans, and the temple attendants began bringing in food.

Calvino said, "Day two, and I can try my luck with some new faces."

Pratt was far away inside his own thoughts. He responded by saying, "Ay, but to die, and go we know not where."

"Is that Shakespeare's way of saying don't bother, it's a dead end?"

"It's my way of saying I wasn't paying attention."

"I'm sorry I was late, Pratt," said Calvino.

"You look like you just woke up."

Pratt thought it wise to let Calvino change the subject. He looked rough, as if he'd gone to sleep in an alley and woken up in a dumpster.

Calvino stifled a yawn, shook it off like a boxer who'd taken a powerful right hook to the chin.

"I really should cut back on my reading."

"What ever happened to the woman in the film business," Pratt asked, "the one you were making som tam for?"

Pratt secretly liked to live vicariously through what he imagined to be Calvino's life as a single man in Bangkok.

"She found a new chef and kitchen."

"Meaning, you didn't get a call back?"

"I could have opened a vein and bled out. I told myself, forget her. That's show business in the City of Angels."

Calvino glanced around the sala. The white overhead fluorescent light washed over the faces, giving them a shiny, polished look. Most of them were young; it was unusual to see so many farang faces Raphael's age displaying solemn, remote, even anxious expressions of grief. Floral arrangements with hand-written names on banners now flanked the coffin three rows deep. The sala had quickly filled up. Most of the chairs were occupied. The second night of the funeral had brought another surprisingly large turnout.

Pratt said, "I'm trying to remember the name of the financial guy, English, who was murdered, and the killer tried to make it look like suicide."

"Hoadly. Ben Hoadly."

"I'd forgotten it," said Pratt. "Obviously you hadn't. Thanks."

"It's a curse."

Pratt smiled.

"Just the opposite. 'Ignorance is the curse of God; knowledge is the wing wherewith we fly to heaven.'"

"It wouldn't be a funeral without Shakespeare," said Calvino.

He nodded at Gavin, who was already seated in the back of the sala.

"All funerals for the young are tragedies," Pratt said.

Pratt had two children, and Raphael's demise was a reminder that death culled from the living of all ages. It frightened him as a father, and he'd hugged his kids the night before and told them he loved them.

Calvino stood up and looked at the rows of people behind him. Heads turned, and whispers came from the hotline volunteers in the back of the room.

"We can catch up on Shakespeare later," Calvino said.

Pratt removed his shoes and walked to the altar in front of Raphael's large framed self-painting, which had replaced the photograph from the first day. He knelt, lit an incense stick, bowed, and walked back to the front row seat to sit down. Calvino performed the ritual after Pratt finished. The eyes of the mourners watched him from the moment he knelt. This was the man anointed by Raphael. Everyone had a theory to explain how that had happened. Later, as he walked down the aisle, a slow buzz of conversation rose. The mood in the sala changed.

The mourners appeared more relaxed this time, comfortable with the fact that the large photograph of the deceased and his coffin had already been emotionally swallowed and digested. The novelty of Raphael's death had begun to wear off as people entered the next stage of grief—acceptance of the loss as another event in their lives. It occurred to Calvino that Thai funerals are like package tours. The first day people are nervous, disorientated, clutching their bags, waiting at a meeting point with a bunch of strangers. By the second day they are no longer strangers but a group with a mission: to explore the artifacts of the living. The only difference was Raphael's mourners had arrived at their destination to find a coffin, and they could imagine, many for the first time, that it was a preview of their own.

The monks shifted weight as attendants served them food and gave offerings of soap, toothpaste, robes, and candles. The mourners talked among themselves with less self-consciousness than the previous evening. A couple of people stepped outside for a cigarette. Others talked and waited for the food to be served to the guests—monks first, guests second. The order of the universe is sequential, thought Calvino, as he moved to the back and took a seat next to Gavin de Bruin.

"I see the volunteers turned out again tonight," said Calvino.

Gavin watched him look over the volunteers.

"Still looking for the guy who sold Raphael the pentobarbital?"

"Looks like that road leads to a dead end," said Calvino.

"Raphael appreciated your humor. I hope the police find whoever it was. We've had callers on the hotline asking about it."

Calvino raised an eyebrow.

"Word spreads quickly," he said.

"Those who have lost the will to live are a tight community."

"Speaking of the community," said Calvino, "there's something you might be able to help me understand. I read Raphael's web page, and I have a couple of questions."

"I'm not surprised you don't understand everything. But frankly, I don't know any more than what I told you last night. We were sparring partners. He came to me for counseling. He worked the suicide hotline. That's about it."

Gavin smiled. He'd anticipated more questions. He leaned forward, looking at Raphael's self-portrait.

It was Calvino's turn to smile.

"I came across an initial in the diary, for someone whose name starts with the letter 'L,' and I thought you might know who he was referring to."

"You find all kinds of references to people in Raphael's diary," said Gavin. "It is a stunning view of how a child's mind is wired inside a commune. It formed his thinking about relationships between adults, sexual freedom, communal living, cooperation, art, friendship ... and it left a sizeable chip on his shoulder about money."

Gavin gestured at the painting.

"I hope you don't mind that I asked General Pratt if it might be displayed instead of that awful photograph of him in the T-shirt."

Sometimes it was valuable to let someone talk until they reached a point of silence. Sometimes that talk is intended to deflect a question. Calvino wasn't going to make it easy for him.

"This 'L' person is someone I'd like to talk with," Calvino finally continued. "But I need more than an initial to go on. I thought since Raphael and you were close, he might have told you something he didn't write in the diary about a Mr. L or Miss L."

Questioning someone at a funeral was hard enough. But questioning a mental health worker at the funeral of a suicide victim made it doubly challenging. Calvino made a point of looking around the room.

"Is L in the sala tonight? If he or she is, just tell me where."

Shrinks knew all the subterfuges, sleight of hand tricks, ways to reframe the question. Gavin's eyes stayed focused on Calvino, who had stayed on message. He'd dialed into a frequency and was waiting for something to rise above the static.

"Sia L was what people call him. Raphael mentioned Lang, Sia Lang, Sia L—take your pick of names—in passing. He's Chinese. Came here from Shanghai about five years ago and set up a consulting business."

"What kind of consulting?"

"Trade, business, commerce," said Gavin.

"What was his business with Raphael?"

"He had a pipeline into the nouveaux riches from the mainland."

"Chinese buyers for Raphael's art," said Calvino.

"That sort of thing."

"Where's his office?"

Gavin looked surprised.

"Just because I know the name doesn't mean I know how to reach him or exactly what he does. Have you asked Raphael's girlfriend? I vaguely recall she's the one who introduced him to Raphael."

"I'll do that," said Calvino.

Gavin moved to return to his group of volunteers.

"You didn't see it coming?" asked Calvino.

Gavin turned back to face Calvino. To judge by the look on his face, he had asked himself the same question.

"People are always asking us why we didn't manage to talk someone out of it. Why didn't we pick up the signals and intervene? Why didn't I stop Raphael? Sometimes it works that way. Mostly it doesn't. Someone like Raphael, who wants to die, isn't reachable through talk. When the time comes, they don't warn you they're really going to do it. They just do it."

Calvino looked at the group he'd joined the previous evening at the Bamboo Bar.

"But aren't hotline volunteers supposed to be experts at getting to suicidal people before they kill themselves?"

Gavin glanced at the others in the row as if seeking to locate one such person. He turned back to Calvino.

"Don't worry, Mr. Calvino. In the case of a suicide there is always enough guilt to around. No one is left short. Also, remember, the hardest people to reach are the ones like Raphael who have worked in mental health themselves. They know all the tricks of the trade. All of our hotline volunteers have previously worked in mental health. Most of us have worked in private hospitals. But in this line of work you become acclimatized to death, violence, and crazy, unstable, and unhappy people. Such people have no brakes on the speed or direction of their thoughts, drives, or impulses. Or if they have brakes, they sometimes choose not to use them.

"Inside a mental hospital, you work with all kinds of patients. You're around them day and night, watching them. You are part of their lives. It doesn't take long before you realize that what goes on inside their heads also goes on inside your own head. The difference is the degree to which any feeling of hope or meaning has been stripped away. Most patients don't cope well once hope and meaning are gone. They feel less than human. Some patients are clearly disturbed; others are there only because they disturb us. We lack the courage to make a fine distinction between the two kinds of patients. Someone should write a Ph.D. thesis about how health workers swim in a sea of the trouble and then can't find their own way back to shore."

"You're saying that's what happened to Raphael?"

Gavin shrugged, his lips firmed up.

"He was an assistant nurse in a private mental hospital. He worked, boxed, and painted. He left his job and traveled to Thailand. He was burnt out. He joined our hotline as a volunteer."

"Did he quit the hotline volunteering because he lost people?" asked Calvino.

Gavin looked away, catching the eye of a member of the hotline, gathering his thoughts as if asking himself what was the truth of his relationship with Raphael Pascal.

"He left after the second suicide, a woman. Beyond that I really don't know. He was a friend I met through Muay Thai, and he also worked with me as a volunteer, at my suggestion. I gave him advice, but it wasn't on a formal basis," said Gavin.

"Don't look surprised," he continued. "Our line of work is like that of a house painter: his house is likely to be the one most in need of paint. He sees the damage and flaws in everyone else's house but doesn't see the damage in his own."

Gavin wandered back to his friends, and Calvino returned to his seat next to Pratt.

"Nothing more about the pentobarbital," said Calvino.

"Do you think he's holding back?"

Calvino shook his head.

"I doubt it. He's got no reason to."

That wasn't what Pratt had wanted to hear. Pratt's attention was firmly tuned in to the narrow bandwidth of the drug connection. It made him blind. Calvino's Law: Once you dial into a man's mental bandwidth, not only do you understand the station he listens to, you understand that other stations are out of range. Calvino had been there and understood the trap. For him Raphael's death played out over the broadband, and the more Calvino looked, the more he realized that how he killed himself mattered far less than how he lived and touched the lives around him. The signals from the night world of his models were particularly amplified in his head. The sala was filled with many of the same women. Sia L or Lang was a rock under a river, and all that the outside observer could see was how the water on the surface parted.

"Did you find out anything else?" asked Pratt.

It was one thing to remain silent; it was another to lie.

"Gavin said Raphael quit working the phone hotline after a second caller killed herself."

"It's hard to let go of those who die on your watch. The sense of responsibility lingers long afterwards."

Pratt had hoped for more. The displeasure registered in his expression, a mixture of disappointment and frustration, and it made Calvino wonder why. Nothing out of the ordinary cast doubt on the conclusion that Raphael had killed himself, and there were no leads on how he had acquired the drug to do the job. Given the many women who had gone in and out of his studio, the odds of finding that one person who had information about the drug transaction were small.

"There is always doubt," said Calvino. "But in this case everything points to suicide."

"There is pressure in the department to open up the case."

"Open it up? Normally, they'd close a case like this. You can pick it apart, but all the parts will just fit back again, like reassembling a rifle. It's the same weapon; nothing's changed. He killed himself."

"What concerns me is the how," said Pratt. "Someone supplied him with a restricted drug. That made it too easy. I don't like that easy part. I want it stopped. It should be hard to kill yourself."

"Do you really think your bosses are worried about the pentobarbital, Pratt?"

Pratt sighed.

"Raphael's not the only one who used it. That's the concern."

"Why focus on Raphael and not the other cases?"

"One was Chinese and the other Japanese. Nothing turned up in either investigation. But Raphael's case is unique."

"How so?"

"Two of his models used the same drug. That's unlikely to be a coincidence."

Calvino shook his head in disbelief.

"I didn't know," he said. "In the land of the living, no one is talking."

"Raphael had painted each of them," said Pratt.

"And you didn't tell me."

Pratt looked wounded by the implied accusation, until he reflected that the withholding of this information had been intended to protect Calvino.

"Murder is on the table."

"Whose table?"

Pratt looked straight ahead and was silent for a moment.

"Your table, Vincent. You are the one who stood to gain financially."

"Pratt, how do I have a motive? I didn't know about his intention to leave me the paintings until I read the suicide note."

"Imagine how someone who isn't your friend might read the situation. He came to your office. He gave you a painting. You sat for him at his studio. In other words, you knew him. He became more than just a missing person you found. He told you things about himself."

"Someone seriously thinks I arranged his death because I wanted his paintings?"

"You can roll your eyes. But it doesn't stop suspicions from being raised. Look, you've been down this road before."

Calvino felt the prickle of sweat running down his spine. Memory of that road made his heart race. Pratt jogged his memory about the killing of a young mem farang—bullet wound to the head from a gun shot at a party in Bangkok.

"Remember the name Samantha McNeal from a few years back?" asked Pratt. "Quentin Stuart," he continued, "the Hollywood writer who got you involved in that case? Turned out it wasn't suicide after all. Raphael's death might be a repeat."

"I was never a suspect in her murder."

"True," said Pratt. "The theory is you befriended Raphael, saw the potential in his art, and planned his death. You found a way to slip pentobarbital to two of the models, and forged at least one of their suicide notes."

"The Thai hookers wrote their suicide notes in English?"

"The custom is to look for patches and to ignore holes," said Pratt.

"Raphael was a kid, but yeah, we were friends. What's your advice?"

"Find the pentobarbital dealer."

Suicide was the one crime you never saw in police re-enactment photographs in the media. No photo-op— nothing in it for the brass, no pointing at a body by the suspect, and no neatly framed package of guilt for the world to swallow. Unless it was or a high-profile Thai or a farang, you never even read the news of the death.

Such deaths slipped under the darkness of night and were forgotten like passing nightmares. Sometimes in life, though, there were deaths that remained in memory and refused to go away. Out of all the random deaths, Raphael's suicide floated to the surface in the department. It had turned into that rare man bites dog case as a senior police officer decided that an air-tight suicide was a murder case instead. To the police that meant someone had a good reason to kill. In Thailand police work was all about who and what to follow. The cynic said follow the money, the psychologist said follow the big face, and the historian said follow the chain of command. But after you followed them all you found yourself at the base of a mountain that was impossible to climb.

FOUR

RAPHAEL PASCAL, WEARING a faded T-shirt with a dreamy-looking Caravaggio self-portrait on the front, had arrived at Calvino's office unannounced. Calvino wasn't in, and Ratana asked him to make an appointment. That didn't stop him from sitting down in a chair beside her desk, taking out a sketchpad, a pen, and ink from his backpack and drawing Ratana.

"You don't mind if I draw you?"

In his experience, very few people ever answered that question in the negative. When he was done, he carefully removed the sketch from his pad and presented it to her.

"It's ... it's beautiful," she said, looking up at the young artist.

She phoned Calvino and told him that there was a young artist in the office who wanted to see him. She didn't mention the sketch. Her style was to leave the reason for the appointment open-ended. Often a potential client was vague about his real reason for wanting to see a private investigator. Sometimes he or she would be embarrassed about the details of a personal problem and would only disclose the facts face to face with Calvino. At other times the caller gave no hint of a problem because he or she didn't have a problem, or least the kind of problem a private investigator might solve. Instead such callers wanted to sell Calvino something. It could be insurance, a time-share in a resort, shares in a hot company, or tickets to some event. Ratana acted as his gatekeeper, and through long experience she had developed good instincts that allowed her to spot the grifters, the time-wasters, the confused, and the hopeless, not to mention those who had no way of paying for the services of a private investigator.

"What's his problem?" asked Calvino.

She sniffed her nose at that question the way a dog sniffed the air for signs of trouble.

"He doesn't have a problem. He's interested in Galileo Chini."

"Is he a reporter?"

"He's a painter," she said, locking eyes with Raphael.

"You still haven't told me his name or why he wants to see me."

She smiled.

"He wants to meet you. As I said, he is a huge fan of Galileo Chini's art."

Calvino's Laws stated a cardinal rule: No one gets in the door without a legitimate reason to hire a private investigator.

"He wants to talk about art?"

She looked at Raphael as she replied, "I know the rule. But yes, he wants to talk about art, and I think you should make an exception."

She gestured to Raphael.

"What is your name again?"

He told her.

"It's Raphael Pascal."

"The missing person," said Calvino. "I found him."

"And now he's found you," she said.

Ratana blushed. Her boss was right. Raphael Pascal was the subject of a missing person case. She couldn't recall another case where the missing person had simply showed up at Calvino's office. Now he had been found. The case was closed. But what was he doing in the office? Ratana could no longer think of Raphael as having ever been missing. His presence filled the office. How could that presence go missing? She admired the image he'd sketched of her. She felt he had seen deep into the place where she truly existed, and no woman was ever immune to a man who possessed such a power.

Calvino's great-grandfather had been a well-known Italian painter who had received a royal invitation to come to Bangkok and paint. Arriving in 1911, Chini had stayed for three years. His paintbrush was his camera; he'd captured his images of Siam during his time there and then left for Italy, never to return. In 1913 his great-grandfather had finished one of his most famous oil paintings, *Last Day of the Chinese Year in Bangkok*. It was easy to miss at the Uffizi as it was hung on a wall in the corridor outside one of the galleries.

It was a few weeks after his meeting with Calvino later that day that Raphael Pascal came to the office a second time, carrying a large framed painting, which he carefully set down against the edge of Calvino's desk. The painting was inside an envelop of bubble-wrap. The multi-thousand bubble eyes, like those of a giant insect, obscured what lay beneath. Calvino looked at Raphael up and down, observing the blotches of paint on his wrists, hands, and neck. Raphael still looked like the kid he'd recently found, fresh from an athletic contest at his school. Lean, fit, dressed in a T-shirt, jeans, and track shoes, he could have emerged from a crowd of graduate students at one of the local universities.

Most painters, like most musicians, had hard-won gravitas etched into their faces and frames from a lifetime of suffering. Obscurity, poverty, and meager earnings wore their bodies and souls down to a pencil stub. Raphael's taut skin had some skid marks, like a racecar track, and a few of those lines ran laps under his eyes, but he bore no other physical signs of hardscrabble living. He had a raw energy, and at present it was focused on Calvino's face. The study couldn't have been more than a minute or so but seemed like much longer, as if the artist was absorbing every detail. Calvino noticed that Raphael's intensity and concentration in that extended moment added a dozen years to his own face.

"Paul said he sorted out things," Calvino said as Raphael sat down in the chair across from his desk.

"Oh, that. I didn't come to talk about him."

"Why did you come?"

"To talk about art."

"What do you know about art?" asked Calvino, sitting back in his chair, sizing Raphael up.

"What an artist looks for is what other people hide. They don't want anyone to see a certain way they smile, hold themselves, their wrinkles and sagging jowls. That's only on the surface. Art goes much deeper. People go to great lengths to hide their loneliness. Their emptiness because they instinctively know they are hollow. Art shows the true face. That's what makes it dangerous. You are a private detective. You understand better than most how difficult it is to find and reveal what others wish to remain secret."

The way he tilted his head and smiled made it obvious that in his world there was nothing more important or valuable to discuss than art and artists.

"I thought I'd already covered everything I know about Galileo Chini. Why do I have the feeling you're after something beyond Chini?" asked Calvino, as Ratana brought him a glass of water. "You want some family secret? Is that it?"

Ratana's entrance had broken Raphael's concentration. He sat with one hand on the large bubble-wrapped package.

He drank from the glass, swallowed slowly, and put the glass down.

"Mr. Calvino, I'd like to paint you."

"Paint me?"

Raphael nodded.

"Yes, it's for the last painting in a series. I've been unable to complete it. Why? I hadn't found the right person. Not until you came to my door looking for me—and all the time I'd been looking for you. Isn't life funny that way?"

Calvino knew that if you want to flatter a person, tell them you're a painter and you'd like to paint them. Their ego will drop like a bloated elephant and sink straight to the bottom pit of your personal vanity trap.

"Is it your habit to go to a private investigator's office and ask to paint him? Maybe you should ask yourself, 'What would Caravaggio have done?' "

Raphael smiled as Calvino looked at Caravaggio's eyes on his T-shirt. They were dull and clouded.

The question left Raphael embarrassed, and the mature, wise face deflated to a child's chastised mask of rejection.

"You're right. That was quite stupid of me. Caravaggio would have got you drunk before asking to paint you. I wanted to give you this."

He leaned forward and began unsticking the bubble wrap. When he finished, he stood the framed painting on Calvino's desk.

"Your great-grandfather, Galileo Chini, inspired me to come to Bangkok. I painted an homage to his Chinese New Year painting."

Calvino stood up from his chair and paced in front of the painting. It was a beautiful reproduction of Chini's great work, updated with modern Bangkok details—high-rises in the distance, a Toyota taxi, a woman in a Chinese dress carrying a Gucci bag, a Rolex on the arm of the man running in the foreground. Otherwise, the colour and contrast, and the play of the light from the fireworks had been faithfully depicted.

"How much do you want for it?"

"I'm not selling it you. I'm giving it to you."

"Look, kid, just come out and tell me what you want." The distant voice of his relatives in New York sang the chorus that no one ever gave you anything in this life, and someone who rolls in with something free is going to cost you an arm and leg at the end.

Raphael was staring at his face again, measuring some aspect or feature, taking in the coordinates. He moved like a tailor making mental notes about fabric and texture, and seeking a way to stitch the elements together.

"I like the painting. What if I give you some money?"

"I'll trade the painting if I can paint your portrait."

"There are a thousand guys who'd be happy for you to paint them. Take the money and go back to your studio and paint."

"Did you ever box?" asked Raphael.

Calvino had been asked a lot of questions in his office, but this was the first time someone had asked him about his boxing career.

"Why do you ask?"

"You have the face of someone who's been in the ring."

"How would you know? From TV or the movies?"

"I belong to a Muay Thai gym," he said, laying the painting flat on Calvino's desk and sitting back in his chair. "I know what a face that's taken a fist looks like."

Calvino sat down as well.

"You're a boxer and a painter. You don't find that combination very often in Bangkok. As far as I know my great-grandfather didn't take up Muay Thai when he

116

lived here. It's the kind of thing he probably would have mentioned."

"I love it. Muay Thai has taught me a great deal as a painter about what to look for in a person's face. I saw it in your face."

He had Calvino's attention.

"That's a new one."

"When you came to my studio and I looked at your face, I saw that your face shows a history of punishment. That's rare. Most people are the same. They can't take a single punch. People don't see the layers of damage carried in a face after it's healed."

"What layers do you see?"

He thought the kid had a high opinion of himself.

"Pain. That's what I see. Every time someone hits you in the face, you feel the pain. The effect on most men is the same. The pain pisses them off. They get angry and lash out at windmills. What Muay Thai taught me is to take the hit in the face but not to respond with anger. The secret is to reach inside and shake off the pain. Absorb it, own it, and make it your slave. You control your feeling of rage, and slowly that stops the pain from taking you hostage. You stay cool and calculated, dancing on your toes, waiting to land a counterpunch. You wait to throw that punch to force your opponent to submit. You learn that the highest goal of violence isn't to inflict pain but to force submission. I want to paint you because I see the face of a man who knows the secret deal he makes with anger when he experiences pain."

The kid was either one of the best bullshit artists he'd come across in all of his years in Bangkok, or he was the kind of creative dreamer, or visionary, who lived on another mental planet and checked in, now and again, to planet earth, plucking out an earthling to paint. Calvino leaned to the side, pulled out his wallet, and counted out twenty thousand-baht notes.

"I'm probably making a mistake. I should throw you out of the office."

"Are you afraid of being painted? Some people are."

"But I'm not."

"If not fear, what?"

The kid had a point, and Calvino looked at him across his desk, thinking that what was starting that afternoon would send ripples down the stream of time. He was climbing into a kayak with a young and over-confident farang who was trying to escape the rapids and rocks of his past. That usually didn't end well. But it was a hot afternoon in Bangkok. The rapids seemed far away, and he hadn't seen the rocks.

Ratana had come back into the office with the sketch Raphael had done of her and put it on his desk. It was two against one.

"Okay, here's the deal. You take the money for this painting, and in return I'll sit for another painting. But it isn't going to turn into an eighteen-month endurance event. I'll sit a maximum of two times, an hour each. If you can live with that, we have a deal. I buy the finished painting for ..."

Raphael beamed.

"I can finish the series. Thank you."

"What number am I in the series?"

Raphael smiled as if that was something he rarely did.

"Number six."

"And the first five paintings?"

"I will show them to you."

"If I don't like them?"

Raphael laughed.

"You aren't the only one who can take a punch, Mr. Calvino."

"Vinny. Call me Vinny."

FIVE

First Sitting

Raphael's studio was sparsely furnished. It had the noir basics: sofa, wooden dining table, bookcase, chairs, fridge and small oven in a tiny kitchen, bathroom with a toilet and shower, mattress in a second room, end tables, lamp, and rechargers connected to half a dozen power strips. Most of furnishings looked second—or third—hand, the wear and tear having left ugly gashes, dents, and scrapes. His belongings were meager, giving the studio a camped-in public place feeling like a squalid park where a bum had squatted for a time on the way to someplace else. Austerity was rarely a choice. Artists were no different from anyone else—they'd rather be in the Ritz than on a park bench. Now and again, Calvino had come across someone like Raphael who tested his rule of thumb about the nature of expats, art, and young people.

Walking into Raphael's studio, he asked himself who would consent to sex in such a dump?

The answer turned out to be many women. But Calvino didn't know that right away. Women wandered in and out all day long. They'd help themselves to whatever was in the fridge. They'd sit and watch him paint and then leave. His attention might turn away from the nude model he was painting and he'd smile at someone newly arrived, exchange a few words, and return to his paints.

What the description above leaves out was the vast number of Raphael's paintings. They were scattered like leaves after a tropical storm—disordered, chaotic debris flung into every corner. And the painter looked like a castaway floating in a raft of his paints.

And not just paintings, but dozens of different brushes, ranging from the very fine to one as large as a boxer's gloved fist, and a bewildering variety of hues in dozens of tubes of paint. The tubes lay scattered in no discernable order, nestled in the further painterly debris, including a collection of castoff bowls, bottles of turpentine, and rags torn from old shirts.

Calvino sat on a chair, and Raphael cleared a seat for himself as big as a foxhole amid the supplies on the floor. He sketched Calvino's face a half dozen times, scattering images on the floor that showed different profiles. Then, selecting a large canvas and working from a cross-legged position, he fell into a pattern of glancing between Calvino a few feet away and a painted image that slowly mapped the contours of Calvino's face. The women would come in and sit on the sofa, eat pineapple or mango, and talk to each other. The numbers rose and fell like a third-world stock exchange.

There was no air-conditioning in the room. Sweat rolled down Calvino's nose and dropped onto the floor. Raphael worked in Muay Thai shorts, barefoot and shirtless. His face glistened with sweat in the natural light that streamed in from a high window.

Raphael had been painting for nearly an hour. He painted with a clear urgency, using quick brush strokes and smoothing the surface of the canvas with his thumb. Working non-stop, he cruised almost silently through the heartland of their first session until it was interrupted by the arrival of an attractive young Thai woman in high heels, short shorts, and a skimpy top with long sleeves. She hadn't knocked. The door was unlocked and she let herself into the room. She confidently walked over to where Raphael sat and looked at the painting and then at Calvino. She squatted down and kissed Raphael on the cheek. None of the other women who had come to the studio had displayed this kind of affection. She had kissed him to establish her special position as The One, though Calvino knew that the girl who seems to be The One doesn't always last.

Raphael lay down the brush and searched under a pile of rags until he pulled out a wallet. Her eyes caught fire as he removed two thousand-baht notes and held them out. She took the money, kissed him again, and stepped back. The smell of her perfume lingered. He stopped to clean a brush and the turpentine fumes wiped out the soft fragrance of crushed rose pedals.

"She models for me," said Raphael. "Ning, that's her name."

"Can she take a punch?" asked Calvino.

Raphael smiled.

"Maybe. Most of my models work in the area. Massage parlors, bars, and nightclubs. They get beaten up. A customer or a boyfriend lands one. Most of the time it doesn't do a lot of damage. They come here to cry. One of them said I made her feel safe."

He nodded at Ning, pointing at her with his paintbrush as if measuring a feature of her face. A few feet away she began to disrobe, and Calvino wondered how long this interruption would last. She folded her clothes neatly and placed them beside a chair. Then she sat naked on the chair with a paperback book open in her hands, eyes downward, staring at the page. Calvino caught the author and title: Leonardo Sciascia's *The Day of the Owl*.

"Is it a good story?" Calvino asked her.

Ning looked up and smiled.

"My English no good. Sorry."

"You proved her right," said Raphael.

"How so?"

Ning turned the page of the book she couldn't read, breaking eye contact with Calvino.

"She told me that most of her older customers just want to talk. They don't want to fuck her. My other models say the same. Old guys pay a woman to smile and listen to stories about their lives. Men like that don't hit women. It's younger guys who do that. They should know better, but they don't."

"Violence is for the young," said Calvino. "A man can handle being punched in the face when he's twenty-something. Add twenty or thirty years, and the same punch puts a man down."

"I see it at the gym. Not a lot of old guys in Muay Thai training. But life is full of surprises, and you can never be sure. I think you're a guy who can still take a punch."

He waited for Calvino to say something.

"Why does that matter so much to you?"

Raphael shrugged.

"Not so much to me. It matters to women. They have no respect for a man who can't handle violence. They feel unsafe."

After a few minutes of intense work on Ning's painting, Raphael put down his brush and searched among the paint tubes for the right hues to produce the color of her painted nails. He looked over at Calvino.

"She's been giving you the eye. She can't make up her mind about you. Are you one of the old guys who doesn't want to just talk but wants to fuck her and give her a taste of the rough stuff? I can give you her phone number if you want."

Raphael was testing him and now waited for him to react.

"I hate standing on line," said Calvino.

He paused as if he wanted to say something else but stopped himself.

Raphael squeezed paint from a tube and screw back on the lid.

"She's a beauty. Aren't you, Ning?"

"I go home now," she said.

Raphael looked at his cellphone to check the time. She was right; the time was up. By the time he'd looked up, she had slipped on her bra and bright-blue-sleeved top. She stood up and stepped into her jean shorts.

"It's you she can't make up her mind about," said Calvino.

"You got that right. It takes a long time to decide whether to trust a man. You have to earn that trust."

He watched Ning walk past another woman who'd just come through the door.

"Tomorrow, you come back, and I finish the painting, okay?"

She waied him and kissed him again on the cheek before leaving.

It was a performance that Calvino was to witness a number of times as he waited to see whether his own sitting was concluded. In any case, Raphael's life was too interesting to walk away from, and Calvino had no urgent business to attend to. Like others who came to the studio, Calvino found it easy to fall into the rhythm of the endless cycle of models and half finished paintings.

Raphael was twenty-six years old but to the superficial observer could have passed as a teenager. The trouble was that in reality he was far too old for his years. His preternatural skill caught people off guard. The kid also had charm that wasn't lost on his models or on Calvino, either, who thought he could be his son. He had warmed to the idea of Raphael painting him as the old guy who could take a punch.

Over the course of the afternoon, other models not unlike Ning floated in and out of Raphael's studio as he painted. He'd turn, look up, and nod only to immediately return to his work, fiddling with his tubes of paints and brushes. Raphael didn't bother to introduce the other women. They were young and pretty, and there was a market for that combination. Some he gave money to; for one of the girls he fished out a cellphone still in the original box, and she snapped it up with the speed of a house lizard's lightning tongue targeting a mosquito.

Calvino had known other men who had a string of women. But this wasn't a string of pearls, evenly spaced; it was a pawnshop jewelry case with the cheap stuff laid out side by side with the expensive pieces. From where Calvino sat, reviewing the parade of models was like watching a carnival filled with entertainment and beautiful women. How many men would have given anything to live Raphael's life? The answer: many. It was the kind of performance that made people confuse the preternatural with the supernatural. Raphael's talented, skillful shaping, with raw passion, of the horror and the beauty of the universe was a step away from making him a cosmic prophet.

The last woman who came to the studio that day was nicknamed Pink. She had rows of scars on her left wrist. The puffy, ragged white lines had been made by a knife or a razor. They were like old scorch marks left by tiny emergency flares lit against a dark sky, screaming for rescue. They were ladder rungs dating the years of self-hate on her wrists. Had anyone noticed, had anyone cared? Not until she had stepped inside Raphael's studio and he used his paint and brushes to lift the veil of darkness, and for the first time she saw herself.

After she left, Raphael said, "Her boyfriend has a meth habit."

"When I see those cut marks," said Calvino, "I see a crude barcode someone cut into their flesh, and when you scan it, the message tells you all you need to know about hurting."

"I'm used to seeing that shit," said Raphael.

"Self-mutilation isn't something to get used to," said Calvino.

Raphael looked at Calvino's canvas and glanced up at his subject. He'd seen a different shape around the eyes come into focus as Calvino pushed back a ripple of anger. It was interesting how the emotions used the face as a billboard to communicate, and how the words spoken were just bad subtitles of that reality.

"That reminds me of the director of the hospital where I worked. He said the same thing the day he approved my leave of absence. He knew I wouldn't come back. I saved him the trouble of firing me."

Calvino wasn't expecting a confirmation and wasn't sure whether his being lumped together with a hospital director was Raphael's way of dealing with older authority figures. Raphael would have known what the scars meant for Pink's future. Potential customers would have a hang-up about a prostitute cutting herself, using her wrists as a public message board of her state of mind. It destroyed their illusion of the happy hooker and left in ruins the possibility of a guilt-free sensual encounter. In Raphael's world, though, it was a perfectly natural and understandable act of communication. Everyone who read that ladder of pain knew the story without having to be told.

"Were you a patient?"

Raphael stopped painting and smirked as he studied the canvas.

"I was an assistant nurse. Like I said, I *worked* at the hospital," he said, looking up at Calvino. "It was a small private mental hospital outside of Montreal. It had only sixteen rooms for the patients. Each one had a private room. My job was to make certain that they didn't destroy stuff and that they took their meds, and to stop them from killing themselves. Most of the patients were young women. The doctors couldn't do much for them except pump them with drugs. That kept them dreamy and manageable. An important term in a mental institution is 'managed care.' Scary, once you know what it takes to manage people who resist. I learned about women by working in a mental institution. Some of the sanest women on the planet are in these hospitals. Their parents, boyfriends, and relatives don't know what to do with them. I did what I could."

Calvino had seen many young men who'd burned out in Thailand. They didn't last long. It was no longer the tropical paradise to heal a troubled soul. Maybe it never had been. Raphael was part of the new generation that had lost what Calvino's generation only treasured as they aged—they had lived in a time when there had been a chance to go missing. Back then, no one would find you. No one would pull you back to the world you'd fled from.

"Is that why you took a leave of absence? Burnout?" asked Calvino.

Raphael resumed painting again, concentrating on Calvino's mouth, which motored from neutral to disapproving to happy, through constant muscle changes.

"I painted a number of the patients. You know what happened?"

"Someone turned you in for violating hospital rules," said Calvino.

"That came later. The director, doctors, and nurses were happy enough at the beginning. They had less resistance, less trouble from the patients once I started to paint them. The reports to the families had less bullshit when they said progress was being made in the treatment. Art therapy

126

enjoyed a brief victory. In the hospital around the doctors and management, no one called it art. It was recreational, or free space for the patients. They called it handicraft activity with staff supervision. Fucked up, right? But private hospitals are weird places. My modest victory in the name of art was short-lived."

"Van Gogh painted when he was in a mental asylum," said Calvino.

Raphael nodded in agreement.

"He did some of his best work inside the cage."

"What happened to make it go sour?"

Calvino was starting to like the kid.

"You really want to know?"

"There's some reason I found you hiding out in Bangkok. I never got a real explanation."

"Here's what happened. I asked the patients' permission before I painted them. Some said later that patients aren't legally capable of giving consent. Their minds can't cope with such decisions. They don't understand what it means to agree. But I asked the patients; they agreed. That was good enough for me. I also asked each of them to write out their personal story. I told them they could write whatever they wanted. Most wrote about the corner they turned that led them to a private room in a private mental hospital. Some of the best writing I ever read was in those stories. I left space on the canvas for them to write. A couple of patients wrote and wrote, turned the canvas over and filled in the back in tiny hand-written script. Stories filled with frustration, anger, rejection, hate, doubt, and despair. Powerful stories," he said, pausing as he looked for a tube of paint.

He talked as he worked, never losing track of his paints or his story.

"The main actors in these stories were family members, usually fathers and mothers, and the stories were about how butting heads with their families caused them endless amounts of grief. Then a few of the parents saw the painting of their daughter during visitors' hours. The patients were proud of their paintings and couldn't wait to show their parents."

"What was the problem?" asked Calvino.

"The problem came when one patient's mother read her daughter's story. She was totally pissed off and said that I'd put hateful ideas into her daughter's head. I said the stories weren't mine; I had only put a pen in the patients' hands. Soon the mothers and of course the fathers got into the act. They didn't want to read these stories, and they were highly embarrassed that doctors and other members of staff had read them. They'd heard the stories before and blocked them out. But seeing them written out on a painting was an experience that shattered them. Writing down these feelings made them official and public."

"After pushing your patients' noses into the shit, you can't have been surprised that others didn't think it improved their looks," said Calvino.

"You could say that. But it wasn't just words in the air. These were words attached to the painting of the person who told the story. That made the parents crazier than their daughters. They complained to the hospital director. This was a private hospital. Parents were paying a lot of money to treat their children, and they were being repaid with open hostility. They wanted a cure, they said. Painting and story-telling were telling just one side of the story and distorting the truth. I said all stories are inaccurate and distorted. So what? It was the patient's story. If she wanted to share her personal feelings, I had no problem with her writing it down on the canvas. The patients were too fragile and easily misled, I was told. The parents wanted me out of the hospital and away from their children. They got their wish."

"That's why you were fired?"

"How many times have you broken your nose?" Raphael asked, avoiding the question about his dismissal.

Calvino showed three fingers.

"You got the boot?" he asked again.

"In part. I'll come to the other part. Let me work on getting your nose right."

Calvino shifted to a more indirect line of questioning.

"What happened to the paintings?" asked Calvino.

"The director confiscated my paintings and locked them in a storage room. He said I'd need a court order to get them. I thought, why bother with courts, judges, lawyers— the people I'd have to pay for a key to the door. Even if I had the money, I couldn't see how they'd take my side against the hospital. I decided to cut my losses. I came to Thailand, asking myself what value is there to life if you can't paint the truth?"

"Have you found an answer?"

"Sure have. The money is in painting beautiful lies."

A woman wore off-duty outfit favored by the fish-tank girls in an upscale soapy massage parlor, showed up. Big breasts, narrow hips, dressed casually, jean shorts and an orange and brown sleeveless top that ended four inches above her navel. As a showcase for waist and legs, she couldn't have chosen a better outfit. She looked like Cinderella a couple of weeks after the ball. Unlike the previous model, this one displayed her success with pride; her bare arms were free of scars.

"Can you loan me two thousand baht?" Raphael asked Calvino.

It wasn't really a loan request. Raphael wanted a gift to make a gift.

The girl not so much stood as posed before Calvino, hands on her hips, smiling at him as he slowly pulled his wallet out, opened it, peeled off two notes, and handed them to Raphael, who raised his passing hand like a quarterback. He was becoming conditioned to Raphael's steady stream of girls who climbed the stairs to his studio. None of them stayed very long. They came with a purpose and were in and out in a few minutes, boyfriends waiting in the street on motorcycles. The studio was an analog space that had the density and speed of the digital world. These real flesh-and-blood women floated in and out of the studio as if made from pixels.

The last woman to arrive weighed no more than forty kilos. At five feet, one inch tall—trim, compact, and perfectly proportioned in her short shirt—she might be mistaken as having been grown from a futuristic bonsai starter kit. She was the size of a golf trophy the winner could display on his mantel. Raphael stretched out his hand and pressed a cellphone into her tiny hand, which folded around it like a Venus flytrap disguised in the form of a Japanese miniature tree. The first thing she did with the cellphone was take a selfie of herself alone, and then she sat down next to Raphael and took several more photos of herself making faces as a kind of facial sign language right next to Raphael, whose expression remained unchanged. She kissed him on the lips and like a fairy disappeared into the kitchen.

"You can take a girl's photo or let her take her own photo. They like to look at their own pictures. It's proof they exist. They post their selfies on Instagram or Facebook for their friends and customers. New customers send a message after seeing the photos. I've paid them, too. I don't judge them, and I don't judge their customers. I feel, though, that you should pay women for modeling, talking, or fucking. If you are an artist, you should give them more money because they make money for you when you sell a painting."

"And you've explained this to your models, and they understand it?"

Bangkok was filled with men who thought they understood what a working girl wanted, and most of the time what they understood was wrong.

"It's simple, Vinny. The reason their heads are messed up is men want to fuck them for free—or photograph, film, or paint them for free. That's bad karma. I say pay them whether you fuck them or not. It's a show of respect. That's what they want from a man. Respect. Besides they need the money for their families and their boyfriends."

A steady stream of women filtered through Raphael's life like bees around a hive. The difference between the beauties and the burnouts among them was measured, like the distance of stars, in the amount of time on the job. Or if not stars, then combat veterans bearing physical scars, reminders of having been shot, stabbed, sandbagged, or shoved down a flight of stairs. But the deeper scars weren't visible. Inside their world, everyone suffered one kind of wound or another; each had multiple purple hearts.

"Jenny, wait until I find your painting," said Raphael. "Sit down over there."

He pointed at a chair. She sat and waited.

Raphael rose from the floor and walked around the studio looking through piles of canvases. He found what he'd been searching for, a painting of the bonsai-size girl, and took the canvas over to where she sat and handed it to her. He gave her a pen and told her to write her story. Jenny lowered her head, looking at herself in the painting. There she didn't look small; she looked larger than life, her eyes shiny, large, focused in an intense stare at something. On closer examination, the naked woman's elongated torso was attached to anatomically questionable legs, hips, and breasts—she was painted as a human tree of life. She had African-like tribal scars on her belly. The skin was puffed as if a colony of night crawlers had burrowed underneath. A pail had tipped over and poured water onto root-like feet disappearing into the earth.

She wrote on the canvas, holding the pen in one hand and her cellphone in the other.

"It won't take long, Vinny," said Raphael. "You can walk around if you want. I've been waiting for Jenny to come around and finish the canvas. It's done only once she's added her story."

"The same drill as in the hospital," said Calvino.

"I guess it is. Except Jenny's sane. Most of the time anyway."

She looked up from writing.

"What you say about me? Talk Thai."

Calvino told her in Thai that Raphael was only saying good things about her. She looked skeptical.

"Why he paint me as ugly ghost?"

"What did she say?" asked Raphael.

"Why did you paint her as an ugly ghost?"

"She's not a ghost. She's springing alive from the earth."

Calvino failed in translating the explanation into Thai. He wasn't certain he understood it himself.

"Jenny's painting is number two in the Six Degrees series. I've spent months trying to get her to come back and write her story. She's been here three times before and run out each time, saying she wouldn't write anything."

"It's not only artists who are temperamental," said Calvino.

He could see his image starting to emerge from his own canvas, now resting on the floor in front of Raphael. He could draw no immediate judgment, looking at the image upside down and incomplete.

Calvino looked up, and framed in the door of the bedroom was a large golden-furred dog. Raphael called her.

"Charlie, come join the party."

The golden retriever carefully stepped around the stacks of canvases and walked over to Raphael, licking him on the cheek. Raphael put the paintbrush between his teeth, stretched out, and scratched Charlie's neck. Jenny, who had taken to sitting on the floor, ignored the dog.

"She wants to go for a walk and take a piss," said Raphael. "Every day about this time she wants out. It's like clockwork."

Charlie was approximately the same size as the bonsai girl on the floor.

"I want Jenny to finish what she's writing. Can you do me a favor?"

"If we're finished today," said Calvino, "I'll take her out for a walk."

Calvino called her name and Charlie walked over to him.

"Golden retrievers are real sluts. They'll go with anybody," said Raphael. "Still, I think she likes you. Her leash is under the sofa somewhere. I think. Don't remember for sure."

Calvino found it under the sofa and attached it to Charlie's collar. Jenny continued to work slowly on her story.

"Take your time," said Raphael.

Calvino walked down the pavement with Charlie in the heat, stopping as she squatted, sniffed, and then signaled that she was ready to move on. She gave Calvino time to think about his great-grandfather who'd lived in Bangkok more than a hundred years ago. Bangkok had always been a city that attracted artists, writers, con men, hustlers, outlaws, and rejects. Bangkok was the preferred refuge for outsiders on the run, for the desperate, and for losers looking for one last chance to grab a berth on someone else's dreamboat. Chini, an artist, had a different story; he'd been invited to Thailand. He'd lasted three years before returning to Italy.

Calvino's grandfather once told him in Florence that every artist could be judged by the quality of his mistakes. It had been Salvador Dalí who said, "Mistakes are almost always of a sacred nature." Raphael was two years into his resident artist period, and artists like everyone else make mistakes—they choose the wrong city, the wrong partner, the wrong models, colors, friends, or dealers. Sometimes they paint mistakes as a provocation in a "catch me if you can" test of wits. Caravaggio's men had two-meter-long arms; Titian's had two left hands. Were they really mistakes? Raphael's tree-of-life version of the bonsai girl took liberties with the human body, and some people would have called the choices mistakes.

Charlie looked up at Calvino, ears pricked, head tilted. The dog pulled him toward a side soi. Twenty meters inside the soi was a vendor selling chicken livers and gizzards on wooden skewers. Calvino bought one, pulling the cooked meat pieces off one at a time. Charlie's concentration never wavered as each piece slipped down her throat. After Charlie swallowed the last piece of gizzard, Calvino checked his watch and wondered if Jenny would ever complete her story.

SIX

Second Sitting

CALVINO WAS RUNNING late for his second and final sitting. He climbed the stairs two at a time until he reached the landing of Raphael's studio. The door had been left halfway open. He pushed it back and walked inside. In the paint-splattered main living area a window with partly drawn tattered curtains looked out onto a brick wall. There was no sign of Raphael, only the smells of turpentine and paint.

He called out Raphael's name.

There was a long silence.

"Bedroom," moaned Raphael in a low voice that trailed off.

A moment later a young, tall, leggy woman with blue eyes flew out of the bedroom like a wildebeest crossing a crocodile infested river. She had long blonde hair matted with sweat, no makeup, and a five-hundred-dollar nose job. Working her left arm into a rumpled sundress, she raised her right arm to drink from a half-empty bottle of Mekhong whiskey—Thai firewater made from ninety-five percent sugar cane and molasses and five percent rice. She smiled at Calvino and offered him the bottle. There was only one way to deal with the strong smell of Mekhong. He tipped the bottle to his lips, felt the burn, and handed it back.

"I prefer vodka to this shit," she said, slurring her words as he passed the bottle back to her.

"Is he okay?" he asked, nodding toward the bedroom.

"Raphael tried to drink me under the bed," she said, "but his bed is on the floor. He passed out, and when he opened his eyes, he drank some more."

"What's his problem?"

"He boom-boom too many ladies. Thai ladies, Korean ladies, Russian ladies, Kenyan ladies."

She stopped as if auditing her memory for any omitted nationality.

"And too many ladies like him too much. The Thai ladies call him a butterfly that paints. And a painting butterfly is no good for a lady," she said, as she opened the studio door and left.

Calvino stuck his head into the bedroom and Raphael was in bed with the sheet over his head.

"Didn't we have an appointment?"

"Where is she?"

"Who?"

"Kristina. Forget about it. My head feels fuzzy. But I do some of my best work when things go out of focus."

He lowered the sheet and sat up on his elbows. He looked around, saw Charlie next to the bed, rolled over to the other side and looked on the floor.

"The bitch ran out with my bottle?"

"Who?"

"Kristina. I think that's her name. She's from Moscow."

He cupped his head in his hands.

"Fuck, my head is exploding."

"Why don't I come back another time?" said Calvino. "When you're feeling better."

"Stay!"

Raphael looked up, smiling.

"I didn't mean to shout."

"Being painted by a drunk isn't the way I want to spend my time."

"You're right. I'm an asshole. A drunk. A loser. A fuck-up. But look on the bright side."

"Which is?"

"Those are the qualities that make it easy for me to fit into this neighborhood. No one expects much from you. That's a good thing, isn't it, Vinny?"

"Feeling sorry for yourself?"

Charlie walked around the bed, smelled Calvino's leg, and licked his hand. She knew an easy mark when she met one. He patted her side.

"I'll be okay."

He belched.

"I'm feeling better already. Kristina tried to outdrink me. Moscow bitch. I told her I'm from Montreal. No one outdrinks someone from Montreal."

He swung his legs over the edge of the mattress and onto the floor. He pushed himself up and wobbled, his legs shaky, then fell back on the bed. Laughing, he stood up again.

"I need a joint and a cup of coffee."

In the kitchen Raphael poured two mugs of coffee and pushed one along the counter toward Calvino. He was dressed in the same Muay Thai boxing shorts that he'd worn the first time Calvino had come around.

"You know what I forgot?" he asked.

"Our appointment?" asked Calvino.

Calvino shook his head, looking at Raphael's thin limbs and bony chest, his hips braced against the sink as if he were about to puke. He'd gone too many rounds with the Mekhong bottle and didn't want to admit the Russian prostitute had won the last round.

"I forgot to pay her."

"She'll be back," guessed Calvino.

"They always come back."

That was the pull of youth. It wasn't always just about money. The women did return to Raphael in a way that would never happen again in Calvino's life. They cut a young man slack because youth itself had value when shared. Women like Kristina did sleep with older men, but because they paid, not because they valued the experience.

"They won't always come back," said Calvino.

"I know that. But I painted her," said Raphael. "Maybe you saw her in my painting?"

Calvino shook his head.

"I missed that one."

"I'll show you."

Shuffling across the floor, he squatted near the sofa and sorted through a pile of paintings. He pulled out one of a blonde Russian woman standing nude, stopping a fleet of Rolls Royce Silver Clouds. It was Raphael's interpretation of the man in front of the tanks at Tiananmen Square.

"What freedom means to a Russian woman is different from what it means to you or me, or the guy in front of the tanks in Tiananmen Square. Or Charlie."

Charlie lay on the floor; she was balanced on her back, hind legs splayed open, her muzzle and legs twitching as she ran inside dreamland.

"Do you like it?"

"She stops traffic," said Calvino.

"She is powerful."

He stared at his painting, eyes wide open, as if seeing some new detail in it for the first time.

"Her weapon is her body. She uses it to stop wealth in its tracks. One day that will end. They will run over her. But not today, maybe not tomorrow."

Raphael turned the painting over and then turned it upside down.

"She didn't write her story. I told her that she had to do that on the painting. Then we started drinking. She was naked. Sitting in that chair. One thing led to another. I got distracted. Put down my brush and took her into the bedroom. She wanted to drink vodka. I gave her Mekhong. We fucked. And then you were standing over the bed."

He scratched his two-day growth of beard looking at the painting.

"Sometimes the model doesn't write much. One of my models wrote one line: 'Life sucks and so do I.' You can read into that whatever you want."

He found the painting with the one-line story and showed it to Calvino.

"See? I didn't make it up."

He touched the canvas with his forefinger. The paint was still wet. She must have been in the studio just before the Russian, thought Calvino.

"I've painted other Russians," Raphael said, digging through a pile of paintings and pulling one out. "Anna."

Calvino looked at the overly large dull, dead eyes of a young woman in her late teens, early twenties, reclining nude on Raphael's sofa. One breast was voluptuous and the other shriveled like that of an old cancer-stricken woman. A hipbone nearly stuck through her sickly yellow skin. Sitting on top of her ravaged body, he'd painted the face of a sublime angel. Calvino counted six toes on her right foot.

The model's hand-written story matched the mood of Raphael's painting: "Mother said I was born to be whore. A Russian woman never disappoints her mother."

Short and sweet like a hurried suicide note.

Raphael waited for Calvino's reaction.

"The story fits Anna to a T."

"T as in Teflon," said Calvino.

Raphael cracked a big smile.

"Exactly. Nothing sticks to Anna," he said, lighting a joint and taking a long pull.

He walked back into the kitchen and returned with a bowl of dry dog food for Charlie. She wolfed the food down in less than a minute from the moment Raphael placed it on the floor. It's the breed, Calvino thought. Slow eating has been deleted from the genome. There are few rivals to a golden retriever as a meditation on the meaning of appetite, hunger, and panic in a world of scarcity.

"After our first session, I started to think about Tremblay, the guy in Canada that Paul Steed said wanted to find you."

"Eric goes way back to the commune days. I've not seen or heard from him in eight years."

"Any idea why he'd go to the trouble of looking for you in Bangkok?"

"Conscience," said Raphael.

"What does that mean?"

"He was my godfather. But Eric was neither a god nor a father in my life. He wasn't all that interested in staying in touch. He was a busy man. Selling pot in British Columbia."

Raphael grinned as he took another hit from his joint, raising his chin and letting the smoke curl out of his nose.

"He asked Paul to find you because he felt guilty over being a lousy godfather?"

"Fuck if I know. But it sounds reasonable."

"Did he offer to help you with your troubles at the hospital?"

Raphael shook his head.

"It was too messy for him. He always liked to keep a low profile. A drug dealer avoids other people's problems. And when one of the patients in my ward killed herself, he left town."

"You left out the patient who committed suicide," said Calvino.

Raphael's face fell. He looked tired, intoxicated, hands shaky as he picked up a paintbrush.

"Her name was Lindsey Wagner."

He told his story as he resumed painting Calvino. Raphael's troubles had begun after he'd experimented with mixing patients' personal stories with his surreal images to represent their suffering and pain. His painting project might have gone on forever. The hospital was a small, closed community. No outsiders came to meddle with what they were doing. Painting at that time enjoyed a reputation as a form of therapy, an activity to engage patients, bring them out of their shell, heal them, and bring them back into the community.

But there was art and then there was Raphael's art. Raphael's kind of painting wasn't part of any studies of how to treat mentally ill patients. The bottom fell out of his world one night when Lindsey, a twenty-three-year-old bipolar woman, walked out of the facility and hitched a ride into the city. She walked into a small bistro and ordered a glass of red wine. A few minutes later, the waitress returned with the wine to find Lindsey had stabbed herself in the chest with an eight-inch knife. She sat at the table, slumped to one side, glassy-eyed, leaking blood and quite dead. The waitress dropped the glass of wine. It smashed on the floor. She screamed. Police vehicles with red lights flashing arrived. An ambulance with sirens blaring arrived. The TV news cameras pulled to the curb and set up shop. An inquiry followed. Exhibit one was Raphael's painting with the patient's signed suicide note written in a felt pen: "Father has no soul, Mother is unbearably shallow and mean. Me, I'm a shadow tired of waiting for the sun."

In Raphael's painting a Medusa's crown of coiled serpents rose out of the young woman's head. Her mouth was open and shaped in the oval of a perfect scream, and her eyes were dark and filled with anguish. Fingers were pointed at Raphael for having created this nightmare. It was hinted he was somehow responsible for her death. He explained he'd done something no one had bothered with—he'd released the patients' demons and given them voice, partly in their own words. These were people who others believed had nothing to say of value beyond clues to their insanity.

They'd been shorn of their right to speak directly, frankly, and without filters.

"The hospital tried to hush up the scandal," said Raphael.

"And you took the fall for the hospital," said Calvino.

Raphael shrugged.

"It was more than the hospital. Her parents said I was anti-family and likely Satan. The police said I was a pornographer. A social worker said I was a corrupting influence. A doctor said I had exercised too much power over the patients and got in the way of their medical treatment. The local press ran a story suggesting that I was mentally ill and should be committed as a patient, and certainly shouldn't be on staff. I had accomplished something."

"Which was?"

"Hating and blaming me brought everyone together. No one had to feel any guilt or take any responsibility. No one asked how she'd escaped. Lax security? That was pinned on me. The feeling was I should be fired. I saved them the trouble and resigned. They gave me three months' payment and I left. The deal was I'd leave the country. The hospital was afraid of a lawsuit. They wanted me far away. I know I told you I'd been given a leave of absence. Actually I was told to get myself absent from Canada as soon as possible."

"When you're down, everyone wants to put the boot in," said Calvino.

"The key is not to get knocked down. Stay dancing on your toes. The first rule of boxing."

"When can I read your story?" asked Calvino, half as a joke and half as a challenge.

"Tell you what, I'll see that you get to. But today, I want to finish your portrait. And you write your story."

"You want me to exchange my story for yours?"

"It's up to you, as some of my models tell me," said Raphael. "No rush."

He sorted through tubes of paint—cadmium yellow, magenta, cobalt deep blue, until he squeezed indigo onto his palette, mixing it with transparent white. He worked on an area below Calvino's right eye. He held up the paintbrush, closed one eye, and measured an aspect of Calvino's face. He painted quickly and with a sure eye and hand. The shape of Calvino's face, like the painting itself, appeared as a work in progress. It was a face that had taken more than one punch, like the moon, whose cold, isolated dents were visible from far away and would be there as long as there was a moon.

When he lay down the brush and wiped his hands, Charlie sensed her master was done. She strolled into the kitchen and returned with a leash in her mouth. The dog looked at Calvino, trying to send a message he'd understand.

"Hey, Charlie, time for a walk?" Calvino said.

She barked, her tail swinging back and forth, thumping against the sofa with the strength of a helicopter blade, causing some of the paintings stacked there to shift threateningly. The disruption didn't seem to bother Raphael.

Charlie nudged Calvino's leg.

"She likes chicken livers," said Calvino.

Raphael brushed his knuckles against her head.

"Charlie, you little whore, you took Mr. Calvino to your favorite barbeque stand. That's okay. It means she likes you."

"She likes liver."

The Russian model named Kristina barged into the studio without warning. She had sobered up and changed clothes. She wore a tracksuit and running shoes, and her hair was tied behind her head.

"You swine, where is the money you promised?"

Raphael fished a pouch from his Muay Thai shorts, and found a crumpled up hundred dollar bill.

"You ran off before I could pay you."

She took the money and smiled.

"No one cheats Kristina," she said.

"Could you write a little more of your story on your painting for me?"

"Why would I do that?"

She pouted her lips as if blowing a kiss.

"Because you are beautiful and you promised me that you would. The story you wrote doesn't seem finished. Would you like a glass of Mekhong? Mr. Calvino is leaving. He's taking Charlie out for a snack and a walk."

Raphael winked at her and she laughed as if they were sharing a private joke.

Calvino could see that the kid had a way with women. He made it easy for them to like him, and for someone so young to take a personal interest in them colored him a blotch of titanium white on the ivory black canvas that was their life. As he left to take Charlie for a walk, Kristina was already kneeling on the floor writing on the canvas.

When Calvino returned to the studio, Kristina had gone. Raphael showed him what she had written: "If tears were pearls, the world would be my oyster."

SEVEN

RAPHAEL ARRIVED EARLY at Calvino's office with his finished painting. Calvino wasn't in. Ratana looked happy to see him standing in the door smiling, holding a framed painting.

"Raphael, come in," she said. "No need to take off your shoes."

Glancing at the wall across from her desk, he noticed that she'd framed his sketch in glass and black wood. She saw him smile as he reviewed his sketch of her. He'd signed it with an oversized letter "R" like the curving canine of a saber-toothed tiger.

"I love it. John John says it looks just like Mommy."

Raphael smiled. Ratana positively glowed with pride.

"I'm glad your husband likes it."

"My eight-year-old son."

"Children are the best judges of art."

In reality this true image looked nothing like what the model thought she looked like. There was art for decoration, art for revolution, art for questioning ... and then there was art to get an appointment, a document, or an official stamp in a world of gatekeepers. Painters, like magicians, learned they had power with gatekeepers. Like everyone else they secretly wanted someone with talent to express it in their likeness.

Painters like Raphael know that secretaries, embassy and immigration officials, cops, women, men, and anyone in uniform can all be bought for a sketch of their likeness. Great (and obscure) artists have worked that weak spot for centuries, and the results hang in every museum in the world. Art establishes a connection between the personal and the official in a way that money never could. Money is common, impersonal, tainted—gatekeepers secretly despise themselves for giving in to the monster of cash, and hate and blame those who corrupt them with it. But a flattering sketch of their face registers as Renaissance gold. The portrait of a person in uniform has the potential to transform the subject into both a human being and an immortal god. A successful portrait is a miracle—water into wine—and it transforms the painter, too, into a prophet.

"Are you all right?" she asked, the smile vanishing as she focused on the damage to his puffy, black and blue face, the lip larger on one side than the other.

He touched his cheek.

"It always looks worse than it is."

As he explained his Muay Thai training, Ratana took out her medical kit and put alcohol on a cotton ball to dab his face. He winced from the sting.

As the two of them waited for Calvino's arrival, Raphael sat down with his back turned to the door and sketched another, more detailed portrait of Ratana in the style of Rembrandt. He'd nearly finished sketching her left eye when Calvino strolled into the office.

"You're early," Calvino said.

Raphael turned around, his face glistening under his right eye from the alcohol.

"My studio filled up early. Too many women, and I knew they'd soon start fighting. It's happened before. I needed to get out. I hope you don't mind."

Calvino smiled, shaking his head. The kid could charm a snake out of its eggs. He couldn't help wondering how anyone could remain so polite whatever the circumstances. He told himself it was a Canadian thing.

He took a closer look at Raphael's damaged eye.

"You look like you walked into a wall."

"My Muay Thai partner today had one or two issues with his wife that he needed to work out. He found my face was the perfect canvas to paint his anger."

The puffy area under his right eye left only a medieval arrow slit to peer through, and his nose was bloated, clogged with blood in the right nostril. He tore out the sheet with his sketch of Ratana from his pad and put it on her desk.

The eyes of her portrait were sad, thought Calvino. All the women in Raphael's paintings had sad eyes, as if caught at the moment of realization that they had no control, and enduring life without that illusion was the saddest of epiphanies, and the most difficult to accept.

"It's for John John," Raphael said.

"Thanks, Raphael," she said, looking at his latest sketch of her.

Raphael picked up the wrapped painting and followed Calvino into his office. Ratana smiled, raised her hand, and gave a little wave.

"Sit down," said Calvino. "Ratana will bring you a glass of water. So what's in the package? It's smaller than the one you did of me for the series."

"It's another portrait of you," said Raphael, "but this one's for you to keep."

Calvino searched in his desk drawer for scissors. He cut away the bubble wrap with the excitement of a child on Christmas Day. Raphael sat holding a pen and watching Calvino's face as the private eye examined his painting.

"I have a pen for you to write out your story," said Raphael.

"Hold on, kid. Give me a minute."

He rested the painting against his computer monitor and stepped back a couple of steps. Was that really him? The person in the painting had a battered, scarred boxer's face with bloodshot eyes, the upper lip puffed out, one ear swollen, and a ragged stitched cut under the left eye. Vincent Calvino's face resembled a middleweight prizefighter at the end of a long, undistinguished, and punishing career. Through a combination of shadows and light, Raphael had captured a proud, determined face, weary from a string of losses, but with a flicker of ambition intact and unwilling to stay down for the count.

"Until I saw this, I thought your face looked a busted mess," Calvino finally said, looking over at the young painter. "You look positively untouched."

"You don't like it?"

"It's not what I'd call flattering. The one you painted for your series, I liked that. But this? I look like …"

Calvino's voice trailed off in disappointment.

"Is that what you wanted? Flattery? Decoration? The A-list movie star face?"

"You didn't let me finish. I look like someone who leads with his chin."

He smiled at the young painter as Raphael again raised his hand toward Calvino.

"Take the pen."

Calvino accepted the pen and pulled the canvas closer. He sat in his chair, scratching his chin as he studied the portrait.

"There's no place for me to write my story."

"There's a place on the back. Turn the frame around."

Sure enough, the back of the painting bore a pasted-on white panel. Calvino wrote: "Busted flesh, busted face, the stakes are high, but bets are for suckers. I can always deal from a new deck, but my face was dealt just once. I get to play it only one time. Every defeat leaves a trace. Every victory vanishes without a mark. A lousy gambler keeps on bluffing, but his face gives him away."

Raphael read Calvino's story. He nodded a couple of times but his expression never changed. Calvino figured Raphael had read a lot of stories. He couldn't help wanting the artist's approval, and he couldn't help but think of Kristina's story about the tears and the pearl. A better story occurred to him: "Inside each painting is a frozen tear suspended for eternity. After you paint an ocean of tears, the time comes for you to build a boat and float away on that sea." But it was too late. He'd already written something else.

"Now your painting is complete."

Raphael started to walk out of the Calvino's office.

"Complete? What does that mean?" asked Calvino.

"A bridge from the outside is connected to what's inside."

"Hold on, where are you going?"

Raphael stood in the door.

"Back to the studio to paint."

"I haven't paid you."

"You don't like it. No need to pay for it."

He wanted to trade it for the first painting even though he knew that one was part of the series. He wanted it.

"How about switching this painting for the one that's number six in your series?"

Raphael's swollen eye closed altogether as he tried not to laugh. "Vinny, it's not like putting the strawberry back and taking the chocolate donut. This is art. Your great-grandfather was a great artist."

Calvino sighed, thinking how blood thins down over time and how his knowledge of art could be written down in a tweet.

"Give me some time to get used to it. Learning to come to terms with your face is an art in itself."

He called for Ratana to come into his office. She slipped in behind Raphael.

"Have a look at this."

She looked admiringly at Raphael Pascal's version of Vincent Calvino.

"It's you."

"I was afraid you might say that."

Raphael waited until Calvino turned his attention to him.

"What do you think?" Raphael asked.

"I look like a rejected stunt double who Sylvester Stallone thought looked too beaten up to play him when he was supposed to look beaten up," Calvino said. "Come on, kid. I love it. It's the same mug I shave every morning, so yeah, I am familiar with that look. That's why I keep my eyes closed when I shave. Your painting doesn't give me that luxury. But I am starting to warm to it."

"That's why I like to paint working girls. They know a man's flattery has no value. It's worthless. But they play the game. A customer's cash card is the prize. You know why they come to my place? I see them for who they are and I don't make fun of their stories. I pay attention to them when they model for me. The whole package—face, body, and mind—is hard to live with. Like the truth, we avoid it unless it flatters us."

All the while, Calvino sat in his chair staring at the painting as Raphael spoke. The artist had no impression that Calvino had heard him.

"If you don't want it, toss it." Raphael said.

He paused and stared at the man looking at his own picture in a painting. Calvino sat quietly, hands folded under his chin.

He was looking at himself for the first time in a long time. He saw a man who wore his years well. But if you examined the face closely you found years of good weather fading to the dark years of raging storms. Raphael had painted Calvino's face as it was and also as it was becoming in the future.

When Calvino looked up, the artist had gone.

Part III

ONE

CALVINO LEANED BACK in his desk chair, legs on the desk, ankles crossed, his black funeral tie loose around his neck, moving the last of the whiskey around the side of the glass before drinking it down.

Pools of late-afternoon light streaked across the office, cutting his legs in half at the knee. His tailor-made black cotton jacket hung on the back of the chair. He looked relaxed and comfortable, like a mortician at the end of a long day of death. He carefully removed his .38 Police Special from its leather holster. He hadn't taken his gun out of the desk drawer for months. He wet a cloth with cleaning oil and ran it down the barrel. The smell of the oil drifted through the air of the small office.

Ed McPhail, drinking on the sofa across from Calvino, had sunk deep inside himself. It was his way of taking in the big picture. Watching Calvino oil his gun, he raised the old specter of Chekhov's gun rule—you show a gun in Act One, the person showing the gun is sending a message that he will use it in Act Three. Calvino gave his usual reply: "Life isn't divided into acts. Guns are displayed thousands of times every day, but only rarely is one used to kill a person."

McPhail poured more whiskey into his glass.

"I'll stick with Chekhov."

"Pratt quotes me Shakespeare, you quote me Chekhov."

"Calvino, you inspire people to quote the dead."

"Raphael ..." Calvino said the name slowly, drawing it out, as he turned the gun over in his hand. "Why is it that the dead sound so wise?"

"The wise don't kill themselves," said McPhail.

"Socrates," said Calvino. "He was wise ... and lucky."

"How was he lucky?"

"He got to choose his poison. And so did Raphael."

"What are you going to do with the gun?"

McPhail hadn't taken his eyes off the weapon since Calvino had removed it from the holster.

"Clean it."

He turned the .38 Police Special over and applied more oil to the cloth.

Calvino had wound down his investigation business. He hadn't taken any new cases lately where he'd needed a gun and had stopped carrying one since the coup. He missed the heft of the .38, the way it felt on his body as the gun rode inside the shoulder holster like a friend you could trust. The point was to scare a man into backing down. Only when there was no other choice was killing an option.

At the best of times, a foreigner found carrying a handgun guaranteed complications for everyone involved. A coup was the worst of times. A phone call from Pratt wouldn't clear up things quickly as it had once done. The military and soldiers were in no mood to coddle foreigners. Besides, they didn't want guns in the hands of anyone who wasn't one of them. There was no American-style Second Amendment in Thailand. Calvino made a mental note to search whether in human history coup makers had ever given a constitutional right to bear arms to the people they'd stolen a government from. He decided it was a waste of time looking. McPhail lit a cigarette, leaned his head back on the office sofa and stared at the ceiling as Calvino cleaned his handgun. He patted the seat on the sofa with one hand, thinking this was where hundreds of crying expat wives had told Calvino their stories of a husband's infidelity. He lifted his head, smoke exhaling from both nostrils like a dragon, and studied Raphael's painting of Calvino. Within a thickly braided gold frame like one you'd find in a museum, it hung on the wall next to Calvino's law school degree and private investigator's license.

"Man, degree, license. It's your story," said McPhail, pointing at each frame as he looked back at Calvino.

Calvino touched the barrel of his .38 Police Special.

"Not even an executive summary, McPhail."

It had been McPhail's idea to meet at Calvino's office before going on to the wat for day three of the funeral. McPhail wanted a second look at the portrait Raphael had painted. He'd seen it the first time not long after Raphael had dropped it by Calvino's office. Now the painter was dead and McPhail thought he might look at the painting with different eyes as a result. He reconsidered it again. What mysteries had he folded into the colors and lines?

"I know I asked to have a second look. Man, I am looking at it. I looked at it before."

He reached forward and flicked his cigarette ash in the ashtray on Calvino's desk. There were two other butts with lipstick on the filters inside the ashtray. Vinny's been a naughty boy, he thought.

"And?" asked Calvino.

"And what?"

McPhail had lost his train of thought. Somewhere there was a missing train and it was touch and go as he chased it down the tracks. Calvino waited a minute.

"Have you changed your mind about it?"

"Is it really you, Vinny?" McPhail asked, looking away from the painting and inhaling from his cigarette. "If that was his style, he committed suicide just in time. Sooner or later someone would have saved him the trouble."

"It's art, McPhail."

"The value's gone up. Dead artist. Think about it, Calvino. I'd sell the fucking thing if it were me."

McPhail was more interested in the lipstick color on the cigarette butts than Calvino's painting. He felt it gave his imagination more to work with.

Calvino unloaded the .38 and cleaned the chamber.

"Raphael believed life was a series of crashes and near-death experiences. He had a theory about motion. You know, movement. Up, down …"

"And round and round," said McPhail. "Pump and grind. What else is there?"

"Raphael saw tragedy in the limits of how we can move."

"He should have lightened up. If you can get a girl to perform more than two movements, you've got a winner. But all of this talk about six like it's a magical number. Raphael and his six this, six that. Motion. What did he expect? That life came with a book of instructions?"

"I'm about finished," Calvino said, the smell of gun oil rising thickly from his hands. He put the gun back in the holster.

"The way he saw your face, man, it makes me very sad. He had to be depressed. With all the women in and out of his studio, he should have been on top of the world. How could he stay depressed with all those women jumping his bones? It don't make sense. I saw them at the funeral. Dressed in their finest seduction threads, giving the eye to foreigners. Tens and Nines. Quality women. Man, I'd have paid him good money to take on his artistic angst. What can you do with someone like that? He gets caught up in his own self-made tragedy and kills himself. That's fucked up. If I'd come to Thailand at his age …"

"You'd have been dead twenty years ago."

McPhail laughed, helping himself to another healthy shot from the office bottle of Johnnie Walker Black.

"Probably. But I'd have been a happy stiff. I wouldn't have killed myself. I'd have brought along Johnnie Walker to do that job."

"Raphael saw life as little more than a series of illusions and traps."

"That's bullshit."

"Not really a trap. More like bait set in a trap. If you believe there's no meaning in life, no purpose, what's the point of trying to be happy? Happiness doesn't mean anything for someone like that."

McPhail huffed, sucked on his cigarette.

"So sell the painting."

He picked one of the lipstick-stained cigarette butts out of the ashtray.

"You didn't bring one of those hookers back here last night?"

Calvino grinned.

"You caught me red-handed, Ed."

"Fuck you," McPhail said. "The lipstick looks incriminating."

He dropped the red-smeared butt back into the ashtray.

"What's wrong with you, Ed? You see a gun and immediately think I'm going to shoot someone. You see an old cigarette butt with lipstick and assume I screwed one of Raphael's models."

McPhail's face twitched as he stood up from the sofa and stretched his arms, trying to come up with an answer through a haze of cigarette smoke and Johnnie Walker Black.

"Shouldn't we being going to the wat?" he finally replied.

One of the things Calvino thought was consistent about McPhail was that whenever he was stumped, he announced it was time to go.

Calvino fixed the knot in his tie, grabbed his jacket, and headed for the door. His hand reached for the air-con remote.

"You forgot your gun," said McPhail.

"Don't fall for that old Chekhov quote, McPhail."

"You want me to take it?"

"That would be a mistake."

McPhail picked up the ashtray, sighing as he looked at the cigarette butt.

"What are you doing?" asked Calvino.

"I wouldn't want Ratana to see the lipstick."

"They were from one of the suicide hotline volunteers."

"The hot blonde. I knew it."

"The other one."

"The old fat one?"

"McPhail, you should run for president."

"Yeah? Given the current state of your problems, you should just fucking run."

McPhail held his hand over the ashtray and let the ash and butts fall into the wastebasket.

On the staircase to the street, the full heat of the night hit McPhail like a white lightning moonshine.

"Slow down, Calvino. You forgot to mention how much you paid for the Stallone portrait."

"Two grand US," said Calvino.

McPhail caught his breath as they walked to Calvino's car.

"Man, you do have money to burn. Twenty C-notes. Remember that next time you bring me into a case for a hundred bucks."

"Earlier you said that after Raphael's death it would be worth a lot more."

"I was thinking a two hundred dollar painting might jump to four hundred."

Calvino laughed as he pointed the remote at his BMW and the lights flashed.

"Always aiming for the big time. I love that about you, Ed."

TWO

ON THE THIRD and final day of Raphael Pascal's funeral, the sala was about half-full if you were an optimist, or half-empty if pessimism was your sugar daddy. Or alternatively, through Calvino's eyes, it looked like what Goldilocks said about the third porridge. It seemed about right. Mourners at farang funerals peeled off over the course of the three-day ritual, drawn like iron filings toward the strong magnet of other social obligations—fleshy liaisons in air-conditioned rooms with soft music, a distraction promising pleasures a million miles away from the sound of chanting monks and the smell of incense. It was nothing personal, no disrespect intended, but three straight days of sitting on hard chairs, glancing at the same faces lined with grief, was never going to win a competition with the attractions of Bangkok. Calvino's Law: We are wired for pleasure. Death is a temporary short-circuit that the living pretend to repair.

McPhail stood outside the sala, smoking with a couple of other mourners. As they gestured, the cigarettes' hot red ends sliced through the darkness like tiny SOS flares. The smokers huddled, their nicotine stained fingers and teeth working in a lifelong harmony with their cigarette. Irony was cheap as they puffed away in the shadow of a crematorium.

Pratt, dressed in a white shirt, black tie, and black trousers, stood away from the smokers outside the sala talking with a tall young Thai woman, all legs in a black pantsuit outfit with a window cut out to expose her midriff—a lush, tight white belly that hinted at the luxurious candy lurking beneath the remainder of the fabric package. She stopped midsentence as Calvino walked up. Pratt introduced Calvino as his friend and urged her to continue.

"Don't let me interrupt," said Calvino.

"Pim had an appointment with Raphael on the day he died," Pratt explained.

Pim nodded.

Calvino thought he recognized her from one of Raphael's paintings. He wasn't sure. There had been so many faces, so many paintings.

Pim fled in fear to an inner quiet space, closing him out.

"You saw him last Wednesday?" Calvino prodded.

Pratt said, "It's okay to tell Khun Vincent your story. He was Raphael's close friend."

Calvino smiled. No quote from Shakespeare, he thought. Pratt had used Raphael's trademarked phrase, "tell me your story," and Calvino wondered if she made the connection to the stories added to Raphael's portraits. But this was no time to interrupt the flow of what she had to say.

Pim sighed and pressed her lips together, watching other people in the crowd of mourners as if drawing inspiration. She tentatively stepped out of her safe space.

"I go to Raphael's studio Wednesday morning, eleven o'clock. His door is locked. I think that's strange. Raphael say he never lock his door. Everyone always welcome. People come and go all day long. Wednesday, I can't go inside. I ask myself, 'Why he do like that?' "

"Did you knock?" asked Calvino.

He made a fist and pretended to strike an invisible door.

She made her right hand into a fist, striking an invisible door in front of her, a little crime scene re-enactment. She repeated the gesture.

"Yes, like this. Bam-bam."

"But Raphael didn't answer the door?" asked Calvino, glancing at Pratt, whose face showed no expression. "Did you try phoning him?"

"His phone ring but no answer. I think, maybe he *mao* on Mekhong. I bang on the door again. I don't think he hear. Music inside very loud."

"What kind of music?" asked Calvino.

"Farang music."

"How many times did you knock?"

Pim half-closed her eyes as if she'd gone into calculator mode.

"Many times. I too angry with him to count. I busy girl. He waste my time. I pay taxi. I cancel morning appointment with client. Pim angry with him. I ask why he do like that to me."

"What'd you do?"

"I write him note and put it on his door."

"What did you write?"

She paused, trying to remember.

" 'Why you not want to see Pim? What I do wrong?' And I leave my private phone number in case he lose it."

"You put it on the door?" asked Calvino. "How?"

From her handbag Pim pulled out a book of yellow heart-shaped stickers with happy faces. Inserted in the left hand corner was Pim's headshot, her name, and the number of her escort service, along with a small space to write a note. Calvino couldn't help admiring how professionally produced it was. She peeled one off and handed it to Calvino. A small removable strip on the back revealed a sticky surface underneath.

"You mind if I keep this?" asked Calvino. "One question, Pim. The lyrics, the words to the song you heard, would you remember them?"

She replied with a blank look.

" 'Should I Stay or Should I Go?' "

"Up to you," she said.

Calvino smiled, thinking part of the charm of the Thais was how they often took everything literally. Words didn't stand for things other than what they appeared to mean.

"Those words are the lyrics to a song." He stepped closer and sang, " 'Darling, you gotta let me know, Should I stay or should I go? If you say that you are mine, I'll be there till the end of time, So you gotta let me know, Should I stay or should I go?' "

Calvino's singing turned the heads of a number of mourners.

"The Clash," said one of the volunteers, who smiled at Calvino on the way into the sala.

"I don't know," said Pim. "Maybe yes, maybe no. I was too angry to listen to the words."

Once a songbird flew out of the cage and started to sing, it was difficult to shut them up. Pim's face flushed with anger as she relived the moment at the studio door. Getting it off her chest to Pratt seemed to have done her some good. She'd sung her song and all that could be expected from her was a repeat performance.

McPhail moved to Pim's side, inhaling on his cigarette.

"Hey, buddy, aren't you going to introduce me?"

Dropping his cigarette butt and grinding it out with the heel of his shoe, McPhail smiled at Pim.

"Baby, you are so beautiful I'd drink your bathwater."

"It's always good idea to first boil your drinking water, Ed," said Calvino.

"McPhail, later," said Pratt. "We're going inside. The monks have arrived."

McPhail grumbled under his breath, "First you give away the retriever, then take away the babe. What've I done to you, Calvino, to cause you to hate me?"

The three men watched as Pim used McPhail's interruption as cover to return to the sala. Pratt sighed, shook his head, and followed her.

"What'd I say?" McPhail asked Calvino, as the two of them stood alone.

"Nothing, Ed. But you need to work on your timing."

"My mother said I grew up dancing to the wrong music."

"You should always listen to your mother."

As Pratt re-entered the sala, he had to admit to himself that McPhail was right. Pim wasn't hard on the eyes.

After three nights of interviewing mourners, he had finally found one who not only had some useful information but also possessed the kind of eye-candy packaging that so easily distracted an interrogator. Pratt reminded himself that he was on the job. He had retired from the police force, but it was his habit to think of himself as still on the job, even though it was only through an informal arrangement hatched out of friendship with a junior in the department.

He struggled to keep his thoughts on the case. And there was a funeral to attend. He hoped that if an angel of death was in his own future, she would appear looking like Pim.

Sitting in the back of the sala, as on the previous two evenings, Gavin de Bruin was flanked by a small contingent of suicide hotline volunteers, returned like frontline troops who'd left the fight briefly to mourn one of their own. On his way to his seat, Calvino invited Gavin to join him on the first row, reserved for family and VIPs. Gavin elected to stay with his troops.

That evening there was a new addition to the front-row mourners. Ratana sat in the front, dressed in black and touching a tissue to her eyes. Calvino sat in the folding chair next to her, looking past her as he spotted Paul Steed and Tuk.

Those two stick close together, he thought.

Their heads slightly bowed, they whispered to one another. Tuk sobbed as the monks chanted. She wasn't alone in her grief. Other women in the sala, a number of whom Calvino recognized from the studio, sat dabbing a tissue to swollen, tear-filled eyes. Raphael's brigade of desirable women hadn't missed a day—and that was a true paradox. Their raw, sensual beauty of youth, tuned to the emotional chords of any man, decorated the sala as much as the floral displays. It was a measure of the pull the deceased had over them.

On the previous nights Calvino had wondered if he'd ever unravel the mystery of how Raphael had left all of these women crying their eyes out—not one or two, but a busload of women working their tear ducts in a sniffling chorus. The third night was their final performance. The curtain was slowly lowering on their little drama, which had pulled them out of their usual evening routines. On this last night, he had come up with an answer for their grief—Raphael had been one of them, understood them, loved them, and never judged them. The same was true for the suicide hotline volunteers and the handful of young Thai men from the Muay Thai gym, shy and humble, who slipped into the sala on the final night to say their goodbyes. Looking over the crowd, it might have been a political convention where every group represented at the funeral claimed Raphael as its own.

Calvino turned around in his chair, nodded in Gavin's direction, and silently mouthed, "Talk later," a gesture that Gavin acknowledged.

Pratt helped two lay staff from the temple distribute robes, candles, incense sticks, and food offerings to the monks. The staff did the heavy lifting of baskets of food and robes. On the first two nights Ratana had slipped into the sala silently, made her wai to the coffin, and quickly disappeared into the night. She'd been the phantom lady.

Raphael's death had upset her in a way Calvino hadn't seen since she'd lost John John's father. His funeral had been at the same wat. Memories had flooded back, and she'd fled from them two nights in a row. She had determined to master those feelings on this last night.

"I know it's hard for you," Calvino said.

She returned a small smile.

"It's the first time since John's funeral," he continued, guessing at the truth.

"I suppose I haven't come to terms with his dying. I never will."

When he asked her if she was okay, she said, "I can't explain why I feel this. I can't believe it." She paused and added, "He was so young and talented. He had everything to live for."

Those at John's funeral had said the same things. She looked uncertain whether to change the subject.

"Do you want to talk about it?" he asked.

"The last time he came to the office I was so busy. He wanted to talk. I didn't have the time. I should have listened to him. It might have helped."

Her answer could have been about either her dead boyfriend John or Raphael.

A dozen people in the crowd appeared burdened with a full weight of guilt, believing that had they said something, done something different, shared a laugh perhaps, it wouldn't have come to this. They'd failed him some how. That's what the dead did to the living: left them with a deep, abiding sense of failure.

"It's never one thing, Ratana. Like dying of old age. It's never one organ that fails; everything falls apart."

"He was only twenty-six years old," she said.

It was the same age her boyfriend John had been when he'd been killed in Bangkok. Shot.

"You don't have to be physically old to die of old age," he replied.

"What's that supposed to mean?"

"Raphael felt he'd done what he wanted to do. His work was finished. He saw no point in waiting for nature to show him to the exit. Some people are impatient with rules made for the living. It's too much trouble. They do what they want to do and are in a hurry to get on with leaving."

"I wasn't paying close enough attention. That's what hurts. If I ever stop paying attention to you, please tell me."

"You'll be okay."

Ratana stood up, walked over to the monks, and knelt with an armful of flowers. She had asked to play a part in the final ceremony. Calvino suspected she'd cleared it with Pratt, and he'd told the laymen who served the monks, who had passed the word on to the men in robes. Ratana edged down the row of monks balanced on her knees, placing roses on the scarves that the monks used to avoid physical contact with women. Calvino watched—and everyone else seated in the sala watched—as this mysterious woman with a tear-streaked face made merit for Raphael.

Who can say what causes some people to react strongly to the news of the death of someone they have met only a few times? Something in this connection, made in a couple of brief meetings, had seeded a lifetime's worth of vivid memories. Who could say whether sending merits to the dead was just another empty ritual, a superstition, or wishful thinking? In a sala, with the body on one side and the row of monks in front of the living, anything was possible but nothing was likely. Calvino watched Ratana placing the flowers before each monk, thinking we all live inside the small slip space of doubt, and these monks gave a slender ray of hope that the doubt would be resolved in our favor.

Once the monks were gone and the food servers started handing out bowls of rice soup, the mourners fell into a rotation of eating and conversation. Pratt waved off the food server. He had work to do. Calvino took a bowl of the soup from the server and set it on the empty chair next to him. He watched Paul Steed across the aisle, with his head hovering like a vacuum above the bowl. Some men had an appetite that knew no bounds. Eating next to the dead didn't affect their enjoyment. The Thais had no problem eating next to a coffin. But foreigners usually lost their appetite. Their stomachs cramped at the sight of food. Unless they'd lived in Thailand a long time, and in that case they stuffed their gobs with the best of them.

Ratana had returned to her seat after passing out the flowers. To the other mourners she looked too young to be the mother and too old to be the widow. Dressed in black, her hair pulled back from her face, she reminded Calvino and Pratt of the funeral days for her own partner.

"It doesn't seem real," she said, looking at Calvino and then at Pratt.

Pratt knew that no smile could heal what he saw in her face.

" 'Are you sure that we are awake? It seems to me that yet we sleep, we dream,' " Pratt said, quoting *A Midsummer Night's Dream*.

Shakespeare's words worked as they'd done for four centuries.

"It is like a dream," Ratana agreed.

It's time to wake up, thought Calvino. He crossed the aisle and sat in a folding chair next to Paul Steed. Tuk sat on the other side. Calvino leaned in close for a discussion, close enough to read Tuk's reaction to his questions as she looked at Paul. She clutched Paul's hand. Paul played his role well. He'd been at her side when Calvino had examined Raphael's body in the bedroom. He'd held her hand. He hadn't let go of it.

"Last day," Paul said.

Puffing his cheeks with air, he slowly exhaled, shaking his head. He munched a shrimp and returned his plastic bowl, now empty. His appetite seemed as strong as ever.

"The soup is good. You should get a bowl, Calvino."

Calvino hadn't come for the food.

"Help me remember a couple of things about our conversation at the studio."

"Remember what?" asked Paul, matter-of-factly.

"Start with the time Tuk found the body."

Paul scratched his chin, eyes looking up as if searching a mind cloud. Apparently it was a cloudless day. He nudged Tuk with his left knee. That always got a woman's attention.

Paul smiled at her, reassuring, squeezed her hand, his tone comforting.

"Honey, what time was it on Wednesday when you found Raphael?"

Her eyes fluttered and closed as if she were remembering something pleasurable.

"I don't know. About twelve?"

"How did you get in?"

She had her eyes on Calvino, the kind of eyes that knew how to look at a man who is looking for some sign she's being less than genuine in her answers.

"What do you mean?" she asked.

"Was the door to the studio locked?" asked Calvino.

She shook her head, blowing her nose in a tissue. When she looked up, she flashed a half-hearted smile. Reading the smile, Calvino saw a touch of disdain mixed with pity that he hadn't really known Raphael as well as he thought or he wouldn't have asked the question.

"Raphael never lock the door. 'Open door policy,' he always say."

"You're sure it was noon?" asked Calvino. "Could it have been an hour or two earlier? Or maybe you spent the night?"

Paul wrapped an arm around Tuk.

"She's already told you noon. The same as she told the police, so why not lay off her? She's had a rough time, Calvino."

It wasn't the time or place to butt heads with Paul Steed. Calvino let Steed play out his protective role. Surely Tuk was wise enough to know Paul was a nobody and his protection meant nothing.

"Are you coming to the cremation tomorrow morning?" asked Calvino.

Paul read Calvino's question as a little victory.

"Yeah, Tuk wants me to."

Calvino half-turned in his chair as he heard Pratt calling his name from behind.

"Pratt, come over here a minute. There's someone who thinks he knows what a rough time means."

"Paul, this is my friend, Pratt."

Paul let go of Tuk's hand to wai Pratt, and Pratt returned the wai.

"We met at Raphael's studio," Pratt said, as Paul tried to smile.

"Hi," Paul said as he swallowed hard. "I remember you of course."

Suddenly Paul Steed seemed to be a man of few words.

Paul remembered everyone had called Pratt by his old rank: General. Calvino had said Pratt was retired, but to judge from the weight he pulled in the room, retirement hadn't sidelined him. What really made Paul Steed curious was why a Thai police general had taken a personal interest in a farang suicide case.

Paul looked nervous as Pratt asked Tuk a vague question to break the ice.

"Khun Tuk, how are you feeling?" he asked her in Thai.

"Very sad," she said in Thai, giving him a deep wai.

"It takes time," said Pratt.

There was that "time" word again, chasing her, haunting her.

With the pleasantries out of the way, Calvino handed his cellphone to Pratt.

"Take a group picture of us."

Pratt took several shots.

"Come on, Tuk, you're included," Calvino said.

Another series of shots, and Pratt handed back the phone.

"I'll shoot you copies," said Calvino to Paul. "I still have your email address at the office."

Paul pulled a card out of his wallet and handed it to Calvino.

"My new email address is on my card," Paul said. "See you tomorrow morning at the cremation."

Paul and Tuk hurried to leave the sala.

"He looked scared, Pratt."

" 'Suspicion always haunts the guilty mind.' "

"Guilty of what?" asked Calvino.

Pratt watched Paul with Tuk on his arm outside the sala.

"That's the question," said Pratt. "He was your client. I thought you might know."

Calvino saw Gavin cross the room with a Thai man in his early thirties, slim, moustache, short hair, and a hawk-like face.

"I want you to meet Chatri," said Gavin. "This is Raphael's Muay Thai coach."

The coach had trouble with English in getting his tenses right. It was much harder than making a fist.

Calvino and Chatri exchanged wais, locking eyes as if both men were searching for the man behind the formality. Calvino broke the wai first.

"It's a good name for a Muay Thai coach," said Calvino. "Brave knight."

Chatri's face softened.

"You know Thai," he said.

"It's all about finding the right coach," said Calvino.

That made the coach laugh.

"I know you are Rap's friend. I am sorry for him."

He grabbed both of Calvino's hands and pumped them.

"Did you ever see him outside the gym?"

"Sometimes we go for noodles," said Chatri. "He ate Thai food like a Thai."

That was one of the ultimate compliments a Thai could bestow on a foreigner.

"Did you have any reason to believe he wanted to kill himself?"

Chatri shrugged.

"You never know a man's heart," he said.

"Did he have any conflicts with anyone at the gym?"

Chatri shook his head.

"Did he ever invite you to his studio?"

The answer was clear from the look on Chatri's face. The relationship was bound to the gym and ring.

"Did he ever ask you for advice?"

"I was his coach. I teach him everything I know."

"I don't mean Muay Thai moves. More along the lines of passing along the name of someone who could help him get something he wanted."

It was a fishing line with a necklace of hooks he tossed into the water.

"One time he asked about changing money ... if I know anyone. I tell him maybe I know someone."

"Why don't I take you to lunch sometime, Khun Chatri?"

Chatri pulled a name card from his pocket and gave it to Calvino.

"You phone me anytime."

After another exchange of wais, Chatri slipped away.

"Chatri's a good guy," said Gavin. "I asked him to come. It's awkward. A foreigner's funeral, not speaking English very well, the distance, many reasons for him not to bother."

It was true that Gavin had gone out of his way. Calvino was a private investigator and not a cop. It gave him freedom of movement, but it also made him a target as cops didn't much like outsiders sticking their nose into crimes they were investigating. He had liked the coach who had taught Raphael the clinch and other Muay Thai moves. He had locked into a man who had the eyes of a wolf and the heart of a dove.

"Funny thing to ask your Muay Thai coach, where to exchange money. Any bank exchanges money," said Gavin.

"There are different kinds of exchanges. It's like the exchange of gunfire. It can be hostile or it can be friendly fire gone wrong."

"I notice that you are fond of gun metaphors. I suspect it goes with your line of work," said Gavin.

Calvino had exposed himself. The shrink was right—he thought in terms of weapons, ammo, ambushes, and explosions. A quarter of a century in Bangkok was bound to change a man's metaphors.

"I got to like the kid and his art. That's enough reason for me to want to know if someone was involved in his death. You mind if I ask your volunteers a couple of more questions? I'll keep guns out of the conversation."

Gavin relaxed, looking at the other mourners pass.

"You saw the other night at the restaurant that I'm not their gatekeeper. Talk to them all you want. That's their job: talking to people who need someone to care."

One of the volunteers, a middle-aged farang, stopped beside Gavin and said, "In our line of work, we learn that it's the bottled-up emotions that are volatile. When they reach a critical mass, they explode."

"This is Jim from Chicago."

"Hello, Jim from Chicago," said Calvino. "How well did you know Raphael?"

"Well enough to come to his funeral three days in a row."

"The other night, I saw you at the table. When I asked about pentobarbital, you didn't say anything. Any idea how he got his supply?"

Jim shook his head, and a couple of other volunteers who had joined them also gestured they had no knowledge of the supplier.

"Didn't know then, don't know now. Wish I did," Jim said.

"It's not difficult to get drugs in Thailand," said Gavin. "So I'm told."

"I've heard there's a vet upcountry who is a source ..." said Jim.

"Who told you that?" Calvino interrupted.

The mem-farang volunteer, the same one who had left behind two lipstick-stained cigarette butts in his office ashtray, cleared her throat.

"I did. But it was just a rumor. There's no proof one way or another."

"I was about to say that Raphael had his own sources," said Jim, shooting a glare at the woman next to him. "No need for him to use a country vet. The women he knew weren't simple country girls with boyfriends and uncles who knew where a friendly vet could be bought. Come to think of it, other than Gavin, Raphael was better connected than any of us to Thais in Bangkok. So if he wanted a final exit drug, all he had to do was make a call. Or ask one of his models or Thai friends to make the connection. They adored him. You saw the Thais showing up every night in the sala. If he'd asked any one of them, they would have hijacked the moon for him."

The others in the group nodded their agreement.

The number of volunteers continued to grow until about eight or nine people surrounded Calvino and Gavin, like homesteaders circling wagons in hostile country. Another volunteer in his forties elbowed to the front where Calvino stood. He looked like an older version of Raphael. Ronnie, a California psychiatric nurse, had known Raphael as well as any of the others. Unlike the other volunteers Calvino's had interviewed, Ronnie had visited the studio a couple of times. The two men had got stoned and drunk Mekhong together and talked about suicide cases, theories, methods, and notes.

"Raphael's playfulness is why no one can be sure," Ronnie said. "He talked about suicide at the hotline office as if he'd planned it for later that day. He was going to do it as soon as he got back to his studio. But there was always some model walking around nude and begging him to paint her and give her money. It seemed like a weird reality TV show, as if that was how he made his reality real and fresh in his mind. He needed the threat of death for life to be real. But after a while I started to think it was an act, a convincing act, but killing himself was part of Raphael's identity. When I was his age, killing myself wasn't in my head. But I was never inside Raphael's head. From what I saw on the outside, I thought he wouldn't do it."

"Because he was bluffing?" asked Calvino.

"Maybe he was," he said with a shrug of the shoulders. "But I don't think he was the bluffing type."

"His old man killed himself," said Jim.

"His father sounded a little crazy," said Gavin.

"The apple doesn't fall far from the tree," said Ronnie.

It was the kind of cliché that must have caused more than one hotline caller to jump off a balcony.

"Most men would have traded lives with Raphael in a heartbeat," said Jim.

"The women …" said Ronnie. "No one had more women than Raphael. But it made no difference. All the beautiful women in the world couldn't push him back from the edge once he'd decided it was time to jump."

To Calvino it seemed that Raphael had used his models to walk a narrow rail between his world and their world, carrying a paintbrush as a balance pole. The way he did it, you would think, there's a guy with perfect balance—no net under him, but he's not going to fall off the beam. Even if he did, one of the nude beauties would rush forward to catch him as he fell.

"Jump off or get pushed off … it makes a difference," said Calvino.

"Only to the living," said Gavin. "We always want to solve the puzzle of a death or know the mystery. All I see is his coffin. I've come to say goodbye. There's no mystery in that."

It was no surprise that collaborators like Gavin de Bruin used mystery as their default explanation when one of their own hit the panic button and exited from the acute phase of being lost with no hope of rescue. Blame, shame, mystery collapsed into the singularity of sorrow.

THREE

CALVINO LOOKED OUT at the hundred-eighty-degree arc of the Bangkok skyline beyond his condo balcony. At night the high-rise towers along Rama IV and Sukhumvit Road rose like glass and steel silos thrusting against a black, starless sky. It was a big city skyline, all grown up and sophisticated in high heels, lipstick, and makeup, out on the town, painting it red, painting it yellow. He stared out at the city, taking in a balcony jumper's view of Bangkok. He was high enough from the ground that going over the side would be guaranteed to get the job done.

Tuk had her story and timeline nailed except for one small detail. Why had she lied about Raphael's studio door being unlocked when she arrived on that Wednesday? Or had it been locked after she arrived? Pim was clear that she'd found the door locked at eleven o'clock. Faced with the stark reality of being shut out, she had turned around and left, fuming over her lost chance to score cash.

Lying, confusion, and inattention were some of the mental states that explained differences in perception. And it wasn't just the women; Raphael's own mental state required closer examination. Judging from his pattern of behavior, it was out of character for Raphael to lock his door.

Calvino knew that people commit acts that are out of character all the time. They act out of emotion. That's what makes them unpredictable, and it's what makes them interesting. When they die, such inconsistencies leave gaps and mysteries, as well as surprise and shock. In Raphael's case, killing himself was both expected and unexpected, like the state of his door. Locked and unlocked. But there was no in-between state for the door. The state of Raphael's door, unless it had entered the quantum world of Schrödinger's cat, which was alive and dead, had to be decided one way or the other.

Pim worked as an escort at an agency that also employed Tuk. One of the two professional sex workers was lying or had entered a quantum relationship with the truth. In their line of work, lying was part of the tradecraft; except for the rare dyed-in-the-wool romantic or idealist, hiding the true state of the "cat" was tolerated, expected, and necessary.

Calvino stepped back inside the condo, closing the sliding glass door. He flopped on the white leather sofa, reached up, and tapped the space bar on his laptop, which lay open on the coffee table. The screen lit up and he mindlessly scrolled through dozens of pages of Raphael's website.

He wasn't sure what he was looking for. Pages of Raphael talking about art, death, his father, the commune, Montreal, his private hospital experience, and his diary of day-to-day painting in Bangkok. He'd been thorough in his record-keeping of dates, places, names, opinions, ideas, and emotions. His painter's eye adapted well to the world of words, where he captured again the models who tripped through his life. He drew a clear picture of how kids raised in a commune received a different kind of education and how their attitudes and values set them apart. It occurred to Calvino that the commune had been closer to a Thai upcountry village than to a big city like Montreal. It had marked him. The girls read that mark as making him one not unlike them.

Calvino wondered if the diary might have been a collaborative project, a part of Raphael's therapy once he had become active on the hotline. Full name: Bangkok Suicide Prevention Hotline. The volunteers had name cards with a number. Had the thoughts and ideas of other volunteers contributed to the stories Raphael wished to tell? It also seemed at times to be Gavin's website. Every so often something in the text popped out as something Gavin might have said, such as, "Marcus Aurelius believed death was either annihilation or metamorphosis."

Whatever the authorship, Raphael's pages of notes alternated between being a guide to living life and building a case for death.

He noticed that the section on Raphael's father sounded a little different from how Raphael talked and how he'd written in the diary. Calvino thought about what Pratt had once said: "Most crime investigations overlook a suspect's father. He's the model for a boy. Know the father, know the man, and you will know why a man did what he felt he had to do."

One of the best people who ever has lived was my father. That is a large statement. You may accuse me of overstatement, but I will set out what he taught me as a model for living, and you can be the judge of whether my father's beliefs and actions explain my own.

Flavio worked as an automobile mechanic and restorer. In his spare time he was a graphic designer. He took several night courses on technique, but in reality he taught himself the art of design. Each night I sat at the long kitchen table after dinner and the plates, cups, saucers, and cutlery were cleared. Other kids and members of the commune hung around, too. We all watched Flavio sketch designs for CD sleeves and book covers. He looked to ancient history for inspiration. Norse legends, Greek gods and heroes, Roman emperors, Irish folklore, Anglo-Saxon myths ...

He always had a couple of regular freelance assignments, but CD producers wanted modern, upbeat images of beautiful women or scenery. What Flavio loved to draw, they rejected. He worked at night on the "commercial shit," as he called the music industry assignments. One of the reasons given by the elders in the commune for us leaving was Flavio had sold out. "Fuck them," my father said. "Fuck the CD companies, fuck the elders." We packed up our belongings in a U-Haul trailer and drove away. I remember looking out the rear window of our car as the commune, the only home I had ever known, disappeared over the horizon.

My father, in a different time and place, might have had the chance to be recognized as a great graphic artist. In our new neighbourhood in Montreal, working-class people didn't talk about art or design. They worked in jobs where they got grease and oil on their hands. Their view of graphic design wasn't much different from those in the commune—it was useless, sissy shit that real men didn't get involved in. Flavio was a real man and the insults hurt.

Flavio's world was torn between the people who assigned graphic design jobs and those whose cars needed the services of a mechanic. He loved getting his hands dirty, working on cars, repairing them, seeing the face of a car owner after he got the car purring again like a well-fed cat. He had the hard hands of a working man or a boxer, not the soft hands of a graphic designer who worked with his fingertips.

Throughout the years, I'd be browsing in a record shop and I'd see one of my old man's graphic art designs on a CD sleeve. It wasn't an accident. I'd gone into the shop looking for my dad's artwork. We had the CDs in boxes around the house. I knew his style by heart. I'd go through stacks of CDs before I found one of his graphic designs. I'd pull it out as if I'd stumbled over it, hold it up so anyone around me could see what a fine cover it had. I'd take it to the front and show the clerk.

"My dad designed the sleeve," I'd say.

"You want to buy it or what?" would be the response.

I'd think about that glint I'd seen in my father's eye as he worked at the kitchen table. Not the long table at the commune but the short table that the three of us sat at every night in the city. I'd ignore the stupid clerk and take the CD to the cashier and ask him if he knew the artist who designed the cover. The cashier would shrug and treat me like a lunatic.

"You did?" he'd guess.

"No, you idiot, my father was the artist."

A shrug, a crooked smile with the lips writing out: *You sorry little fuck, get a life.* But, the employees on the shop floor remembered me. They understood what I was looking for. When I'd go in, one of the clerks would direct me to the latest batch of CDs that were still in the box in the back. They'd already gone through them looking for my father's name on the art credits.

"Your old man's an artist," they'd say. "That's cool."

They'd stopped shrugging. Their smiles were no longer crooked.

What I didn't tell them was my dad almost never received any money for his artwork. Artists weren't working for money; everyone knew that money tainted and corrupted a true artist, made him a whore. For the music industry it was a good line when they wanted something for nothing and you could make a profit on a myth.

Flavio fit the artist stereotype, and he was content to receive copies of the CD or food or drinks. He had the same attitude toward money when fixing people's cars—he got eggs, chickens, vegetables, fruit, and a live goose now and again as payment for work done. He wasn't interested in money. He'd met my mother in a commune in Quebec. They'd moved out (or been forced out, depending on how you looked at their leaving) and set up house in Montreal. But what they shared and valued was never the same once they left the commune. Their anchor, compass, polestar ... whatever you wanted to call the commune as a feature of their life ... no longer kept the lid on the compromises that normal people have to make when they live in the world.

Flavio, the man with the blond hair, the mechanic, the artist, worked the moving parts, selected the colours from a cupboard deep inside his heart. He worked with passion, losing himself in repairing cars and designing CD sleeves. Recreation? He cooked Italian on special occasions. Most of the time, he acted like a man who had no ego and accepted what people gave him. If he could help others, bring something good into their lives, whatever they chose to give him he accepted as sufficient payment for his services.

My mother questioned his views. She called him stupid and told me that my father was useless. She said that Flavio would never have enough money to buy two sticks to rub together. We would live in eternal cold. She'd changed. Her attitude was like someone who'd never lived in a commune. For her the commune had been an interval in our life, a timeout, where she'd gathered admiring friends and memories before moving to make our place in the real world. My father said the values of sharing inside the commune were also in the real world. But you had to look hard or you'd miss them. You had to seek out the people who believed like you. My mother and father had never fought when they lived in the commune. Now they fought all the time, as if without the commune they both had found they'd mistaken the true nature of the other person they believed they had known. Flavio would look up from his sketch on the kitchen table, emit a long sigh, light up a joint, and pretend that my mother's voice was a strong wind that would soon pass ...

My father had this enormous pride whenever he stood next to his vintage 1957 yellow Cadillac Eldorado. He puffed out his chest, sucked in his gut. He had restored it to mint condition and parked it in a heated garage all winter. Mother bitched about the heating cost. He didn't care. People saw that car and cooed like songbirds. It was in perfect condition. His car restoration work had a waiting list that stretched for a year or two. Car lovers were willing to wait months for Flavio's magic touch. He never rushed a job ... a restoration had no fixed timeline. Every part of the work had to be perfect. I'd watch him as he spent hours working on backseat upholstery that no one would ever look at twice.

He didn't believe in a lot of rules; he felt that they only set a man up for failure. But he had one rule he kept to—he never drove the Cadillac in the ice and snow of the Montreal winter. Each year when spring came, he backed that beautiful yellow Cadillac Eldorado out of the garage and sat in the driveway listening to the Clash singing "Should I Stay or Should I Go."

It wasn't just another song for Dad, it was a philosophical question he asked himself every year. He loved that car. The Eldorado was his mirror. He saw reflected in that car his dedication to perfection and a work of art. It wasn't just a machine to drive; it was a condition or state of beauty he'd created with his imagination and hands.

You'd think he'd have driven that Cadillac Eldorado all around Montreal to show it off. But you'd be wrong. Dad never drove the Caddy out of the driveway. He was afraid he might have an accident. And then he'd have to start all over again, trying to put the smashed-up metal back into its original condition. It was the Humpty Dumpty fear that he could never fit all the pieces back together again. The real problem was his own fear that without that Cadillac he would lose an important part of who he was. His favourite piece of artwork was his life work, and to ruin one would be to destroy both.

My mother's smug remarks about the uselessness of that car stung him. In one way she was right. It was a car. He didn't use or treat it as a car. Nothing made her crazier than seeing him sit in the Eldorado in the garage and listening to the Clash. Except, of course, the day each spring when Dad backed the car out of the garage and into the driveway, leaving the engine idling as he sat alone inside it like a teenager, smoking a joint and listening to music, banging the heels of his hands against the steering wheel.

"It would be nice to have cash rather than eggs and chickens," my mother said.

She was talking about the latest auto repair, a valve job on a 1968 Buick, for which the owner had paid Dad with chickens, eggs, cheese, and a quarter of a goat.

"It isn't the money," Dad said.

"What is it, then?"

He looked up from his sketchpad. I sat in the chair beside him, drawing on my own sketchpad he'd bought me. He always had some money socked away for art supplies.

185

"The flow. Being in the zone. No money needed in that space. You fly, fly above the clouds. You never want to come down."

I looked up from my drawing of the geese at the commune, drawn from memory.

My mother responded with hot, wounding words forged by the heat of anger.

"Fly? We live on the ground. Look at your feet. You need shoes. Look at my feet and Raphael's. We need shoes. You're selfish. You don't see that your space isn't big enough for a family, which needs money to buy shoes. You say you never want to come down. You've let us down."

Then she said something I never forgot: "I wish I'd stayed."

I could tell by the way he looked at her ... as if he had been violated, dumped, rejected and dismissed in those four words. Something had broken deep inside him, and as an expert restorer he saw that it was beyond his reach to repair.

"Take it back," he said.

She left the room, crying. He stood with his hands trembling, his mouth slack and eyes wide open, staring blankly at the ceiling. He looked like he might pass out.

My mother's expression of regret about her choice was the last straw. It drove Dad from his place inside the "flow" and over the edge. It would be easy to blame my mother. Dad's mind was a complicated space. Maybe it was some combination of pot, the Clash and his visions about design that made him decide it was time to flip the switch. He had tried programming his life with a long series of 1s. That had failed and he was left with the 0s. Once a man flipped to 0 on the dial, he vanished.

The year I turned nine years old, I watched as Flavio, his hair cut the day before, wearing his favourite shirt, slowly backed the Caddy out of the driveway with the Clash's "Death or Glory" cranked up to full volume. I stood on the side and watched my father. He was smiling. I waved at him, and he winked as he rolled down the window.

"Now you be good boy," he said.

"Where are you going?" I asked.

"I'm joining the flow." He inhaled on a joint and blew out the smoke, listening to the lyric. "I'm going to glory." He followed "glory" with a big grin.

I had seen him stoned lots of times, and he would laugh and joke around. It was a bargaining grin. I have thought about it for years, and I think Dad had struck a bargain with himself ... he was going to take a huge risk, but he was convinced the odds were in his favour.

All of this happened fast. To describe it and read about it takes much longer than the actual chain of events did, one following another. I stood on the side of the driveway as that beautiful yellow 1957 Caddy backed into the street that crisp, clear day. It was one of the picture-postcard beautiful Montreal spring days. Dad rolled down the window, stuck his hand out and waved. We exchanged a couple of words before he and the car disappeared. "I am proud of you," he said. "Paint the world as if you were given the personal mission to restore the image of nature. Do that, son."

I knew that people said that kind of thing when they were stoned. But I told him I'd do my best.

I believe he had looked at himself in the rearview mirror and seen a man he'd avoided seeing his whole life—a fearful man. Mirrors don't lie. They reflect a man's reality, whether he wants to see it or not. He faced himself, his fear, and kept on going. He found the courage to drive the vintage car, all nicely washed and polished. He reversed it into that glorious spring day and into the street. He shifted gears into first and slowly drove forward. He gathered speed as he turned the corner at the end of our street.

Flavio drove in the direction of the old commune. I also think it is possible Dad wasn't sure where he was going. He was just going. He had entered the flow. Riding in the slipstream of flow was itself the experience. It didn't aim at going anywhere in particular ... it was pure movement.

I see my dad in my dreams. Riding in the driver's seat on the road, out of the neighbourhood, strapped inside his pride and joy.

That night, when he didn't come home, I sat looking at his latest sketches on the kitchen table. Mother paced back and forth beside the stove, saying, "He's not coming back. I know it."

A few days later she cleaned the kitchen table, taking away his plate, crumpling up his drawings, along with my drawings of the commune geese, and threw them in the trash. That was the day we received news from the police that he wouldn't be coming back. I can't remember if she cried, but I think I would have remembered if she did. I cried for both of us.

My dad had taught me a final lesson, a sequence of signs or goals ... Don't idle forever in the driveway. Get your real life into gear. Park yourself inside the flow and unplug. Death or glory.

It didn't matter which one came up. All that mattered was the crazy idea ... it is always in your power to reverse out of a life that has run its course. Get out while you are still able to mount a horse and ride off into the sunset. Become part of the flow. Don't chase it. Be it. In Dad's case, it had taken him a long time to decide to drive out of his life, but once he did, it was metal to the floor, chasing the tail of the flow like a snake chasing its own tail.

Did he catch it? That's the question I've asked myself over time.

The police found my dad slumped over the wheel of his vintage 1957 yellow Cadillac Eldorado with a plastic pipe rigged from the exhaust through the side vent window and into the car. Dad drove into the country and parked in a field about five hundred meters from his old commune. At the funeral someone said Dad died with a smile on his face. People interpret a smile in all kinds of ways. The way I read Dad's smile was that he hitched a ride on the back of Pegasus, the white winged horse that I'd seen him sketch many times.

I learned about Greek and Norse legends at my father's knee. Later I learned that my father's preoccupations were a mental contagion that tends to run along the racetrack of DNA. I saw the theory at work at the hospital. What chance did I have with two crazy parents? Spalding Gray's mother committed suicide. Years later Spalding Gray, his acting career in the ditch, jumped over the side of a Staten Island ferry. The body was found days later. Like Flavio, he climbed onto the back of the white winged horse.

My dad was thirty-five years old when he died. He had disappointed his wife and likely fucked up his son's head too with all his talk about the flow, design, restoration and life at the commune. He lived long enough to know how fleeting happiness is, how none of it comes easily. All those years that he had started the car and backed it into the driveway, cranking up the sound of his favourite band, then pulled the Caddy back into the garage and danced like a high priest after a successful cult ritual ... those times had been dress rehearsals for his escape. He had finished working on the last restoration and had got paid in cash. His last graphic design for a book cover had been sent to the editor. It was a good time, it was the right time. He had nothing left to do or to prove before entering the ultimate flow state.

For some time I too have been carefully planning how to reverse that vintage 1957 yellow Cadillac Eldorado out of the driveway, my own driveway. Flavio provided his son with a lesson in driving.

How surprised Dad would be if he knew Pegasus had dropped me into a third-world military dictatorship, where artists and political activists are thrown into attitude readjustment camps or locked away in prisons. I like the edge of danger. Guns and power. A Lord of the Flies boy blowing into a seashell, sounding the horn, calling the other boys to do what they are told. What joy in seeing the powerful fangs bared! I have watched people who look and dress and act pretty much the same turn against one another. They have learned to hate each other's guts over the issue of who should run things. It is theatre, and I paint the puppets, nude or dressed, with their strings and without their strings. They arrive all day long in my studio, and I see how their strings make them twitch, turn, bow, fuck and eat. What beautiful puppets I have collected. I have taught them to listen to Dad's music as they sit naked on a chair in my studio.

But none of this theatre of the mind is enough. Just like money was never enough.

My dad was right about that. He was right about most things.

The women who sit for me know how to pull the strings of their customers. Those small, slender fingers restore men like Dad used to restore vintage cars. They slowly bring them back to the day when they were shiny and new. But there is a difference ... Dad loved vintage cars. My models despise the men for their ignorance, gullibility and childlike innocence. Reality and theatre blur when a customer is fucking them. They enter the anti-flow where everything freezes in time. My models work in the land of make believe, hired by rich sleepwalkers who want to share a dream that they are awake. For them sex isn't just pleasure; it is the key of a door to their dream world.

I make it a point to never lock my door. Reality always finds a way in. Why make it hard? Let come through the door whatever wants to find you.

A man wakes up. Then what? Dad knew the answer. He woke up.

"Death or glory ..." So the song goes. I hear the voice of my mother who said, "Never forget, he loved that Cadillac more than he loved us." At least he loved something, and died inside what he loved, I told her.

Dad was an artist. That's all you need to know. His first love was his art, which he used to restore the harmony in used-up, battered things.

Once my father read me a letter sent by a friend from the commune. I was a kid at the time. What do I remember and what has my memory added?

> *"Something is decaying in art. Murdered and mutilated, packaged and slipped into the stream of commerce. No one sells a cow; they sell steaks and hamburger after the butchers finish with the cow. Most artists are butchers working in bloody aprons*

and with knives. They can cut the meat only in so many ways. Most people want hamburger. The same could be said for film and books and music. The artist has gone through the abattoir door and into the marketplace. We forget the slaughterhouse. It no longer exists except as a vague memory about the history of meat. What comes out of the package is dead meat—they have lost the vision of Pegasus."

Butchers don't improvise. He was a mechanic. He was not an artist. The subject of his work was dead. Nothing he could do with a knife could change that. He could not restore the animal; he could only dismember it. Serving up flesh for a hungry man was a trade. Restoring a car, though, was an art.

From today's newspaper: "9th March 2016. Police were called to the Patong Hill Shooting Range at 1:54 p.m. after receiving a call about a shooting." It sounds like a joke. Of course there was shooting. That is the purpose of a shooting range. The target of the shooter at the shooting range is supposed to be a paper one and not the shooter's own head, a target made of bone, flesh, and brains. The bullet makes no distinction.

When the police arrived, a small crowd had gathered near the body. A Thai member of staff identified the dead man as a Mr. Andres, a 40-year-old Estonian man. Police said that Mr. Andres had shot himself in the head with a .45 STI Eagle handgun. The staff knew who he was because earlier he had left his passport at the rental counter. He had killed himself with a rented handgun, which the police found clutched in his right hand. Another employee of the range said he thought Mr. Andres had looked unhappy and frustrated.

He had smoked three cigarettes before going out to the shooting range, where he had fired seven consecutive rounds at the target. At that point he had aimed the gun at the area behind his ear and shot the eighth round into his head. He was recorded as dead at the scene. The police were notifying Mr. Andres's embassy.

Self-shooting stories involving farang are rare. Such a death requires planning. Most suicides aren't planned. Jumper stories are mostly about an unplanned moment. They depend on a spontaneous impulse rather than courage.

What would my dad have made of my Thai models as an art form? Would he have admired their courage for selling themselves to men driven by spontaneous impulse? Or would he have seen them as butchers working with meat? I think he'd have understood them as restorers of vintage vehicles. A clue is in the messages I read on Tuk's iPhone as she slept in my bed. Sometimes I watch her sleeping and wonder if she's dreaming of a faraway place with cool drinks, good drugs, white horses, infinity pools and the sea. That was her plan, she told me. She was working on it with the same devotion as my dad who restored vintage cars.

Paul: Are you ready?

Tuk: Yes, darling. Kisses. (^人^)

Paul: You haven't changed your mind?

Tuk: I do like you say. You worry too much.

Paul: Sure you ＼,ⓓ凸ⓓ''、

Tuk: I no lie to you.

An artist doesn't tell lies. Tuk's art was polished, sharp and hard like a Gurkha's knife hidden behind a long, passionate kiss.

FOUR

RAPHAEL'S CREMATION SERVICE began at 10:30 a.m. A handful of people attended. Three days of sala attendance and then the early morning wore most people down to the emotional bone. For those who came, staying out of the cone of direct sunlight was the first priority. Gavin and one of the hotline volunteers, the one named Ronnie, found a piece of shade to stand in. Not far away Paul and Tuk, Ratana, Pratt, P'Pensiri, Oi, and McPhail, along with several young women, waited in line to climb the steps. Crematorium workers worked behind the scenes. Undercover police watched from the shade. The main cement courtyard, which baked as the sun beat down, was empty. The crematory oven radiated its own waves of heat. Solar waves bounced off the pavement under the feet of the mourners, who filed one by one up the stairs to the open oven door. Raphael's coffin was positioned inside the main chamber.

Each mourner said a little prayer of goodbye, waied the coffin, and tossed their wood shaving orchid into the mouth of the furnace. Afterwards, the door closed with a bang, and the natural gas jets opened, heating the coal and wood in the combustion chamber and raising the temperature inside to 1150 degrees Celsius. The heat quickly vaporized the water content of Raphael's body, and in the next stage the meat and bone would combust, vaporizing and going up the chimney as smoke. Around a couple of hours did the trick, leaving behind the ashes and charred bones of a man who had once been called Raphael Pascal.

Back in the courtyard, standing in a patch of shade alone was a Chinese man in a business suit. Calvino hadn't seen him at the funeral. He asked a couple of people if they knew who he was. No one knew him. Calvino wandered over to the man and introduced himself. He asked him how he knew Raphael.

The Chinese man clicked his tongue behind his perpetual smile.

"My principal instructed me to arrange the shipment of the 6 Degrees of Freedom series he bought."

"Where is your principal?"

"Hong Kong."

"Your principal has a receipt of payment?" asked Calvino.

The Chinese man's smile widened to show pure white teeth with a gold cap on an upper canine. It made his bite look worse than his bark. He handed Calvino a business card.

"It was a cash transaction."

"Paid to Raphael?"

"Paid to his agent, Mr. Lang. I expected him to attend the ceremony. He phoned half an hour ago to say he'd been delayed."

Afterwards, on the drive back to the office, Ratana said, "No one from his family came."

She was right. His maid and landlady weren't family, any more than Calvino was—or the professional Chinese fixer attending for business purposes. The embassy hadn't found any family. Ratana was taking that news hard. Not to have one's family at the funeral was the worst thing for a Thai. Everyone died. Most in Thailand died and were buried with family surrounding them like bearers to the next life. How would Raphael know where to go? How could he not be afraid or angry at being abandoned?

"Someone from his family should have come to say goodbye," she said.

Calvino glanced over at her.

"He told me his father's funeral was on a clear, blue April day when he was nine years old, and he ate an ice cream cone Eric Tremblay had bought for him, and that everyone from the old commune came. They had been his family, scattered to the winds after the commune had disbanded and brought back by his death to celebrate what had been lost."

FIVE

SEVERAL DAYS AFTER the cremation, perched on stools, ankles hooked over the metal hoops, Calvino and McPhail occupied prime territory overlooking the congested Soi Cowboy, teaming with touts, cops, taxi drivers, pimps, boyfriends, and illegal immigrants selling fake brand-name watches. They were the extras in the play. The stars were the girls in tiny bikinis lining the street. Cast and extras moved in coordinated fashion as if an invisible director had stationed herself at the Soi 23 end of Soi Cowboy.

"I can never remember. Is it a gaggle of geese or, or ... something else? It's on the tip of my tongue," said McPhail.

"Skein of geese," said Calvino, watching a group of male Chinese tourists in shorts and sandals scuttle past, goose-like, necks twisting 180 degrees, wondering if they'd taken the wrong turn on the large march. Women in bikinis and high heels trying to wave them over, broadcasting their siren calls from both sides of the soi, startled the Chinese. These were young women, the men noted. Not only that, these women smiled at them, wanted to meet them.

"Watching them is like watching a waterfall."

"With no possibility of a rainbow," said Calvino.

"It's been three days since the cremation, and I still need a stiff drink," said McPhail, calling the waitress over and handing her his empty glass. "Can you smell the smoke from the chimney? I mean now. It stuck inside my nostrils, you know what I mean?"

McPhail shook his head as if to dislodge the smell. He yanked a tissue out of a box and blew his nose.

"It's fucking still there, in my nose."

"For a gathering of loons, it's called a raft."

"Look at those Chinese floating into Soi Cowboy on a raft. Which reminds me, who was that Chinaman at the cremation?"

"A patron of the arts in Hong Kong sent his envoy."

"He looked like a vulture. Do they buy art?"

Calvino watched a man being collared by a girl in a bikini.

"He says his patron bought paintings from Raphael. And he wants them."

"You told him to go fuck himself, right?"

"I told him I needed the name of the person who sold his principal the art."

It hadn't been what the Chinese suit had wanted to hear. But he could see Calvino had made up his mind. He'd coughed up a name: Lang.

"Give him the painting Raphael made of you. That should scare him back to China. If it's that freedom series thing, it's jinxed. You said so yourself. The models are all dead except you and an escort girl."

Calvino nodded, holding up his glass.

"I found out more information about that woman the police say killed herself five days ago."

"Which woman?"

"Holly Lam. A picture of her ran on the timelines. But who remembers a photo of a dead woman when there are all those pictures of food and videos of road rage, barroom fights, and a dancing dog in a clown outfit? No one, Ed, remembers anything anymore. I scrolled down the timeline until I saw a photo of a beautiful luk khrueng woman. Holly Lam. I'd seen the face before at Raphael's studio. He'd painted her as part of the series. Chinese-Thai father, Danish mother. Blue eyes. Twenty-three years old. The cops reported that Holly had overdosed. Pathology says she swallowed pentobarbital. You don't take that drug for a high. You take it to die."

"Copycat suicide. Nothing new. Move along, folks."

"She modeled for Raphael."

"So you said."

McPhail was still digesting his connection to another dead escort service girl. McPhail was getting himself into deep waters. He frowned as he sucked a lungful from his cigarette and slowly exhaled.

"I fucking hate this smell of burnt flesh inside my head," McPhail said. "Cigarette smoke helps."

"I kept thinking to myself, Thai-Chinese father. That's interesting. Chinese buyer of the series. The girl modeled for the series. She worked at the same agency as the two other pentobarbital suicides. Could there be a connection? Could there *not* be a connection?"

"There are a billion and a half Chinese. Try working out *that* connection. I'd stick with the copycat suicide angle."

Suicide does have a contagious element, thought Calvino. McPhail had that half of it right.

"The three women all worked for the same escort service. Copycat is when a stranger reads about a celebrity killing herself and decides if it was good enough for her, why don't I try it?"

"Hasn't Pratt been telling you some of his cop friends think it was murder? This pentobarbital stuff is better than a gun. No sound. The victim looks like a suicide. A perfect crime."

"A big part of a homicide investigation is identifying the murder weapon and connecting it to a suspect," Calvino said. "Maybe you can trace the pentobarbital to the person who sold it to the deceased, but even if you can do that, you still don't have a smoking gun. Prostitutes commit suicide. That is what people expect. No one is that interested in the details. It's good riddance as far as most people are concerned. There's little incentive to investigate the apparent suicide of a worthless woman who has been out corrupting husbands. Society is glad she's dead."

"You're right," said McPhail. "And anyway, people fuck up their suicides. If you make it too hard, they live but end up wearing diapers and connected to machines. I say let them make a clean break. Drink down a bottle of pentobarbital. But this particular string of suicides carries a bad smell."

McPhail blew his nose and looked at the snot in the tissue before crumpling it up and putting in the ashtray.

"It's black soot from the crematory. I'm blowing Raphael out of my fucking nose. How depressing is that?"

McPhail's attention returned to the parade of Chinese mainland tourists squinting under the garish neon lights, a little disoriented, slack jawed, as if a school bus of fourteen-year-old boys had been slipped a key to the girls' locker room.

"Mao must be spinning in his grave," said McPhail as the last of the stragglers in the advance column passed.

"He's in a mausoleum," said Calvino.

"Stuffed with pentobarbital."

"Actually he's full of embalming fluid."

McPhail raised an eyebrow.

"Why don't the Chinese do another autopsy? Open him up live on TV? Sell worldwide rights? Think of the audience. The money. 'Budweiser Presents: The Inside of Mao's Head.' And while they're at it, an autopsy on some of these brain-dead tourists they're sending to Thailand would also be entertaining."

Calvino bantered with McPhail, killing time before his appointment to meet Pratt across town at a nightclub called Finders. Pratt wanted to check out whether any of the people Holly Lam worked with had any information about how she got hold of the drug.

"I'm meeting Pratt at ten. Finders," said Calvino. "You know the place?"

"Hi-so nightclub on the other side town."

The phrase "other side of town" was shorthand for "might as well be on Mars."

"What else do you know about Finders?"

McPhail said, "Of course I've heard about Finders. This morning I saw a Facebook-sponsored window, or someone emailed me a promotion."

"You're on everyone's list, McPhail."

"I am famous. So where's my drink?"

He blew his nose again, lit a cigarette, and looked around for the waitress. All McPhail remembered from the bombardment of social media information dumps was the name and visual image of the nightclub. It really could have been on Mars as far as he was concerned, as it was located at the impossible distance of twelve kilometers from Soi Cowboy. McPhail's attitude reminded Calvino of New Yorkers he had known in the Village who had taken enormous pride in never having traveled above 14th Street in twenty-five years.

"Did Pratt say why he wanted to meet at that nightclub? Doesn't seem his style. Or does he have a secret life I don't know about?"

"The latest suicide victim worked at the nightclub."

"I thought you said she worked for an escort service."

"Moonlighting during the day, working at the nightclub after ten. Plus she modeled for Raphael. Pratt wants the story."

"Tell him to go to a library."

"I'll pass along your suggestion."

Calvino looked at his watch.

"Time to go," said Calvino, pulling his chits out of the cup and waving to get the attention of a waitress.

"But you just got here a few minutes ago," said McPhail, lighting a cigarette.

"Tuk's picture is on the same escort agency website. She's goes by the name Rabbit."

"Why didn't they kill her before she started blabbing to the cops?"

Calvino looked at him as he paid the bill, wondering if McPhail's time-scrambled questions explained something about the way he saw his life moving.

"McPhail, her painting wasn't part of the series. I'm the only one in the series who's still alive. Six paintings. Number five was Fah, killed by her ex-boyfriend. Number four was Holly Lam, who went out with pentobarbital. Fon was number three, again pentobarbital. Number two was Jenny, twenty-five years old, who died in January, same drug. Number one in the series was Raphael's self-portrait. What are the odds that string of suicides was a coincidence? Only Fah's death destroys the perfect set. I figure she was murdered before her suicide could be arranged."

McPhail rolled his eyes. "Was Fah the movie chick you had a date with?"

"No, that was Fon. Fon is Rain. Fah is Sky.

"Charlie Brown that's a big rain cloud hanging over your head. Man, you're number six. Your lucky number. Have another drink to celebrate your good luck."

"Later. I've got to go."

"Are you packing?"

He looked for a sign of a concealed gun. Calvino just laughed.

"It's back in the office."

"What if there's trouble? I should go along to watch your back," McPhail said.

He seemed a bit hurt, his eyes sad and shoulders slumped as the waitress put the drink in front of him.

"Pratt will be watching it."

"Okay, got it. Time to shove off."

Calvino slid off his bar stool and stuffed two five-hundred-baht notes into McPhail's chit cup.

"I have no idea why the kid made me executor in his will," he said.

McPhail smiled at him and said, "Hey, he trusted you to do the right thing."

"What *is* the right thing, Ed?"

"Don't ask me. I've been doing things wrong for too many years."

Calvino was about to step down to the street when McPhail grabbed his arm.

"Wait a sec, Vinny. What if this meeting with Pratt is a hoax?" asked McPhail.

"What gave you that idea?"

McPhail sipped his drink. His nose seemed to have cleared from the cremation smoke.

"I got a bad feeling. I smell a hoax in that nightclub. Seeing you're the only one in that series still alive, you gotta be careful."

"You mean setup, not hoax. Pratt's going to ask the staff a few questions and try to connect some dots. We'll have a couple of drinks and a few laughs and I'll drive back to the condo."

"Don't say I didn't warn you."

"I'll keep that in mind, Ed."

"Vinny, one more thing. What was Holly Lam's name at the escort service?"

"Honey," said Calvino.

McPhail flipped him a two-fingered military salute.

"Honey landed in the wrong hive."

Calvino left McPhail flirting with one of the chrome-pole dancers. He threaded his way through the crowd toward the Soi 23 end of Soi Cowboy, where he'd parked his car. Calvino drove the back streets until he reached Sukhumvit and then headed across town. The online report of Holly Lam's death had been buried under the avalanche of daily news, submerged in a sea of noise, wedged into the margins among pictures of cats and dogs and plates of steaks, shrimp, or salad.

The first day of Raphael's funeral, another foreigner, a young woman, had been found dead. Holly Lam had two connections to Raphael. She'd used the same drug to kill herself. She'd also sat for Raphael. Holly Lam had modeled for one of the Degrees of Freedom paintings.

Holly, or Honey, was the fourth degree of freedom.

He remembered the painting. It was striking in color and structure. Raphael had painted her face in detail, a realistic face, looking out from the painting. That was the start and finish of the realism. Holly's head was attached to a fetus body with a caterpillar-like ribbed cocoon, with a dozen legs and arms, some short, some long, tangled around musical instruments—a violin, a banjo, a guitar, a keyboard, and a saxophone. She was contained in an oblong womb. Bees swarmed as a halo above her head. Birds emerged from the flow of her hair. The flock found a breach in the womb wall and broke free. Intently watching the birds escape, off to the side of the fetus head, a calico cat, eyes wide open, waiting patiently, had its claws extended.

The story she'd left there amounted to only one line. Holly had written the shortest of the stories for the Degrees of Freedom series. Calvino recognized the phrase. It was a quote he'd heard Pratt use over the years. He'd asked Raphael how she had come up with the line. He said she had copied it from her T-shirt.

"Who is it that can tell me who I am?"

When Calvino casually told him he had come across the phrase in a painting, Pratt slowly said, "*King Lear.*" He looked at Calvino for an explanation. "She got it from a T-shirt," said Calvino.

Pratt had emailed him the small English-language press report about the woman's death. He later gave him a summary of the autopsy report, which was positive on pentobarbital. Calvino checked her name with the list of women Raphael had used as models. There was a match. He photographed the painting of Holly Lam and emailed the JPEG to Pratt with a message: "Remember the attached painting in that series by Raphael? You were surprised to find a hand-written quote from *King Lear.* Holly was the model. She had used Shakespeare to tell her life story."

Pratt had answered: "Police officers at the scene found a bottle of prescription medication. They suspect it was for sleep. She had checked in as a guest of the hotel the day before. Miss Holly was last seen on Sunday at approximately 10:00 p.m. Police officers at the scene said they were unable to determine the cause of death; the body was transferred to the Police Hospital Forensics Laboratory to determine the cause."

McPhail had one thing right: the widely shared belief that a bright line existed between what was a hoax and what was real had vanished years ago. Ever since then people had spent their days and nights digging out from under the rumors, legends, lies, half-truths, propaganda, and jokes that dusted their minds like fresh snow. In Bangkok, when a foreigner was found dead, whether by suicide, accident, or an act of violence, the speculation machine cranked up. A chorus of bar stool philosophers tripped over themselves, some digging into the subsoil of falsehood, other shoveling it into another hole.

Everything and everyone was suspect. People stopped complaining about hoaxes. They'd been folded into life as another wing on a bird. It was no longer an embarrassment to be hoodwinked in a neighborhood run by hoods. Information moved faster and faster, and everyone ran faster too, only to fall farther behind.

What kind of escort service girl quotes *King Lear* to describe her life story in a suicide note?

Question: "Who is it that can tell me who I am?"

Answer: Doesn't compute.

McPhail might have stumbled on to something, thought Calvino. What if the suicides had been part of an elaborate game, a brilliantly planned and executed hoax? He had to go deeper.

SIX

PRATT SAT IN the back of the nightclub with two other Thais—one a waitress and the other a Thai man in his thirties who looked like he might be the manager. A dozen tables circled an area for a band. A guitar, a piano, drums, and a saxophone had been left on stage by the band, who were huddled around their own table drinking beer. They'd finished their first set when Calvino walked in.

Pratt spotted Calvino immediately. His posture and gait were better than a fingerprint, Pratt thought. Calvino looked like he'd climbed out of a foxhole after surviving an artillery barrage and was keeping low, looking for snipers in the tall grass. Pratt caught his eye and gestured to him. Calvino would take a bullet for him, thought Pratt. There weren't many men he could say that about. Explaining what that meant to a fellow Thai would have brought an amused smile. Calvino was, after all, a farang. He stood on one side of the line, and the Thais stood on the other. And so it had always been.

The two other Thais smiled in their shy way, supine and squirming that a foreigner would be invited into the middle of a discussion about the suicide of an employee. It was like a metal rod had been sucked out of their spines.

Within a minute of Calvino sitting down at the table, the waitress left, and a couple of moments later the manager also found an excuse to slip away. That left Pratt and Calvino to take stock of each other.

"I hope it wasn't personal," said Calvino.

"We'd wrapped up. They were about to leave as you sat down."

The same waitress Pratt had interviewed at the table then came back and asked Calvino what he wanted to drink. Calvino smiled at her but she was all business. She'd switched into full waitress mode, ready to serve a farang customer who sat with an ex-cop. She looked at him as a spider might do, peering out from her web.

"Miss me?"

She cocked her head.

"Not really," she said.

He turned to Pratt.

"She didn't miss me. Honesty—now that's as rare as a single-malt whiskey in Soi Cowboy."

"Can I have your order, *ka*?"

"Johnnie Walker Blue," he said.

She wrote down his order and left without making eye contact. It was the kind of expensive drink order that flashy Chinese made to impress on the staff that they were rich. The problem with vulgarity was, at the nightclub level, it magically transformed the drinker into a man of power and influence, as did his car and jewelry and the submissive women he arranged around him like furniture. The more the customer spent, the more important and rich he was assumed to be. In Bangkok money bought face, and in places like Finders it didn't matter where the money came from.

The waitress returned with his drink order and smiled. He tipped her a hundred baht and she waied him. The system of respect operated on the same principle as a streetside vending machine. Put your money in the slot and your product comes out of the chute.

"Discover anything useful from them?" asked Calvino.

Pratt stared at his glass as if some reflective quality compelled his attention.

"A couple of things."

"Such as?" asked Calvino.

He scanned the early crowd filtering through the entrance to the nightclub. Smartly dressed, stylish clothes and haircuts, flashy handbags and watches. Heads down, the flicker of light from their cellphones illuminating their faces like medieval candles. Some clubs specialized in entertaining the well-off middle class who emerged from their working day lives to unwind. Finders wasn't that kind of club. Like silhouettes cut out of black-and-white patches, the patrons huddled around their drinks, confident that their fast money, women, and cars entitled them to respect and privileges.

"Four suicides ..." said Pratt. "Raphael and three of his models—Jenny, Holly, and Fon—all of whom worked for the same escort agency. It turns out that Holly and Fon also worked for a time at this nightclub."

"Until they switched to the escort agency," said Calvino.

"Better money and hours," said Pratt. "That was the manager's opinion."

"Was he surprised when Holly and Fon killed themselves?"

"In his world, nothing surprises him, he said. 'Pentobarbital,' I said, 'you know about that drug? And he said, 'Coke, ecstasy, and meth.' Later he added Rohypnol to the list. He asked me if pentobarbital was a psychedelic. I told him no one knew."

Pratt thought for a moment and said, "It turns out one of the partners of the club also has an interest in the escort agency."

Calvino smiled.

"Let me take a guess. He goes by the name Sia Lang."

"How did you know that, Vincent?"

Pratt leaned forward, hands cupped around his glass, waiting for Calvino to say something more about the Chinese gangster from Shanghai.

"Raphael mentioned the name."

"What did he say about Sia Lang?"

"They'd done some business together. Before you ask what kind of business, I think you should ask Lang. I don't know. Maybe Raphael wanted to paint a Chinese gangster and call it *Chinese New Year, Bangkok, 2016*."

Pratt caught Calvino's reference to Chini's Bangkok New Year painting. Calvino was right in thinking that although much on the surface had changed, burrow underneath and things were much the same as in Chini's time.

"The point, Vincent, is Raphael painted models who worked for Sia Lang's escort service, two of whom were recruited from this club to work as escorts, and all of them dead."

"Pull Lang in. Talk to him in that special language he'll understand," said Calvino.

"It's not that easy."

Calvino got the picture.

"He's got someone higher up protecting him," said Calvino.

Pratt went quiet, the wheels turning in his mind, and Calvino had a pretty good idea of what was about to come out.

"When devils will the blackest sins put on, They do suggest at first with heavenly shows," Pratt said, quoting *Othello*.

"The devils don't make it easy for you, Pratt."

"There are no angels," said Pratt.

From the way Pratt looked at him across the table, with his mixture of worldly wisdom and the heavy load of resignation that wisdom leaves, Calvino felt the chill that came whenever Pratt lowered a barrier.

"It makes sense you getting involved in the funeral arrangements," said Calvino. "You had to consider how to deal with the police presence at the funeral and ..."

There was always a reason, and in a land of angels with their wings clipped, it was a struggle to get off the ground, and those trips to paradise required cash.

"About the crematorium," said Pratt, as the band members rose from their table and headed back to the stage. "I saw you talking to Mr. Wang Tao at the cremation."

Calvino grinned.

"How did you know his name?"

"I ran a background check after one of my men took his photo. Wang Tao is a partner in a Hong Kong law firm that represents some of the wealthiest families there."

"He gave me his name card," said Calvino. "He said his client had bought Raphael's series. I asked for a receipt."

Pratt's broad smile wasn't the one he used to express approval.

"How did he react?"

"As if a forest elf had unzipped his pants."

"How was it left?"

"Tense. And I asked Wang Tao, is that why you came to the cremation?"

"And he said, 'I came for the ashes,' " said Pratt before Calvino could answer the question.

The band started on a standard cover of Steppenwolf's "Born to be Wild."

"How did you know that?"

"He's already received an export license to remove the ashes from Thailand to Hong Kong."

Calvino snapped his fingers.

"Just like that? The guy gets fast track treatment. No embassy involvement. No consent of the executor. No questioning of who is his client and why he wants Raphael's ashes."

"There was no family, Vincent."

"What's he going to do with the ashes?"

Pratt sighed and gestured for the bill.

"Does it matter?"

"Maybe nothing matters, Pratt."

It was a sentiment Raphael might have agreed with.

The manager came over to say the drinks were on the house. They rose to leave, and the manager waied Pratt.

As they left the club, Pratt stopped as two couples pushed through the entrance. They had no idea they were pushing against a retired general. Pratt let it pass. He turned to Calvino as if nothing had happened.

"Wang Tao agreed to our request to take less than half of the ashes," said Pratt. "

"Did he reach some understanding with the police? How do I know how much he helped himself to?"

"He left ashes, that's the point."

"He left behind a mini-Raphael pile of ashes," said Calvino.

Calvino had returned to the wat the morning after the cremation for a ceremony that accompanied the collection of the deceased's ashes. He'd looked around, thinking Paul and Tuk would show up. Or Gavin. Or P'Pensiri or Oi, the maid. He was alone. He walked to the front of the crematorium where attendants laid out the ashes like a three-year-old's drawing of a stickman figure. He immediately saw what was wrong. The right arm and right leg on the stickman had vanished. The head and left side of the ash body remained on the double amputee figure. An attendant brought his boss to tell Calvino that Wang Tao had been to the wat at the crack of dawn with a permit and collected the ashes. Not long after Calvino arrived at the crematorium for a final ceremony, one of the crematorium workers shaped the ashes into a new, compact stick like body.

Outside the nightclub Calvino and Pratt continued the conversation next to Calvino's car. The heat of the night hit

Calvino like a sucker punch. Pratt shook off the heat like a man with a secret power to control his body temperature.

"Tuk also worked out of the same escort agency," said Calvino. "She modeled for Raphael. She was his girlfriend. Chances are she asked her friends to model for him."

Calvino shifted his weight, folding his arms as if suddenly cold.

"Correct," said Pratt. "They sat in his studio. He painted them. They committed suicide. And he followed them."

"This is the evidence for the department's suicide-murder investigation?"

"As you said at the funeral, some things don't add up," said Pratt. "Tuk's three friends are dead, but she's managed to stay alive. Then there's Pim, who showed up for a morning appointment on the day of Raphael's death and found the door locked. Raphael always kept the door unlocked. Why was it locked that day?"

"I've asked myself the same question," said Calvino.

"Any answer?"

Calvino shook his head, thinking that sometimes a piece of a puzzle falls through the cracks and never can be recovered.

"Just door stories, but nothing that explains the lock. Did the police find suicide notes for each of the three women?"

"You know the answer."

Calvino cocked his head.

"You overestimate my abilities."

Pratt shook his head.

"It's not your abilities. It's the paintings. For that series each of the women wrote a note."

"Raphael asked the models to write their stories. Why do you call them suicide notes?"

"Maybe they didn't call them that at the time, but their words are consistent with what we find in suicide notes. They were written in their own words. I've read what they wrote for Raphael many times. Each time I find gloom and intentions that are dark and depressive. Do you agree?"

"Holly pirated Shakespeare."

"If it was actually her idea to use that quote or someone suggested it to her because she was drawning a blank screen."

Someone who was clever enough, knew psychology, and used just the right "gaslighting" techniques could convince someone else to kill themselves—or if they weren't up to the job, give them an assist: lace a drink with ten grams of pentobarbital. When it's only a prostitute who is found dead, no one is going to look beyond the motive of suicide once the drug turns up in the autopsy report.

"There are six paintings in the series," said Calvino, opening the photo file on his cellphone. "Here they are. Have a look."

He showed the paintings in order. Calvino stopped at the sixth painting.

"You're number six," said Pratt.

Pratt looked up from the phone.

"I am looking at the only person in Raphael's series who is still alive," said Pratt. "Be careful, Vincent."

"That's the second warning I've had tonight."

"And the first one was?"

"Beware of a hoax. That's from McPhail."

"Don't worry. I never confuse your McPhail quotes with Shakespeare."

Calvino was looking at his own image as painted by Raphael Pascal. Somehow he represented the sixth degree of freedom.

"And you believe that if you can trace the source of the pentobarbital, it might lead to a murderer," said Calvino, "and even if it doesn't, you'll put the dealer out of commission, save a few lives."

"What better way to spend our time on this earth?"

"None. That's why I'm here."

"Let's find the sonofabitch," said Pratt.

"And what if that guy is protected?"

Pratt shrugged.

"You aim the arrow to strike Achilles' heel."

Calvino opened his car door.

"Keep an eye on me. As the last model in the series left, I might be in a good position to find him. Just by being alive."

"It's not a joke, Vincent."

"Okay, I get it. It explains the surveillance team at the funeral and the cremation. The drug dealer or murderer might be milling around the crowd, sizing up the last member of the 6 Degrees of Freedom club left alive in Bangkok. "

"Are we looking for one murderer?" said Pratt. "Or two or more killers? It's a complicated case. With Raphael dead, who else had a motive? Who profited? There's only one person. The one who owns the six painting series stands to make money from the six paintings. Three women model for an epic artistic tour de force and each snuffs it, using the same hard-to-get drug. But the sixth person, a farang, rides the huge news story of dead prostitutes in Bangkok and the underground art world. That might inflate the price of the art and the farang becomes incredibly rich."

"Pratt, you're talking to me, but this isn't you. Where's this coming from? Inside the department?"

Nodding, Pratt explained: "You fit their story. You own the paintings. You sat for one of them. Think how it looks through the eyes of my ex-colleagues on the force. I've explained that someone has tried to frame Vincent Calvino. Over the years, like you said, you've made a lot of enemies. Have you been set up? Possible. But it's more likely a way to clear five cases and make a hero out of the boss. It's because he knows your Calvino Law—The only safe solution is not to do your job, let someone else do the work, and if it works, you take the credit."

"What's the play? I hand over the paintings to this Wang Tao and he flies them back to Hong Kong for his client, and suddenly I'm no longer a person of interest? Is that what they want?"

In Thailand circumstantial evidence was good enough to send a man without power connections for a lethal injection of a kissing cousin of pentobarbital. The irony wasn't lost on either Pratt or Calvino.

"You've been set up as the fall guy."

"I'm not even Burmese."

"It's not funny, Vincent."

"Okay, who set me up? Raphael?" asked Calvino shaking his head. "That doesn't make any sense. "

"I didn't say it was Raphael. But did it make any sense for him to name you executor and give you all of his paintings?"

"I told him about my family background in the arts."

"You let him flatter you and you dropped your guard."

"Pratt, I had no beef with him. None."

It was as in a Muay Thai match, when an overconfident boxer drops his hands, feeling invincible, and then in the blink of an eye a knee smashes into his rib cage. Calvino remembered Raphael sitting in his office with the updated Chinese New Year painting modeled on Chini's original, and he started to sweat.

Pratt was right—he had allowed the family Chini connection to mushroom inside his head, filling his mind with the idea he knew something profound about art. Part of his identity had come from his great-grandfather's paintings in Thailand a hundred years earlier. He'd let himself believe he had inherited the fine art gene from him. Instead what he'd inherited was a story that connected a long dead family member to Bangkok. A man can be defined by the depth and length of his connection to the country he lives in. Calvino wanted to believe he was more than a private investigator taking shitty cases on the margins of Bangkok, that he was from a long line of artists who had come to Bangkok to test their vision and limits. Of course a young painter would seek out someone like him; it was obvious Calvino wanted to seal his connection to a long line of artists. The bullshit had been recycled into something real and tangible, something he believed in about himself.

"Like I said, Pratt. Why would Raphael want to set me up? That would be evil. He'd have no reason to do that."

" 'Good without evil is like light without darkness which in turn is like righteousness without hope.' "

"What Shakespeare tragedy does that come from?"

"Unfortunately it isn't from one of his tragedies. It's from *All's Well That Ends Well*."

In the noir landscape of Bangkok, the default was tragedy; things rarely ended well. The evil might slink away in a pseudo-defeat and lie dormant for a few years or even generations, but the seed never died. It sprouted into a sapling, and the sapling into a redwood the height of a high-rise, with balconies for the latest class of newly arrived jumpers. Shakespeare had understood that only in a comedy do things have the potential to end well. But life as Calvino knew it was a tragedy with some comic moments, and tragedy was the gravity well with noir world of losers and winners orbiting at the bottom.

"How long do I have?" asked Calvino.

Pratt remained silent for a long moment.

"Three, four days, maybe a week, to hand the paintings to Wang Tao. Otherwise, you go into the system."

Calvino understood what that meant. Once inside the gulag of generals with their photo ops, press conferences, prosecutors, courts, and prisons, there would be little that Pratt or anyone could do for him. He'd become another news cycle loser profile story. The kind of story the winners send out as warnings.

"I'll see what I can do," said Calvino, taking his wallet out.

"Give him the paintings," said Pratt. "Unless you have evidence a Hong Kong billionaire is lying about having paid for them."

"The rich don't lie or cheat, is that it?"

"Most certainly they do. But their lawyers are skilled in hiding lies in the legal packaging."

"Go easy, Pratt. I used to be a lawyer."

"And that's why you aren't one anymore."

Calvino thought he'd have no better opportunity to tell Pratt about the notebook of monthly bribes paid to the police and other officials. He had no doubt that Pratt would recognize names in the notebook.

"Pratt, the rich can't make all evidence of crime disappear," he said. "The more there is at stake, the greater chance someone will take a shot. If they can get away with it, even the rich can be victims. The difference is the rich send the Wang Taos like gunboats to grab what they think belongs to them and punish those who stand in their way. Or do you see it a different way?"

"What are you getting at, Vincent?"

Pratt knew him well enough to know the vague exploratory statement had something like a basket of cobras underneath.

Calvino wanted to tell the truth and believed that withholding the truth was a kind of lie, but he knew that once he lifted the lid on the information in the notebook, the outcome was predictable—Pratt would be the one the wolves would drag down.

"Just thinking out loud, Pratt."

Meanwhile he was thinking in silence … about the work history of the models, their access to Raphael's studio, and

Raphael's connection to Sia Lang, who had interest in both the nightclub and the escort agency. He was thinking that the missing notebook would have Finders' manager and owners sweating silver bullets.

"Take care, Vincent."

Calvino smiled and got into his car. He sat with his hands on the steering wheel, staring ahead at the parking lot, watching Pratt walk away.

Justice in the third world was the original IKEA model—do-it-yourself, only the box of pieces came without an instruction sheet. You didn't even have a diagram of what the final thing should look like. It wasn't fair. It wasn't just. It had always been like that. Socrates warned of the monsters under the bed. Pratt had pulled back the bed coverings and Calvino had squatted down and had a good look at a set of beady eyes staring back from the shadows. The time still wasn't right to tell Pratt what he'd seen. Calvino needed more time. But he had no more than a week, and after that what was under the bed would fly out and aim its talons at his throat.

SEVEN

CALVINO SEARCHED THROUGH Raphael's studio, bedroom, kitchen, and bathroom, and checked out the landings, the stairs, even the building's front entrance. He thought he'd examined every last corner. He'd turned up nothing. The chances of finding another notebook seemed to have dwindled to nil as he sat on the studio sofa and waited for P'Pensiri, Raphael's landlady. She had approached him on the first night of the funeral to tell him in her respectful, quiet tone, befitting the occasion, "Keep Khun Raphael's apartment for the rest of the month. He's paid the rent. You might need it."

P'Pensiri had turned out to be a prophet. He had found himself spending more and more time inside the apartment. The night before he had fallen asleep on the sofa and woken up with the sun shining in his face. When he opened his eyes, he saw two women standing over him, whispering.

P'Pensiri stood beside Oi, Raphael's maid. Two of Raphael's beneficiaries appeared to him as if in a dream.

"Khun Vincent, I thought for a minute ..." Khun P'Pensiri said, stopping herself short in finishing the sentence.

Calvino finished it for her: "That I was dead."

P'Pensiri laughed nervously. Oi, out of breath, eyes darting around the room, looked like she'd sidestepped a stampeding herd of elephants.

"You're early," said Calvino.

As lateness seemed to be part of the Thai DNA, P'Pensiri was one of those people who just kept on surprising him, making him question how shallow his knowledge was of his adopted country.

"I brought Oi along. I hope you don't mind. She needs to clean the apartment. She's afraid of ghosts, but I told her not to be silly. There are no ghosts. I'll go with you and you can see for yourself."

"I didn't see any ghosts," Calvino said, winking at the maid. "I've looked around but found nothing that the police hadn't discovered."

Oi looked sheepish, lips twisted into a forced smile. She disappeared into the kitchen and a moment later appeared with a broom and began to work the floors. The maid hadn't struck Calvino as someone who feared ghosts. It had taken genuine courage to tell him about the notebook. If she was nervous, it was presumably from her fear that Calvino might mention the notebook in the presence of her employer. The tension soon left her, though, and she hummed under her breath as she worked the broom on the floor of the bedroom.

"She's the best maid I've ever had. She's more like a sister," said P'Pensiri. "Oi's family got on the wrong side of the old military government in Burma. When that happens, and you lose, you end up working as someone's maid. If you're lucky, that is. She had enough relatives who got a bullet instead."

P'Pensiri seemed like a wise woman, but as with all the wise, there were gaps in her wisdom, ones you could drive a truck through. She was an accidental millionaire. In a way she had won the lottery. Development in Bangkok had exploded in her district, and developers, contractors, and politicians were getting rich from it. She could glide the rest of her life, one of those people who never had to start her engines. It was enough to be alive and preserve what one had. She also had the bubble and squeak sweetness of an auntie. It said everything that someone who was writing a will would think of his landlady. Or maybe Raphael had felt guilty about killing himself in an apartment she owned.

P'Pensiri had resisted the chance to clean out the valuables before anyone in the building who had access to it, perhaps half of the working girls in Huai Khwang, beat her to it. Calvino had seen how, in Thailand, death provided a cover for finger-pointing at the poor—look at their greedy and opportunistic behavior. From there it was a short step to saying, "You can't trust the poor. They steal from the dead." Whether descending on the homes of victims of plane, train, or car crashes or of a man who jumped off a balcony, taking what could be carried off or stripping the apartment was their one chance for some do-it-yourself redistribution of wealth. P'Pensiri was rich, and the rich could afford to be generous as her clan had accumulated enough plunder to relax.

But then, putting aside Marx, ethics, and moral philosophy, another explanation for P'Pensiri's self-restraint was her belief in the supernatural. The locals, especially the educated ones, wouldn't admit it, but they were afraid of angry ghosts. Oi didn't seem to be afraid of ghosts, but with P'Pensiri, Calvino wasn't so sure.

A young farang who had committed suicide, in their minds, would return (if he ever left) to his place of death for nightly hauntings and revenge against the living. Besides, a room left vacant by suicide was hard to rent to a Thai. After returning to the scene of a dead farang over the years, Calvino hadn't ever witnessed a ghost. But he had seen a lot fearful people worried about ghosts.

P'Pensiri reached into her handbag, pulled out two keys, and pressed them into Calvino's hand.

"All the locks will be changed today. Here's a new set of keys."

The keys were attached to a chain with one of those button-eyed monkeys on it.

"Thanks, P'Pensiri," Calvino said with a smile.

"Stay as long as you like. After you finish, lock the door from the inside and close it. Tomorrow a young foreigner is coming to look at the apartment. I know it's not the end of the month and the rent is paid. So if there is a problem, I can wait until the first."

"If I don't rent it, I'll return the keys, Khun P'Pensiri."

She gestured with her hand as if it were a trifle matter.

"Of course, Mr. Calvino. Take as much time as you need. If I may ask, what are you looking for?"

"I don't know," he said.

"That's a problem," she said.

"Problems don't get any bigger than this one."

She walked to the door and looked around the room, sniffing her nose as if she'd caught a bad scent.

"I'll leave Oi to clean the place. If you decide to keep her, you can count on her doing a good job."

He caught Oi's eye as she looked up, waiting for his reply.

"Let me think about it."

"If I can be of any further help, Khun Vincent, phone me."

After P'Pensiri left, Calvino found Oi washing dishes in the sink.

"Khun Oi, you knew the notebook was hidden in the water heater on the wall. And I've been thinking … how did you know that? I've looked at the water heater, and I don't think the cover would have just fallen off."

She wiped her hands on a towel.

"I knew from the screws on the case. I cleaned that case before. The screws were rusted. Who put new ones in the old case? Next time I brought a screwdriver. Inside I found the notebook."

She looked at him, waiting for him to say something.

"I have the notebook," he said. "Why did you tell me about it?"

Oi studied him as she had done at the funeral—the way you look at someone with power when you need to make a decision how it will be used and whether you will become a target. The Burmese had a lot of practice in making such assessments.

"Raphael trusted you," she said. "I think he not trust many people. I don't know what to do with it. I thought maybe you know."

"Any idea how the notebook got in the casing?"

She shook her head.

"I don't know who put it there."

"That's what I was asking," said Calvino.

In Thailand the maids, especially the Burmese ones, were the hidden intelligence center of many households, and important support players in many household dramas.

"Why didn't you give it to P'Pensiri?"

"Is that what you would have done?"

Calvino slowly shook his head. Oi nodded, looking Calvino in the eye without blinking, as if to say, I have hidden things for others, but I have nothing to hide.

"Things like this are dangerous. If you are a woman, they can do anything to you. Better for you to have it."

"But why didn't you tell Raphael?"

"He was a boy in a young man's body. I asked myself, would you tell your son about a mafia book? Or would you stay silent and watch him to see if he knows about the hiding place? But he walked by the water heater all the time without looking at it. I say to myself, my boy doesn't know. Someone knows, but not him."

EIGHT

HALF AN HOUR before sunset, Calvino rode the lift sixty floors to the hotel rooftop. The doors opened to an exclusive restaurant with a fish-eye view of Bangkok. Lang sat at the bar flanked by two bodyguards. His white silk shirt, the color of a cloud, was open at the throat, and the crease in his tailored trousers was sharp enough to cut a cobra in half.

Two young Thai women in flashy glamour dresses and open-toed high heels worked their fingers massaging his back and neck. They played him like a couple of pros who'd studied Wolfgang Amadeus Mozart's piano sonatas for four hands. Lang was enjoying his wine, the view, and the concert treatment being given to his middle-aged body. He nursed a glass of red wine. It was served in a glass the size of a small globe. He swished the wine around, creating a mini blood-red tsunami, splashing and rising as it gathered speed. Lang had boxed himself in, making it difficult for any outsider to get in close without appearing obvious. Chinese men like Lang came in groups. Like Zero-dollar tour owners, they were insiders who threw money around to buy respect and loyalty. Those occupying the outer fringes protected the princeling in his self-imposed cage in the center.

Loitering at the railing, Calvino held on tight as he looked out at the helicopter view of the city. Thousands of high-rises like Lego castles extended as far as the eye could see.

The ghost of hot money danced to the beat of heat waves bouncing off the vast infrastructure. The rooftop attracted those who had painted the history of Bangkok in cement, steel, and glass. They weren't artists. They were copy artists, recycling hot money, leveraging their future bets. Calvino watched Lang for a couple of minutes before approaching him. He made his move as Lang ordered another round for his entourage. They had relaxed, and relaxing was the one thing a bodyguard is trained not to do. As he walked up, Lang was half-turned away on his chair, eyes half-closed, as skillful hands massaged his neck.

"Mr. Lang, you are a difficult man to reach."

Sia Lang's eyelids opened like a reptile's, two dull pupils enlarging as they focused.

"You're the foreigner who has called me."

That was so like the Chinese attitude—Calvino was the foreigner, but he, from China, was the local. So far Lang hadn't appeared in public or said anything that wasn't part of the role he'd learned from watching Hong Kong Triad movies. His bodyguards tensed and Lang raised a finger, which they understood as a signal to back away.

"Wang Tao sends his regards," said Calvino, standing close enough he could smell the wine on Lang's breath.

"What do you want?"

Not who are you, or where are you from, or did you follow me here? None of the niceties or formalities came out of his mouth. His lips had gone firm, dispensing with his smile like a snake swallowing its own tail. The Chinese immediately got down to business.

"Wang Tao tells me his client in Hong Kong paid you for a series of paintings."

"How is this any of your business?"

"I have the paintings. Wang Tao says you have a receipt of payment."

His expression changed.

"You must be Vincent Calvino."

He reached out to shake Calvino's hand. His right hand sported a ring with a walnut-sized diamond. You could have cut glass for a city's worth of windows with that diamond.

"I was in Shanghai when Raphael killed himself. I was sorry to hear about it. Raphael had the receipt. I gave him the money."

"How much money did you give him?"

Sia Lang squinted as if trying to remember a trivial detail, a small amount.

"I recall the net was 150K."

"How much was the purchase price? The gross amount?"

Those last two words collapsed Lang's smile again as fast as a shophouse gate pulled down at closing time.

"Of course, I received a commission. Fifty percent. That's standard. Check any art gallery. They charge at least fifty percent. Raphael had no problem with the deal. You'll tell me he's dead and you can't confirm what Raphael thought about the deal. I can tell you. He was happy with it. Very happy."

A little moan of pleasure tumbled from his lips as he wrapped his arm around one of the women while the other one continued to massage his shoulders, her fingers locating the right spot to apply pressure.

Some loose ends remained. Wang Tao was in town to turn up the heat on Lang to make things right. The only pressure Lang liked was from the hands of a woman working a kink out of his shoulder. It didn't help Lang's nerves that Wang Tao had mastered the executioner's one-eyed squint as if looking down a rifle barrel.

"I was about to contact you. I'm just settling back. I told Wang Tao to stop worrying. I'd take care of it. But lawyers are professional worriers, and he flew to Bangkok so he could worry here rather than in Hong Kong."

Lang grinned as his two bodyguards laughed at their boss's little joke at the expense of Wang Tao. Calvino thought Lang was lying about his intention to contact him but was telling the truth about settling back into the Bangkok groove.

"You've seen Wang Tao?" Calvino asked.

"He's camped in my office. I came here to get away from Wang Tao. He thinks I have the paintings. I told him Raphael's executor has all the paintings. It's out of my hands."

He looked at Calvino, the smile creeping back to his lips.

"It's in your hands, Mr. Calvino. Good luck."

He turned back to his women. Calvino tapped Lang on the shoulder.

"I'm trying to understand something."

"What don't you understand, Mr. Calvino?"

"Why Raphael didn't mention the sale. He talked a lot about the 6 Degrees of Freedom series. But nothing about a 150K payday. I find that strange, don't you?"

"What are you saying, Mr. Calvino? That I didn't give him the money?"

Calvino saw one of Lang's bodyguards pulling back his jacket, showing a holstered gun.

"I wasn't there. I don't know."

"Exactly right. You don't know."

"You supplied Raphael with the models. Unfortunately, after they sat for him, they had a higher than average mortality rate."

"He requested troubled girls," Lang said, looking at the woman massaging his shoulder. "Come around to my nightclub some night and I'll introduce you to a nice, untroubled girl. Someone to take your mind off all these questions."

"You supplied the models and the buyer, and he supplied the paint and canvas," said Calvino.

Lang smiled.

"I think you understand the situation very well."

"Only one small thing troubles me."

"What's that, Mr. Calvino?"

"Raphael mentioned a nightclub notebook listing payments to the cops. Of course, it is the kind of crazy thing an artist would say."

Calvino started to leave when Lang's hand reached out and pulled him back. Lang almost spilled out of his chair as Calvino spun out of his grasp.

"You have the notebook?"

All the fun drained from his voice. Lang's serious side was delivered with a face distorted by anger.

"So such a notebook does exist?" Calvino asked, knitting his eyebrows together, lips pressed flat, eyes unblinking. "That's shocking news. I wonder how Raphael got hold of it?"

"Mr. Calvino, do you enjoy the view from this restaurant?"

Calvino looked out at the landscape of tall buildings.

"Nice view."

"But not such a nice view on the way down."

"Wang Tao told me about the ashes," said Calvino, not breaking eye contact with Lang. "He said the ashes were part of the deal for the series. He said you still owed him the ashes of the last model. He's come to collect them, along with the paintings."

Lang broke the eye contact first.

"You can tell Wang Tao that his client will have them the day after tomorrow," Lang said.

Calvino narrowed his eyes and leaned forward, looking straight at Lang.

"Let me see if I understand this. You've promoted me from being another Frisbee tossed aside to my new role as your errand boy."

"It's good when a man knows his role," said Lang.

"It's even better when a man keeps his promises."

It wasn't that Calvino didn't take threats seriously. He did. But a threat from someone like Lang, despite its razor edge, issued from something deep inside: his own fear. If Lang had double-crossed the Hong Kong buyer who had enough money to fund a Panzer division, he'd have had no qualms about sticking it to Raphael. Perhaps Calvino frightened him because he could see through him, and there was no shield against a man who could enter the deepest part of your mind and take the lid off the box of deceit and expose them for all to see.

NINE

THE NEXT DAY, Calvino slipped the new key into the shiny new double-bolt lock and turned it. The bolt slid back stiffly and he slipped into Raphael's studio, closing the door after McPhail.

"What a dump," said McPhail.

"You should have seen it yesterday, before the maid came to clean."

"No way a maid's been inside this pit since Custer took an arrow at the Battle of the Little Big Horn.

"I did say yesterday."

"How much did Raphael pay for this dump?"

"Eight thousand baht a month."

McPhail stuck his head in the bedroom.

"Nice little pad. Is it for rent?"

"You said it was a dump."

Raphael hadn't been much interested in housekeeping, and the stream of women who visited him in the studio had no intention of providing maid service.

"I've had a look around and changed my mind. It's still a dump, but it has possibilities as a bolt-hole."

Calvino thought about P'Pensiri as he put down a bag with three large bottles of Chang beer and sat on the couch.

"Have a beer," he said, handing McPhail one of the bottles.

"Did you bring an opener?"

"Try the kitchen drawers."

Calvino watched as McPhail prowled around the studio for something to pop the cap. He disappeared into the kitchen and emerged drinking the beer straight from the bottle.

"You should come and have a look at kitchen, Vinny," said McPhail.

"What did you find?"

"Well, for starters, I found an opener in the kitchen drawer," McPhail said.

"What else did you find in the kitchen?"

"A rat the size of a cat."

"I mean anything unusual?"

McPhail rolled his eyes. "Vinny, I said that I saw an enormous rat. I looked at him, and he looked at me. Mr. Rat stood his ground. Me? I didn't pay much attention to anything else until I opened my bottle of beer."

"You still want to rent the place?"

McPhail tipped the bottle back.

"I'm considering it."

"You know that old line about smelling a rat?" asked Calvino.

"The rat in the kitchen was big enough to use deodorant."

"I told the landlady that I'd rent it."

"What are you going to use it for?"

"Inspiration," said Calvino.

McPhail drank heavily from the beer bottle and then came up for air and belched.

"Now that's inspiration."

Calvino raised his arm and gestured across the room.

"I keep feeling there's something I'm missing."

"Like what? A body?"

"A dead body smells. You can't hide one unless you have three-foot-thick walls. Even with deodorant."

"Man, the cops have been through the place. And you can bet the hookers have been through it too. If the cops and the hookers couldn't find anything worth taking, you can be sure there's nothing to take."

"Maybe they weren't looking in the right place."

McPhail disappeared into the kitchen again with a second bottle of beer and started making noises.

The idea of further inspection of Raphael's studio had been seeded in Calvino's mind at the rooftop restaurant. He'd made a point of memorizing the faces of the two bodyguards. The chances of running into them again had gone up from improbable to highly likely, and that had been his intent. The question was how long until someone came looking for the missing notebook. Judging from the look on Lang's face, Calvino didn't have much doubt that it was something Lang wanted badly. That made him wonder again what else Raphael or someone else might have stashed in the studio.

It hadn't mattered that none of the usual evidence of a crime scene was present anywhere in the studio: no broken glass, no blood stains, no reports from neighbors of loud, angry voices—the usual bits of evidence that pointed to violence and struggle. But the hidden notebook complicated the neat, clean picture that Calvino would otherwise have in his mind. What if Lang had stiffed Raphael for the paintings, and Raphael had found a way to get the notebook and use it as leverage for the money he was owed? Lang might have had him taken out with a lethal dose of barbiturates. Or maybe Lang had made a deal he never intended to keep, murdered the painter, and walked away with the cash, blaming the dead artist and his executor. Lang was an angle shooter, and in Calvino's experience people who shot around corners sooner or later ran into a sharp shooter who fired back.

Calvino had decided after the meeting with Lang that he'd have to show Pratt the notebook. He'd hoped to avoid that outcome. Once a ball starts rolling down the side of a mountain, it gathers speed. The cops investigating the studio would lose face; the senior station commander and deputies would be reassigned to inactive positions. It wouldn't be a good time to be around those looking for revenge.

Calvino gazed again at the studio. The old adage was to see a room without observing it. He walked into the bedroom and concentrated on the double-sized bed on the floor and the spot where Raphael Pascal had lain curled up in the fetal position, looking not unlike his self-portrait dressed in Muay Thai trunks, number one of his series, which featured a nude model with a knife in her chest.

It hit him. Of course the police must have got wind of the missing notebook.

Suicide represented a criminal law paradox—the merger of killer and victim. The offender was dead. Raphael's suicide note and a heavy dose of pentobarbital discovered in his blood should have sealed the verdict of another farang suicide. But it hadn't done. Why had a gecko crawled up the ass of someone with rank? The notebook exposed corruption. Removing that gecko overcame the decision to take the suicide at face value. Which meant that threatening Calvino with a murder charge had nothing to do with the evidence and everything to do with the notebook. Calvino sighed as he realized why the cops had turned an easy case into a hard one. Only the weight of heavy money could explain such a shift.

A murder charge needed supporting evidence or a confession. They were short of both. Not that it mattered, as evidence could be "found" and "confessions" extracted. Those were details that would only occupy the mind of farang. A dark shadow had fallen sometime between the initial investigation and the funeral. A decision by someone high up had gone down the chain of command to rewrite the history of Raphael's death.

"Someone doesn't like you, Vinny," said McPhail said, returning from the kitchen.

"You find something else in there?"

McPhail winked and set his empty beer bottle on the floor.

"Let me show you something."

Calvino followed him into the kitchen. The doors on the cupboard underneath the sink had been pulled open. McPhail got down on his hands and knees, and his head and shoulders disappeared inside the cupboard. He then backed out holding a wooden panel and returned again, emerging this time with something wrapped in a blue bath towel.

"This is where Mr. Rat disappeared into. Look what I found behind the panel."

Calvino unwrapped the towel. He felt the 597 gram heft of a Glock 19. He checked the chamber and clip. It was loaded.

"What the fuck was a painter doing with a Glock?" asked McPhail.

"You're assuming it was his," said Calvino.

"Maybe he was using it for rat control. Except it was hidden. If it wasn't his, whose was it?"

"Dozens of people came in and out of the studio every day."

"We've got drugs. We've got weapons. Another fully furnished Bangkok apartment. What could possibly go wrong?" asked McPhail. "Isn't there another beer left?"

"It's yours."

"What are you going to do with the gun?"

Calvino held the gun in his right hand.

"I'm thinking."

"Now it's got your fingerprints on it," said McPhail. "I'd ditch it, if it were me. You don't need the headache. Fuck the cops. They've got nothing but their dicks in their hands. Leave it alone."

McPhail was missing the point. They knew the hand they held was always a winning one; that's how the game worked. There were no losing hands among the cops once a big shot made a decision about a case.

Calvino wrapped the Glock in the towel again.

"You want me to put it back?" asked McPhail.

"I'll keep hold of it," said Calvino.

"Right, give it to Pratt. He'll get someone to run a check on it."

Calvino smiled. The reality was Pratt couldn't handle it, and to put him in the position of trying something impossible was pointless.

"You've done nothing wrong, Vinny. That counts for something."

"In the scale of how things are measured in Thailand, that counts for nothing, Ed."

The Thai attitude for what counted and who counted was ancient. It functioned like skin that covered the body. It stretched back centuries and was written down in something called the Three Seals Code. A person's value, like that of opium, depended on the weight. From the small bronze chicken weight of a few grams to the monster chicken weighing in at over two kilos, small and big chickens measured different values. It was the same with people. It wasn't how much a person physically weighed. Their personhood had an intangible weight that was precisely understood. The scales of justice adjusted depending on your weight. You were assigned a number divisible into the number of rai, the Thai measurement of a piece of land. You measured a man or woman according to the number of rai they were in theory entitled to receive. Heavy or light, it all depended on the weight of your family name, the extent of your wealth, and your title and position. The system had never been devised to serve as an objective truth determiner or justice dispenser but to preserve the weighing system where your rank was your destiny. Harmony itself had weight. And a high-ranking cop's opinion carried an elephant herd of weight against the word of an ant-like foreigner.

"What else do you want to do here?" asked McPhail, finishing the last beer.

"It's hot inside. Why don't you go back? I need some time alone."

McPhail didn't argue.

"Before I decide to rent the place, clear it with the landlady whether it comes with ammo."

"Sure thing, Ed," said Calvino.

As McPhail left, Calvino sat on the sofa, arms stretched out on the back. As with Calvino's inheritance of Charlie the dog, McPhail had found a new bolt-hole but wouldn't need to find excuses not to rent it.

The only question on Calvino's mind was who would come first—Lang or the cops? He'd sealed his fate by dropping a hint to Lang about the notebook. That blood had hit the water and the sharks would be gathering to feed soon.

Calvino phoned P'Pensiri, who told him that as far as she knew, the police hadn't been back to the studio. In any event they didn't have a copy of the new key.

The cops missed the notebook and the gun on their first sweep. So did I, Calvino thought. He hadn't seen either one coming. He told himself that after all these years, he should know that when a man gets in real trouble, he should stop looking at the ambushes and traps as if they were meant for someone else. No one had been looking to build a murder case against him at the beginning, but the case was now well past the beginning.

Calvino's thoughts returned to his experience in examining the crime scene. When a man dies, you check his body for signs of violence. You examine his clothing for anything out of the ordinary: rips, tears, lipstick, strands of hair, missing buttons, blood stains, alcohol, or cigarette smoke smells.

Raphael had been dressed as a boxer. Calvino hadn't considered the Muay Thai boxing shorts as anything significant in themselves. It was hot working in the studio during the day, and wearing shorts was practical. In fact he didn't have much clothing outside his Muay Thai gear. Slipping into boxing shorts to paint was a perfectly natural daily act for Raphael. If he'd been dressed in a shirt and tie, that would have told a different story.

That was logical, but Thai cops didn't always follow logic. They marched to the sound of the status of the drummer. There were big drummers and medium-sized ones, but most of the universe of music came from the small drummers working the village circuit. Seeing it from their point of view, the fact that Raphael had dressed in the Muay Thai outfit dealt them a murder card to call the suicide hand. The suicide hand was about to fold. Calvino felt like a small drummer living under curfew.

"Why farang do like that?" Incomprehension was densely packed in that question, one asked hundreds, if not thousands, of times each day.

Raphael had chosen the shorts not to keep cool but to make a statement. It wasn't just the shorts; his hands had been wrapped too. He wanted to go out as a boxer in the clinch. Raphael's diary entries supported that line of thought. But Calvino could imagine a Thai cop's eyes glazing over listening to his theory until he would finally say, "Farang think too much."

Murder? The autopsy report revealed bruises were found on his body. He was, after all, a boxer, and he would have received scrapes, cuts, and bruises at the gym. But there was no evidence that anyone had pried open Raphael's jaws and stuffed ten grams of poison down his gullet. All the evidence at the time the body was found pointed in one direction: suicide.

But there was also a way to read the scene as murder. Only later did the pieces of a larger puzzle appear. Three models for a painting series who had died from a suicide drug, and a fourth who died by other means. A brothel's police pay-off notebook hidden in a water heater. A handgun found behind a panel under the kitchen sink. A Chinese gangster who pocketed big money paid by a Hong Kong billionaire in return for delivering a series painted by an obscure farang artist hiding out in Bangkok. And then there was the arrival of a Hong Kong lawyer to bag Raphael's ashes and collect six paintings. Of course, at the time Calvino had seen how Raphael ran his atelier like a commune—part safe house, part sanctuary—for prostitutes. An investigator could have arrived at a story of murder simply by putting those pieces together.

Pratt had told him this was the way the evidence was being read. Raphael curled up in his Muay Thai boxer shorts was the image of an obsessed man. He was dressed up to be a message that any rookie cop could read—farang boxer fights his last fight in Bangkok slum. Someone got the better of him.

Calvino's thoughts circled back to Raphael's note. The presence of a suicide note normally was a game clincher. But it wasn't absolute. To cast doubt on the authenticity of the note was simple enough in Bangkok; one had only to consider the possibility that it was forged. A mini-industry of forgers worked the back streets making perfect replicas of passports, ID documents, driver's licenses, press cards, and university degrees. There was no shortage of criminals who were artists in that domain.

It was Paul Steed who had found Raphael's note.

Normally the police were quick to credit other "found" suicide notes, like the one found next to the body of a farang who the cops said had hanged himself in a high-ceilinged room. They waved the note as conclusive and downplayed that there been no chair or other furniture he could have used to stand on. Even the fact that the dead man's hands had been tied behind his back was not important according to the police. A murder investigation would cause too much paperwork, and that had been enough motivation to bury the details of tied hands and absent chairs. The suicide note, the police handwriting expert said, was that of the deceased. Case closed.

In this case, though, Raphael's suicide note was in his own handwriting, but that hadn't stopped the threat to open a murder case. Still, the murder charge wasn't a done deal. That was something. It meant the cops were after something that Calvino, in their mind, could deliver but only under threat.

It was irrelevant whether the cops thought Calvino had killed Raphael and maybe his models as well. All that mattered was piecing together circumstantial evidence in a creative way to construct a possible case. They'd done that already. Didn't the killer sometimes show up at the crime scene? Calvino's client, Paul Steed, had called him to the studio, according to the two men. But what if Calvino had been at the scene from the start, and the phone call was his alibi? That was the problem with reality; you could fit pieces together to tell almost any story you wanted. The only requirement was that the story be plausible. It didn't have to be true. The test was believability, and the listener's faith that the storyteller believed it to be true. That was usually enough. Calvino had to admit as he walked out of the bedroom that the police had a plausible story. It didn't matter that it was false. Calvino's worth was as light as a feather.

The only way out of that double bind was a demonstration that contradicted their reading of the evidence. When he was a kid in New York, a teacher had asked him, "Do you know how many times you can fold a piece of paper in half?"

"Fifty times," he remembered answering. The teacher smiled and shook her head. "People usually say seven or eight times. The fact is you can fold it twelve times. To fold paper 103 times, the paper would have to be the size of the universe. That's a fact." After McPhail left, Calvino had the feeling he'd miscalculated the measurement of Raphael's universe. There were more folds to be discovered.

He kneeled beside the bookshelf, pulled out Sciascia's *The Day of the Owl*, and flipped through the pages. As he glanced up, Calvino eye was level with the shelf below the one with the Sciascia. It was filled with art books on Caravaggio, Lucian Freud, Francis Bacon, Rembrandt, Rubens, and Tournier. Squeezed between the art books and Gabriel García Márquez's *Memories of My Melancholy Whores*, he saw a volume titled *Upholstery Bible: Complete Step-by-Step Techniques for Professionals*. It seemed oddly misplaced. He pulled out the "bible" and flipped through illustrated discussions of upholstery tools, webbing, stitching, piping, and chaise longues. At first he thought Flavio Pascal must have handed it down to his son. But when he turned to the publisher's page, he saw the "bible" had been published long after his father's death. Calvino opened his cellphone and searched the title on Amazon; he discovered the book had been a bestseller in England. Written by an adult education teacher from Colchester, it outsold and out-ranked the Nobel Prize winner Gabriel García Márquez's *Memories of My Melancholy Whores* on Amazon.

Since when did the light turn green to let everyone to order up their own reality? You got the hard, cold reality dished up with tools, fabrics, and step-by-step instructions and illustrations. The thing with melancholy whores is there were no instructions. It was all up in the air and then falling down like a monsoon rain. It often made no sense. What appeared to be making up reality was a desperate attempt to explain incoherence and irrationality.

He opened the upholstery book to the section on chaise longues. On the page was Raphael's thumbprint set in purple paint. Calvino turned around and looked at the only upholstered piece of furniture in the room, in fact in the whole studio: the sofa, paint splattered over the black covering. It looked old. It looked vintage. Wasn't that the goal of restoration—not to make something look new and restored but to make it appear that it was showing its age discreetly? Re-upholstery was Botox for furniture. Calvino put the book back on the shelf. He rose to his feet, walked over to the sofa, and sat down. He'd sat on the sofa many times without thinking much about it. He stuck his hand down the sides and pulled out a couple of one- and five-baht coins and a handful of lint tangled with dog hair. Hiding guns, drugs, and the forbidden was an art form, one that seemed, like gladiator battles, to belong to the remote pre-digital past—except in Bangkok, where gladiators continued to battle.

Calvino had thought it likely that one or more of the models had used Raphael's studio as a safe hiding place. The book on upholstery made him question Raphael's role— had he known about the gun and the notebook? Model or artist? Which one had chosen the places to hide contraband? Or, as with the members of the Freedom Place commune, had a number of people cooperated?

An artist like Raphael, who created the persona of an artist and who, like Caravaggio, worked out his beauty and violence on the canvas, might have been oblivious to working girls casing his studio for temporary storage of stolen artifacts from the nightlife. The case for the models: a convenient, accessible location and a resident painter totally focused on his painting. However, that view failed to take into account Raphael's curiosity. For example, though Tuk may not have known it, Raphael had an interest in tracking her secret text-message life. He'd mined her text messages and copied them into his online diary. He knew the women who came to his studio all had secret lives. His art was an exploration of such lives. Another factor, thought Calvino— an important one—was Raphael's history of training as a boxer. A Muay Thai trained boxer learned that deception was a necessary part of landing a fist, an elbow, or a knee on the opponent's body.

Raphael was an artist and a boxer and the son of a restorer, an upholsterer, someone who got under the surface of the old and broken and made it new again ...

Calvino rose from the sofa and squatted down in front of it, running his hand across the seat. It was impossible to tell whether the covering had been restored. There was only one way to find out.

He walked into the small kitchen and slid open the top drawer of the built-ins next to the sink. Nothing. He checked the next drawer and found what he was looking for. He pushed aside the spoons, knives, and forks and picked up a box cutter. Using his thumb, he pushed the blade open. He examined it closely for signs of use. The shiny blade gave up no secrets. He carried the box cutter to the sitting room. Sitting on the edge of the sofa, he ran his free hand across the back, feeling for any irregular lump. He found none. His hand crossed over the seat. Again, Calvino felt nothing out of the ordinary. The surface, flat and even to the touch, suggested that nothing lurked submerged underneath.

Flavio Pascal had been an expert restorer of cars, and that, Calvino reasoned, would have involved a number of related skills, not the least of which was re-upholstery. The front and back seats of a fine vintage car had the luxury and design of Victorian private clubroom leather chairs. The seats were an intricate and elaborate expression of comfort and style. Flavio was a skilled craftsman in the restoration business. If there was a gene for skills of that sort, Raphael might have inherited it. There was only one way to tell.

Calvino plunged the box cutter blade into the right side of the seat and cut a straight line from left to right. He glanced at the bible of upholstery. He'd made a wrong cut, but it didn't matter. He pulled back the paint-splattered black Naugahyde covering, peeling it like tough skin. The plastic coating resisted. Calvino used the blade to cut vertically at the ends of the first cut. He was able to fold back the seamless material. Calvino recalled a legend about Naugahyde that he'd heard as a boy. Unlike leather, which required the killing of animals, Naugahyde was the skin from the mythical horned, grinning Nauga which shed its skin naturally.

Once he had the skin pulled back, Calvino dug his hand into the guts of the sofa, removing hunks of foam. Below the foam he reached a layer of padding from animal hair, and beneath that were the burlap-wrapped laminated boards used for the frame. Between the padding and the frame he found a small duffel bag sealed with duct tape.

Calvino cut through the tape. He pulled the zipper on the duffel bag. Inside was a diary the size of a paperback. The book looked well thumbed through, with some of the pages torn, others stained or smudged with what looked like ancient bits of dirt or grease in the shape of a fingerprint. Calvino carefully flipped through the three hundred or so pages, none of which were empty. The author's neat, exact handwriting showed a measured and thoughtful mind behind the pen. Flavio Pascal had written his name and the date on the first page of the diary. Nearly thirty years had passed. He designated his location as Freedom Place, twenty-three miles east of Montreal, Quebec. Calvino read random passages. Yellowing tape held a clipping placed on page one. It appeared that Flavio had cut it from a brochure and pasted it into the diary:

We are dedicated at Freedom Place to releasing the chains of cultural and psychological restraints. We walk toward a horizon where the degrees of freedom open; our goal is to spread our knowledge. Come and walk with us on the only journey of a lifetime that matters. Our commune is a place where we relearn how to live together, grow food without chemicals, care for animals as sentient beings, and heal our rivers, seas and land to health. We seek to restore our planet to its natural state and to co-exist within nature as totally free men and women. We have 60 acres of farm and woodlands, and 36 cottages. We are educators, homesteaders, ecological builders and land caretakers. We are restorers of the Earth. Join us on the voyage.

Calvino put the diary back in the duffel bag. He picked up the box cutter and cut through the black Naugahyde covering on the opposite side of the seat. Inside he found a second, much larger duffel bag with the logo of a Muay Thai gym on the side. He pulled it from the messy guts of the sofa. This bag had more heft, close to ten kilos. A small library of diaries would have weighed as much, thought Calvino. He sliced through the duct tape double-wrapped around the bag. Zipping it open, he stood staring at stacks of hundred-dollar bills, each one holding a hundred Ben Franklins. On top of the stacks was an envelope addressed to Vincent Calvino. He opened it, one knee on the disemboweled sofa. The paper inside looked like old pages of a rare book.

Dear Mr. Calvino,

Even though you were clueless what you were getting into, you now will understand that I have shown my great faith in your investigating skills, or you would not be reading this letter.

I have no doubt you will find my secret. And if I am wrong, what then? That's simple. It will have been the money's karma and it will find its rightful place in the world.

If the money had been left in the open, it would have evaporated long ago. That might have been sweet in a way. I wouldn't have cared, really. But it would have drawn the wrong kind of attention. Once you are fingered as having lots of cash, your models look at you the wrong way. You never will see another honest face. If you can't see honesty in a model's eyes, how can you paint her? You can't!

Please give the cash to the Bangkok Suicide Hotline. Talk to Gavin and figure out how to do this while causing him as few problems as possible. When (not if) problems come up, pay who needs to be paid and give the balance to this charity. Ask Gavin to call it the Flavio Pascal Fund, or some other title that uses my father's name.

You will have found the diary too, and that should answer a lot of questions.

I assumed from day one that you knew it was Eric, not Paul, who had really sent you to find me, and why. Over a couple of months, I found I was wrong. I don't think you had any idea that you were being used. Except in your line of work, that should come as no surprise. The diary will give the scoop on Eric Tremblay and my dad, Flavio Pascal.

Let me give you a few of the basics. Flavio was the only member of the commune who found himself on a trumped-up charge before the whole community, which was being asked to vote him out because he failed to increase freedom possibilities. Sounds like a joke, right? But it really happened to him.

That night Flavio and Eric got into a fight, and Dad knocked Eric down, broke his nose. It took a couple of minutes with cold towels before he opened his eyes and staggered to his feet. The next morning about dawn we got into Dad's car. My mom put me in the back and she sat up front. She didn't need to say she'd made up her mind. She just got into the car and slammed the door and said, "Go, Flavio."

I found out later that the real reason Eric had wanted Flavio out was the conflict over a woman. Eric had a thing for my mother. Tremblay made her choose between him and Dad. Stay or go. She chose Flavio. Sticking beside a good mechanic would mean she would never starve. Dad kept a diary of their time in the commune and he gave it to my mother and made her promise she'd give it to me on my 18th birthday. To her credit she did.

By then she had taken up with a lover and moved out of Canada. She no longer cared what Flavio had written about her, Eric, others in the commune, or their life together. Also it was her parting shot, her separation from the past, so she could disappear into her future without baggage. Dad and I were a link to a time she wanted to forget. The old diary was passed along, and that meant she'd closed the book.

On my 18th birthday she threw a party for me and invited Eric Tremblay. The commune had folded years earlier, but a couple of people from the old days came. So the birthday party was really a reunion of the Freedom Place commune. Everyone brought me a present. Handmade crafts, jam and a bench for my paintings. Eric said he had something special. The money of the future, he told everyone. He transferred to me $5,000 of nearly worthless bitcoins. They were down in value, he said, but that was only temporary.

It was one of the few accurate predictions Eric ever made. The small change ended up as big dollars. My 18th birthday turned out well for me but only brought regrets for poor Eric. He had lost my mother, and now he had lost his bitcoins too. Losers excel at losing. Eric taught me a valuable lesson. I took a discount when I found a

Chinese guy named Sia Lang to arrange the cash exchange for the bitcoins. God bless the Chinese for being able to do any kind of deal. But don't trust them, either.

Given the history of the money and the people involved, I saw nothing but bad karma. It's not only people but money, too, that can have bad karma. It stinks of disloyalty, revenge, drugs and bad blood. Eric's old drug money turned to dust before it exploded back to life. Giving it to Gavin's group may clean the scent.

My mother said to my dad not long before he killed himself: "I wish I'd stayed."

My life would have turned out a whole lot different had she stayed with Eric in the commune. What she taught me was this: we are all guests, and you can stay or leave. We all have that choice. I don't wish to stay. You, on the other hand, will make the harder choice, which is to stay on.

You must be wondering what other surprises I've left to cause you a headache. I can say with conviction, you've found the grand prize. There is also a consolation prize—the 6 Degrees of Freedom series and my other paintings. See they find a good wall somewhere.

Raphael Pascal

Part IV

ONE

GAVIN DE BRUIN lived in a small house nestled inside one of Bangkok's few remaining family compounds. It was one of those lost-in-time spaces that had been overlooked or forgotten in the development shuffle. It wasn't the kind of place where foreigners lived. The first thing that ran through Calvino's mind was that Gavin was living Thai-style. The style didn't come with an oath like the Italian Mafia, but the underlying rules that Tony Soprano and Thais lived by were pretty much the same. The family kept to itself unless it needed something from the outside. He looked up at the high-rise buildings flanking the compound—towering structures of glass and steel, dotted with tiny figures moving past the distant windows like workers manning a panopticon. Gavin's good fortune, or it might have been pure luck, was to have found a small house inside a Thai enclave of the old style, meaning it was built after World War II. It was a place where the modern world outside the gate seemed far away.

Calvino pushed the buzzer on the side of the compound gate. A maid came out and opened it, and Calvino drove his car inside. She pointed at Gavin's house, and Calvino parked in front. He got out of the car and walked to the door. As he removed his shoes, the familiar figure of a large golden retriever heading toward him at full gallop appeared as he knelt down with a bag of grilled chicken livers. She'd gathered some speed and her force knocked him over. She barked and licked his face. He sat up on one elbow and showed her the bag.

"Hey, Charlie, did you miss me?"

Charlie sniffed the plastic bag with the two sticks of chicken livers and hearts.

"Or did you just miss your liver treats?"

It was a question Calvino sometimes asked himself about the women who passed through his life like icy comets only to return months or years later. Charlie sat, ears erect, tail sweeping the ground behind her. Her head was level to one of a pair of large water jars. She took a drink and resumed her position, waiting for Calvino to pull the chicken livers off the skewers. He fed her one piece at a time, her gentle mouth taking the morsel and waiting expectantly for the next. Gavin appeared at the door and watched Calvino with the dog for a couple of minutes.

"Charlie never forgets a friend," said Gavin.

"A dog's definition of a food source."

"It's also the meaning of friendship for many people."

"Nice place," asked Calvino, looking at the whitewashed, wood-framed cottage with ceramic tiled roof, with its small courtyard featuring two large water jars with lotus floating on top and fish swimming below. The ochre-colored pottery in front of a traditional house often signaled the owners lived in a time closer to the Bronze Age than the digital one.

"Why don't you come inside?"

Calvino rose to his feet as Charlie finished the last of chicken livers. A dog's instinct isn't much different from that of human beings, he thought. Feed one, and they stick around; leave them unfed and they wander off, sniffing the ground, looking for a reliable food provider.

"I missed her, too," said Calvino.

He followed Gavin inside to a nondescript sitting room. Side tables, a reading lamp, a bookcase, a couple of chairs, and a Naugahyde sofa all had a second-hand look. Piles of books and newspapers sat on the floor near the reading lamp. A couple of unwashed coffee mugs and plates on the table indicated Gavin didn't use a regular maid service. He lived like a bachelor, Calvino decided, a lifestyle with which Calvino had plenty of familiarity.

Charlie nosed her way through the door and walked into the sitting room, tail wagging, tongue lolling, ears up, waiting for someone to give her more food. Gavin pulled a dog biscuit from a box, and without a command she automatically sat on the floor. He gave her the biscuit.

"How did you find this place?"

Calvino was impressed not so much by the luxury of the small house—it was in fact very modest—but by its existence and that a farang should be occupying a house built not for rental but a family member.

"My landlady and her family live in the compound— Khun P'Pensiri. You met her at the funeral. She owns a lot of property in the area. Jacking up the rent isn't her style. And she likes foreigners and is very wealthy. She's been to Holland three or four times and loves the Dutch people."

"P'Pensiri ..." said Calvino. "Just the other day, she met me at Raphael's studio and gave me a set of keys. She'd had the door locks changed."

"I got him the studio."

"Lucky break for him."

Calvino reached down and gave Charlie a pat.

"Not as it turned out," said Gavin.

He watched Calvino falling for Charlie's considerable charms.

"Have a seat."

Gavin nodded toward the sofa. He disappeared into the kitchen, leaving Calvino and Charlie in the sitting room.

The houses in the compound were built in the architectural style of the 1960s, a combination of two-story and single-story wooden structures, whitewashed, with an outside half-enclosed area used for cooking. The verandahs on two of the houses had deck chairs and tables for cool drinks at sunset—except that there were now only three or four hours of direct sunlight not swallowed up by the adjacent high-rises. It was after eleven in the morning that the sun cleared the one on the east side, and around two in the afternoon that the sun disappeared behind the one on the west side. A couple of decades ago most of Bangkok had been dotted with compounds containing modest houses. It was a reminder how Bangkok Thais and regional Thais had long lived in the same style of house. Now only a few enclaves remained inside the city's inner core, and Calvino found himself inside one, looking around as if he'd stepped out of a time machine.

The main room lacked any outstanding features. It was decorated and furnished with the simple basics, preserved like a fly caught in amber from a much earlier time. Some framed photographs of the seashore and mountains hung on the wall. He recognized a lamp whose twin was near the bed in Raphael's studio. The artificial leather sofa was also the same shape and style as Raphael's, though the one in Gavin's house wasn't covered with blotches and streaks of paint. The feel of the place was similar too, which made Calvino realize that he didn't see one of Raphael's paintings hanging on the wall. The windows, with curtains drawn, looked out at the driveway and the grassy areas of the family compound.

Not too far beyond the compound walls, the neon signs of the entertainment world were switched off at this hour, leaving gray, fake Greek pillars and flashy enormous blowups of smiling women exposed to harsh sunlight. Here, once the compound gate was shut and locked, there was no view of the massage parlors, restaurants, and nightclubs— no evidence, even, that such a world existed. But unseen though it might be, that glitzy world was still hurtling at the speed of light toward what was left of the old order in places like this. It was only a matter of time before these walls and this compound got swallowed up.

Inside Gavin's cottage, for now, that other world seemed to occupy another universe. As Gavin disappeared into his kitchen, Calvino walked to Gavin's bookshelves. He tilted his head to the side to read the titles and authors on the spines of the books, mostly popular books on psychology, sociology, and politics, along with a few novels set in Bangkok. Calvino stopped at a row of books grouped under a common theme: *Myths about Suicide, The Suicidal Mind, No Time to Say Goodbye, Why People Die by Suicide.* He pulled *Myths about Suicide* off the shelf and was leafing through the pages as Gavin reappeared from the kitchen with a glass of water.

"That one has some very good insights," said Gavin, handing the water to Calvino. "Cool water. It's a Thai tradition I like," said Gavin.

Calvino nodded his agreement, sipped from the water glass, and slipped the book back onto the shelf. Lately he'd been finding that libraries should be the first place an investigator looks. Motives, intentions, inclinations, nature, and more were written in the books a person chose to read and keep.

"Your job is to get inside people's heads, right?" said Calvino. "Once you open that door, you look around and figure out the source of a client's fears and anxieties, and you go in and redo the electrical wiring or plumbing in the neural networks. And that little renovation job restores the client to a life where he can deal with fear and anxiety."

"Please sit down, Mr. Calvino," Gavin said.

He showed no reaction to Calvino's speech about what he did for a living. Calvino suspected shrinks were used to hearing patients saying much the same thing, as they sat in their chairs looking supportive and thoughtful.

"Vincent. You can call me Vincent."

Gavin took a seat on the sofa as Calvino sat on one of the stuffed chairs, sipped the water, and put the glass down on a plastic coaster with tiny shells embedded.

"Your collection of books on suicide is a good conversation starter," said Calvino.

Glancing at his bookshelf, Gavin replied, "Most psychologists keep up to date on the literature."

"Maybe you'll write a book about Raphael?"

"No, I don't think so. Client–patient privilege is one reason. Another is I have no desire to write about suicide. I am much more interested in the psychological states of people who go to the edge but step back. Frankly, I find books addressing childhood-related problems more useful and productive."

"Did you ever sit for Raphael?"

Calvino shifted the subject deliberately. He saw that Gavin was an expert in directing a conversation down the paths he chose.

Gavin smiled, shaking his head.

"Professional ethics?" asked Calvino.

"In a fashion. There was a line. As far as I know, none of the hotline volunteers sat for Raphael. He preferred to paint …"

"Strangers."

"He needed the psychological distance."

"Or he might have felt a psychological closeness to working girls," Calvino suggested. "Artists and hookers have a long shared history."

"It's possible. He was searching for a personal connection. Perhaps he was looking for someone like his dad. You read his diary. His track record at the mental hospital in Montreal revealed a need to personally connect to patients. The most vulnerable of people are young women in a private hospital. He felt most of the patients had been abandoned by their father and mother. Raphael was like the tourist who goes to the wat and pays the man standing in the road with a wooden cage to set the birds free. The vendor opens the cage door; the birds fly out. The tourist feels good, feels he's made merit. But by the time he's left, the birds have returned to their cage. Raphael wanted to destroy the cage. He wanted to live free."

"Like his father," said Calvino.

"Is that the reason for your visit today? You want to talk about Raphael's father and Raphael's state of mind?"

Calvino made his hands into a bridge, forefingers touching his lip.

"Has anyone ever told you that you are psychic?"

"I was being sarcastic," said Gavin.

"I wasn't. I push hard for people, Gavin. That's my nature. But I need to know who I'm putting my neck out for. It makes a difference if you believe someone is on the side of right. Then you push, you take a stand, even if you might get hurt. The thing is, Gavin, in the real world, when you push, people push back hard. And if they have power, they can push very hard. That's where I am, at the fork in the road, and I have to make some difficult decisions. Did Raphael ever tell you that he put aside some money for your suicide intervention group, and he wanted to donate it in the name of Flavio Pascal, his father?"

Gavin's smile disappeared.

"You're serious?"

He paused, trying to read Calvino's face. Was he joking?

"He lived hand to mouth," said Gavin.

"How a man lives and what a man owns can be two very different things. Before we talk about Raphael's donation, I have a couple of things I'd like to clear up."

"Of course, I don't mind. Please, what can I tell you that you don't already know?"

"The police don't believe Raphael committed suicide."

Gavin laughed, shook his head.

"Is that why you've come to see me?"

"The police aren't laughing. They think he was murdered."

"Did someone confess?"

It was a fair question. The police had techniques to extract confessions when the accused refused to cooperate. Calvino shook his head.

"No one has confessed."

"The police must have something up their sleeve. What with a suicide note and the autopsy report, I'd say they have their work cut out for them, wouldn't you, Vincent?"

He paused as Charlie nudged his hand, wanting to be scratched around the ears.

"Do the cops have a suspect?"

"Me. I'm their suspect."

"That's ridiculous," said Gavin.

"Thanks. I'll see that you're called as a character witness," said Calvino, flashing a smile. "I'd like to know about the background of Raphael's secret website."

"Such as?"

"Was that your idea?" asked Calvino, turning the conversation.

"He saw me professionally. We talked about the need to express feelings, doubts, rage, and ideas. Writing them out, as he knew from his own work in the hospital, is standard therapy. If you'd ever had therapy, you'd know."

"I know about the diary-keeping technique."

Calvino had written out his thoughts for a therapist; he did know the drill. But he wasn't going to let Gavin distract him with his own history.

"From firsthand experience?"

Calvino nodded.

"Did he talk to you about the models who came to his studio?"

Gavin nodded.

"He had many women in his life."

"I'm interested in the ones who modeled for the 6 Degrees of Freedom series. Four of them ended up dead, three by suicide. A string of related suicides makes for the kind of story the cops hate."

Gavin shook his head.

"He never mentioned that. It's strange. We were close. I'm surprised that he would have withheld such information. Are you sure Raphael knew this?"

"I don't know. What about a Chinese businessman they call Sia Lang? Did he ever mention that name? Shanghai Lang?"

Gavin showed no flicker of recognition at Lang's name.

"I don't recall him telling me about someone named Lang. I don't think he mentioned that name in his diary. He was brutally honest about himself when he wrote. He had so many women floating in and out of his life, coming to his studio. I imagine he'd have difficulty keeping track of them. Who were these models who killed themselves?"

Calvino explained the basic details for the three suicides—each of the women had worked at the same club. Each was young, from upcountry, with a history of drugs, failed relationships, and abusive fathers. Each of them consumed enough pentobarbital to kill a bull.

"Raphael's death was last. Over the past year Holly Lam, Jenny, Fon, and Fah died. All except Fah killed themselves. Fah's ex-boyfriend shot her in the head six months ago. There are six paintings in the Raphael's series. All the sitters except for one are dead."

Gavin leaned back on the sofa.

"You're number six."

"The sole survivor." He had started to think of himself as the clueless man in a cartoon who'd been painted into a corner.

"And that makes you a suspect in the eyes of the Thai police?"

Charlie had edged across the floor and flopped beside Calvino, laying her head on his foot. Calvino shrugged as he stroked Charlie's floppy ear.

"They've got a flea in their ear. Once that happens, all their attention is devoted to stopping it from itching. Meanwhile, I'm trying to find a way to get the flea out."

"How can I help?"

"I want to know if there's a record of Raphael counseling them on the suicide hotline. I know it's confidential information."

"That's a problem, but putting it aside, the callers are anonymous. They rarely give us their name. And we don't ask them. The callers are worked up, emotional. They're depressed, embarrassed, resentful, needy, and angry."

He got up from the sofa and walked to the front door.

"Let me show you something."

He led Calvino to a small house at the end of the compound. A motorcycle and a couple of bicycles were parked in front. He stepped into the common driveway.

"Come over here," Gavin said. "Take a look."

Calvino looked up as Gavin pointed toward the roof.

"Pensiri had a problem a few years ago with jumpers from that building. In three years, she had two people jump from windows. I convinced her to have a suicide hotline in this cottage and write on the roof in big, bold Thai script, "Suicide Hotline. Call us. We will help." And we gave our phone number. After we painted the sign on the roof, there were no more jumpers." He pulled out his cellphone and opened up a window, scrolled down to a photo of the roof taken from a nearby building. He showed the screen to Calvino. The sign painter, in the playful fashion of the Thais, couldn't resist using the "O" in Hotline to paint a bright yellow a happy face. He couldn't help smile. Calvino handed the phone back to Gavin. "So far so good," said Gavin.

He rapped his knuckles on the wall, which was not made of wood.

"You're superstitious," said Calvino.

"We all are, Vincent. But we can't really help ourselves. We are, after all, only human."

Calvino cupped his hands over his eyes. From that angle he wasn't able to read the sign. But he imagined from the Jpeg on the cellphone that from the windows ringing the compound, the message could be read loud and clear.

"Let's go inside," said Gavin.

He opened the door and Calvino walked inside. The main room had several old-fashioned wooden office desks and a couple of tables with chairs. Backpacks were on the floor near the chairs. A coffee maker, a large jar of instant coffee, spoons, and mugs lined a table. Three volunteers sat at desks in the main room. Calvino recognized a couple of the faces from Raphael's funeral. One of them was on the phone, so Gavin spoke in whispers. Calvino could hear only one end of the conversation, punctuated by pauses: "How many pills did you take? … What is the name of the drug? … Where are you? … Are you with anyone? …"

Another phone rang, and a second volunteer picked it up. This was a Thai girlfriend of a farang on a condo balcony, crying, pleading, and screaming loud enough that her broken English mixed with Thai leaked into the room. The volunteer replied in Thai, again pausing to record the answers. With each pause, the volunteers made notes by working a computer keyboard. The volunteers acknowledged Gavin and Calvino's presence in the doorway with a hand wave and nodded. There were no smiles. Calvino listened as the hotline volunteers worked the phones. A caller would suddenly end the call. Another person would phone, and the volunteer would start the empathy building process all over again. Gavin said they worked four-hour shifts—the longest four hours of my life, one of the volunteers had told him.

Walking back through the compound, Charlie trailed behind Gavin.

"You've seen our operation. It's done on a shoestring. We try to have someone on the phones 24/7, but that doesn't always work out. Volunteers burn out, leave for home, or find a job that can pay them. The turnover is high. Finding replacements is difficult. I pay a small amount out of my pocket. We get a donation now and again."

Calvino thought the shoestring was about to be upgraded to a silver slipper. Watching the volunteers working the phones, checking their email, drinking their coffee, made it easier to understand what Gavin had told him.

"You can see there's not much privacy among the hotline staff," said Gavin, as they strolled back to his house in the compound. "Everyone hears what the other volunteers are saying, and that's how we designed it. At the end of a shift on the phones, we ask the volunteers to suggest how they or one of the others might have handled something differently. But that doesn't mean we know anything about the hotline callers' identities. Asking the callers to expose who they are, even in a small way, doesn't work. I'm afraid it's impossible to know whether any of the women who modeled for Raphael called our hotline."

Once they reached Gavin's little house, they stopped outside. The high-rise towers loomed above like a forest canopy. Calvino wondered if one of the figures at the windows in the distance was reading the sign on the roof. Charlie scratched on the door, wanting to be let inside.

"I wish I could be of more help," said Gavin, sounding sincere.

He waited for Calvino to speak as he could see the investigator had something bothering him.

"Okay, let's assume he didn't talk to them on the hotline phones. Did he receive any personal calls there that anyone remembers? One of your staff might have mentioned an overheard conversation. That wouldn't be eavesdropping. Working that close together, of course you hear what the other person is saying."

"Nothing like that was reported, Vincent."

Calvino stopped himself, thinking he was starting to sound desperate because he was. He needed a lead.

"Did you ever meet any of Raphael's models?"

"Frequently. It would have been hard not to. You were at his studio. So you know one or more young women were always hanging out. They wandered in and out of his studio day and night. It was a daily affair, with some new face always showing up. I never knew him to chase them away. In fact, he encouraged them to come around. He did little else but paint and ship out paintings by FedEx to overseas customers. He'd meet me twice a week for a session, we'd see each other at Muay Thai, and on Monday nights he'd join with the volunteers to help out on the hotline. But he socialized in his studio. He brought the party to his place."

"For a struggling artist, Raphael had lot of cash to throw around."

" 'Struggling artist' was a misconception when it came to him, one he happily promoted," said Gavin. "But he sold plenty of paintings on the Internet. He deliberately created a mystique about himself by keeping a very low profile."

"As if he was hiding," said Calvino.

"He cultivated mystery. He told me once that was part of the reason he liked the anonymity of the hotline. He could be himself without anyone knowing him."

"So you agree that he made money from his art? I thought you said he lived hand to mouth."

"You must understand: there were many hands and mouths in his life. Yes, he had buyers in Germany, England, France, Canada, America, and the Netherlands. Many people—buyers, critics, admirers, and collectors—wanted to meet him. He was never available. He trusted me with his address and number. But I don't think he gave details to any of the volunteers. They knew him as Rap. I understand you paid him two thousand dollars for a painting. That wasn't unusual. He might finish a dozen paintings in a day. He painted every day. The volume added up. He was as frugal as a Dutchman in the way he lived. I don't think cash was much of an issue. He bought the women cellphones, tablet computers, motorcycles … paid their rent, gave them money to go home to visit their mothers …"

Calvino silently replayed the names of the places Gavin said Raphael's customers lived. One missing place popped into his head as Gavin finished.

"How about Hong Kong? Did Raphael say anything about a big buyer wanting to buy his 6 Degrees of Freedom series?"

Gavin's training told him Calvino had listened only to the first part of what he'd said and ignored the rest.

"Yes, but it wasn't Hong Kong. It was Shanghai. I don't know the buyer's name. Sorry."

"Do you know the name Wang Tao?"

"Sorry, Vincent," Gavin said, shrugging. "With me, Raphael wanted to talk mainly about his father and mother, his hospital work back in Canada, and some other problems he had there."

Calvino was testing for signs of a hidden link to connect Raphael with Wang Tao and Lang. Neither of the two men was someone he could imagine as a patient talking to his psychologist about in an hourly session. But he felt he needed to clear the possibility. Besides, he wanted to make certain Gavin was the right kind of guy to hand over a lot of money to and not the kind to hatch a plan to help himself to it.

Gavin opened the front door of the cottage, letting Charlie in first, and then stood aside for Calvino to enter. The two men entered in silence as they collected their thoughts. Calvino sat on the sofa and waited as Gavin made a cup of coffee for himself, spooning a couple of teaspoons of instant coffee into a mug and filling it with hot water. There was no evidence of a woman in the room. He wondered if there ever had been a woman there other than a maid.

"You have a girlfriend?" asked Calvino.

"Had. She left six months ago," Gavin said, sipping his coffee. "She wanted the lifestyle of the rich and famous. She found I was a mistake. And I found that catching someone is easy but letting them go can be difficult.

"That seems to be the theme of Raphael's life: letting go of the past," said Calvino.

"It's a common problem. His diary tells the story. Abandonment at nine years old created a big hole in Raphael's life. It messed him up. Inevitable, I would say. If you look at the patterns that shaped his life, what eventually happened seems a foregone conclusion. At the private hospital in Canada he helped patients whose chaotic lives were connected to their family problems. He had them sit for paintings. He had them write out their stories. He was fired for being compassionate. He found his work with the patients healing. The patients found the art healing. But it was unconventional, and people distrust novel therapies. The hospital administrator wanted an assistant nurse to give medication, check they hadn't slit their wrists, and clean up their shit, blood, and tears. Raphael exceeded his pay grade. Rather than supporting him, his employers were suspicious of his motives. What was he after? I don't know if Raphael had the answer. You might see him as a messed-up kid looking for a father figure in all the wrong places to compensate for his loss."

"That didn't work out, did it?" said Calvino.

"Raphael had two father figure substitutes. I am about the same age as his father when he died. The patient's transference to his psychologist is expected and normal. He also had a second father figure in Bangkok: Vincent Calvino. Think about it. You are about the age as his father would be if the old man had never left home and was still alive and living in Montreal."

"Raphael saw me as a father figure?" Calvino said, grinning.

He tried to imagine how he could be a father figure to anyone. He'd found Raphael to clear a missing person case. As far as Calvino could remember, he'd never experienced the role reversal where a target thought of him as the find.

"You must have sensed that possibility. You're an intelligent man. It didn't hurt that that your famous great-grandfather painted in Bangkok a century ago. Did you ever see a photograph of Raphael's father?"

Gavin got up from the sofa and disappeared into the bedroom. Calvino heard the sound of a drawer opening and shutting. Then Gavin reappeared with a printout of Flavio Pascal.

"Raphael combined elements of you with those of his father in the painting he did of you."

Calvino saw only a slight resemblance. Raphael's father was more handsome. The shape of the nose and jawline of Calvino in the portrait drew inspiration from Flavio.

"He showed you my portrait in the series?" Calvino asked.

"He was proud of it. Yeah, he showed me. I asked if he'd copied his father's features into the painting, and he said, not intentionally. He was being honest. But the unconscious mind plays its games with all of us."

Number six in the series had been a tribute to Raphael's father. He'd used Calvino as the sitter for the final installment, in the role of father stand-in. Calvino reviewed in his mind the fate of the other sitters: the hookers who sat for him, all suicides or murder victims—check. Raphael's self-portrait, and he also killed himself—check. Calvino had been chosen as the father figure to represent Raphael's actual father who had killed himself—check. On the cosmic checklist, six dead souls in a series of paintings: 6 Degrees of Freedom. Except Calvino, a stunt double, was still alive.

"I keep asking myself," said Calvino, "why did he leave Tuk out of the series? They were close. She slept in his bedroom in the afternoons while he painted in the studio. He'd check her cellphone for messages. When she wasn't looking, he read her exchanges with customers and her boyfriend. With most men, it would become an obsession to shove a blade into the boyfriend's guts, but not with him."

Gavin shrugged, replying, "I talked to Tuk briefly the second day at the funeral. I didn't find anything suicidal about her."

Calvino had read her as a pro, a working girl who was a fighter, one who had learned the ropes by watching everyone from the managers to the other fighters to the customers who arrived wanting to be entertained. She was a survivor, someone who might get knocked down but would quickly get back on her feet, weaving and bobbing.

"Funny what people say at a funeral," Gavin added.

"What did she say that was funny?"

"Not really funny. It was more unexpected. She said it was the fourth funeral she'd been to with him, but this time he was the one in the coffin.' "

"What do you think was she saying, exactly?"

"I was confused too. I asked her to explain. Her boyfriend had disappeared for a moment, so she seemed more relaxed. She said that one girl who'd modeled for him had killed herself, and it gave her an idea. Tuk suggested painting other girls who were ready to kill themselves. She said he asked her to help, so she helped. She found the girls for him. After the sittings were done, they went to their funerals together."

"Any idea why she volunteered that information?"

"Her boyfriend came back before I could ask her any more questions, and I took his posture as disapproval of my presence, so I went to talk with someone else."

"You said Raphael mentioned how he and I met," said Calvino.

Smiling, Gavin replied: "He did. He said someone was looking for him. That you found him."

"He said I found him?"

"That's exactly what he said."

Calvino sat back on the couch, exhaling deeply as he settled in.

"Strange," he said.

Charlie pawed his hand, hoping for a scratch.

"Would you mind if I borrowed Charlie for a few days?"

Gavin replied with a wary smile. He was about to say that Calvino had seemed anxious to get Charlie out of his office and life. As with all relationships, there had been ups and downs, regrets, missed moments, and long loose strands of blonde hair all over the place.

"If you want, take her with you. Promise to bring her back, though."

The counselor wanted a promise. Calvino wanted the truth. Promising to tell the truth was never straightforward. Everyone wanted something, including the judges who made witnesses swear an oath before they testified to what they presented as the truth.

"I'll return her in a few days."

Gavin reached over and ruffled the fur around Charlie's neck.

"She likes you."

"Golden retrievers love everyone."

"Allow yourself to feel special, Vincent. No one will judge you for it. Be a good judge of yourself. Take an oath to tell yourself the truth."

The idea made Calvino grin, smiling from the eyes.

He said, "Do you know the oath that Thai courts use?"

Over the years, Calvino had heard it read out many times. He knew it by heart, much as Pratt knew Shakespeare by heart.

Gavin shook his head. He didn't have even a vague idea.

"It goes like this: 'I swear before the Emerald Buddha, the City Guardian, Siamdevaraja, and all the secret gods, that I will speak before the court with total honesty. If I tell even the slightest lie, all destructions and calamities shall suddenly befall my family and me. But if I tell the truth to the court, I and my family shall have only happiness and prosperity.' If you are a foreigner, the court assumes you have no secret gods or family who you worry will be destroyed by your lies. You're simply asked to promise to tell the truth."

"Come back if you have any more questions."

"About Raphael's donation ..."

Gavin tilted his head to side.

"Put it in an envelope, and when you're in the neighborhood, you can leave it with my landlady or one of the volunteers if I'm not here."

"It won't fit in an envelope," said Calvino.

Calvino stopped himself from telling him the amount of money in the duffel bag. He stared at Gavin, waiting for words that never came from his mouth—how much money did Raphael donate for our suicide intervention group? That silence reassured Calvino in an odd way. Even when provoked, Gavin wasn't someone who focused on money. Like Raphael Pascal, he used other tools to measure value in the world. No amount of cash would change his world. The question was whether it would change Gavin.

TWO

MCPHAIL HAD AGREED to give Calvino a hand returning the six paintings of the series to Raphael's old studio from Calvino's private storage locker, where they'd been removed to for safekeeping. McPhail had expressed doubt that the studio was a secure enough place for them. Calvino told him that P'Pensiri had changed the deadbolt lock. He failed to mention that he was hoping someone would be coming to take them. He'd be ready. It had taken over an hour to carry the large canvases one by one up the stairs and into the studio. The heat of the day had both of them sweating and cursing as Charlie tagged along happily behind. Sweat fell from McPhail's face and splashed onto the sixth painting. The painting, encased in bubble-wrap, was unharmed. Calvino watched McPhail wipe his brow with the back of his hand.

"McPhail, your sweat's dripping on my painting."

"What the fuck do you expect? It's hotter than hell."

He looked at the wet smudge on the back of his hand and wiped it on the leg of his jeans. After Calvino had leaned the paintings against the wall, the two of them sat on the couch, drinking cold Singha from a cooler next to the sofa as Charlie napped on the floor. Calvino had packed the cooler with ice. He took out a cube and rubbed it on his wrist.

McPhail touched the seat of the sofa.

"What happened to the sofa? It looks new."

"Ratana found someone to reupholster it," said Calvino.

"What the fuck for? Why waste money on junk? But at least it was interesting junk. Now it's boring junk."

McPhail ran his sweaty hand across the new Naugahyde covering. All signs of paint had vanished. It no longer looked like part of an artist's studio.

"I saw the book on upholstery. We'd found the gun ..."

"I found the gun."

"Okay, you found the gun. And we'd found the notebook ..." said Calvino.

"The maid told you about it," said McPhail.

"Okay, the maid told me. So I went looking in the sofa and found the cash and the diary."

"Want my advice? Burn the diary, keep the money."

"Thanks, Ed."

"Okay, keep the diary and give me the money. How much did you say it was?"

"I didn't say."

"What happened to Tuk? I thought she was coming to see the paintings."

McPhail had hit a sore spot. Tuk had just texted Calvino to say she couldn't make their appointment. She was already an hour late.

"She messaged me: 'I have customer. Cannot meet today.' "

"And you texted her back what?"

" 'Tomorrow?' And she said okay. And I asked her, 'How much is your customer giving you?' and she texted, "5,000 baht."

"How did you leave it?"

"I said, tomorrow, but come on time and I'll give you 10,000 baht."

"A bidding war. She must have loved that."

Calvino looked annoyed, staring at his phone for a message that was coming through. He dialed her number and she picked up on the fifth ring.

"Tuk, meet me tomorrow at the studio, okay? Two in the afternoon?"

He repeated the amount he would pay her. McPhail was off the sofa, drinking from a freshly opened beer bottle. Calvino had measured the paintings and the wall earlier, leaving a mark for the drill hole for each. Plugging in a power drill, McPhail now pressed the shaft against the wall and pulled the trigger switch, drowning Tuk's voice.

"Wait a minute," said Calvino.

McPhail stopped as Calvino walked into the bedroom and shut the door. The drill cranked up again.

"What's that noise?"

"We're hanging Raphael's series in the studio."

"All of them?"

"All six paintings."

It wasn't clear whether it was the news of the paintings being hung or Calvino's repeated offer of a ten thousand baht reward that worked to soften her attitude. Suddenly she was cooperative. He figured it was probably the quote to pay double her fee. It would be her new benchmark, one she would keep on her mental whiteboard from then on when a customer asked for a price.

As Calvino returned to the sitting room, McPhail tightened the bit and drilled again. Dust from the bricks behind the plaster poured out of the holes. Sturdy screws were inserted into plastic anchors fitted into the holes. The paintings were hung, and McPhail stood back, sipping his beer, admiring their work.

"How long are you keeping the paintings here? The place doesn't look all that secure. That deadbolt ain't gonna to stop anybody coming in."

"Until tomorrow, maybe longer."

"So … she's stood you up?"

"She had a better-paying client."

"Competition is a bitch," said McPhail, smiling as he opened another beer bottle. "Outbid by the one percent. It's not like the old days before Ayn Rand screwed up their heads. Remember those times?"

"What do you know about Ayn Rand?"

"How about *Atlas Shrugged*? 'Run for your life from any man who tells you that money is evil. That sentence is the leper's bell of an approaching looter.' "

Atlas Shrugged hadn't been among the books in Raphael's bookcase. Calvino had found no leper's bell, no evidence of looting.

"You want my take on nostalgia, McPhail? When were those good old days in Bangkok? It's always been a refuge for losers pretending they were once winners. It wasn't all that great in the past. Just in the parts we choose to remember. We forgot the rest."

"Look at how he painted you," said McPhail, who stood at eye level with the subjects of the paintings, admiring his own work in hanging the pictures. "These are lost faces, Calvino."

McPhail looked at the paintings one by one.

Staring at the one with Jenny as the model, he said, "You're looking at the face of a cashier. 'You pay money now, okay? Many customers are in line behind you. Next.' You didn't see faces like that in the old days. How he could refer to these women as Degrees of Freedom is a mystery. There are no free people in these paintings."

"What would you have called them?"

McPhail thought for a moment and smiled.

"Run for Your Life."

Calvino glanced at McPhail as he lit a cigarette, and then turned back to look at the paintings. It wasn't just one painting; the group projected a feeling that was greater than the individual portraits. Looking at all of them from an angle, he saw something he'd not seen before: each of the models wore a leper's bell hanging around the neck. He pointed out the detail to McPhail.

"The bell rings," said Calvino. "We don't pay attention to the motion. We listen to the sound. That was Raphael's point. Six degrees of freedom is no real freedom in the grand scheme of things. People are distracted. They're confused and frustrated. Their money buys them freedom. The reality is, we set traps and we step into traps set by others."

"You think this trap with the paintings is going to work?" McPhail asked, opening another beer and drinking from the bottle.

He walked back to the painting of Calvino.

"I'll get back to you on that, Ed."

"At least Raphael didn't paint you as a total monster," said McPhail.

"The women aren't monsters, McPhail. You're looking at the faces they hide from customers. That doesn't make them any less real."

"What does it make them?"

"Human."

The Thai, Chinese, Khmer, Russian, Burmese, and Laotian women who migrated to the two-square-mile radius of the Huai Khwang MRT station stared out from the paintings. They were free; they were imprisoned. They were lepers; they were goddesses. Contradictions of lives moving in different directions but all coming back to a central geographical point, as if returning to a sparrow's cage hanging on a vendor's pole outside a temple.

"I don't like the faces," said McPhail.

He wasn't giving up on his memory of the faces of an earlier generation of bar girls. It had defined him and a generation of farang like him. That world had passed.

The faces he remembered had vanished. He was finding it difficult letting go of what he had known as a young man, when the world was his oyster. Being left with nothing but the shell was a hard lesson in late life. As far as he was concerned, freedom or not, the women's faces Raphael painted were not from his world. A new generation saw Bangkok through different eyes; they arrived long after the rice farmer's daughters in their cheap sandals and street market clothes, looking for a farang husband. The search for a farang husband wasn't on the bucket list anymore.

"I want a woman who likes the feel of mud between her toes," said McPhail.

"No, you don't, or you'd have married one."

The earlier generation of Thai women had moved down the highways from Isan on non-air-conditioned country buses. Inspired by friends, neighbors, and relatives who had told them stories of the great riches to be had in Bangkok, they had walked away from their dirt road villages, places with outdoor toilets, no phones, and chickens running around unfenced houses that were cobbled together from corrugated metal, bricks, and wood, shabby structures on stilts. They wore nineteen-baht sandals and an amulet from their mother. In Bangkok they discovered freedom, money, drugs, excitement, friends, and farang. Reborn, they returned to their village wearing gold chains, pretty new dresses, and high heels, arm in arm with a foreign boyfriend, surprised to learn the family had arranged a village wedding and the monks were already chanting sutras at the house. The seed was planted in the village for other girls who dreamed of boarding the bus to Bangkok to try their luck.

The problem with memory, Calvino thought, is that it drags an anchor of sadness into the harbor of the present. It explained why some men never sailed out of the bay. McPhail's riff on the disappearance of the women from the old days ended with, "They're all cynical, hardcore snakes. I call it the Goldman Sachs Effect. Think about it, Calvino. Like a hedge fund manager, the incentive is to pocket the largest-sized bonus possible from the smallest-sized dick."

It wasn't Shakespeare or Ayn Rand but McPhail who successfully channeled the wisdom from Thai Visa.

"How does the greed for money explain why the models killed themselves?" asked Calvino.

"That's easy," said McPhail. "It's hard times. Think about the big drop in tourists. Fewer suckers. The party isn't as much fun; it doesn't pay like it used to. They saw through their money god, who'd gone on leave without absence. No customers, no money ... What did they have to live for? Nothing."

"Why assume it was Raphael's idea?"

"What idea?"

"Getting the models to drink pentobarbital."

"Who thought it was his idea? The cops?"

McPhail drank his beer, looking thoughtfully at the bottle label as if reading it for the first time. In the unfolding chaos, Calvino hadn't told McPhail that Raphael had attended their funerals or that Wang Tao had claimed their ashes after cremation.

"Someone might have brewed up a death cult, mixing in human sacrifice and connecting it to art. Think about it, Ed. A rich man looking for a unique art series not commissioned for thousands of years."

"The suicides were set up by some rich, bored guy?" asked McPhail.

Calvino shrugged.

"I get it," said McPhail. "Who the fuck knows? Raphael ran with working girls used to running with the rich crowd in the fast lane. They didn't know when to step on the brakes. Pills, balconies, razor blades were the only ways they knew how to stop. You said he wrote pages and pages about suicide and death. These are vulnerable girls. Only a small push and they go over the edge. Occam's razor."

McPhail had articulated Raphael's point—life was Sisyphus rolling the boulder up the mountain every day. Freedom of movement as the clock arms circulated was not real freedom. It was a mockery of freedom. The clock hands circled, a slave to the sun, and pulled lives around a circle as they struggled to break free. Raphael's death had completed the paintings. The series depicted the last motions of a free man. He'd gone as far as he could go, had reached in every direction as far as he could reach, and had found himself back where he started.

The faces in Raphael's series stared into the void at dark images from folktales, legends, myths—the nightmares that people found hard to shake off, things no one could shield themselves from, the dark things, relentless in their pursuit. Surrounded by Raphael's paintings, it was as if the images absorbed the viewers' thoughts the way an absolute darkness robs a man of speech. All of the faces shared a common mood—desolate, deserted, haunted by vapor trails of pain, chimeras locked in horror, terror, fear, and humiliation. The figures carried a deep secret of darkness within. But they weren't alone; they were part of a group of six images. Raphael's masterpiece was a study of freedom of movement inside darkness. Each subject struggled toward the light.

Each one of them thought the same thought Raphael had heard from his mother when he was eight years old: "I wish I'd stayed."

Calvino had hung the series in groups of three paintings, two rows side by side. He'd followed a specific order or sequence with the first painting beside the second one, three positioned next to four, and five hung opposite six.

"Raphael left instructions. Each one was to be six centimeters from the one to its side and to the one above and below it," said Calvino.

"They'd gonna give me nightmares," said McPhail.

"Number five is Fah. Her name translates as Sky."

McPhail stared at the image of Fah's face the artist had captured, one filled with a kind of raw pain that could drive a person to madness, one that between breaths, when her eyes and mouth were as wide open as humanly possible, allowed for the ejection of a supernova-sized scream. He'd never seen anyone capture hopelessness and despair any better.

"She's hurting."

"That's why he positioned her in the 'down' position. Each of the paintings has a position. It has a freedom of its own. And each model is asking herself the same question, 'Do I stay or do I go?' "

"Raphael was a freak. People want something beautiful to come home to after working all day. She's dressed like a mental patient. Institutional bed rails like prison bars behind where she's sitting. One look at that painting and you want to slit your wrists. I don't even work, and I want to slit my wrists when I look at this."

He turned to Calvino.

"She killed herself, right? Slit her wrists?"

"She didn't overdose on pentobarbital. Her ex-boyfriend shot her in the head."

"In your picture you're staring at Fah with eyes sad enough to fall out of their sockets. She's done something to you. She's passing along her pain like an electrical current."

McPhail was right. The artist had painted the two to be hung side by side so the eyes lined up between Calvino and Fah.

"And there's Vinny, facing that storm and not looking away. That's the one thing Raphael got right in the painting. He saw that quality in you, and you get the feeling that Fah never saw that look before, and that's why she's screaming. But what does it matter now? She's dead. Whatever she had boiling inside her, I could understand if it wasn't the boyfriend that killed her. That hardly matters because her world had been scheduled to end anyway."

"He combined my face with his father's."

McPhail rubbed his eyes, slowly lowered his fists, and took another look at the painting of Calvino.

"What he got right was that look," said McPhail, "the look of a guy who walks shoulder to the wind. It's dark and you're squinting because you can't see much. You're fighting against the rain coming down heavy. You've figured out something. But you know if you keep walking forever you'll never be free of the storm."

McPhail had provided a translation of Calvino's profane law of motion: If forces outside your control won't stop you, nothing will stop you, unless you stop yourself.

It was also a good description of Raphael Pascal, an artist who saw he'd never walk free with the choices that being alive allowed. Six degrees weren't enough. If death was oblivion, then that was better than being an ant tied to a stick with six ways to move. Calvino touched the space above and below the paintings and the corridor between the two rows with a measuring tape. A space of six centimeters separated each pair. Raphael had painted on six separate canvases; together they formed a pattern representing the six degrees of movement. Raphael connected the images and weaved themes that overlapped and supported each other in a unified whole.

Freedom in Raphael's corner of reality had limitations. No matter what we dreamed, the confines were in those six degrees of movement. And no matter the direction of the motion, the first step remained identical: stay or go. The *Hamlet* moment, and the player can't move on until a decision is made.

"Something's bothering Pratt," said Calvino.

"Did he say what it was?"

"The paintings, me, Paul, Tuk, Raphael, Gavin, the landlady."

"You forgot Charlie."

Calvino looked down and patted her on the head.

"Charlie's the only one who was in the room the whole time. She knows the whole story."

"Have you talked to Paul? After all, he's the one who hired you to find Raphael."

McPhail slowly rolled his cigarette between his index finger and thumb.

"I've talked to him," said Calvino. "It was like talking to a rock in the Grand Canyon."

"He appears out of the blue and hires you to find a missing person, and a year later that missing person becomes your new best friend. This young friend then writes a suicide note making you his executor and leaves a fucking hidden stash of cash. Yeah, I'd start asking how much of this is coincidence."

McPhail was right. Paul had hired Calvino to find a missing person. Missing persons cases were Calvino's specialty—locating their apartments in places where the farang thought they were off the grid and unfindable. Or an expat hired him to find a wife or girlfriend who'd run out on him. No one disappeared for long in the modern world.

"When I found him he was painting in this studio. The door was open. I just walked in."

Raphael had looked up from the floor where he sat next to a canvas in progress, a naked model on the sofa, and asked Calvino if he wanted something to drink, and told him that if he did, to go to the fridge and help himself. There had been no attempt to ask Calvino who he was or what he wanted. Most missing persons tried to evade or hide. If caught, they denied they were the person who was missing.

Raphael had concentrated on his painting. Calvino had waited until Raphael put down his brush before stating his business.

"Are you Raphael Pascal?" he'd finally asked.

The artist had beamed as he answered, "That's me. I'm sure we've met, but I can't place your name. You came to buy a painting?"

"No. My name's Vincent Calvino. I am a private investigator and I was hired to find you."

"I didn't know that I was lost. You want my phone number? I can show you my passport."

"You don't want to ask who hired me?"

Raphael had shrugged and picked up his brush again.

"Does it matter?"

"That I can't tell you."

Raphael had smiled innocently, like a boy who'd beat the odds, winning a chess match against a grandmaster.

THREE

CHARLIE CURLED UP into a tight ball, head buried in her paws on one end of the sofa, as the two of them waited in the studio. As Charlie slept, Calvino listened to the Clash coming from Raphael's laptop in the bedroom. The lyrics of "Dictator," out of time by thirty years, arrived as if written yesterday to a time and place with better guns, once again tearing away the freedom to dance and sing in the streets, the music replaced by a strongman's speeches.

In the heat of the room, Calvino's mind drifted past the music, the rotating blades of the fan, the melody of Charlie's soft snore. He closed his eyes, thinking of Tuk. She had her own internal time machine, running, running, never late, always on Tuk time. It was a dimension in which the phone regularly went unanswered. He imagined her as having just stepped out of the shower in a five-star hotel, toweling herself in front of the mirror. He imagined her last appointment, some midlevel executive on an expense account flying in from headquarters in Melbourne, Chicago, or London, sitting on the edge of the bed pulling on his socks. Fifteen minutes earlier Calvino had called her again, but she had turned her phone off. He'd sent her a text message. He'd waited for her reply. No one could type faster than a hooker with a john hovering around as she typed, but once that hovercraft landed on her, that was it for a while, fast typing or not.

Calvino was dressed in a pair of Muay Thai boxing shorts and a Tiger Muay Thai T-shirt, the tiger of the logo showing fierce eyes and large, sharp incisors. He waited in front of the oscillating fan, the sweat seeping through his T-shirt. Charlie's eyes opened and shut again. She'd checked out what she needed to know and was back in dreamland. Beyond the shiny, newly upholstered sofa, the floor was speckled with layer upon layer of paint, giving it an uncanny resemblance to the green, blue, and red microwave map of the early universe. He lifted the last bottle of Singha from the cooler and took a long sip. Wiping his face with a towel, he let the bottle slip onto the floor. Closing his eyes, he rested his head back. The fan turned slowly, fluffing Charlie's fur as the air current passed, but Calvino didn't see it.

It had been nearly a year since he'd been hired to find a missing artist from Montreal. Raphael had been holed up in a part of the city with only a handful of farang scattered among the old-style apartment houses. But among the photos of his paintings that he'd uploaded to Facebook was a Bangkok cityscape. Calvino had studied the painting and recognized the neighborhood. He knew that painters often left cookie crumb trails to their location. They painted the shapes and structures of their physical world, and in Raphael's case, he used color as a GPS to pinpoint his studio, neighborhood and models. The Facebook cityscape showed rows of high-rise buildings dotted with the female heads of his models—straight headshots, profiles, three-quarter profiles, and so on, with naked breasts adjusted to the angle of the head. Raphael had advertised his neighborhood. All that was missing was the GPS coordinates. Calvino had printed out the landscape image, and after some searching, matched it with buildings in Huai Khwang. He had taken the MRT to the area, approached a motorcycle queue, and showed it to the motorcycle drivers. One of them said he knew where to find the street and drove him straight to Raphael's building.

"Are you Raphael Pascal from Montreal?" Calvino asked aloud.

The beer and heat had made him drowsy, and he'd nodded off long enough to start babbling in his sleep.

"No, I am Tuk," she said with a giggle, standing in front of him naked, her dress folded and on the chair.

Still lodged inside his dream he awoke with a jolt. He propped himself up on his elbows, eyes wide open, looking at Tuk's slender body. It had been honed expressly for the purpose of attracting and holding a man's attention. No background noise of life interfered with the message it signaled—supple, narrow waist, large, firm breasts, and long, tapered legs. A mirage of an ideal body that might have been manufactured from men's holographic dreams downloaded from the latest neurographics software. She loved the power she had. Every day she used that power and money vaults opened.

He reached over and turned down the music.

"How did you get in?" he asked, doing his best not to pull her onto the sofa.

She inched forward. All he had to do was lean forward and grab her. She laughed at him, shaking her head, her long hair stirring with the wind from the fan. She opened her right hand and in her palm was a key.

"But I didn't have to use it," she said. "The door was unlocked, as always."

Tuk's command of English seemed unaccountably improved.

"Did Raphael give you a key?"

"Of course. Wouldn't you have given me a key?"

She made it personal, and with good reason. Her world was nothing but personal and impersonal smudged together, never in one location or the other.

"Why are you naked?"

"Isn't it obvious? You called me. I am here."

"Put your dress on. I want to talk."

Her lips pouted and she fluttered her eyes. She looked confused as to what to do next.

"I can talk dirty, if you want."

"I want to talk about you and Raphael."

Her shoulders slumped slightly as the smile slipped from her face, and her initial seductive pose was transformed into a casual Asian-style squat on the floor. She sat in that position with her arms balanced on her knees.

"I've talked, talked until I can't think of anything else to say. What do you want me to tell you?"

A hurt tone was in her voice as she stood up, walked over and slipped on her dress in one graceful movement. She stood before a chair that Calvino had positioned opposite the wall with the series of paintings.

"Like I told you on the phone," he said, gesturing at the wall, "I hung them for you."

He towered over her as he joined her in front of the paintings.

"You didn't tell anyone I was bringing Raphael's six paintings here today?"

She shrugged to signify that she had no intention of adding any words on the subject. Instead she gazed at the paintings.

"Why do rich people like this? If I were rich, I'd buy pretty paintings of myself in a beautiful room—you know, a five-star hotel suite with lots of flowers."

"You know these rich people?"

"Many of my clients are rich," she said, pride coloring her tone of voice.

By the time she stood in front of the third painting in the series, she was muffling a yawn with the back of her hand. The yawn taken care of, she pulled out her phone and scrolled through her last batch of text messages. If she had briefly had any interest in the paintings, it had vanished. The paintings in Raphael's series appeared to mean nothing to her beyond the fact that she had slept with the crazy farang who had painted them. Tuk seemed more concerned about the money Calvino had promised her. She worried whether, now that she was dressed, she'd have a hard time collecting the ten thousand baht. He watched her thumbs work the phone, sending a return message to someone.

"You're a busy woman," said Calvino, leaning in close to her, "But I need your full attention."

He could read some doubt in her eyes.

"You'll pay me like you said on the phone?"

"I'll pay you for some information."

"You're playing Rap's music," she said, keeping the beat with one hand.

"Did he talk about music with you?"

"Not too much. Talking isn't my business. You're my first talking client. I'm losing my talking virginity today. Never mind. You give me ten thousand baht, I'll give you words. Tell me what you want me to say."

"If talking were a new business model, everyone would be a millionaire. I want you to tell me what you remember from your last week with Raphael. Just talk about what you did together. His mood, your mood ... What did you talk about? Whatever comes into your head, even if you think it's not important."

Sitting on the floor, she nodded and then leaned back on her hands to cross her legs.

"He liked sex. But I didn't want it. He didn't complain to me. He wasn't weird in bed. But he had power."

As Charlie stretched beside Tuk, her front paws clawed the wooden floor, and Tuk looked straight into the dog's opened eyes. Charlie sniffed the air, her large black nose quivering as she picked up the scent of Tuk's perfume. Tuk looked annoyed as she pushed Charlie's head away.

"That dog stared at me sometimes when we fucked," she said. "Sometimes she'd bark, or yawn, or scratch her nails on the floor. He told me she's a jealous girl. I told him all girls are jealous."

She seemed to have become comfortable enough to let down her guard.

"What music was Raphael playing when he died?" asked Calvino.

"Same as you play now."

She cocked her head, as if thinking about the music, but what was really in her head was the question of how much longer she would have to wait until she could leave. Rising and walking to the bedroom, she climbed onto the edge of the bed next to the laptop and gazed at the menu on the screen. She looked up as he appeared at the door.

"What do you want now?"

Calvino was a hard case. He was one of those farang who, like a dog, sniffed at a pair of shoes to find out where the shoes had been and who they belonged to.

"What do I want? I want you to show me what happened."

"Show you? No problem. I show you everything, okay?"

She held out her hands, her fingers touching his, and he found himself on Raphael's bed with a beautiful woman and Clash's "Dictator" filling the room from the computer speakers.

FOUR

WAKING IN A sweat, Calvino pulled himself upright on the sofa and struggled to shake off the dream. There was urgent business to think about. He tried to clear his head of the dream fog.

Over the phone Tuk hadn't immediately warmed to the idea of a re-enactment of the day Raphael died. Calvino had judiciously avoided using the word. Instead he'd said, "I want you to come around so the two of us can recreate the day. I'll even bring along all six of the paintings in the series and hang them on the wall."

"Same as the day he die?" she'd asked skeptically.

"I won't make it sad. We'll have fun."

"Fun" had been, like superstition, a magic word promising infinite possibilities. That's why people paid big sums for both.

Police re-enactments seen in the media often featured a grim-faced suspect pointing at something. Surrounding him would be uniformed and plainclothes cops, along with a gaggle of grinning onlookers. The finger pointer would be cast as the defeated villain in Thai criminal-law theatre, in a drama that was also part press conference. It was always a big face day for the cops. The re-enactment followed the suspect's confession—and no one in the press ever raised their hand to ask the length of the rubber hose used to extract it. That would have been rude. It would have spoiled the big celebration.

But Calvino had his own version of a re-enactment—off-stage, private, and personal. As far as Calvino remembered, the local cops hadn't yet used a re-enactment as bait to set a trap for a criminal. It was an old practice in need of a modern revival, he thought.

Calvino dressed in the same Muay Thai outfit that Raphael had worn. The paintings were hanging on the wall. As she entered the studio, Tuk checked the paintings, not as an art critic would do but more in the manner an inventory clerk whose job was to check things off on a list.

"Satisfied?" he asked Tuk.

She nodded.

"Having fun?"

She enigmatic smile might also have registered her experience of pain or boredom. Buddha like smiles covered a universe of emotions.

"Same Muay Thai gym clothes," he said.

In preparation for the re-enactment, the clothing had been a detail that Ratana had put together so the top and trunks matched. Calvino had asked one of the girls in front of the One Hand Clapping massage parlor, next to his office, to wrap his hands like a Muay Thai fighter. The girl had disappeared inside. For a while he'd looked up at his window, which overlooked the sub-soi, wondering if he'd scared her away. But a couple of moments later she'd returned with the mamasan, whose job it was to handle customers with unusual requests.

"It looked better on him," said Tuk.

Thai women could be brutally honest when it came to age, weight, crooked teeth, and whiteness of skin. He'd clenched his wrapped hands.

Tuk had paced in front of the paintings until she got bored. Less than five minutes had elapsed.

"Now what you want me to do?" she asked.

"Let's go to the bedroom."

Her eyes lit up as if he'd put the key into the sex drive and started the Formula One engine. She grabbed his hand and pulled him onto the track, ready to race.

Tuk had said that she'd been in the bed with Raphael the day he died. She claimed to be his girlfriend, an ambiguous status, given the traffic flow in his studio. The evidence of their relationship leaned in her favor. She had slept the afternoons away in his bed. Raphael had taken the opportunity to search through the text messages on her phone, making notes on his laptop.

Tuk slipped out of her dress and sat knees pressed together beside Calvino on the bed. Charlie flopped in the corner of the room, her eyes on the two of them in the bed. She was observing a repeat performance, but as a critic Charlie was silent on whether the later version equaled the original. Which was better—the movie or the novel? In her world past, present, and future collapsed into the moment.

"I touch him," she said, her hand sliding inside the Muay Thai shorts.

"What did he say?"

"Feel good."

"And ..."

"Same as you, he get hard," she said with professional pride, massaging him.

The eyes of a pro were never bovine; they radiated like sparks from a flywheel attached to a brain in overdrive.

He firmly pushed her hand to the side. It was easy to slide into the clinch inside and outside the ring. Tuk offered no resistance and arched her back, stretching her arms over her head. It wasn't something that Raphael or her clients did.

Confused and angry, she asked him again, "So what you want to do?"

"What did Raphael want you to do?"

"I show you. You don't like."

"He wanted something else."

"What you mean?"

"You made him a drink."

She nodded.

"I always make his drink."

"Show me," said Calvino.

On the floor beside the bed, an arm's length away, a new bottle of Mekhong and two glasses waited. Calvino leaned over, picked up the bottle, and offered it to her. She didn't hesitate, grabbing it firmly by the neck. If the bottle had been a newborn kitten, it would have suffocated. She twisted off the cap and poured a couple of amber fingers of the rotgut into one glass.

"Aren't you going to pour yourself one?" asked Calvino.

He held the second glass, watching her pour the Mekhong. After she'd finished twisting the cap back on the bottle, he handed her the glass.

He touched his glass against hers. She made no attempt to drink.

"Did you drink with Raphael the day he died?"

Her mouth tightened, her tongue licking her lips—one of the involuntary tells a person can't help but flash an instant before responding to a question with a lie.

"I drink with Raphael. It help me relax. Help me forget. Why you ask me that?"

"I think you arrived at the studio early that day. Around nine or ten in the morning."

For a working girl who was chronically late, showing up anywhere that early in the morning would be, like the licking of lips, a tell. She was withholding some piece of information.

She drank from the glass before setting it on the floor next to the bed.

"I think afternoon. I always come in afternoon."

"Except this day. This day you came early."

She slightly bowed her head, eyes averted.

"I not like farang look at watch all the time."

"That morning you locked the studio door. Why?"

The question caught Tuk off guard, like a knee to the groin in a Muay Thai match. Her eyes expanded into full moons orbiting an alien planet.

"I don't understand."

For a call girl it was the usual fallback position. The mantra was always the same three words: "I don't understand." A variation had a broad following, too: "You misunderstand me." Both phrases were recycled year after year, deposited by the millions into a vast library where questions about theft, murder, plunder, corruption, road accidents, broken promises, and broken heads and bodies went unanswered. To play stupid was to play smart.

Tuk rolled out of the bed, stepped around Charlie, and walked into the studio. Calvino followed her to where she stood by the front door.

"The door was locked. Why?"

A small ripple of emotion crossed her face. Calvino had seen in the sala when she had knelt and waied Raphael's coffin. She understood a reality that she refused to confront.

"I think he not pay attention to me. Other girl come and he paint her."

"So you locked the door to keep Raphael to yourself?"

Tuk nodded but avoided Calvino's eyes. Turning away from the door, she marched across the studio and back to the bed, arms folded across her chest. Charlie lifted her head. She looked hungry. Tuk ignored her. She was caught up in her own cloud of sadness, confusion, and anger. Calvino sat beside her again. She was playing tough, but Calvino figured her as the kind of woman who would crack once someone pulled on a thread of truth, and the whole Oriental carpet of deception would unravel.

"I tell police everything. Why you ask me questions now?"

"You told the police a story."

"They believe me."

"But I don't believe you told them the whole story."

He looked at her glass beside the bed and refilled it.

"You're not drinking."

She didn't answer. Calvino sat on the bed across from her, close enough to reach out and touch her.

"Paul told me the truth," he said.

He saw a tiny twitch and a blink. It was enough encouragement to continue.

"He said when he came to the studio that day, you told him that you'd put pentobarbital in Raphael's drink. You'd bought some on the black market. He mentioned Sia Lang's name. Does that ring a bell for you? It should. He's the big boss at the escort agency."

The mention of Lang's name drained the blood from her face. Lang's agency had a casualty rate equal to the first Allied platoon to hit Omaha Beach on D-Day, and that was pretty damn high. She drank heavily from the glass and shuddered as the flame shot from her mouth down her throat. Calvino refilled the glass. Two or three glasses of Mekhong was as effective as shooting an elephant with a .22 handgun.

"Paul said you were afraid that Raphael was getting tired of you. You thought he had a new girlfriend. That made you angry. He kept cash in the studio. The two of you decided to take the money. But you had to deal with Raphael. Paul forged the suicide note. He had dozens of Raphael's old notes to choose from. They were in a file on his computer. Raphael had advertised his death wish. His models were killing themselves. Death was all around him. You took him to the funerals of the models. Maybe Sia Lang and you let Paul believe that he was running things, but Paul was a front. The real action was happening elsewhere. The question is, who was the biggest fool? Paul, Raphael, or me? Or was it you?"

A smudge of shame flickered in her eyes, fleeting like the brush stroke of a painter who had used the wrong color. Realizing her error, she quickly corrected it. It was too late. Calvino had noticed.

"Someone used you, Tuk."

"I go to sleep, and when I wake up, Rap is dead."

"When you woke up, you phoned Paul. That tells me something important."

"What you mean?"

"You didn't phone Sia Lang. Isn't that what you were supposed to do? Wasn't that the plan—phone him after Raphael was dead? He would come and get the paintings."

"I was afraid," she said, wrapping her arms around his waist and burying her head in his chest.

"Afraid of Lang," whispered Calvino. "He wanted the paintings."

Raphael Pascal had set himself up. All that remained was for any criminal to come along and recognize how easy he'd made things. What Tuk had going for her was there were many plausible stories about Raphael's death; Raphael imagined himself as reliving the life of Caravaggio—a realistic painter who descended into a violent underworld where knives, swords, and fists inflicted damage.

Caravaggio ignored the risks of going out into the night after bouts of heavy drinking and in the presence of heavily armed men, all looking to impress young women and each other. Venturing repeatedly into that world was playing the odds; it was a suicide pact whose fulfillment was unpredictable but inevitable. He'd been a role model for Raphael and countless other artists who danced with death. His premature end cast a disturbing, ugly legacy of a time when death, corruption, and power curled inside a death-cult fetish. Raphael followed a long tradition in the art world of such perverse deaths and surreal images. Without his violent death at thirty-eight years of age, would Caravaggio's art have achieved the same recognition and reputation? Didn't this disguised suicide, or at least suicidal behavior, burnish his reputation, fusing his art with more vitality, urgency, and darkness?

"You tell me we have fun. Why so serious? Talk, talk! Boom, boom much better."

The instinct for distraction was universal. The quality of execution of "Look, there's a squirrel" depended on the education of the distractor and the distractibility of the audience. In the case of a hot, young naked woman willing to take a man through the tight turns of the track, the distractor didn't need much education.

The skin around Calvino's eyes tangled into a spider web as he swallowed his laughter. He smiled at Tuk, thinking about how a black widow spider telegraphed the same offer to the males of her species, and the male always took the bait.

"Let's stick to business," he said.

But he regretted that reply as soon as it came out of his mouth. That was her point—she was trying to stick to business. She had let herself be lured outside the mental space she was used to entering to service a customer. She shriveled at this farang's idea of talking about the dead as another kind of business. It had become too personal and confusing with Calvino. Her old formula, with its charms and seduction, had failed to melt him. None of it was working.

"Did you care about him?"

She thought about the question.

"Caring too much is bad business," said Tuk.

She was right; caring brought a walloping punch. The heart of the matter wasn't that a working girl took a man's money for sex. People took money to endure all kinds of treatment. The problem was the state of mind that went with the money. Tuk was a professional who instinctively kept a psychological distance from men. She had mastered the covert tradecraft that reinforced that distance as an invisible force field. It created a gap that could never be crossed—not with money, love, promises, threats, or oaths. Maybe Tuk, against her better judgment, had tried love as a temporary bridge over that gap with Raphael, but it couldn't hold the weight of the future. Tuk wouldn't risk another attempt; she'd learned that in her world the only survivors were love-bridge burners.

Calvino got up from the bed.

"Get dressed."

He left the bedroom before she was out of bed.

She didn't protest. From the sitting room he listened to her dressing. She took her time, leaving him to wait alone. Once she had dressed, Tuk emerged with a sheepishly warm smile. She walked over to where he stood beside the paintings and squeezed his hand.

"I like you," she blurted out.

He believed that she meant it. He glanced at her and smiled.

"That's good. Now you can tell me the booking arrangement for the models. The ones you kept a secret from the cops."

"I tell the police everything."

"Did you tell Paul everything? Does he know Raphael and you went to the funerals of the models? Does Paul know about Lang's deal with the buyer in Hong Kong? Of course, Paul knew all of this, right? What he found out was that Lang had handed Raphael a lot of cash, the same cash Paul asked you to help him find. Who offered you a better cut? Paul or Lang?"

She slapped him in the face. Like turned to hate in a heartbeat.

"Lang want you dead. I said, no. I tell him you a good man," she said. "Raphael trusts you very much. So why you want to make a big problem?"

That day the Clash had been playing on the laptop on a continuous loop for hours. The lab report that Pratt had shown him stated that the bottle of Mekhong and the glass found in the bedroom had tested positive for pentobarbital. Pratt had also given him a copy of the autopsy report, which concluded that Raphael had consumed ten grams, more than enough to hurl him into the next life. Calvino had initially assumed that Tuk had coiled around Raphael, feeling his breathing go shallow, his skin cold, as he drifted away. But that was before he found out about Lang, the bitcoins, and the art collector in Hong Kong whose lawyer had come to Raphael's cremation.

Finding Raphael Pascal, another young farang, dead from suicide should have made things simple for the police, an easy case to close. A one-day news story no one would remember after a week. But journalists were always looking for some juice to keep it alive. Raphael's use of the exit drug, along with so many women he knew, had made a lot of noise in the police department. A death cult nesting in Bangkok wasn't something the senior brass wanted their masters to find out. It came down to the economy. Tourism had to preserve the image of a tranquil, fun and relaxing destination. If word got out that young foreigners and their escorts had a pipeline to death drugs, the tourist trade might take a body blow. Mothers worried their sons and daughters would swallow the wrong drugs. Rather than admitting that something about contemporary global life had visited Thailand, creating a personalized death cult, the way out of the problem was to identify the one man who benefited most from the deaths and pin everything on him. Problem solved. Let someone else pick up the ashes.

"Did Raphael know that Lang's buyer wanted tragic deaths for each of the models?" he said.

Her lower lip trembled.

"He want model who think like him. He think they want to die just like him."

He gestured at the paintings on the walls.

"You knew these women from the escort agency. Did you know what was going to happen to them after they modeled for Raphael?"

She raised her eyebrows.

"I'm country girl. I don't think too much. It's not good to think in my business. Do you understand me?"

"Tuk, just say it. You delivered them, gift-wrapped, to the studio."

Her face clouded up and the storm broke.

"He want beautiful girl to paint. I don't want him looking for beautiful girl. Farang don't know many bad girls want to lie and cheat him. My friends not do like that. I think what I do help everyone. But I am stupid girl."

She said this without irony. Tuk had the classic working girl's fear—she was afraid of losing control of her customer to the next pretty, young face who walked in the door of her world, turning heads. She had found Raphael and was going to protect her property. In the trade, one of the rules was a friend didn't poach a friend's customer, and in return you didn't poach theirs.

"I help my friends, sure."

He gestured at the paintings.

"They're all dead, and you knew they were going to die."

"You can't say like that," she said, angry because he was blaming her for their deaths. "I tell you the truth. I not put drugs in their drinks. I don't know who does this. I am honest with you. I put the drug in Rap's glass. He see me. After I give him drink, he say, 'That smells like death drug.' And he looks at the glass, and I tell him, Lang pay me to. Then I say, 'I am joking you,' but I wasn't joking, and he knew it. He look at his glass and again at me. He say, 'Aren't you going to make special drink for yourself?' He give me a big smile like he want to see me make another drink, like he is happy. I say, 'Not for me, I have to work later.' He laugh and laugh. 'That's brilliant, Tuk,' he say, 'truly brilliant thinking. How could I possibly miss a world that bring Lang, Paul, and you together?' He smell the glass again like he teasing me.

"And I say, 'It has no smell. You say you want to kill yourself, but I think it is not true. You play with death. You not serious man. More like funny boy. Why you like this game? Why you ask me to bring crazy girls who want to die? You do business with your paints. I do business with girls. We no different from gangster or hit man. Not any anger. It is business. I bring girl. She model for you, she go away and kill herself. And you? Do you try to stop? Do you say, 'Why pretty girl like you want to die?' No, you ask for another girl to paint before she kills herself. Why you do this? I think, okay, I make you the last drink. I leave you to decide. Drink? Not drink? What will you do?'

"He stand by the door, holding a glass. I think handsome man. *Jing jing.* I still think he's joking me. But he not look at me. He look at the glass. I start to laugh. He says, 'Why you laugh like that?' I say, 'Look at your feet.' He look at his feet. I say, 'Don't you see the color? You drop red paint, green, black, and yellow paint on your toenails. Your feet look like Christmas tree. I never see feet like that on a man. They look like child's feet. Girl look at your feet and she want to be your mother. Take care of you. Give you a kiss and hug.' He think what I say for a minute. Then he opens a drawer and takes out paper and pen. He sits on the floor and writes something. I see him count money from his wallet. He lays the money on the floor with the paper. Thai money, dollars, euros.

" 'What's that?' I ask him. 'Ask your farang boyfriend, Paul,' he says. 'You my boyfriend, *jing jing*,' I tell him.

"Then he come and sit on the bed. Put his arm around me. Kiss me here," she said, pointing to her nose. "Then he pick up the glass. And I am scared. I don't want him to die. I say was a joke. I say, 'Are you sure? Give to me, I throw out.' He smile and drink until the glass is empty. He give glass back to me, and I put it on the floor, next to the money. He laugh and he push me back and climb on top of me, whispering. 'What you say?' I ask him. I can't understand. He not speaking English. He talking in French. We lay down and he touch my breast. Suck my nipples like a baby. He lift himself up and goes inside me. He stays there a long time, holding me tight. Like Muay Thai man."

Raphael had died in her arms. She described his last wish.

"Last thing he say to me, 'You want to stay or you want to go?' I tell him, 'I stay with you.' He squeeze me hard, and say, 'Thank you.' I feel him go. He stop breathing and I cry, holding him."

The tears returned as she squeezed Calvino tight.

"Then you called Paul Steed?"

"I am scared. I see the money Rap leave on the floor. I am surprised. It's not big money. I think Lang or Paul not satisfied they see little money. I think why they do all this for that little money. I'm afraid they think I take the big money and lie, no big money in the apartment. But I worry Lang not believe me. I call Paul. I know he'll believe me. Police come and see. Everyone see. I not take big money."

She'd changed her story for an audience who'd given her no choice. This version might be true, but in her world truth was malleable. The smooth surface of her revised version of events had a polished, shiny quality that gleamed the way people imagined to be the hallmark of truth. Raphael had finished the last painting in the series. He'd decided against Caravaggio's example of picking a fight in a bar. The days of swords and knives and finishing the bloody business in the streets may not have ended in many places, but it was a rare event in Bangkok. Cellphones with video cameras and CCTV cameras patrolled the streets and bars. Nothing happened in private, and murders competed for attention. Murders were an attraction but they had to be special. Besides, it would have been a derivative death. It wouldn't be his death. It would be a copycat of a dead artist's death that had happened four hundred years ago.

"I go now," she said.

Calvino counted out ten thousand-baht notes into her outstretched hand. Her lips silently moved counting off the numbers in her head. Satisfied that she'd been paid in full, Tuk turned to leave, blowing him a naughty kiss.

"Any time you want to talk again, you phone me," she said, folding the money into her handbag. "Not free. Nothing free," she said.

She leaned in the doorway, and Calvino imagined that she was re-enacting Raphael's pose in there. Calvino didn't try to stop her from leaving and wondered why she lingered, standing in her high heels, looking at him on the bed. He had all he could get from her. Her last words had meant the most—she'd let her guard down and been honest. They were the words of bounded freedom. Raphael would have appreciated them. She had seen something in Calvino that reminded her he understood that free didn't exist.

"You forget something?" she said with a crooked smile, laughing as she tilted her head.

Calvino wondered what she meant.

"Tell me," he said.

"Money for taxi," she said.

Tuk couldn't stop herself from making the classic doorway request. Calvino counted out another two hundred baht from his wallet, folded the money, and pressed the notes into her hand.

"Did Raphael give you taxi money?"

She threw her head back and laughed.

"Of course not. But you not Raphael."

Calvino dug another two hundred baht from his wallet and handed it to her. She slipped it into her handbag and closed the door behind her.

He thought of her day-to-day job of trolling for small money. She was like a fish trawler captain face to face with that once-in-a-lifetime chance to score the big haul. The small and big glided through the layers of the system. Paul had paid him two grand to find Raphael, Calvino had given the money to Raphael for a painting, and Raphael had left it to Tuk in a suicide note. Pleasure acted like gravity, sucking money into its orbit. It was so obvious. What good were Calvino's Laws if a man forgot they were date-stamped with his age? As with many things in Thailand, there was a two-tier pricing structure for fucking someone your own age. Maybe it was as simple as that Raphael had been very young and had treated her better than any other man had ever done, never made demands, never got angry with her about customers and her boyfriend, and given her money without asking for anything in return. He'd treated her like a human being. She'd taken his money, but he had never made her feel dirty or small or a whore. By asking for taxi fare, Tuk was revealing how she felt about herself in the moment before her departure.

FIVE

CALVINO HEARD THE sound of the front door opening. He shook his head, smiling. It had to be Tuk returning for something she'd left behind—a brush, a phone, lipstick, or maybe her wounded pride. In one way Calvino's immediate reaction was right, but in a more important way he was dead wrong.

P'Pensiri was the first one through the door. Behind her were two uniformed police officers. One of them was a colonel. Behind the cops was a Thai in civilian clothes, whom Calvino recognized as Wang Tao from Raphael's funeral and later seated at Lang's table at Finders. He had pegged him as one of Lang's men. In fact, Wang Tao was in town checking up on Lang and sorting out the business of the series of paintings. He watched as Wang Tao, in his role as Hong Kong lawyer, stared at Calvino without smiling. They filed into the studio past Calvino, who stood at the door. Wang Tao finally allowed himself a smile like a cat spotting an open birdcage as he stood before the wall of paintings.

"Khun Vincent, I hope you don't mind, but these men have come to remove these paintings," said P'Pensiri.

She introduced the policemen.

"I do mind, P'Pensiri."

She sighed, looking him with a sense of amusement and disappointment as he stood in the door in his Muay Thai workout clothes.

"As you should," she said. "But Colonel Panit has his orders. As the owner of the property, I have no choice but to comply."

"What are the orders? Whose orders?"

He looked like a boxer arguing with the referee, knowing that such arguments were never won.

"He is to take possession of Raphael's paintings. Not all of them."

Calvino locked eyes with the smug-faced Wang Tao.

"He wants those six," Wang Tao said.

He nodded at the wall and smirked as he looked at Calvino's hands, wrapped and ready to slip into a pair of boxing gloves.

"You need a court order," said Calvino. This brought a small smile from Wang Tao's stoic face. As if to say, Calvino's Western mind was disconnected with the reality of how the system actually worked.

He'd wanted to say, "I used to be a contender," but his gut told him the reference would be lost on Wang Tao and others in the room.

"There's nothing to smile about, Mr. Calvino," said Wang Tao. "The police don't need a court order to collect evidence from a suspect in a murder investigation. Failure to comply is itself a sign you are trying to hide something. It is evidence of guilt."

Colonel Panit and the others were happy to let Wang Tao do the talking. All the while, they kept their eyes on this strangely dressed farang as if he might do something crazy. P'Pensiri had followed the English-language conversation with ease. Colonel Panit understood about forty percent and the other officer heard only noise.

Colonel Panit huddled with the others, gesturing toward the paintings and eventually handing P'Pensiri a piece of paper with Thai writing.

"Colonel Panit asks you to sign this document," she explained.

"And if I don't sign?" asked Calvino.

Colonel Panit shook his head.

"We can go the friendly, nice way. Or we can go the other way. Up to you. I think you sign either way," he said. "The friendly way is best. Believe me."

All eyes were on Calvino. He gave the appearance of a boxer struggling to find his feet after being knocked down with a lightning-fast knee to the solar plexus, the nerve fibers sending pain signals through the stomach and diaphragm. The colonel nodded to the junior ranking police officer, who stepped forward and removed a set of handcuffs from his belt.

"I believe you, colonel. Let's do nice."

The colonel and the others except for Wang Tao smiled with relief.

Calvino didn't bother to ask how the police and Wang Tao knew the paintings were hanging at the studio. Wang Tao offered Calvino a cheap ballpoint pen. He thought about asking Colonel Panit to read the Thai script to him. But did it really matter what the paper said? Calvino took the pen in his wrapped hand and scrawled a signature at the bottom and handed the paper and pen back to Colonel Panit. The Thai in civilian clothes and the junior officer began removing the paintings and stacking them against the wall near the door.

"Careful," said Wang Tao. "Those aren't bags of rice you throw into a warehouse bin. That is fine art, and valuable. Please be gentle."

A piece of shophouse advice for handling art didn't extend to the women in Wang Tao's circle. Calvino thought of Tuk's role. She'd done a splendid job. She'd not let him down with a sudden lapse into sentimentality.

Tuk had done what he predicted she would do. She'd told Lang that he had a chance to get the paintings. The rest was merely execution of the plan to deliver the 6 Degrees of Freedom series to the Hong Kong buyer's lawyer.

"Wang Tao, you never said who you represent," said Calvino.

Wang Tao's head snapped up to meet Calvino's eyes. He'd forgotten about Calvino as he busily supervised the removal of the paintings. At that instant Calvino had dissolved into irrelevance.

"That is confidential information, Mr. Calvino."

"I understand. Ash robbers have their code of silence," said Calvino, smiling. "Thanks for the heads up. When my time comes, I've decided against cremation. If your client sends you back for my funeral, feel free to take an arm or a leg. Think of me as the South China Sea."

He'd noticed that P'Pensiri had watched him as he signed the document. She'd arrived at the apartment in full makeup, her hair freshly combed and set. On her right hand she wore a large emerald ring, and on her left a glittering ruby nestled in a tiny backwater of diamonds. On her wrist was a Cartier watch on a diamond bracelet. There was an art to reading a Thai from their appearance. What Calvino saw written in her jewels and makeup was advance knowledge that she needed to equip herself with every signal of respect and privilege to carry out her role in an official task. The P'Pensiri who attended Raphael's funeral and who had given him the new key to the studio door disguised another P'Pensiri whom he was meeting for the first time in the company of Colonel Panit. He watched her check the time on her Cartier. In Thailand, telling the time was a minor function of what a watch told others about the time teller.

After he signed the document, he asked P'Pensiri what it said. She turned to Wang Tao.

He pulled a paper from his briefcase, saying, "I will read you the original English. It says that, as executor of Raphael Pascal's estate, you consent to deliver six paintings to the legal representative of Wang Tao to settle a claim against the artist. That you freely agree to the transfer of the paintings and that Raphael Pascal's estate waives and releases all claims, actions, or lawsuits based on ownership of the paintings and will defend any counterclaim."

"Can I have a copy?" Calvino asked the lawyer.

Wang Tao handed him the paper he'd been reading from.

"For your file," he said.

"Nice doing business with you," said Calvino. "If you see Sia Lang, please ask him when I can expect the money from the sale."

"That isn't my client's business," said Wang Tao.

"Probably not. What exactly is your client's business?"

"Ceramics," said Wang Tao without missing a beat.

"A vase and toilet bowl merchant inspired by the Terracotta Warriors and Horses. A specialist. I get it. Your client interest follows a long Chinese tradition of human sacrifice art."

P'Pensiri stood beside the door as the paintings disappeared from the wall and down the corridor. A black unmarked SUV idled beside the curb below. As the last painting was removed, Colonel Panit left with it. Only Wang Tao and P'Pensiri remained inside the studio.

Calvino stood, arms folded and one knee slightly bent. Looking away from the blank wall he caught the lawyer's wary eye, which seemed to fear that this aged Muay Thai boxer was aiming the knee at him. He took a step back.

"It's been memorable, Mr. Wang Tao."

Calvino lowered his knee and smiled.

"Irony is a white man's luxury, Mr. Calvino. If you are over-indulgent it can choke you."

Calvino broke into a good-humored grin.

"You know, that's funny. I was just thinking that working for the mafia on a fat retainer guarantees a life of luxury for a lawyer."

Then the grin withered away.

"But if you cross a line," Calvino continued, "and that line is always moving, you can get run over by a bus. It's the same in New York, Hong Kong, or Bangkok. If you fuck up, you're gone. Someone else is assigned your files and files the billable hours. A little lesson to remember—you are dispensable."

"I have a small lesson for you in return: if you are patient in a moment of anger, you will escape one hundred days of sorrow. It is the patient man in a time of trouble who is indispensable."

Just as Calvino had become comfortable hating Wang Tao, he couldn't stop himself from respecting him in that moment. He had said something true and straight. He felt that state of puzzlement of hating and admiring someone at the same moment.

Wang Tao turned away, as if nothing behind him had any further significance. He left behind not so much the feeling of the death of innocence as the feeling that innocence, wherever it was reborn, would be coldly, methodically betrayed.

Then only P'Pensiri, sitting on the edge of the sofa with knees locked together, remained. She stared at her cellphone to avoid making eye contact with Calvino, or else she no longer knew how to make eye contact. A silence filled by the traffic sounds outside fell between them in the empty studio. Calvino was the first to speak, unwrapping his left hand with his right hand.

P'Pensiri's driver appeared at the door, slipped off his sandals, lowered his shoulders in the servant's submissive posture, and walked in.

"Raphael was set up," said Calvino as she nodded at her driver. "I am so disappointed. His most valuable paintings are gone."

"You did your best, Mr. Calvino."

He watched the obscure family compound owner show another face. The kind of face that Raphael would have painted, one curated by ambition and desire—a double face, the light side warm and embracing, the dark side crackling with electrical storms.

"You really think so?"

"I must go, Mr. Calvino. If you decide to rent the studio, you have my number."

The chill of winter echoed in her voice.

"Goodbye, P'Pensiri."

She replied with a perfunctory wai, the kind dispensed to a social inferior. It was the goodbye of a woman who had realized that her ambition showed in her tone, her posture, and the nature of her wai.

Wang Tao practiced a form of equilibrium that played on contradictions and doubts, as he marshaled all forces to achieve harmony. But P'Pensiri lacked this skill, and that left an opening through which Calvino could see how fragile her world was. She had the eyes of a woman looking at the ceiling and fearing it was about to come crashing down. It's true that she appeared strong and determined, but she left with worry lines across her painted face. Wang Tao and P'Pensiri, the alpha-omega of the world buried within everyone.

But there was always a clue in plain sight that the mind games couldn't hide. Tuk had found one of Raphael's—a true artist who lived and breathed his work wouldn't notice he'd splashed paint on his feet. Instead he would dance to the Clash, as his father had done, with naked feet, animating his abstract art. But he was up against much larger forces than he could imagine. It was inevitable that Raphael would discover his day of the dead creation would never match the Terracotta army, but that didn't stop him from taking the commission to create an entourage for the journey into the land of the dead.

SIX

RATANA WAS WAITING for him as he arrived at the office at mid-morning. She wore an apprehensive, worried look that hard earned experience had taught him to expect an unpleasant disclosure. Bad news scrolled across her face like a Bloomberg stock market quote following news of a big terrorist attack.

"What's the problem?" asked Calvino.

"Gavin is dead."

She'd said it—delivered the one simple, declarative sentence that had been bottled up all morning, waiting for its audience to arrive.

"When?"

"Last night. The news is online. Photos. Terrible."

Calvino hadn't been online; he'd kept his cellphone switched off. After leaving Raphael's old studio, he'd retreated deep into an inner place mentally protected by "no entry, do not disturb."

"How?"

"Hanged himself with his own belt. At his house."

Ratana followed Calvino into his office, where he sat down in his chair and switched on his computer. He scrolled through the early news report about the Dutch national who had committed suicide and left a note: "I wish I could have done more. Sorry if this causes you trouble. But it is my time. My choice."

Calvino rang the hotline number. It was busy. He rang again until he got through.

"Put Ronnie on the line," said Calvino.

Ronnie was one of the people he remembered from the funeral and later at the hotline office. A couple of moments passed and Ronnie came on the line.

"Vincent, we are in an emergency meeting."

"Who found the body?"

"Janet," he replied.

Calvino remembered her from the Bamboo Bar. Janet was the nervous, silent type, someone he had difficulty seeing in the role of talking someone out of killing themselves. She had issues with her mother and an older sister, who married a Wall Street banker.

"Who did she phone?"

"She phoned me. I went to Gavin's bungalow. He hanged himself on the bathroom door. He was sitting on a chair, leaning forward, the classic exit position. I checked for a pulse. There was none. Then I called the police."

"Did Gavin say anything about the money Raphael left to the suicide hotline?"

"News to me," said Ronnie.

"Are you certain?"

He heard Ronnie call out to others in the hotline office, "Did Gavin tell anyone about some money Raphael left for the hotline?"

A murmur of voices followed. Ronnie came back on the line.

"No one's heard anything about it."

Calvino lowered his head until his chin touched his chest. He set the cell phone on his desk. He stared at the screen, listening to Ronnie's voice, tiny and distant, coming from the phone: "Hello ... hello? Are you there? Can you hear me? Are you okay?" The usual drill offered by the volunteers at the suicide hotline. Calvino had a glimpse of what it was to experience darkness deeper and blacker than could be described. He felt a force of hopelessness dragging him into the darkness, and he no longer had the will to struggle against it.

Ratana had never seen a tear run down Calvino's face before. It frightened her to see him this way. Someone had found his vulnerability and used that advantage to tear him apart from the inside. She thought of a winged garuda, a mythical creature, half-man, half-bird, a Thai symbol on permanent loan from Hinduism. The birdman had swooped down and released its pent-up violence.

She walked next door to her office and phoned General Pratt. An hour later Pratt walked into the office carrying a box of assorted homemade cakes. He'd stopped to buy them at the Villa Market around the corner from the office. Cakes cheered Pratt up when he felt depressed, which wasn't often. Ratana told Pratt that she was worried that Vincent was becoming sad again, the way he had been after Rangoon. But she left out the tear she'd seen on his cheek. One small, clear pearl that slipped down the contour of his face and splashed onto his desk. What she had witnessed seemed a violation. Vincent wouldn't have wanted her to see him with a tear that he couldn't call back.

Pratt found Calvino standing at the window, looking out at the One Hand Clapping sign on the massage parlor below in the sub-soi.

"I thought I had another couple of days," Calvino said.

He slowly turned from the window.

"I've got a problem, Pratt."

"What kind of problem?"

"Raphael had a lot of cash. He hid it in the sofa. The one covered with paint in the studio."

"How much cash?"

"Three quarters of a million dollars," said Calvino. "Raphael left it to the suicide hotline. I delivered it to Gavin,

314

and Gavin is dead. He was found by a hotline volunteer hanging from his own belt. The police are calling it suicide. They found a hand-written note. I talked with the hotline office. No one knew anything about the money. I doubt you will find it listed on the police inventory."

"Was this drug money?" asked Pratt.

"No, nothing like that. It was legit. His godfather had given him bitcoins for his eighteenth birthday, when the value was almost zero. He cashed out using Sia Lang as his broker."

Pratt raised an eyebrow. The wheels turned behind his eyes.

"You're sure about Sia Lang being the fixer?"

Calvino nodded.

"Raphael left a note with Sia Lang's name on it. I found it with the stacks of hundred dollar bills. Why do I have the feeling you're asking a different question?"

"Did Raphael have the expertise to check the hundred dollar bills?" asked Pratt. "Or do you have that expertise?"

Calvino stopped breathing for a couple of seconds as the possibilities rolled out from Pratt's use of the word "expertise." It was so blindingly obvious. How could he not have seen what had been in play? Sia Lang had passed off counterfeit hundred dollar bills to the tune of $750,000. He'd bet that Raphael, being a down and out artist, someone who despised money, wouldn't know a phony from a real hundred dollar bill.

"It's not only down and out artists who are fooled, Vincent."

"The counterfeits were good enough for someone to kill Gavin to get them."

"You have someone in mind?" Pratt asked.

"P'Pensiri's compound is secure. There's no way you could get in or out without someone noticing."

"The evidence for suicide was substantial, Vincent."

Pratt had already talked to one of the officers who had been on the scene of Gavin's death.

"What if he had the money in a duffel bag, or they found it hidden under the bed at his bungalow, or he handed it over, saying, help me convert this into Thai baht?" Calvino waited for a moment as Pratt thought about the possibility.

"And you're saying that this someone lives in the compound?" asked Pratt.

"Maybe the same person who unlocked Raphael's studio door for the cops and a Hong Kong lawyer?"

"Why are you smiling, Vincent?"

"At P'Pensiri's bad call. She allowed Sia Lang's men to take away Raphael's paintings. I signed a paper acknowledging my consent to the delivery. But is P'Pensiri an art expert? Are the cops? Is the Hong Kong lawyer? None of them are. They just assumed they were the originals. I find that innocence almost touching in a place like Bangkok, with people like this. The reproductions I had made of each painting were good enough to trick the mind. They never stopped to question if they were originals."

Pratt felt a sense of vertigo. He'd had cases of murder and forgery. But Raphael Pascal and his art project had spawned a crime spree and a death cult. Sia Lang had passed off fake US hundred dollar bills, and Vincent Calvino had passed off a series of fake paintings to Sia Lang. Which meant that Sia Lang had pocketed the proceeds of the bitcoin sale on Raphael's behalf, and Calvino still had the original paintings. The insiders riding the Ferris wheel of fakes were dying at an alarming rate.

"Do you have any proof of delivering the money to Gavin?"

"None."

"That makes it difficult. Whoever took the money, if we questioned them, would say, 'What money? We didn't see any money.' We can go back and look again. That's the end of it."

Pratt walked to the window and stood beside Calvino. They watched an old lady make an offering at the spirit house in the sub-soi. She knelt, holding the burning incense sticks, the breeze buffeting her white hair. Faith. Why is life a test of faith in others and oneself, Pratt asked himself.

"The officer who came to Mr. Pascal's studio was also one of the officers who went to Gavin's house. He remembered me from the earlier investigation. He phoned because he thought the cases might be connected."

"Do you see a connection, Pratt?"

"It is an interesting theory. And I believe you about the money. Don't get me wrong. But there's nothing to back your words up in a courtroom."

"Unless the thief finds out about Sia Lang's con and demands he exchange the counterfeit bills for the real thing," said Calvino.

"You have someone in mind and a plan?" asked Pratt. "For instance, your ex-client Paul Steed and his girlfriend?"

"Paul's not smart or connected enough to play in this league. Tuk is the same—a small goldfish in a big lake. Paul and Tuk are the kind of people that smarter, more connected people use as tools. All of which leads me to an interesting theory," said Calvino, smiling as he used Pratt's own phrase, grateful that he'd supplied the punch line.

"I wouldn't dismiss Paul that quickly."

Calvino returned to his desk, sat at his chair, and turned to his computer.

"Here's how it went down, Pratt. From the beginning I had the sense of a setup, but I wasn't sure. I tend to give people the benefit of doubt, especially an old client who paid his bill on time. I go to the studio after getting Paul Steed's call. The year before I'd found a missing person for

317

him. He's in the studio with a girl named Tuk. The dead guy inside is the ex-missing person from the year before. I find Raphael Pascal dressed for a Muay Thai fight, but there's no fight left in him. He's dead on the bed. His paintings, framed and unframed, are scattered in every spare space on the floor. What better distraction than a suicide note, with cash neatly stacked in piles? A dog named Charlie lying in the corner of the bedroom. A half-empty Mekhong bottle and a glass next to the bed. Two drinking glasses. The Clash playing on a perpetual loop on the computer.

"The woman in the studio with my ex-client is distraught. I read the suicide note. I'm named executor. You were right to let me take all of the valuables. That was the safe call. If not, we both know what would have happened. Within twenty-four hours his studio would have been stripped clean as a bleached bone. Of course, in most situations, removing valuable items that might be evidence of murder from a possible crime scene would guarantee a case would be thrown out. Here no one blinks an eye."

"The point is I persuaded the officer at the scene to let you take custody of Mr. Pascal's valuables," said Pratt. "Now he's being punished for violating procedure."

"He was punished because the paintings were supposed to go to Sia Lang," said Calvino. "Don't you see, we interfered with their plans to take the series and, who knows, maybe the rest of the paintings. Now Sia Lang has a problem. I have the art. He's sweating it because he's already sold the paintings and pocketed the cash. He has a habit of doing that. I am surprised he's still alive."

"Ratana said that your client, Paul Steed, was a software consultant," said Pratt. "He had no direct contact with Mr. Pascal prior to his death. Steed knew Tuk, but she knew a lot of men."

"Steed hired me to find Raphael Pascal," Calvino said, opening Paul Steed's client folder on his screen. "But what

318

Paul really wanted was the bitcoins. Or he'd take the cash. Paul doesn't seem too fussy."

"Maybe he has a way to the cash," said Pratt.

"I figure he found out that Sia Lang had handed over the cash from the bitcoins. Paul knew that it would be a pile of money. He hired Tuk to find it. She tried but couldn't deliver. I don't think anyone other than Raphael knew where the money was hidden. Paul would have helped her search the place after Raphael was dead. Hours went past before I got the call. I think that Sia Lang wanted Paul to find the money. He could finger Paul Steed with his police friends. They'd bust him for running a counterfeiting ring and then slap a murder charge on him for killing his partner in crime, Raphael Pascal. But he didn't find the cash. I found it but passed it on."

"If that is true, Sia Lang won't know who stole the money, or even whether it was stolen, or where exactly it was. He doesn't know the money was discovered," said Pratt, following the logic of Calvino's argument.

"I will let him know who has the money."

Pratt clenched his jaw.

"Walk away from it, Vincent."

"How can I, Pratt? Colonel Panit said the police were thinking of dropping their murder investigation in return for six fake paintings owed to certain people. I was in the middle of a game that I didn't understand and should have walked away from while I could."

It seemed to Calvino that certain games require nerves of steel, the amorality of a shark, and the planning of a grand chess master. Gavin had been one of the good guys. But that doesn't matter in the game. The rules don't protect the good guys. In fact, just the opposite: one of the bad guys' rules was to use the Gavins of the world as cover. That was a good enough reason to find a way to pour a handful of sand into their gears, if for no other reason than the pleasure of watching the whole thing blow sky high. Perhaps it was the only way to light a candle of hope.

"You should've given them the originals. It's not normal times," said Pratt. "People like these will come after you."

"When was it ever normal times in Bangkok, Pratt? Remind me."

Pratt walked to the door.

"If you don't report the delivery of the paintings by tomorrow, they'll issue an arrest warrant. Just so you know."

"Colonel Panit said the case against me would be dropped," said Calvino. "That by delivering the paintings, everything was settled."

"Nothing was settled."

Pratt looked away, not wanting to think that Calvino had for a moment believed him, while Calvino had read Pratt's reaction as a flash of guilt.

"It's not your fault, Pratt."

" 'The fault, dear Brutus, is not in our stars. But in ourselves.' "

"I've not betrayed you, my friend."

"Cooperate with them, Vincent. Don't get in their face. Give them the original paintings. Forget about the money you found. Go back to your life. While you can."

Calvino rose from his desk and the two friends walked into the outer office. Ratana looked up from her keyboard.

"These people have big money and power," said Pratt. "Bigger than you, bigger than me. Let karma take care of them."

While Pratt had managed a weak smile, Ratana was surprised to see that he was in worse emotional shape than Calvino as they emerged from their meeting. She had phoned Pratt to come around and shake Calvino out of his depression. Calvino no longer looked depressed; it was as if it were a condition that was transferable, leaving the original victim depression-free.

They exchanged wais and then Pratt was gone. Calvino went back to his office, sat on the sofa, and stared at the painting Raphael had done of him as he listened to the sound of Ratana on the keyboard in the next room. He thought of the sadness in Pratt's face, his disappointment and frustration at not being able to stop the process, not being able to stop him. Pratt carried the full burden of the unfolding disaster on his shoulders. He'd wanted a way to lighten the weight but had failed. Calvino had pulled him onto the scene with the body. Now he had a dog in the race, whether he wanted one or not, and it wasn't Charlie. He hadn't said it in so many words—he should have asked Calvino directly to phone the police now. But it was too late. It was done. The most Pratt could do was to shelter his friend as best as he could from the debris soon to fall from the sky.

Calvino called out to Ratana: "Phone P'Pensiri and make an appointment for me to see her tomorrow."

"What should I tell her the appointment is about?"

"A dog named Charlie. She's looking for a home."

It wasn't Julius Caesar who came to Calvino's mind. It was a line from William Blake: "It is easier to forgive an enemy than to forgive a friend."

SEVEN

THE DAY PAUL Steed had come to his office with the missing person case, Calvino had asked for a photograph of Raphael Pascal. He'd done a Google search and come up empty-handed. That was unusual, he thought. Someone in the visual arts selling to the public would have pictures of themselves at openings, in their studio, and with their paintings, photographs taken at the time of an interview or review. Yet with Raphael Pascal a Google search returned no image at all.

Steed had emailed him a photo of Raphael and another farang in a restaurant booth. Both were smiling into the camera, the older man with an arm around the shoulders of the younger man. Calvino had asked who the other man was in the photograph. Steed had answered that it was a friend of Raphael's father who was worried about the welfare of the young painter because he had disappeared in Bangkok and had been out of touch. It was a run-of-the-mill missing person case. At any given time hundreds of people are lying low in Bangkok, Phnom Penh, or Saigon, for a thousand different reasons. Finding them had become much easier in the new technological world. The notion of hiding out in remote places as an escape from one's past was quickly drifting into legend.

Calvino had studied the features of the young man in the photo on his screen. He hadn't paid enough attention to the older man in the photo. Later, when he'd read through Raphael's letter he'd found with the diary, he had run a Google Image search. The details had appeared on his screen. It was a matter of scanning through the layers of Eric Tremblay's life, which were scattered among websites, including one devoted to his musical career. As with bits of driftwood, if you get enough, you can build a table, a chair, even a house. Not a particularly beautiful one, but one that functions.

Calvino found a couple of things that stuck out. Eric Tremblay was a fifty-two-year-old epileptic who lived in the same commune that Raphael's parents had once lived in; he'd stayed on after they left. There was an old photograph of Eric Tremblay with an arm wrapped around Raphael's mother on his left, and his father on the right. They seemed like one big, happy, cozy family. There was a later one with Tremblay, his mother and father, and a small boy seven or eight years old that looked like Raphael. Tremblay had been born into a well-off family of doctors, judges, and lawyers, but he'd followed a different path. Having dropped out of McGill University in his third year, he'd drifted to British Columbia and back, eventually returning and joining Freedom Place. After that he still made regular trips back and forth between Quebec and British Columbia. Eric had health issues and was taking medicine for seizures.

His passion was New Age music. He played the bamboo flute and recorded meditation music. He sold his music tracks to private mental hospitals like the one he had been in, along with spas and hotels. He wrote about his operation and his recovery. His interprovincial travels between the pot farms in British Columbia and the commune in Quebec earned him a criminal record for smuggling. He'd been convicted twice and served eighteen months in prison the second time around.

Calvino checked the time in Quebec. It would have been around eleven in the evening in Eastern Canada. The name Tremblay was like Smith or Jones there, and Calvino's first half-dozen search attempts by Skype turned out to be the wrong man. The seventh Tremblay was the man he'd been looking for, and there he was on his computer screen.

"My name is Vincent Calvino. I was hired by Paul Steed to find Raphael Pascal in Bangkok. He said that you'd sent him to find Raphael."

"Paul went looking for him but couldn't find him. He hired you?"

"I found Raphael. Paul never told you that he'd been found?"

"When?"

"About a year ago."

There was a long pause. Calvino saw Tremblay staring into the camera on his computer, trying to control his breathing, a dark storm brewing behind his eyes.

"That's a surprise."

A lawyer's trick was to ask a question that only someone with detailed knowledge could answer, and to which the interrogator already knew the answer. It worked to flush out the liars.

"How well did you know Raphael?"

"Know him? I was his godfather. His parents were my closest friends."

"Aren't godfathers supposed to keep track of their godchildren?"

"Frankly, after the family left the commune, I was pretty much cut off. I wasn't a good godfather. Except for one time when Raphael turned eighteen. I told Paul about it. He may have told you about it."

"He didn't mention it."

"It was back in 2009, when someone paid me in bitcoins. The value had tanked. I had about five thousand of them. It was Raphael's eighteenth birthday. I gave him the bitcoins. He was very excited because he thought it was a lot of money. I told him to hold on to them. They were only worth about thirty Canadian dollars at the time. It wasn't much, but it was the thought of the present. You know what? I was right all along. Damned if those five thousand bitcoins didn't shoot up like a rocket. A few years ago they were worth about a million Canadian dollars. I thought that Raphael, being an artist like me, might have forgotten all about them. It was a long time ago. And I said to Paul, 'When you find Raphael, let him know his godfather did the right thing by him. Also tell him that his godfather wouldn't mind a little contribution for his own stash.' But like so many things, I let it go and didn't give it much thought. I figured Raphael was like his old man, dug in somewhere, unable to find a way to pull his custom restored Caddy out of the drive and hit the road."

He paused for a moment, threw a couple of pills into his mouth, and drank from a glass of red wine.

"That's better. So you found Raphael. Can I get you to phone him and ask him to Skype me?"

"Raphael is dead."

Calvino saw the tired eyes with bags like flat tires underneath expand in size. He shook his head.

"No, it's not true. Why wasn't I told?"

"By whom?"

That shut him up as his mouth went crooked on Calvino's screen.

"I guess you're right. Nothing from that time ever turned out the way I wanted it to," Eric said, a bitter tone creeping into his voice.

Eric Tremblay was talking about his youth on the commune. How did one tell a man that when he drops out of people's lives, he no longer has any right to be told anything about them? They no longer belong to him, and he doesn't belong to them. No one in Bangkok had any knowledge of Eric Tremblay's existence or his connection to Raphael. No, Calvino thought, that's not true. Paul Steed knew, and he himself should have known. He'd seen the photograph of Tremblay with Paul when he'd taken the case a year earlier. Paul had glossed over the figure as a guy that he'd met in a bar in New York after a New Age music festival. In any missing person case there was a long list of names, most of them irrelevant to finding the person. Every so often one of those irrelevant names revealed a reason for the disappearance.

"I tried finding his next of kin. But your name didn't turn up."

"What did he do with my bitcoins? Did Raphael sell them?"

Calvino sighed.

"He sold them."

"I hope he made a lot of money," said Tremblay.

He paused and as an afterthought said, "Not that I saw any of it. But that's water under the bridge. I'm glad I finally made a big difference to his life."

"It's made a difference to the lives of a lot of people," said Calvino.

"It's a shame about Raphael. I wanted to tell him about Jessie. He'd remember Jessie LeBlanc, his mother's best friend at Freedom Place. Jessie was appointed curator at a new museum in Montreal. Jessie would have remembered Raphael. She was his mentor, the one who taught him as a little kid how to hold a paint brush."

After the call ended, Calvino leaned back in his chair, thinking it was strange that, as far as he could tell, Raphael hadn't painted his godfather. He wondered if he'd tried and somehow failed to capture what Calvino had seen during the Skype call—a small boy fighting a cobra, its hood raised, the terrified eyes, and the callow adult who carried on the fight in a hundred ways, exhausted, desperate to let go, but fearful of life without the cobra struggle.

EIGHT

LANG HAD DECLINED to take Calvino's calls. Long before Lang's thumb grew callused from hitting the decline call button, Calvino had heard Lang's message loud and clear—"I don't want to talk to him, ever. Our business is finished." That decision might have carried more weight if Lang had been in a different line of work, but he ran a nightclub, and that made it easy to find him. Normally when you corner a lion, the immediate response is unpredictable, but the end result is preordained: hamburger and bones. The safer way to deal with a lion required luck—good timing and the right place. The night was the best time. It was after midnight and time to walk into the lion's den and throw him a juicy bone. Paul was the bone. Calvino had a plan to let him walk under his own steam into the den.

If the plan went sour, Calvino didn't want McPhail or Pratt or anyone else getting hurt. He'd put himself in the center of this maelstrom, and no one could walk him out of it. He had to do it on his own. What he did arrange was to meet Paul Steed at the club. He smiled at the thought of using Paul as a beard, his reason for going to the club. Paul was the man who'd walked him into the minefield, and Calvino had a score to settle with him. Lang would almost buy that package of goods.

Calvino slowly walked through the courtyard, passing the large, identical golden lion-head medallions on either side of the main entrance—spherical manes, jaws open to show full sets of teeth. You entered the door between yin and yang; the dual heads inviting you to believe in the illusion of safe space. A waterfall turned a water wheel over a pool. Lights streaked over the water, and two beams captured the roar of the bronze lions on the club wall. Inside, the floor was crowded. People sat at tables. The chairs being all taken, others stood around talking and drinking, waiting for a chance to sit. The big room sprawled in every direction and featured plush red velvet high-back sofas, some of them sectioned off with gold brocade curtains, and framed reproductions of famous paintings of women in erotic postures. It was a Chinese vision of a hi-so bordello.

Calvino elbowed his way to the bar, stopping cold when he saw Tuk holding hands with a well-dressed Chinese customer in his thirties. Flanking him were two other men, whose manner suggested they worked for him. Sia Lang sat beside Tuk and his own two associates, one of whom had been at the studio to strong-arm him for the paintings. Both had hostesses draped around them like high fashion capes. Calvino lingered, reading the table and the tables around it.

Tuk saw him but didn't. She pretended not to see him even as she was looking at him—it was an old New York gambit. This time he caught her. She allowed him to lock eyes before breaking off. She showed no emotion, turning back to her customer and hand-feeding him a green grape. It was like watching someone feeding a slot machine at Atlantic City. Clubs like this one operated like a casino cross-bred with a reverse petting zoo—those locked in the cage fed food to the visitors hoping to hit a jackpot. He watched Tuk pick up another grape and drop it in Sia Lang's mouth as if rewarding a dolphin. No prophet ever performed a miracle as convincingly as Tuk making the big man in the room execute a back flip for a grape. It was the way the game was played.

There were rules, though. With Calvino showing up, Tuk knew her job was to pretend not to have seen him. She'd been trained to have eyes only for the customer. But Calvino knew there was another, more compelling reason. She didn't want to be the one who had to tell Sia Lang that Calvino was in his club.

He watched Tuk as she spaced the timing between grapes like a veteran bombardier. Plop, plop, swallow, plop—the rhythm of a leaky kitchen faucet. She sat with her boss, whose attention was distracted by a new and younger waitress on her first night. Tuk slowly filled his glass from a bottle of Blue Label. The new girl double-teamed with Tuk—and that was nightclub neon writing on the wall that Tuk was on the way out. Another waitress worked a set of silver tongs, adding ice to Lang's glass. He stuffed five hundred baht in her hand. He made certain others could see the money. Raphael's money—from the 6 Degrees sale, from the bitcoin cash-in—was financing Lang's newly enhanced lifestyle. Using a dead man's money to buy himself face, thought Calvino.

Civilians sometimes wondered what criminals did with their money. All they had to do was watch a guy like Lang to understand that inside his world it bought him influence and power. He bent others to his will. He made them fearful. He also knew when to back off when a bigger, more dangerous gangster dispatched a Wang Tao to Bangkok. The likes of Lang weren't volunteering to help on suicide hotlines, or to change diapers on bedridden old people, or to sign petitions to protest against child labor. And there was a reason—it was the Langs who drove people to phone suicide hotlines, left old people in the gutter, and saw child labor as another revenue source.

It wasn't only Tuk's table. The smell of big, fast, easy money drifted across the room, as the rich showed each other they had the kind of money that Bangkok required to have skin in the game.

Tuk picked up another clump of grapes. Across the room Paul Steed sat at the bar, drinking house whiskey on ice and watching the sharks—literally in this case. It was hard for a bar customer to take his eyes off the display. Suspended from the ceiling, a enormous aquarium contained four baby sharks swimming from one end of the tank to the other, turning, swimming back. Every pass was the shark equivalent of a two-channel life: *Sisyphus* and *Groundhog Day*. One of the four was double the size of the other three. They made way for the big one. Calvino watched over Paul's shoulder as the sharks' white bellies slipped past in the tank, showing a permanent thin strip that formed the mouth and looked like a gruesome smile of a body snatcher at a car crash.

A few other farang customers sat at the bar, talking, laughing, looking into the mirror, wondering why life had delivered them to a stool rather than a harem sofa. There were alpha males and alpha wannabes, and "Lady's in Trouble" drew both crowds, who like blacks and whites at an Alabama restaurant knew better than to try to mingle.

The DJ came back after his break and cranked up the volume on the club's theme song: LA Priest's "Lady's in Trouble with the Law." The lyrics, swallowed by the scattered voices from the main floor and the bar, wove into an indistinct background noise. Only the DJ mouthed the lyrics—"Since I heard from the law, I never look back anymore, from one life to the next, I'll be gone ..." It was a good theme song for Bangkok after midnight.

Calvino saw that Lang had spotted him just as he pulled back an empty stool next to Paul Steed. Calvino thought that was good timing. Lang would wonder what the two of them were saying and assume it had to be about him. Paul had been expecting Calvino, but that hadn't stopped him from being surprised that he actually showed up at Lang's club. He'd thought that Calvino had been bluffing, and only a fool would walk alone into Lang's lair.

Paul had mastered the poker face.

"Some customers drink all night watching the sharks," said Paul, "Others keep their faces in their cellphones."

"And you, Paul, what direction are you looking in? I don't see you at Lang's table. I see Tuk. But where are you? You're here on shark patrol, and then I walk in."

"We talked. I was expecting you," said Paul.

"Look at the sharks, Paul, who are they expecting?"

"Vinny, let me buy you a drink."

He said it in a way meant to suggest that Calvino's arrival was no surprise, no big deal, nothing special. His performance did nothing to ease the tension as Calvino sat, hands folded on the bar, looking at him—that New York City look from someone who has no fear and has a reputation for settling scores with street justice.

"Let's go outside where we can talk," said Calvino.

"It's the tropics, man. It's boiling hot outside."

Paul's eyes now showed fear.

"Lang stiffed Raphael for the paintings, and for the bitcoins," said Calvino. "How much did he stiff you for, Paul? You two had a deal. I am guessing, but I'm willing to bet you didn't even get a ten percent commission. But you're hopeful that you can convince him to pay you something. How's that going, Paul?"

Paul Steed leaned back, his eye-roll sending a message to Calvino as Paul glanced over at Lang's table.

"I wouldn't fuck with him if I were you."

"I'll leave Tuk to do that. I am more interested in the money he ripped off from Raphael."

"Lang isn't just a rich Chinese guy from Shanghai. He's connected. You can't touch him. Don't even think that's possible."

"You know him well? I am impressed."

"I've seen him around."

"You've seen him around?"

"Are you hard of hearing? That's what I said."

Calvino grabbed Steed by the shoulder and squeezed hard.

"You're fucking with me, Paul. You don't want to do that."

The shock wave of pain spread through Paul's face and his eyes bulged.

"You're hurting me."

Calvino released some of the pressure but didn't remove his grip.

"Look in the tank, Paul. That's what can hurt you. When they jump the aquarium they look just like one of us. The instincts are the same. Predators have an acquired taste for blood."

"Don't threaten me, Calvino."

Calvino released him and sat back. The female bartender with short hair and a smile that belonged in the tank above her brought him a drink. The drink had been sent by someone on the other side of the room, she told him, nodding at Lang's table. Calvino looked at the drink.

"What this? The pentobarbital special?"

The waitress shrugged and moved down the bar.

Calvino sipped the complimentary drink and turned back to Paul, who was edging off his stool. He pulled him back onto the stool.

"We're not finished. I had a conversation with an old friend of yours. Eric Tremblay."

"Eric who?"

"Now you're doing what I told you not to do. You're fucking with me. I don't like it when someone plays stupid. Bar girls do that for a living. But you're not in their league."

"I told you before, he's some guy from Montreal. I met him more than a year ago. So what?"

"About the time you hired me. Your story was that you were helping a friend find someone. You'd met this guy in a bar in New York City. Probably sitting at a bar like this one. Drinking shit whiskey and asking why life hadn't delivered more. That guy was Eric Tremblay. He told me about his conversation with you, about Raphael's million dollars' worth of bitcoins."

"He knew Raphael's father. When he heard I lived in Bangkok, he told me his story. He was Raphael's godfather. He was looking for his godson, who'd disappeared in Bangkok. I said I'd help. I contacted you, and you found him. What's wrong with helping someone?"

"The thing is, Paul, you never got back to Tremblay."

There was a way that Paul Steed stared at him that he'd seen before on other men's faces. It reflected that moment when an eighteen-wheel truck of truth crunched a lie. A sudden burst of energy flickered as a guilty afterglow in Paul Steed's eyes.

Paul turned away from Calvino, looking at his drink on the bar.

"So what do you want from me?"

"After I found Raphael, you figured there must be a way to steal the bitcoins. Raphael was an artist who lived in semi-poverty. In your mind that meant for whatever reason he likely had never used the bitcoin account. You couldn't imagine how anyone could live like Raphael when he was so close to that amount of money. And if he didn't want it; you did. It started with you and Tuk. She brought in Lang. That's when you lost control. See that big shark in the tank? Notice how all the smaller ones stay out of its way? The way I see it, you've been pushed aside. You thought once Raphael was dead, Tuk and you would find where he hid the money. Only you didn't find it. I did."

"I don't know what you're talking about. I did a favor for Tremblay. Sure I know Tuk, and I've met her boss, so what?"

"Do you know where he hid it?"

Paul watched the sharks circling, moving side to side, as they patrolled their narrow channel of territory.

"He stitched it inside the sofa," said Calvino, watching Paul's face go slack. "Seven hundred fifty thousand dollars."

Calvino drank from his glass, watching as Paul's face reflected the red neon light from the tank. Steed had proved to be an expert at misdirection. He had made others look where he wanted them to look and made them see what he wanted them to see. His core knew nothing of human compassion. What made him tick was the worst impulse of the human species: to cross the floor and be seated as an equal next to Lang, the big silverback alpha male.

"But there was a problem with the money," said Calvino, sipping his drink, lips pressed together.

Paul glanced at him.

"What kind of problem?"

Calvino ignored his worried tone.

"I'll get to the problem in a moment. First, I believe you weren't certain if Tremblay was making shit up. But you wouldn't know unless you investigated. Or hired an investigator to do the legwork. You hired me. You hired Tuk. You found a way to drink with Lang. You knew the ropes and invested money in the scheme. You were riding high. It was all working out like you'd planned—except how to get the money from Raphael's bitcoins? You helped arrange for Lang to cash him out. No wire transfer. Hard cash. Lang had access to that kind of money, you thought. After Raphael killed himself, you and Tuk searched his studio looking for the cash but didn't find it. You decided if I could find Raphael, I could probably find where he hid the cash too. I was your silent partner along with Tuk. We were part of your plan to take the money."

Calvino glanced over at Lang's table. They were having a great time laughing, drinking, and feeling up the girls.

"But you're not at your partner's table, are you, Paul? He seems to be doing fine. And you're here staring up at sharks."

Paul Steed did an eye-roll and slowly shook his head.

"Now let me clear up that small problem I mentioned before. Lang, your partner, paid in counterfeit currency. If I had to place a bet, I'd place it on the possibility that Lang intended to set Raphael and you up to take a fall on a counterfeiting wrap. He needed to offer someone up. Why not Paul Steed and Raphael Pascal? It would make for a nice story in the newspapers.

"What's with the face?" Calvino continued. "You look disappointed that Lang didn't play nice. Is that really what you expected?"

"They will come after you, Vinny."

"Who is 'they'?"

"Does it matter? You know how things work. It's bigger than Lang. They have nothing on Tuk or me. They don't care about us. We know how to keep our mouths shut."

"Let Lang know I don't have the counterfeit money. P'Pensiri has it. Once she finds out it's phony, who knows what kind of stink she can raise. But the scent will get up the wrong noses, and that is never a good thing, Paul. Deliver that message to Lang. He looks like the type who gives generous tips to messenger boys," said Calvino.

"When they finish with you," said Paul, "it'll be good Raphael painted your portrait, just so you can remember what you once looked like."

Calvino reached over and shoved Paul Steed's face into the top of the bar. The bartender and security came running over as Steed slid off his seat and crumpled onto the floor, leaving a trail of blood.

"My friend drank too much. He passed out and hit his head. You'd better take him to the hospital."

Others at the bar elbowed each other to photograph an unconscious Paul Steed, who was wedged between a bar stool and the bar counter, slumped over, face up, on the floor. A dozen smartphones competed for the best angle. Calvino moved out of the way, clearing space for Paul's ad hoc photo session. Soon Paul's bloodied head would appear on timelines across Bangkok's social media. One of the customers would win the race to be first to upload the photos and select the winning hash tags—#NightclubAttack, #NightclubBrawls, #ThaiViolence, #BangkokNoir, and #LadysInTrouble. Slamming Paul Steed's head against the bar hadn't solved anything, but Calvino figured that if you can't solve a problem, at least you can do something to make yourself feel better.

On his way out, Calvino caught sight of Tuk, who in the commotion was trying to comprehend what had happened at the bar and whether Calvino was involved. He shrugged his shoulders and smiled at her as he worked his way to the door. She'd found a small window of opportunity to connect as Lang and his associates shared a belly laugh from a story one of them had told. The busted head at the bar had triggered a fond memory of someone recalled at Lang's table. Violence in a nightclub was funny to them. It broke the boredom. It got everyone's blood pumping. Criminals have a better grasp of the true nature of things than the rest of us, thought Calvino, and that gives them a competitive advantage, along with guns, over everyone else.

Men like Lang acted like the glove that snugly fit the double-fisted hand of power. It was always the gloved hand that a man saw speeding toward his face.

The echo of their laughter carried across the floor as Calvino left the nightclub. Outside, the night was steaming, and the heat hit his face hard as the door closed behind him. Calvino stood looking at the traffic on the street. Hundreds of cars after midnight, people under the illusion they were going places, when in reality they were lost in bumper-to-bumper traffic, moving at a crawl. Life was a joke. And Bangkok was the punch line.

NINE

OI, THE MAID, came out in her pajamas to open the compound gate. She waited until he drove in to close it behind Calvino's car. Ratana had managed to get him an appointment with P'Pensiri at two in the afternoon. The spot after lunch and before coffee was a confined time when there was no need to feed a guest or pretend that anything other than business will be conducted.

P'Pensiri waited for him in front of Gavin's house. She wore sunglasses with black frames and oversized black-as-coal lenses, and a golden yellow scarf over her head, tied under her chin. She looked like an aging actress trying to disguise her identity in public. Her gloved hands worked the clippers on a rose bush along the fence. She looked up as Calvino stopped and got out. Deeper in the compound, he recognized a couple of the hotline volunteers loading a Toyota pickup with computers, printers, and office supplies.

Calvino closed the car door.

"One minute, P'Pensiri, my friend. I want to say hello to Ronnie."

She saw Ronnie struggling with a computer monitor. Behind the sunglasses and scarf, P'Pensiri didn't look happy as she watched Calvino walk down the compound road to the Bangkok Suicide Hotline office.

He approached the volunteers. Ronnie, the California psychiatric nurse, came out the door carrying a whiteboard.

"What's going on? Looks like you're moving out," said Calvino.

Ronnie handed the whiteboard to Roger Stanton, another volunteer who found a spot for it in a black pickup. As Calvino approached, he saw the pickup had heavily tinted windows.

"We've had a sudden funding problem," said Ronnie, nodding in the direction of P'Pensiri, who watched them from the distance.

"Rent went up from five thousand baht a month, which she waived each time Gavin offered to pay, to fifty thousand, which she now wants in advance," said Ronnie. "A bit of a hike, don't you think?

"Gavin's just died and she's jacking up the rent. I asked her, why the change of heart?" said Roger, walking back from the pickup. "And you know what she said?"

"She needed the money," guessed Calvino.

"That's probably the real reason. But what she said was the hotline wasn't what she expected. The farang in the compound were giving her a bad image. First Raphael, then Gavin. Who would be next?"

He looked over at the cottage at the end of the compound.

"The police and other government officials are asking questions about the business going on in her compound. P'Pensiri doesn't like the idea of people looking over the compound wall. Her way of kicking us out was to jack up the rent," said Ronnie.

"Where are you going?" asked Calvino.

Jim from Chicago tied off the load inside the tuk-tuk.

"We are going to use my place in Lad Prao. At least until rainy season hits and we're flooded or until something better comes up. Whichever happens first," he said, wiping his hands on his jeans.

Calvino walked around to the back of the pickup. Computers, chairs, a couple of desks, and filing cabinets were all tied down. He noticed the Bangkok registration plates on the rear bumper.

"Your pickup?" Calvino asked Jim from Chicago.

"It's not mine," Jim said.

"P'Pensiri's nephew let us use it. I guess he felt sorry we have to leave the compound without any notice. He has that van too. It's no sweat off his back," said Ronnie, nodding at a van twenty meters along the pavement, parked in front of the bungalow used by the nephew.

"Her nephew lent us his truck because he wanted us out of the compound. That's the truth," said Jim. "It wasn't about the money."

"The nephew lives here?" asked Calvino.

Ronnie gestured toward the bungalow at the end of the compound, isolated from the other houses, surrounded by mango trees. Parked in front was a spotlessly clean black van with windows the shade of P'Pensiri's sunglasses. The nephew seemed to love the tint of guaranteed privacy.

"Rune is the son of P'Pensiri's sister, who lives over there," he said, pointing to the largest house in the compound. "Rune and his buddies work out of the bungalow at the far end, out of the way of everyone. They keep to themselves. I rarely saw them during the day. Sometimes if I worked the nightshift, I'd see one or more of them come into the compound and disappear into Rune's bungalow. P'Pensiri says her nephew and his friends have an export-import business."

He paused, looking at the bungalow and then back at Calvino.

"You learn in Thailand not to ask a lot of questions. We did our thing, and the others in the compound did theirs. I was surprised when Rune came to our office and said, 'Hey, you guys need a pickup to take away your stuff? You can use mine.' You could've knocked me over with a feather. This guy had ignored us for two years, had hardly said two words, and suddenly he offers us his pickup. And I said, 'Yeah, thanks, man.' "

Oi stood inside the fence around Gavin's old bungalow, watching Charlie sniff a frog. The frog hopped, Charlie barked. Calvino leaned over the fence and called to her. She looked away from the frog and bolted to the fence.

"Someone's happy to see me," said Calvino.

P'Pensiri was annoyed that the "hello" Calvino had used as an excuse to talk with the volunteers had turned into a long conversation with fingers pointing at one house and then another. She was regretting the decision to meet him. Without Ratana's considerable charm, P'Pensiri would have told Calvino to get lost, though in a highly polite Thai way.

"There's your dog," said P'Pensiri. "Take her. Oi will open the gate for you."

"I'd like to talk before I go."

She lowered the clippers and leaned forward to smell a red rose. She was making a valiant effort to pretend he didn't exist. Clearly she'd be issuing no invitation for him to go inside Gavin's old bungalow or anywhere else in the compound. Like a tradesman he could say what he had to say on the driveway between the houses of the compound.

"I have rented the studio to a friend of my nephew. Please arrange to leave at the end of the week."

She'd shifted from offering him Raphael's old studio to pulling it out from under him. Calvino had seen people like her before. It was as if they knew he could see through their disguise.

In the blink of a shaded eye, she'd snuffed out their deal. It was gone, and the sooner Calvino was gone too, the better. She positioned the clippers around a snarly branch and snapped. He watched the branch fall to the ground.

"Most problems start when someone is too greedy," Calvino said. "Someone you've done business with cheats you. That hurts. You trusted them and they repay you by stealing from you. Sia Lang is a perfect example of a fine-tuned greed machine. He receives from Hong Kong the proceeds for Raphael's paintings but cuts Raphael out. Raphael may not count as he's a foreigner. It's okay to cheat a farang. Before that he passed a large sum of counterfeit money to Raphael. You have to give him credit. He knew Raphael was an innocent. He'd never suspect that someone might pass him phony money. He wouldn't know how to check if a bank note was the real thing or a professional forgery. Like hell's money, Lang gave Raphael paper to burn on All Souls Day. The perfect gift for someone about to commit suicide, don't you agree? Sia Lang's phony money has ended up with some sucker. Some Thai who probably has no idea that the money is fake.

"They say the Chinese are cleaning up in Thailand. Some say the Chinese are calling the shots now. It seems people saying that have a point. It makes me sad, P'Pensiri, the way Thais put up with the Sia Lang's breaking their rice bowls and their faces. My answer is, Lang is in deep with the right people."

Charlie jumped up and rested her paws on the fence. The interruption gave P'Pensiri a chance to move down the fence, away from where Calvino leaned over, rubbing the fur on the back of Charlie's neck. For the most part dogs have no idea of death, Calvino thought. That might explain their personalities—always up, tail wagging, wanting to please. Raphael wasn't coming back, and neither was Gavin.

When Calvino glanced at P'Pensiri again, she was at the end of the small garden, her clippers at her side. Her reaction was a variation of the standard boilerplate—the driver fled the scene of the accident.

He walked along the fence line, Charlie running beside him and barking as if it were a game. He stopped a few feet away from where P'Pensiri stood.

"How much do you want for the dog?"

He had his wallet pulled out and opened.

"Do you really think I'd take money for a dead man's dog? Unlike some Chinese, I have my honor."

"I didn't intend to insult you, P'Pensiri. I wish I'd explained the problem with the money to Gavin. I figure he found out on his own that the money was phony. It was the last straw, and he killed himself."

Oi opened the latch on the fence gate in front of Gavin's bungalow. Charlie, tail thumping, ran straight to Calvino. He opened the door of his BMW and Charlie jumped in as if on a stormy night, on a dark road, she'd crashed and a rescue vehicle had appeared with a familiar driver behind the wheel.

He powered down the back window and closed the back car door. When he turned back to P'Pensiri, she had vanished without a word, without a sound.

"I will open big gate for you," said Oi in a half-trot in the direction of the gate.

She looked back at Calvino, waving for him to follow her. Stopping on the edge of the drive, she motioned for him to roll down his window.

"Thank you for not telling P'Pensiri about the notebook," she said.

"Tuk and you were close."

"She was different from the others. I liked how she treated Raphael. I think in her heart she is good."

Dig deep enough down and you find some good in everyone, thought Calvino.

Calvino checked his rearview mirror. The volunteers leaned next to the pickup. It looked like they were finished. He saw P'Pensiri talking to Ronnie, who shrugged his shoulders. She'd asked him something he didn't know or, if he knew, wasn't saying. Oi stood waiting for Calvino to drive out of the compound. He pulled even with her where she stood clinging to the gate.

"We both know Gavin didn't kill himself and P'Pensiri took the money. Come to the studio this afternoon. Tell her you are going shopping. Don't tell her you are going to see me. I will give you enough money to leave this place and these people. It's up to you whether you stay or go. But my offer is good. Think about it."

TEN

OI DIDN'T SHOW that afternoon. Nor did she come around the following day. Calvino had given up on her. But on the third day Oi came around to the studio. She had changed out of her pajamas and into market-shopping clothes—a gray T-shirt with the Union Jack stamped on the front, a sarong wrapped around her waist, and a large floppy hat pulled forward on her head. Placing two large baskets, weaved from bamboo, on the floor, she sat on the sofa. The weight of one of the baskets tipped it over to the side, and kui chai, sugar peas, and pak choi spilled onto the floor in shades of green. Underneath the vegetables were folded clothes, a hairbrush, a small mirror, a cellphone, a bottle of moisturizer, and a Burmese passport. It wasn't much, but it was all that she owned.

Calvino knelt down and helped her collect her things. He handed her a tube of lip balm. She took it and put it back in her basket.

"Looks like you're planning a trip," said Calvino.

"I'm going home," Oi said.

"Back to Burma?"

She nodded as Calvino rose to his feet and walked over to his briefcase, which lay on a chair, opened the clasp, and took out a white envelope. He held it out. She looked at the envelope and then at Calvino.

"Take it," he said.

"I saved money," she said. "I always planned to return. Now is the time."

Her tone wasn't convincing; her pride shone through.

"Take the money."

He slipped the envelope inside one of her baskets.

"Who did this to Gavin?"

"Rune and his men."

She wouldn't be sitting in the studio unless she had intended to open up. That happened slowly as she crawled her way toward the truth.

"How many men?"

"Two, three, sometimes four men go with him in the van."

"Why are you helping me?"

"Because of what happened to me in Burma and what I see in the compound. That's why I tell you," she said.

She'd had a history of hard men in her life. If Rune had any suspicion she might give him up, she'd be another piece of his work. After Calvino had left the compound, she'd been asked by one of Rune's men what she'd said to the farang when he rolled down the window. She told him that Calvino asked about the dog's food bowl and medicine. Charlie had bought her time. The men had watched her the next day. Long enough for them to get bored watching a Burmese maid clean and cook. Finally they melted away like shadows.

"Did they threaten you?" asked Calvino.

"Men like that don't need to use words," she said.

She explained to Calvino what she had witnessed. She had seen a great deal in her time, and P'Pensiri's compound gradually yielded its secrets, ones familiar to someone of her background.

Men with short hair, muscled and young, all knuckles and teeth, with unblinking eyes, had stood at the windows of the bungalow, pushing back the blackout curtains and watching the hotline crew remove office equipment. She told Calvino that she'd seen such men in the streets of Rangoon in 1988. She had been a young student demonstrating when the army opened fire. She remembered those same wild, wolf-like eyes, full of death and cold, making determined calculations as they raised their rifles. P'Pensiri and others in the compound saw Oi as another insignificant Burmese maid. A chattel. She spoke five languages—Burmese, Karen, English, Thai, and basic Chinese. The Thais treated her like an ignorant peasant. That assumption worked to her advantage. The Burmese secret to well-being in Thailand was simple: do nothing to discourage the Thais from underestimating you. Let the Thai alphas pound their chests and roar. Sooner or later they would trip over their sense of superiority like a ballerina whose ballet shoes were tied together.

She told Calvino about her older brother, Thet, who had been arrested by the Burmese military and tortured. After Thet came out of Insein prison, he was never the same. He sat staring at the wall for hours. He said nothing. Tears streamed down his cheeks. His life had fallen apart, and one day he killed himself. He went into the forest and hanged himself from a Bodhi tree. It was the invisible hand of the military that had tied the rope around his neck. They'd left it to Thet to finish the job.

Oi had liked the idea that she worked for a family where foreigners like Raphael and Gavin worked the phones at the suicide hotline. She'd been proud of her boss P'Pensiri and had done her best to overlook the comings and goings of her nephew and his men. They kept to themselves. She'd been inside their bungalow only once. That had been enough for her to know why they didn't want her cleaning the place. With her family history, she knew firsthand what powerful people were capable of doing. She had no illusions that such men could be controlled. They could only be killed.

She had an uncle who'd been picked up by the Burmese military. When the family got a call two weeks later, it was to identify and pick up his body. The family had difficulty recognizing the dead man. The military said he'd fallen down a flight of stairs trying to escape. Sign this form. Go. Take the body with you. Next. That was the attitude. It matched Rune's attitude.

Rune's crew rarely ventured out in the compound during the day. They came and went under cover of darkness, careful to avoid the suicide hotline volunteers.

Rune was no ordinary rich punk. He held the rank of a police major. The men who worked for him were ex-cops or subordinates from his district station. Rune's home was like a revolving door, with people going from the police station into the night playground where another hidden world came out to dance, sing, fuck, drink, gamble, trade information, and sell and use drugs, all under the watchful eye of a vast, interconnected network that had no name. Carnival magicians don't need names, as everyone knows who they are and what that represent, and how they have the power to make people who cross them disappear.

The bungalow was located in an ideal place, in the heart of the Ratchada entertainment area. Rune had been brought into the family business by his father, P'Pensiri's brother-in-law, who had retired nine years earlier. The father had dropped dead in an interrogation room. His bloated liver had exploded as he exerted himself a little to much with a rubber baton, inflicting blows on a man who'd failed to pay the vig to a loan shark. Rune had inherited a thriving business.

A bar owner who failed to pay his monthly protection received a warning. Every establishment kept a notebook with a record of payments. You showed the book and the initials of the person receiving the money, and you were good until the next month. If you showed the book, and there was no initial, there was a problem. If he hadn't paid after the first warning, the manager or owner could expect Rune's associates to arrive late at night, around closing, when most of the customers and staff had left. In the back room the manager would be counting the take. A man could be a scofflaw, and that was accepted. What wasn't allowed was to ignore the rules of the carnival. There was no room for a scofflaw when it came to complying with the rules of the carnival magicians like Rune.

Wearing balaclavas, they would strong-arm the manager into the back of the black Toyota van, where he'd be blindfolded and cuffed and driven to the safe house. Once inside the soundproof interrogation room, the men in balaclavas would set to work. They had good reason to hide their faces. No one wanted to be recognized by the victims. As the unlucky manager was slammed against the wall, slapped, and punched in the face and stomach, he would never see a face, only a mask.

The manager would pay up within twenty-hour hours, but only after he had learned the true meaning of suffering. They rarely had to burn one. The muscle worked well to terrify the nightclub and bar managers, who would cut their staff salaries, or their own arms or legs, rather than miss another payment to the police. The idea of a call-in by Rune's men had them wetting their pants.

Over a couple of years Oi had watched as Rune's gang expanded their business. Their skills were also a natural to convince gamblers to make good on their bets. Around the World Cup, they had a lot of action. Eventually they stumbled upon a new sideline operation: the kidnapping and extortion of foreigners. Their first grab of this kind was a Taiwanese high roller who'd been fingered by a manager in one of the bars or nightclubs. If the guy had no local connections, they'd play him. They'd hold him until his relatives paid a ransom, and then drive the mark, who was way outside his league, eyes blindfolded, out into the country and dump him in a rice field. They stuck with Asians. They were less likely to be connected to locals with juice. If you didn't have a sugar daddy, then you were anyone's bitch for the taking.

"My bedroom is next to the drive," she said. "One night I dreamed of my brother and then I heard the van engine outside. I sat up and looked out my window. I looked at the time. It wasn't the first time I hear the van coming or going late. I am a good sleeper. I say to myself, this isn't like before. My brother doesn't come to my dreams before. He comes for a reason. I got out of bed and went outside, behind the back of the row of houses. I keep close to the wall. There are no lights on. No moon. It was very dark, but I know the way. In Burma our father taught us to always have an escape plan, just in case."

Rune and his crew worked the late shift, well into the night. With only one or two volunteers on the night shift of the Bangkok Suicide Hotline, Rune and his men could come and go in the van without drawing attention. Whoever was blindfolded in the back would not see the sign for the Bangkok Suicide Hotline as the black van slowed down and parked at the end of the compound. The safe house blackout blinds were drawn. She said some of the windows in the back were painted black from the inside. That side faced the compound wall, but they were taking no chances. Men emerged from Rune's bungalow around three in the morning. The back of the van was open and Oi saw them loading what looked like a body wrapped in a carpet. They quietly closed the rear door of the van. One man climbed into the driver's seat and the rear lights flashed red. Two other men walked alongside the van like bodyguards protecting an important politician.

The van slowly reversed, stopping in front of Gavin's bungalow. The driver climbed out of the van but left the engine running. The other men opened the rear doors of the van, lifted out the body in the carpet, and carried it through the gate where the driver stood as a lookout. She heard Charlie bark a couple of times inside. The barking stopped. She thought they had either killed the dog or given him food. As they were in the bribery business, she guessed it was the food. Killing the dog would have left a big question mark over a suicide verdict. If it came to that, she had no doubt, they could have found a reason—Gavin wanted Charlie in the next life, for example. If the police could ignore the rope burns on Gavin's wrists, they could invent a reason for the death of his dog.

After the van was moved back to Rune's bungalow, Oi had let herself inside Gavin's cottage. She'd moved quietly. Her smell was familiar to Charlie. The dog didn't bark. Once inside, she didn't turn on the lights. She crept through the sitting room and found Gavin's body leaning forward on a chair, a belt around his neck. Charlie stood between her and the body as if protecting her dead owner. Oi reached out and petted Charlie.

"It was dark, but I could see that it was him, Gavin. Like my brother, he was a good, decent man. I knew then why my brother came to me in my dreams."

Gavin had been strangled inside the safe house and moved.

"In the morning the police came with the rescue van. They took away the body. They asked me questions ... 'Did I see anything or anybody?' I told them that I was sleeping. They wrote that down. The rescue people took away the body.

"That night I couldn't sleep. I was scared. My room was hot. I go out for fresh air. I walked on my secret path behind the houses to Rune's house. The family doesn't go there. They are afraid of snakes and rats. I don't know why, but I wanted to see what these men did. I leaned close to the window. It's totally black. I think they use something to keep the noise in. I don't know. I never see with my own eyes. But I hear a distant voice, and it is full of pain. I know that sound. It's the sound a man makes when they beat him and bad things are done to his body. I hear him cry out in Chinese, '*Nan shou!*' And that is not good."

"What does '*nan shou*' mean?"

Oi grimly pressed her lips together.

"When a man can no longer bear the pain. I hear one of Rune's men shout at him in Thai, 'Sia Lang, you dog, you pig, where is the money?' I don't think Sia Lang's Thai is so good. He cries out '*Nan shou!*'"

ELEVEN

CALVINO SAT ON a park bench next to Pratt, watching a couple of runners pass on the track ringing Lake Ratchada. The joggers sweated, mouths open, faces flushed as they disappeared toward Queen Sirikit Center. Calvino slid a Foodland plastic bag slowly across the small bridge of space until it touched Pratt's hand. He quickly removed his hand and stretched both arms over his head.

"I'll take a walk."

Pratt opened the plastic bag as Calvino rose from the bench. Fifteen minutes later the joggers had lapped Calvino twice. He headed back, sitting on the bench, the plastic bag nowhere to be seen.

"How did you get this, Vincent?"

Pratt, like any other cop, understood that thousands of notebooks just like this one were in back offices through the entertainment industry. They were all versions of the same book. Enough of them floated around that together they'd rank high on Amazon. The point wasn't the notebook's existence. The point was how it had found wings to fly out of a manager's office and land on Calvino's shoulder. Like a parrot it could squawk in many tongues that clearly identified the speaker. Notebook identification was standard but released into the surface world never helped anyone's career. Calvino filled him in on Sia Lang's notebook.

Both Calvino and Pratt understood how the system

actually worked. But when some people don't follow the rules of the game, they invite others to make up new rules, ones that are coded for stealing and killing. The black market world, like the surface, visible market world, had its disgruntled workers. The white market world fires the disloyal employee. The black market world hurts the employee. It didn't take a palm reader to conclude that luum sop, the grave, was their future.

"Paul Steed was double-crossed by Lang," said Calvino.

"He worked for Sia Lang?" asked Pratt, gazing at the reflection of high-rises on the lake.

"Paul thought he had a commission deal on some money. Lang stiffed him. Why? Because he could, and Paul couldn't do fuck about it. Paul might be stupid, but he's not a complete moron. He wanted revenge. He took a big risk in trusting an escort named Tuk. He got her to nick the bribery notebook. He used it for extortion. When I met him at the bar, before I smashed his head onto the counter, I'd figured it out—the dynamics of his relationship with Tuk and Lang. It all revolved around one thing: the money. Tuk lifted the notebook, and the two of them were trying to exchange the notebook for a one-third interest in the counterfeit scam and—and this was the hard part—doing that and staying alive. Taking Lang's notebook was a very bad idea. It was only a matter of time before Lang figured out that it was Paul and Tuk. Then they'd be dead. They knew it. But now they won't be hearing from Lang any time soon. No one will."

Calvino gestured like a magician showing his hands after making a dove disappear.

"Lang's been reported as disappeared," said Pratt.

"I caught up with Lang a day before he left our little planet."

"What did you say to him?"

"I ambushed him in the lobby of his condo. I said, 'I've

355

come to collect Raphael's money for the art.' Lang said, 'He's dead.' I was half-expecting him to say that. I smiled and said, 'Maybe in China death settles a debt. But it doesn't work that way in Thailand.' Lang thought about what I'd said. 'You're right, Mr. Calvino,' he said. 'But there is no debt owed. Not after I've deducted expenses.' So I asked him, 'What expenses might those be?' By then one his bodyguards had stepped alongside to give him moral support and he perked up, feeling secure and protected. 'Model fees, entertainment. And funerals don't come cheap.' Then he left. He should've used the money to upgrade his security team."

Calvino had noticed over the years that when people throw around the declaration 'I'd take a bullet for him,' it's usually hot air, rhetoric. Most people run away from a fight. They don't step in the way of a bullet for you. Only certain men are capable of doing that. Pratt had taken a bullet for Calvino, as Calvino had for Pratt, and when they compared their entry and exit wounds, they pretty much matched up. Karma. They'd understood years before that when Thai and farang work together, both must jump over the sword or else lose their legs. They knew that in Thailand, no matter how it looks from the outside, no farang can jump that sword alone. If they try, it's called jumping the shark.

"Who gave you the record book?" asked Pratt.

The first step in assessing the damage was to find out the length of the chain and the names of its links.

"Raphael's maid," said Calvino, a crooked grin crossing his face. "Who also worked for Gavin de Bruin."

"How did she come up with it?"

"Remember the Chinese fortuneteller we met in Rangoon? He was a crackpot, but he said one smart thing, borrowed from Confucius: 'When the wise man points at the moon, the idiot looks at the finger.' The Burmese maid is a finger; what you found in the bag is the moon."

"Full blood moon," said Pratt. "That moon is an omen for the end of times, a prophecy. The sun turns into darkness."

A jogger stopped cold in her tracks, bent over to grab her knees, inhaled, exhaled, did a stretching exercise, and without any warning took off again like someone tuned in to a high-pitch dog whistle. Calvino appreciated her performance. He thought about predictions and prophecies, reading the future from the color of the moon, or reading it in a notebook of illegal payments.

"Oi," repeated Pratt, locking it into memory. "Other than Oi and you, who else knows you have this record book?"

"She's on a bus back to Burma. Out of the picture. She won't be back to Thailand any time soon. And me? In two days I'll be on a one-way flight to Montreal."

The surprise registered in Pratt's face as if Calvino had told a joke.

"Vincent, that's not funny."

"I've bought the ticket. A Canadian named Janet Fortin is the curator at the Freedom Place Museum. It's a new museum funded by a dot-com billionaire whose parents were in Raphael's old commune. Have a look at this."

Calvino reached into his briefcase, pulled out a printout from a website, and handed it to Pratt. Raphael Pascal's self-portrait was on the front. There was a full page and text for each painting in the 6 Degrees of Freedom series.

Pratt looked worried.

"When did this come out?"

"They are working on the brochure. They are planning an exhibition. They have a lot of material. I made certain that the museum received all of his other paintings. I tried to give the museum the dog, but they drew the line."

Pratt exhaled a sigh that seem to go on forever as he passed back the printout.

"You've committed suicide by art."

Once the Hong Kong collector found out that Wang Tao had brought back fakes, there could be a problem, Calvino knew. He remembered Wang Tao's wisdom about patience. Wang Tao would be in no hurry. No hot blood would turn the moon red. It would be a cold, blue moon.

"Do you know the Chinese word for intolerable pain? Or for 'I'm about to die'? It's '*nan shou.*' A Burmese maid taught me that word. She speaks four, five languages. I started thinking, there must be a word for intolerable pain or 'don't kill me' in every language. Sure enough, it's as common as 'mommy' and 'daddy.' In Japanese, they say, '*shini sou.*' In Spanish, as the knife slips into your guts, '*me estás matando.*' It's probably written on Sumerian tablets and Etruscan inscriptions."

"I get the point," said Pratt, "but I am not certain you do."

Calvino's eyes narrowed. "The point is a simple one, Pratt. You aren't young very long. The paint is barely dry before you're dead. You put your finger on the canvas and look at the smudge. That's what's left behind. Paint fast. Paint the truth. Paint until the crematory door slams shut. An immortality project takes rich patron. Raphael found his or he found Raphael. It amounts to the same thing. Artist and patron are two sides of the same coin. They flip that coin to be caught in the future."

"You believe Raphael was involved out of choice?"

"Who says we have anything but an illusion of choice?"

Pratt waited a beat before replying. "What matters, Vincent, is they will come after you."

Calvino shrugged. "The buyer's beef is with Lang. It was Lang who was crying out *nan shou.*"

"They don't care about Lang. The Hong Kong lawyer received the paintings from you. You signed for them."

The frustration made him close his eyes and rest his head back. More joggers trotted past. The sky overhead clouded over and threatened rain.

Calvino laughed, and leaned forward as if to share a secret with Pratt.

"I'd like to be a fly on the wall when Wang Tao has to tell his client about the real ashes and fake paintings. His client's human sacrifice ritual derailed. Come on, Pratt, there must be a Shakespeare explanation of the paintings."

" 'There's no art to find the mind's construction in the face,' " said Pratt, quoting from *Macbeth*. "There are times when I feel Shakespeare was really a Thai transported in a time machine from our time to Elizabethan times."

"Ratana will handle things while I'm away," said Calvino. "I'll take my time in Montreal, go down to New York, check things out. The world's on fire, Pratt. From here all we see are columns of smoke. The old world is burning to the ground. What comes next from those ashes? Who knows? I want a second look before it's all gone."

"A moth is drawn to the flame, Vincent. That's what a second look earns you. Remember, Wang Tao and his people will find you in Montreal, New York, or wherever you go. They don't give up."

"That may be true. But after the exhibition opens in Montreal, it won't much matter what Wang Tao does. The paintings are beyond his reach. I was just the messenger boy who delivered him what I thought the Chinese highly valued—counterfeit goods. Did he really think I'd hand over the originals?"

"Nothing is ever settled, is it?" asked Pratt after a while.

"One thing's certain: if I stay here, the Chinese Mafia will have the local comrades watching my every move," said Calvino.

Pratt blinked and smiled.

"You can count on it."

"I'm a farang. Short of a dedicated miracle I will always be an outsider. That makes me less than human. I can't ask you to stand between me and Wang Tao's terracotta army marching through the land looking for me."

Calvino turned and faced his friend.

"Look at me, Pratt. I know the score. And if you're honest, so do you. That's why I'm going away. Let's see how it goes."

It was true that Pratt sometimes forgot Calvino was a farang. He had stopped seeing him as a foreigner.

Calvino put his arm around Pratt's shoulder.

"Foreigners are always asking themselves, 'Do I stay or do I go?' It's time for me to go, Pratt. You're not the only one who's read Shakespeare. 'Who is it that can tell me who I am?' "

"*King Lear*," said Pratt.

"He also wrote, 'Thought is free.' And I need to spend some time in a space where that's true."

The Tempest, thought Pratt. What an appropriate name for the place to search for freedom.

"Who's going to watch your back?" he asked Calvino.

That made Calvino smile.

"After all these years in Bangkok? An adult crocodile has had time to grow a thick hide and sharp teeth. But it's the wise croc who knows it's all luck whether he's going to have a good swim or end up as a handbag."

"Don't forget me, Vincent Calvino." A slight hitch in his voice gave away his feeling.

Calvino saw something in Pratt that he'd not seen before, the most human of fears. "I won't forget you."

Calvino was about to say something but stopped himself. You can travel around the edge of evil only so long until one day a long tentacle reached out of the shadows, grabbed you and pulled you into the canvas of the dead. The worry of life wasn't death; people came to terms with their demise, it was inevitability of being forgotten, to have existed without leaving a trace, a mark in the memory of those who carried on. All of the good and evil, the art and politics of the world were driven to create a personal wormhole in the collective memory. The most powerful words a person ever heard were the same in every language and in every time: I won't forget you. Even though instinctively from dictator to bar girl, they understand that all memories collapse over the long haul. Memory, in the end, as the last refuge against oblivion was just another phony, false god.

As they walked back together, the rain started. Tiny drops at first, which turned into bigger, more frequent drops. The joggers scattered, looking for shelter. The rain hit the lake like pinpricks. Calvino put the Foodland plastic bag over his head. Some students in their school uniforms running past pointed at the funny middle-aged farang with the Foodland plastic bag covering his head like a giant condom. A foreigner eventually learned he was always on stage when in the street. Thailand was the place for a farang who was a born exhibitionist. There was always an audience appearing out of nowhere to observe the performance. Strangers clocked you, mining your deepest secrets, panning for gold. There were Muay Thai–trained artists with rainbow feet, for instance, dancing and singing and dying in the red tide.

In the bars, clubs, and massage parlors, all the bar girls, the yings, wore badges with numbers—some pinned to bikini tops, others worn on uniforms—and they made their living in motion, fully exploring the six degrees of freedom. Raphael painted the whore love gap, filling in the collateral damage that spread over their lives. It showed in their faces. The real damage went deeper beneath the skin. It wasn't on any flow chart or PowerPoint presentation. It wasn't in the footnotes. But the message was everywhere—women on the game saw men as fungible, things that could easily be replaced, in the same way men who bought their services saw them as fungible. Like loose grains shifting inside a truck in transit to the bakery to be made into loaves of bread.

Inside the place where Raphael Pascal painted was another world, a watering hole where the herd drank and grazed. Circling around the herd were violent, determined men who made their own rules, played their own games, cloaked themselves with immunity, and staffed the money pump stations, keeping the movement flowing through the night, painting their visions on the dream wall of others. That was the face of terror—a world covered with their graffiti, "I was here. I was feared. Remember me."

The same was true of those from the old commune. They'd left it, but the commune had never left them. That old dream wall they painted together had never disappeared, no matter how many times it had been painted over. To say no one could climb over that memory wall and escape was a half-lie.

But the question remained—escape to where?

Inside that half-lie was the darkest of all the half-truths—nowhere.

ACKNOWLEDGMENTS

Over the many drafts of *Jumpers*, two readers provided me with useful and insightful comments and suggestions: Mike Herrin and Charles McHugh. They dedicated many hours reading an earlier draft and their contribution assisted me greatly. I am grateful to both for their efforts.

My long-time copy editor Martin Townsend, whose diligence and meticulous eye has been saving Calvino from unintended mishaps like a special guardian angel, worked his magic on the text. Thank you, Martin.

Thanks to several other friends for their contributions: Luciano Prantera who brought to my attention Sciascia's *The Day of the Owl*. Edwin van Doorn who assisted in selecting Dutch names. And Peter Klashorst, a legendary Dutch painter, who provided inspiration and knowledge about the art world. Peter's painting of me appears as the author's picture on this book.

My wife, Busakorn Suriyasarn, read with patience and care. She knows Vincent Calvino better than just about anyone. She keeps him from falling into the potholes and has saved his neck more than once in matters of Thai culture and language.

SPIRIT HOUSE
First in the series
Heaven Lake Press (2004) ISBN 974-92389-3-1

The Bangkok police already have a confession by a nineteen-year-old drug addict who has admitted to the murder of a British computer wizard, Ben Hoadly. From the bruises on his face shown at the press conference, it is clear that the young suspect had some help from the police in the making of his confession. The case is wrapped up. Only there are some loose ends that the police and just about everyone else are happy to overlook.

The search for the killer of Ben Hoadley plunges Calvino into the dark side of Bangkok, where professional hit men have orders to stop him. From the world of thinner addicts, dope dealers, fortunetellers, and high-class call girls, Calvino peels away the mystery surrounding the death of the English ex-public schoolboy who had a lot of dubious friends.

"Well-written, tough and bloody."
—Bernard Knight, *Tangled Web* (UK)

"A thinking man's Philip Marlowe, Calvino is a cynic on the surface but a romantic at heart. Calvino ... found himself in Bangkok—the end of the world—for a whole host of bizarre foreigners unwilling, unable, or uninterested in going home."—*The Daily Yomiuri*

"Good, that there are still real crime writers. Christopher G. Moore's [*Spirit House*] is colorful and crafty."
—*Hessischer Rundfunk* (Germany)

ASIA HAND
Second in the series
Heaven Lake Press (2000) ISBN 974-87171-2-7
Winner of 2011 Shamus Award
for Best Original Paperback

Bangkok—the Year of the Monkey. Calvino's Chinese New Year celebration is interrupted by a call to Lumpini Park Lake, where Thai cops have just fished the body of a farang cameraman. CNN is running dramatic footage of several Burmese soldiers on the Thai border executing students.

Calvino follows the trail of the dead man to a feature film crew where he hits the wall of silence. On the other side of that wall, Calvino and Colonel Pratt discover and elite film unit of old Asia Hands with connections to influential people in Southeast Asia. They find themselves matched against a set of farangs conditioned for urban survival and willing to go for a knock-out punch.

"Highly recommended to readers of hard-boiled detective fiction"—*Booklist*

"Asia Hand is the kind of novel that grabs you and never lets go."—*The Times of India*

"Moore's stylish second Bangkok thriller … explores the dark side of both Bangkok and the human heart. Felicitous prose speeds the action along."—*Publishers Weekly*

"Fast moving and hypnotic, this was a great read."
—*Crime Spree Magazine*

ZERO HOUR IN PHNOM PENH
Third in the series
Heaven Lake Press (2005) ISBN 974-93035-9-8
Winner of 2004 German Critics Award for Crime Fiction (Deutscher Krimi Preis) for best international crime fiction and 2007 Premier Special Director's Award Semana Negra (Spain)

In the early 1990s, at the end of the devastating civil war UN peacekeeping forces try to keep the lid on the violence. Gunfire can still be heard nightly in Phnom Penh, where Vietnamese prostitutes try to hook UN peacekeepers from the balcony of the Lido Bar.

Calvino traces leads on a missing farang from Bangkok to war-torn Cambodia, through the Russian market, hospitals, nightclubs, news briefings, and UNTAC headquarters. Calvino's buddy, Colonel Pratt, knows something that Calvino does not: the missing man is connected with the jewels stolen from the Saudi royal family. Calvino quickly finds out that he is not the only one looking for the missing farang.

"Political, courageous and perhaps Moore's most important work."—*CrimiCouch.de*

"An excellent whodunnit hardboiled, a noir novel with a solitary, disillusioned but tempting detective, an interesting historical and social context (of post-Pol Pot Cambodia), and a very thorough psychology of the characters."
—*La culture se partage*

"A bursting, high adventure ... Extremely gripping ... A morality portrait with no illusion."
—Ulrich Noller, *Westdeutscher Rundfunk*

COMFORT ZONE
Fourth in the series
Heaven Lake Press (2001) ISBN 974-87754-9-6

Twenty years after the end of the Vietnam War, Vietnam is opening to the outside world. There is a smell of fast money in the air and poverty in the streets. Business is booming and in austere Ho Chi Minh City a new generation of foreigners have arrived to make money and not war. Against the backdrop of Vietnam's economic miracle, *Comfort Zone* reveals a taut, compelling story of a divided people still not reconciled with their past and unsure of their future.

Calvino is hired by an ex-special forces veteran, whose younger brother uncovers corruption and fraud in the emerging business world in which his clients are dealing. But before Calvino even leaves Bangkok, there have already been two murders, one in Saigon and one in Bangkok.

"Calvino digs, discovering layers of intrigue. He's stalked by hired killers and falls in love with a Hanoi girl. Can he trust her? The reader is hooked."
—*NTUC Lifestyle* (Singapore)

"Moore hits home with more of everything in *Comfort Zone*. There is a balanced mix of story-line, narrative, wisdom, knowledge as well as love, sex, and murder."
—*Thailand Times*

"Like a Japanese gardener who captures the land and the sky and recreates it in the backyard, Moore's genius is in portraying the Southeast Asian heartscape behind the tourist industry hotel gloss."—*The Daily Yomiuri*

THE BIG WEIRD
Fifth in the series

Heaven Lake Press (2008) ISBN 978-974-8418-42-1

A beautiful American blond is found dead with a large bullet hole in her head in the house of her ex-boyfriend. A famous Hollywood screenwriter hires Calvino to investigate her death. Everyone except Calvino's client believes Samantha McNeal has committed suicide.

In the early days of the Internet, Sam ran with a young and wild expat crowd in Bangkok: a Net-savvy pornographer, a Thai hooker plotting to hit it big in cyberspace, an angry feminist with an agenda, a starving writer-cum-scam artist, a Hollywoord legend with a severe case of The Sickness. As Calvino slides into a world where people are dead serious about sex, money and fame, he unearths a hedonistic community where the ritual of death is the ultimate high.

"An excellent read, charming, amusing, insightful, complex, localized yet startlingly universal in its themes."
—*Guide of Bangkok*

"Highly entertaining."—*Bangkok Post*

"A good read, fast-paced and laced with so many of the locales so familiar to the expat denizens of Bangkok."
—*Art of Living* (Thailand)

"Like a noisy, late-night Thai restaurant, Moore serves up tongue-burning spices that swallow up the literature of Generation X and cyberpsace as if they were merely sticky rice."—*The Daily Yomiuri*

COLD HIT
Sixth in the series
Heaven Lake Press (2004) ISBN 974-920104-1-7

Five foreigners have died in Bangkok. Were they drug overdose victims or victims of a serial killer? Calvino believes the evidence points to a serial killer who stalks tourists in Bangkok. The Thai police, including Calvino's best friend and buddy Colonel Pratt, don't buy his theory.

Calvino teams up with an LAPD officer on a bodyguard assignment. Hidden forces pull them through swank shopping malls, rundown hotels, Klong Toey slum, and the Bangkok bars as they try to keep their man and themselves alive. As Calvino learns more about the bodies being shipped back to America, the secret of the serial killer is revealed.

"The story is plausible and riveting to the end."
—*The Japan Times*

"Tight, intricate plotting, wickedly astute ... *Cold Hit* will have you variously gasping, chuckling, nodding, tut-tutting, ohyesing, and grinding your teeth throughout its 330 pages."—*Guide of Bangkok*

"The plot is equally tricky, brilliantly devised, and clear. One of the best crime fiction in the first half of the year."
—*Ultimo Biedlefeld* (Germany)

"Moore depicts the city from below. He shows its dirt, its inner conflicts, its cruelty, its devotion. Hard, cruel, comical and good."—*Readme.de*

MINOR WIFE
Seventh in the series
Heaven Lake Press (2004) ISBN 974-92126-5-7

A contemporary murder set in Bangkok—a neighbor and friend, a young ex-hooker turned artist, is found dead by an American millionaire's minor wife. Her rich expat husband hires Calvino to investigate. While searching for the killer in exclusive clubs and not-so-exclusive bars of Bangkok, Calvino discovers that a minor wife—mia noi— has everything to do with a woman's status. From illegal cock fighting matches to elite Bangkok golf clubs, Calvino finds himself caught in the crossfire as he closes in on the murderer.

"The thriller moves in those convoluted circles within which Thai life and society takes place. Moore's knowledge of these gives insights into many aspects of the cultural mores ... unknown to the expat population. Great writing, great story and a great read."—*Pattaya Mail*

"What distinguishes Christopher G. Moore from other foreign authors setting their stories in the Land of Smiles is how much more he understands its mystique, the psyche of its populace and the futility of its round residents trying to fit into its square holes."—*Bangkok Post*

"Moore pursues in even greater detail in *Minor Wife* the changing social roles of Thai women (changing, but not always quickly or for the better) and their relations among themselves and across class lines and other barriers."
—*Vancouver Sun*

PATTAYA 24/7
Eighth in the series
Heaven Lake Press (2008) ISBN 978-974-8418-41-4

Inside a secluded, lush estate located on the edge of Pattaya, an eccentric Englishman's gardener is found hanged. Calvino has been hired to investigate. He finds himself pulled deep into the shadows of the war against drugs, into the empire of a local warlord with the trail leading to a terrorist who has caused Code Orange alerts to flash across the screen of American intelligence.

In a story packed with twists and turns, Calvino traces the links from the gardener's past to the door of men with power and influence who have everything to lose if the mystery of the gardener's death is solved.

"Original, provocative, and rich with details and insights into the underworld of Thai police, provincial gangsters, hit squads, and terrorists."
—Pieke Bierman, award-wining author of *Violetta*

"Intelligent and articulate, Moore offers a rich, passionate and original take on the private-eye game, fans of the genre should definitely investigate, and fans of foreign intrigue will definitely enjoy."—Kevin Burton Smith, *January Magazine*

"A cast of memorably eccentric figures in an exotic Southeast Asian backdrop."—*The Japan Times*

"The best in the Calvino series ... The story is compelling."
—*Bangkok Post*

THE RISK OF INFIDELITY INDEX
Ninth in the series
Heaven Lake Press (2007) ISBN 974-88168-7-6

Major political demonstrations are rocking Bangkok. Chaos and fear sweep through the Thai and expatriate communities. Calvino steps into the political firestorm as he investigates a drug piracy operation. The piracy is traced to a powerful business interest protected by important political connections.

A nineteen-year-old Thai woman and a middle-age lawyer end up dead on the same evening. Both are connected to Calvino's investigation. The dead lawyer's law firm denies any knowledge of the case. Calvino is left in the cold. Approached by a group of expat housewives—rattled by *The Risk of Infidelity Index* that ranks Bangkok number one for available sexual temptations—to investigate their husbands, Calvino discovers the alliance of forces blocking his effort to disclose the secret pirate drug investigation.

"A hard-boiled, street-smart, often hilarious pursuit of a double murderer."—*San Francisco Chronicle*

"There's plenty of violent action ... Memorable low-life characters ...The real star of the book is Bangkok."
—*Telegraph* (London)

"Taut, spooky, intelligent, and beautifully written."
—T. Jefferson Parker

"A complex, intelligent novel."—*Publishers' Weekly*

"The darkly raffish Bangkok milieu is a treat."
—*Kirkus Review*

PAYING BACK JACK
Tenth in the series
Heaven Lake Press (2009) ISBN 978-974-312-920-9

In *Paying Back Jack*, Calvino agrees to follow the 'minor wife' of a Thai politician and report on her movements. His client is Rick Casey, a shady American whose life has been darkened by the unsolved murder of his idealistic son. It seems to be a simple surveillance job, but soon Calvino is entangled in a dangerous web of political allegiance and a reckless quest for revenge.

And, unknown to our man in Bangkok, in an anonymous tower in the center of the city, a two-man sniper team awaits its shot, a shot that will change everything. *Paying Back Jack* is classic Christopher G. Moore: densely-woven, eye-opening, and riveting.

"Crisp, atmospheric ... Calvino's cynical humour oils the wheels nicely, while the cubist plotting keeps us guessing."
—*The Guardian*

"The best Calvino yet ... There are many wheels within wheels turning in this excellent thriller."
—*The Globe and Mail*

"[*Paying Back Jack*] might be Moore's finest novel yet. A gripping tale of human trafficking, mercenaries, missing interrogation videos, international conspiracies, and revenge, all set against the lovely and sordid backstreets of Bangkok that Moore knows better than anyone."
—Barry Eisler, author of *Fault Line*

"Moore clearly has no fear that his gloriously corrupt Bangkok will ever run dry."—*Kirkus Review*

THE CORRUPTIONIST
Eleventh in the series
Heaven Lake Press (2010) ISBN 978-616-90393-3-4

Set during the recent turbulent times in Thailand, the 11th novel in the Calvino series centers around the street demonstrations and occupations of Government House in Bangkok. Hired by an American businessman, Calvino finds himself caught in the middle of a family conflict over a Chinese corporate takeover. This is no ordinary deal. Calvino and his client are up against powerful forces set to seize much more than a family business.

As the bodies accumulate while he navigates Thailand's business-political landmines, Calvino becomes increasingly entangled in a secret deal made by men who will stop at nothing—and no one—standing in their way but Calvino refuses to step aside. *The Corruptionist* captures with precision the undercurrents enveloping Bangkok, revealing multiple layers of betrayal and deception.

"Politics has a role in the series, more so now than earlier ... Thought-provoking columnists don't do it better."
—*Bangkok Post*

"Moore's understanding of the dynamics of Thai society has always impressed, but considering current events, the timing of his latest [*The Corruptionist*] is absolutely amazing."
—*The Japan Times*

"Entertaining and devilishly informative."
—Tom Plate, *Pacific Perspective*

"Very believable ... A brave book."—*Pattaya Mail*

9 GOLD BULLETS
Twelfth in the series
Heaven Lake Press (2011) ISBN 978-616-90393-7-2

A priceless collection of 9 gold bullet coins issued during the Reign of Rama V has gone missing along with a Thai coin collector. Local police find a link between the missing Thai coins and Calvino's childhood friend, Josh Stein, who happens to be in Bangkok on an errand for his new Russian client. This old friend and his personal and business entanglements with the Russian underworld take Calvino back to New York, along with Pratt.

The gritty, dark vision of *9 Gold Bullets* is tracked through the eyes of a Thai cop operating on a foreign turf, and a private eye expatriated long enough to find himself a stranger in his hometown. As the intrigue behind the missing coins moves between New York and Bangkok, and the levels of deception increase, Calvino discovers the true nature of friendship and where he belongs.

"Moore consistently manages to entertain without having to resort to melodramatics. The most compelling feature of his ongoing Calvino saga, in my view, is the symbiotic relationship between the American protagonist and his Thai friends, who have evolved with the series. The friendships are sometimes strained along cultural stress lines, but they endure, and the Thai characters' supporting roles are very effective in helping keep the narratives interesting and plausible."—*The Japan Times*

"Moore is a master at leading the reader on to what 'should' be the finale, but then you find it isn't...Worth waiting for... However, do not start reading until you have a few hours to spare."—*Pattaya Mail*

MISSING IN RANGOON
Thirteenth in the series
Heaven Lake Press (2013) ISBN 978-616-7503-17-2

As foreigners rush into Myanmar with briefcases stuffed with plans and cash for hotels, shopping malls and high rises, they discover the old ways die hard. Vincent Calvino's case is to find a young British-Thai man gone missing in Myanmar, while his best friend and protector Colonel Pratt of the Royal Thai Police has an order to cut off the supply of cold pills from Myanmar used for the methamphetamine trade in Thailand.

As one of the most noir novels in the Vincent Calvino series, Missing in Rangoon plays out beneath the moving shadows of the cross-border drug barons. Pratt and Calvino's lives are entangled with the invisible forces inside the old regime and their allies who continue to play by their own set of rules.

"[Moore's] descriptions of Rangoon are excellent. In particular, he excels at describing the human and social fall-out that occurs when a poor, isolated country suddenly opens its borders to the world.... *Missing in Rangoon* is a satisfying read, a mixture of hard-boiled crime fiction and acute social observation set in a little known part of Asia."
—Andrew Nette, *Crime Fiction Lover*

"The story is delicious. Calvino gets a missing person's case that takes him to Myanmar (Burma), drugs are involved, and the plot takes several wonderful twists that keep the reader mesmerized... It's Moore at his best... Reading a book like *Missing in Rangoon* will open up a whole new world of knowledge that will help the reader to understand the element in the story that the newspaper—and reporter—dared not reveal." —*WoWasis Travelblog*

THE MARRIAGE TREE
Fourteenth in the series
Heaven Lake Press (2014) ISBN 978-616-7503-23-3

It's okay for Thais to believe in ghosts—it's their birthright. But why is Vincent Calvino seeing ghosts, and why are they so angry? Calvino is haunted by a series of deaths in Rangoon and Bangkok, when he stumbles onto a new murder case—but is it a new case, or an old one returned from the dead? A murder investigation leads Calvino inside an underworld network smuggling Rohingya out of illegal camps and detention centers. Calvino looks for the killer in the mystical Thai world of sword and marriage trees.

"[*The Marriage Tree*] will keep the reader up at night, though, as the action is fast-paced and full of enough twists to foment insomnia. For readers who loved Missing in Rangoon, this follow-on book provides something of a final resolution."
—wowais.com

"The plight of the Rohingya refugees has been documented many times, but never dramatised like this.... [W]hen a novelist brings his powers of description and sense of empathy to bear on such a subject, the wholehearted tragedy of these crimes against humanity hits home in a powerful way. The opening is riveting ... The plotting is taut and the pacing sharp."
—Jim Algie, *The Nation*

"*The Marriage Tree* is a top tier crime novel set in a top tier city, Bangkok, to be enjoyed by crime fiction readers everywhere."
—Kevin Cummings, *Chiang Mai City News*

CRACKDOWN
Fifteenth in the series
Heaven Lake Press (2015) ISBN 978-616-7503-32-5

In *Crackdown* visual art becomes a powerful take down tool to push back against the oligarchs. People adjust to the surveillance state and its agents who are emergent forces. Post-coup Thailand is the setting as high tech competes with traditional power in a battle for hearts and minds. It is a noir landscape where Calvino finds himself ambushed as casualties from this battle leave behind a mystery or two. Calvino enters a world of ancient maps, political graffiti, student protesters and murder. The finger points at Calvino as the killer. He searches for allies who will help him prove his innocence.

"*Crackdown* is a superb novel and a wonderful read."
—*The Life Style Detective*

"This carefully crafted politically-aware crime novel ... set in Bangkok during post-coup military rule ... is a book of symbols. [*Crackdown*] is a book of dusty maps and edgy political graffiti. A book of warnings, predictions; a well plotted social document."
—James Newman, Author of the Joe Dylan Private Investigator Noir Crime Series

"Christopher G. Moore's freewheeling intelligence roams over the manifold aspects of modern life, from the 2014 coup to high-tech crime surveillance, map-making, and radical street art. The sum total infuses his latest novel, *Crackdown*, with a richer palette of colors than the endless black and grainy bleakness of so many other noir tales."
—Jim Algie, *Bangkok 101*

Ralf Tooten © 2012

Christopher G. Moore is a Canadian novelist and essayist who lives in Bangkok. He has written 27 novels, including the award-winning Vincent Calvino series and the Land of Smiles Trilogy. The German edition of his third Vincent Calvino novel, *Zero Hour in Phnom Penh*, won the German Critics Award (Deutsche Krimi Preis) for International Crime Fiction in 2004 and the Spanish edition of the same novel won the Premier Special Director's Book Award Semana Negra (Spain) in 2007. The second Calvino novel, *Asia Hand,* won the Shamus Award for Best Original Paperback in 2011.

CPSIA information can be obtained
at www.ICGtesting.com
Printed in the USA
BVOW06s2122190917
495158BV00009B/32/P